T0367881

I Bet You Never Thought

Herbert L. Moore III

ARCHWAY
PUBLISHING

Archway Publishing books may be ordered through booksellers or by contacting:

Archway Publishing
1663 Liberty Drive
Bloomington, IN 47403
www.archwaypublishing.com
1 (888) 242-5904

ISBN: 978-1-4808-6401-6 (sc)
ISBN: 978-1-4808-6402-3 (e)

Library of Congress Control Number: 2018948005

Print information available on the last page.

Archway Publishing rev. date: 07/03/2018

CHARACTERS FOR BOOK

1. Thomas Jefferson Robinson III (Main Character; goes by middle name Jefferson), born 1984

2. Olivia Jacobs (Jefferson's Girlfriend/Wife), born 1984

3. Thomas Jefferson Robinson Jr. (Father of Jefferson; looks like Denzel Washington), born 1952

4. Anna Mae Broussard Robinson (Mother of Jefferson; reminds you of Angela Bassett), born 1954

5. Thomas Jefferson Robinson Sr. (Father of Thomas Jr.; reminds you of Sidney Poitier), born 1928

6. Abigail Everett Robinson (Mother of Thomas Jr.; reminds you of Margaret Avery), born 1932

7. Abe Jackie Robinson (Jefferson's Oldest Brother), born 1975

8. Antoine Isiah Robinson (Jefferson's Older Brother), born 1981

9. Aaliyah Eve Robinson (Jefferson's Baby Sister), born 1985

10. Jin Ho(Tiger) Kim (Jefferson's Best Friend)

11. Jung Ho Kim (Tiger's Father)

12. Soon Yi Kim (Tiger's Mother)

13. Young Jae Kim (Tiger's Older Brother; Nickname Rabbit)

14. Manuela Santiago, born 1986

15. Constantine Santiago (Manuela's Father), born 1958

16. Alejandra Santiago (Manuela's Mother), born 1960

17. Sophia Santiago (Manuela's Sister), born 1985

18. Eduardo Santiago (Manuela's Cousin), born 1978

19. Elena Martinez (Manuela's Housekeeper/Nanny/Confidant), born 1965

20. Carlos Lopez (Constantine's Bodyguard/Driver), born 1950

21. Coach Nick Jenkins, High school Baseball Coach, born 1945

22. Dr. John Ewing (Jefferson's Foot Specialist), born 1955

23. Pablo Medina (Constantine's Business Associate/ Mafia Boss), born 1958

24. Escobar Medina, born 1982

25. Maurice Williams (Class Bully), born 1982

26. Pastor Riley

27. Suzette Boudreaux (Jackie's Girlfriend; Wife)

28. Lionel Jacobs (Jefferson's Grandpa's best friend)

29. Samuel Abraham Robinson (Jefferson's Uncle; his father's brother). He was crazy as all outdoors. He loved to fight.

30. Jamie Rollins (Freshman Pitcher on University of Alabama of Alabama Baseball Team from Huntington Beach California)

31. Butch Sullivan (Senior Right Fielder on University of Alabama Baseball from Marietta, Georgia)

32. Ricky Williams (Senior 1st Baseman on University of Alabama Baseball Team)

33. Pedro Santiago (Manuela's Brother Born 1984 Freshman on University of Alabama Baseball Team from Miami, Florida)

34. Jonathan & Tammy Montana–Old Couple that Thomas and Olivia had met on elevator in New York.

35. Jessica Jacobs–Olivia Jacobs' sister

36. Jason Jacobs – Olivia Jacobs' sister

37. Mark Jacobs (Olivia's Father)

38. Samantha Jacobs (Olivia's Mother)

39. Jeremy Bosch (The boy Olivia cheated on Jefferson with)

40. Maria Sanchez (Pedro's girlfriend)

41. Mr. Sanchez (Maria's Dad)

42. Mrs. Sanchez (Maria's Mom)

43. Isabella Sanchez (Maria's Sister)

44. Selena Sanchez (Maria's Sister)

45. Ricardo Sanchez (Maria's Brother)

46. Jane Johnson (New York Realtor)

47. Sandra Wilson (New York Home Decorator)

48. James Bond (Jefferson's Driver in New York)

49. James Bond Jr. (Jefferson's Driver's Son)

50. Jake Goldstein (Guy Olivia Cheated on Jefferson with in New York)

51. Attorney Jim Mccorqudale (Jefferson's Divorce Attorney)

52. Billy Waters (Olivia's Divorce Attorney)

53. Emily Watson (Olivia's friend from New York)

54. Susan Rockefeller (Olivia's friend from New York)

55. Sarah (Worker from Restaurant in Jefferson's Building)

56. Davey (The bellman at Davey's building)

57. Dr. Wayne Dawson (Jefferson's Orthopedic Surgeon who operated on his damaged ankle)

58. Presario Gonzales (Trainer and Supplement & Vitamin Shop owner in Miami; referred by Dr. Dawson)

59. Ray Donovan (Private Investigator from New York)

60. Mickey Hammer (Private Investigator from Mobile, Alabama)

61. Jeremy Bosch (The guy from Auburn that Olivia cheated on Jefferson with while they were in college)

62. Melissa Cartwright (Manuela's friend from college at the University of Alabama. She is from Wyoming)

63. Rosetta Flemington (Manuela's friend from College at University of Alabama. She is from California)

64. Jason Wheeler (Pedro's friend from the Florida Marlins baseball team)

65. Davey Woods (Melissa Cartwright's boyfriend)

66. Wilma Roberts (Sandra Wilson's friend)

67. Amanda Wilson (Sandra Wilson's Sister)

68. Derek Wilson (Sandra Wilson's Brother)

69. Jacqueline Guy (Sandra Wilson's Friend)

70. Mia Acosta (Presario Gonzales Girlfriend)

71. William (Billy) Lewis (Jefferson's friend from the University of Alabama. They both graduated with degrees in Accounting)

72. Rory Lewis (Billy's father and Multi-Billionaire and owner of Lewis Oil out of Dallas, Texas.)

73. James Stephens (Vice President For Lewis Oil)

74. Bryan Rivers (Chief Operations Officer for Santiago Holdings)

75. Jamie Rodriguez (Assistant Head Security, works for Carlos)

76. Javier Garcia (Jefferson's Driver in Miami)

77. Anabella Padilla (Jefferson's Personal Maid in Miami)

78. Luis Marin (Jefferson Personal Butler in Miami)

79. Jim Dean (Head DEA From Mobile Alabama)

80. Billy Reed (DEA Agent From Mobile Alabama)

81. Susan Johnson (Older Girl from Leroy)

82. Tracy Wiggins (Older Girl from Leroy)

CONTENTS

CHAPTER ONE

The Beginning

It was the first day of school on August 22, 1992. I was a third grader at Leroy High School. Yes, I said high school. Leroy is a high school that is located in Leroy, Alabama which has a population of around 850 people. The school goes from kindergarten through twelfth grade.

I knew everyone in my class except this new Asian kid sitting in the corner. He was new to the school. "Good morning, my name is Thomas, but everyone calls me Jefferson. What is your name?"

He replied, "Jin Ho Kim. But everyone calls me Tiger."

"So why do they call you Tiger?"

"It was a name given to me by my father's father; he said that I had the warrior spirit like the Tiger."

"Well Tiger, if you hang with me, I will teach you the ropes around this school. I pretty much know everyone around the school from the third grade through high school. I have two older brothers and one younger sister. What about you, how many siblings do you have?"

"I have one older brother named Young Jae, but we call him Rabbit because he is fast.

I said, "Tiger, whatever you do, please stay away from the kid sitting on the front row. His name is Maurice Williams. He is the class bully as well as a troublemaker."

"He looks a lot older," said Tiger.

"Yeah, he is two years older than everyone else in the class; he was left behind a couple of years."

Later that day at recess, Tiger and I were sitting on the bleachers about to finish up our chips and soda during recess when Maurice walked up and snatched Tiger's chips and began to eat them.

"Maurice, please give me back my chips," asked Tiger.

"I'm not giving you anything," replied Maurice.

Tiger, quickly kicked the back of Maurice's leg, and as Maurice dropped to one knee, Tiger grabbed Maurice head in a backwards headlock, grabbed his chips and then released Maurice's head. Maurice then fell to the ground. About this time all of the kids were crowding around, Maurice quickly jumped to his feet and proceeded to walk toward Tiger but the bell rang to end recess. Maurice then stated, "I will see you after class, Bruce Lee."

As we were walking back to our class, I asked Tiger, "So are you afraid of what is going to happen when Maurice sees you after the bell rings to end school?"

Tiger responded, "Jefferson no, I'm not afraid."

I then asked Tiger, "So where in Leroy does your family live?"

Tiger responded, "My family purchased 30 acres near St. Stephens, Alabama; just past the old Leroy Post Office landmark."

After hearing his description, I knew of the place that he was talking about. It was the old Mosley property.

"My mom will be picking me up after school today," said Tiger.

The rest of the day went by quickly. When the last school bell rang to dismiss school, I said, "Tiger there is another way that we can go in order to avoid seeing Maurice."

Tiger responded, "No, Jefferson, we will go the way everyone else goes."

I said, "Ok, good luck."

Tiger and I had just exited our classroom and were turning the corner to make our way toward the parking lot when Maurice confronted Tiger. Without hesitation, Maurice charged Tiger. Tiger quickly took two steps back, turned as if he was going to run away, and then jumped and did a kick that hit Maurice directly in the chest. The force of the kick sent Maurice directly to the ground. Tiger quickly pounced on Maurice and hit him with one right punch and then an elbow to the head and Maurice was practically out. Maurice started crying. He was begging for Tiger to not hit him again. Tiger raised up and asked Maurice, "Do you surrender?"

Maurice said yes. Tiger then let Maurice up. Maurice then ran toward the front of the school crying. I was in shock, because everyone from kindergarten to the sixth grade was afraid of Maurice. However, here was this new kid that was half Maurice's size who made him cry like a baby.

I asked, "So Tiger where did you learn to fight like that?"

He responded, "My father taught me."

I asked, "So what do you call it, karate?"

"No Jefferson," said Tiger, "it is called Tae Kwon Do. It is a form of martial arts that is taught in my father's country South Korea. My father's father taught him the forms. It has been passed down from generation to generation for centuries."

I asked, "Do you think that your father will teach me how to fight like that? I want to kick butt and beat people up."

Tiger responded, "Jefferson, we don't use the martial arts to bully people or to show our strength. If we did, we would be no better than Maurice. We only use our skills as a last resort in order to protect our families, friends, the weak or ourselves. One of our oaths is to not attack without reason; another is to show concern and compassion."

Once we got to the front of the school, Tiger and I both saw our mothers waiting for us. Tiger introduced me to his mom and vice versa. Both of our moms introduced themselves to each other. Prior to them saying good-bye, Tiger stated, "Jefferson, I will ask my father to teach you."

I said, "Ok."

The next day when Tiger arrived at school, I was waiting for him to get out of the car with his mom. I quickly asked what his dad said.

"My father said yes," said Tiger. "He stated that you must have your parents' permission."

"Well Tiger, I will ask my parents tonight."

Tiger and I both were shocked to see a new student when we arrived in class. She was gorgeous. Her name was Olivia Jacobs. I was instantly in love. She was a Caucasian girl with long brunette hair and blue eyes. I couldn't stop staring at her.

During recess Maurice came up to Tiger and apologized for starting trouble with him. He now wanted to be our friend. Tiger and I stated, "Maurice, in order for us to be friends with you, you first have to change the way you treat people."

"Tiger and Jefferson, I give you my word that I will stop mistreating people," said Maurice. He said that he would. It would be the beginning of a long relationship between us three.

The bell rang, so the three of us started walking back to class. Olivia and two other girls were walking in front of us. I saw a blue scarf fall from Olivia's purse onto the ground. She hadn't noticed that her scarf had fallen. I quickly picked up the scarf and handed it to her, stating that it had fallen out of her purse. She thanked me and said, "Hi, my name is Olivia."

I said, "My name is Thomas Jefferson Robinson." I then introduced Tiger and Maurice. I was excited the rest of the day.

When school turned out later that day, I noticed Olivia getting in the truck with a man whose truck had Jacobs Construction engraved on the door. While having dinner with my family that night, I learned that her father was Mark Jacobs, the owner of one of the largest construction companies in the state of Alabama. Their family pretty much owned everything in Washington County. Leroy is one of the small rural areas that make up Washington County. Washington County is one of the largest counties in the state of Alabama. Their family lived in Fruitdale,

Alabama. Everyone was shocked to see them relocate to Leroy. My dad stated that it was their 20,000 square foot home being built off Highway 43. They had purchased 200 acres from the Richardson Family.

I was sitting at dinner with my sister Eve Robinson, older brother Antoine Isiah Robinson, oldest brother Abraham Jackie Robinson, my mom Anna Mae Broussard Robinson and my dad Thomas Jefferson Robinson Jr. Well, my full name is Thomas Jefferson Robinson III. I'm named after my father, who is named after his father. I know what you are thinking. Where in the heck did our family get the name Thomas Jefferson? Well, it is a long story. If I'm not mistaken, my grandfather says it has something to do with one of the country's founding fathers, the third President of the United States. He stated that Mr. Robinson was doing some fathering of his own. I'm told that he is my grandfather several times over.

My mother and father are high school sweethearts. They have been married 16 years. They got married right after high school. We live on an 80-acre farm in a 5,000 square foot home next door to my grandparents, Thomas and Anna Mae Jefferson. My father didn't leave home after high school. He immediately started working on my grandfather's farm, as well as taking a job with the Department of Transportation in Mobile, Alabama, about 45 minutes south of Leroy. He farms whenever he isn't working. He normally stays gone for weeks at a time traveling with his job.

My grandfather, Thomas Robinson Sr., worked at the same job as my dad for 40 years prior to retiring several years back. Dad didn't want to leave my grandfather to farm the property by himself when he graduated high school, so he stayed. He turned down several scholarships in baseball. One of the scholarships was to my favorite university, the University of Alabama. He says that he has no regrets, because even though he loved playing baseball, he loved being a husband, father, and farmer more.

My father is a six-foot-two dark, handsome, well-built man. Everyone says that he looks like the actor Denzel Washington. My mom is a beautiful brown-skinned woman with long curly hair that comes down to the middle of her back. I say that she looks like Angela Bassett.

My grandfather Thomas Sr. is a tall, dark, good-looking man as well. He looks real good for 64 years old. He will always let you know his age. His favorite saying is "black don't crack." He looks like a younger Sidney Poitier. My grandfather is a character. My grandmother Abigail is a gorgeous light-skinned Creole woman with black wavy hair to her shoulders. She is four years younger than my grandpa. He always tells her every day how beautiful she is and how blessed he is to have her in his life. He always tells me, "Son, when you get married, get you a woman younger than you."

When I ask why, his response is that they keep you young. I always say, "Keep me young? What does that mean?"

He replies, "When you get old, you will find out."

Let me tell you about my family. They are a hardworking, churchgoing, peaceful family. However, don't cross them. That goes all the way from my grandfather Thomas Sr. down to me, I guess. The town folks in Leroy call my family the Fighting Robinsons.

While having dinner, I decided this was the best time ever to ask Dad to take Tae Kwon Do lessons with Tiger's dad. "Dad, is it possible for me to take Tae Kwon Do lessons with Tiger and his dad?"

Dad said, "What? First, who is Tiger, and second, what is Tae Kwon Do? Then third, what about your schoolwork and chores around the farm?"

Mom chimed in, "Tiger is this new Asian kid in Jefferson's class. I had the opportunity to meet Tiger and his mom the other day. They seemed like nice people."

"Dad, Tae Kwon Do is a form of Karate."

Then my brother Jackie stated, "It isn't karate. It is Korean Martial Arts." Jackie always wanted to do martial arts; however, they don't have a place that offers it with 60 miles of Leroy. He constantly watches old Bruce Lee movies, reads books and purchases Karate magazines.

As it relates to school work and chores, I responded, "Dad, I promise you that I will be able to do all three of my chores on time."

Dad's response was that he would first have to meet Tiger's dad and we would go from there. "I will pick you up from school tomorrow and go by Tiger's house in order to meet his dad."

I said, "Thanks Dad." I hurried up and finished my dinner. Then my brothers and I went outside check on the animals one last time and turn off the lights in the barn.

I was so excited. I couldn't wait until the next day to go to school. Not only was it a Friday, but I was getting ready to become a martial arts fighter.

The next day while Tiger, Maurice and I were walking to class from recess, Olivia came up to me and asked, "Jefferson, will you carry my books after school?"

I responded, "Yes, I will carry your books." I was so excited; my day was going great. Now, I had two reasons I couldn't wait for school to be over. I couldn't wait for three o'clock to come. As soon as the bell rang to end school, I immediately waited by the door to carry Olivia's books. Tiger and Maurice also waited with me. All four of us walked together toward the front of the school.

Olivia asked, "So where do you live, Jefferson?"

I responded, "I live several miles from here on a farm." She was about to tell me where she lived when I stopped her. I said, "Everybody in the entire school knows where you live. Your house is the biggest house in the entire county."

Once we got in front of the school, I returned her book bag. "Thanks Jefferson," said Olivia.

Then Tiger and I walked to meet our parents. My brother Jackie was standing with my father in the front of the school as well. My father and brother introduced themselves to Tiger's mom. Dad, Jackie, and I jumped in the vehicle to follow Tiger and his mom to their house. I asked, "So Jackie, why are you in the truck with Dad?"

He responded, "I want to learn Tae Kwon Do as well."

Once we got there Tiger's dad came outside to greet us. He said, "Hi Mr. Robinson. My name is Jung Ho Kim, nice to meet you."

My father said, "Hi my name is Thomas but you can call me T.J., and these are my sons Jefferson and Jackie."

Mr. Kim said, "I see you have two sons like me."

My father replied, "No, I have a third son and a daughter as well. Their mom picked them up from school early today; they both had dentist's appointments."

Mr. Kim asked, "Are all of your sons interested in Tae Kwon Do?"

Dad said, "As far as I know, these two are the only ones interested."

"Sounds great," said Mr. Kim. Mr. Kim then asked us to walk with him to the building next to their house. When we walked in we were blown away. It looked like about 2500 square feet of space. In the front of the building was carpet, sitting space and two doors. One door led to what appeared to be an office. The other door led to the training room. There was a large 16x16 window on each side of the door that allowed you to see inside the training room. Mr. Kim led us to the entry door to the training room, them he stated that we must remove our shoes and socks and place them in the cupboards along the wall. After we removed our shoes and socks, we walked onto the training room floor. It appeared to be hardwood from a distance, but when we walked on the floor it felt soft. It was made out of a water resistant material. There were mirrors all around the room. Mr. Kim, then stated, "We must bow to the flags at all times." He had the American, Korean, and Kukkiwon (Tae Kwon Do School) flags on the wall.

Mr. Kim then asked me, "Jefferson do you know the meaning of Tae Kwon Do?"

I responded, "No sir, I don't."

Mr. Kim replied, "The meaning of Tae Kwon Do is as follows: Tae means foot or to strike with the foot; Kwon means hand or to strike with the hand; Do means discipline. Discipline is the most crucial of all the elements of martial arts. Without discipline you set yourself up for failure." He continued, "Without discipline, you may kick when you are supposed to strike. Martial arts was developed thousands of years ago as forms of self-defense. Karate originated in Japan; Kung Fu came from China. Tae Kwon Do is a native of Korea. Tae Kwon Do emphasizes kicks more than any other martial arts, making it ideal for improving balance, flexibility and endurance.

"I have Twenty-Seven years of martial arts experience," said Mr. Kim. "I'm a Seventh Degree Black Belt in the traditional Korean Martial Art of Tae Kwon Do, certified by the Kukkiwon. I taught Tae Kwon Do fulltime in South Korea prior to moving to the United States. I only taught my sons since we've been in the United States. I was born in South Korea, and am a graduate of the world famous Yongin University, where I received a Master's of Physical Education Degree. I also have a Master's of Finance Degree from the University of San Francisco in

San Francisco, California. My family and I lived there nine years prior to moving here."

"So what brought you to a small town like Leroy?" asked Jackie.

Mr. Kim responded, "A good friend of mine who lived San Francisco during that time was born and raised in Jackson, Alabama. But he talked about Leroy a lot as well. His name was Bobby Moore."

Dad stated that he knew Bobby.

"Well, Bobby left San Francisco about two years ago and moved back home to Jackson. His father was ill so he moved back to manage E-room Bank. He wanted me to come take over the bank and help expand into other cities/counties. They currently have three locations. Prior to coming here, I was third in command of one of the biggest banks in San Francisco. My wife and I, as well as the family, were a little tired of the hustle and bustle of city life. So I took Bobby up on his offer. I'm the President of the three locations. I'm putting together the blueprint in order for us to open two more locations within the next six months. So what bank do you bank with, Thomas?" asked Mr. Kim.

"I bank with Trustworthy Bank. My family has been banking with them for over forty years. My dad and I own a small 80-acre farm, plus I'm a manager with the Department of Transportation, said Dad. "I've have been there for eighteen years. I was hired there right out of college. I commuted back and forth to Mobile College and obtained my degree in Criminal Justice after high school."

"Well, Master Kim—"

"No, call me Jimmy."

"So what is the cost for you to train my boys in Tae Kwon Do?' asked Dad.

"Well T.J., there is no cost. I only ask that they give me 100% percent while they are training with me. I won't tolerate being late or insubordination; they must maintain self-discipline at all times and show respect and concern for others."

"Well Jimmy, since you are willing to do that at no cost, I'm willing to move some of my banking business over to E-room Bank," responded Dad. "I will also pass the word to some of my friends to come over and meet with you as well."

"Thanks T.J., I appreciate that," said Mr. Kim. "Well, first things first.

Our training days based on my current work schedule are Monday and Wednesday from 6 p.m. to 7:30 p.m. and on Saturday from 10 a.m. to 1 p.m. If you are late and/or miss one of those days, you have to stay double your workout time on the next scheduled workout day. Our training will consist of doing our Poomsae Forms from Yellow Belt all the way to Black Belt. It normally takes someone three years to obtain a black belt. However, if you follow my program and do as you are supposed to, you can whittle that down to two and a half years. We will perform belt promotion tests every eight weeks. Please come to the closet in the back in order to get your uniforms.

"T.J., it was great to meet you."

"Same here, Jimmy," said Dad. He then stated that he would see Mr. Kim—I mean Master Kim—on Saturday at 10 a.m.

"I will see y'all tomorrow at 10 a.m.," said Master Kim.

Jackie and I were so excited to be starting our training tomorrow. Dad stated that he would bring us to practice on Saturdays and we could talk to Mom, Grandma or Granddad about bringing us on Monday and Wednesday afternoons. I'm kind of glad that Jackie will be attending Tae Kwon Do with me, because in a couple of years he will have his license and be able to bring us himself.

"Dad," asked Jackie, "do you think that Isiah will want to attend the training with us as well?"

"Well, said Dad, "your brother is kind of like your Grandpa and me. He is an old spirit in a young body. He likes to kick someone's ass the old-fashioned way, with his bare knuckles and brute strength."

Sure enough, that was the case; when we were having dinner that night, Dad asked Isiah if he would like to take Tae Kwon Do as well; his response was that he wasn't interested.

The next day Dad took Jackie and me to Tiger's house to begin training. It was kind of cool wearing the Gee and our white belts to hold them up. Dad dropped us off and told us that he would be back by 1 p.m. to pick us up.

When we arrived Tiger was standing outside the martial arts studio waiting on us. "Jackie and Jefferson," said Tiger, "you have your belts tied wrong." He then proceeded to show us the correct way to tie our Gee.

We walked into the studio to start training. Prior to walking into the studio, we had to remove our shoes and place them in the cupboard. Then as we were walking through the door to the studio, we had to face the flags and bow then turn and face Tiger and his brother Young Jae, who were Black Belts, and bow, then last turn and face Master Kim and bow.

Then we sat on the floor and began our stretching routine. We had to count and then say 'sir' afterwards. "One–Sir, Two–Sir" and so on and so forth. We had to say sir after every response. We did five minutes of stretching, 50 jumping jacks, and 50 push-ups on our knuckles and several other exercises for the next 10 minutes. We then put on our shoes and went outside and ran several times around their property, which seemed like forever. Then we came back into studio, took off our shoes and went to another section in the back of the studio and stood in a straight line. Master Kim had us imitate him as he was kicking. We did 25 kicks per side, then we did punches, 25 per side. Then we were asked to put our feet together, then as we were squatting move our feet apart and bring our arms directly beside us. Then we dropped to the floor and did push-ups. Then we went to another area in the back of the building, where Master Kim showed us how to punch the punching bags. Then he showed us how to kick the bags.

Then, after training on the bag, he took us in a room directly across from that area. The room looked like a Shaolin Monk Temple. It had several statues in the back of the room; it had two swords in their cases on each side of the room. Master Kim then told us to kneel and cross one leg over the other; then place our arms in front on our knee and just breathe normally. He told us this was the place where we would meditate 30 minutes per day when we train. He stated that meditation is another important element when we are training. It helps us to relax and free our mind. Before I knew it the 30 minutes were over.

Then we were told to put our shoes on and we went outside once more. We did one more lap around their property and had lunch. Then next thing you know, Dad was picking us up to go home. While on the way home Dad asked, "So how do you guys like Tae Kwon Do?"

Jackie and I both emphatically yelled that we loved it. When we got home, we quickly changed into our work clothes and began our daily chores around the farm. I knew at that point that I had another love in my life besides playing baseball, and that was Tae Kwon Do.

That night I went and knocked on Jackie's door; he said, "Come in." He was reading about Tae Kwon Do in some martial arts magazine. He and I both looked at each other and then gave each other a high five. We didn't have to say anything; it was written all over our faces. We both loved Tae Kwon Do. We sat and talked for what seemed like hours; before Dad came in.

He said, "It is time for bed; we have church in the morning."

Sure enough 5 a.m. came quickly; my brothers and I were up doing our daily chores. We were finished feeding all the animals by six and sitting at the table waiting for breakfast. We had forgotten that Grandma was preparing breakfast this Sunday until Dad came over to remind us. We quickly ran over to our grandparents' house to eat. I loved my mom's cooking; but I loved my grandmother's cooking even better. She had everything prepared: bacon, ham, eggs, sausage, fried chicken, grits, omelets, pancakes, and my favorite, biscuits. Nobody made biscuits like my Grandma. She had homemade syrup, fig jam, grape jam, strawberry jam, and peach jam to choose from.

Everything was homemade. Everything was made and grown on our farm. We never had to purchase meat from grocery stores. Whatever food we wanted to eat, we raised right on our farm. We raised chickens, cows, goats, horses, pigs; we even had a catfish pond. We also grew peas, okra, corn, white potatoes, sweet potatoes, peanuts, tomatoes, butter beans, cucumbers, squash, and green peppers. We also had plum trees, pear trees, and pecan trees. I must admit it was great being raised on the farm.

Once we finished breakfast, we were off to church. We were always one of the first families to arrive at church. We always sat on the front row. Reverend Riley always acknowledged when we arrived.

The days and months seemed to go by rather quickly. Tiger and I began to bond. We even became blood brothers by cutting our thumbs then pressing them together to join our blood. We made a pact that nothing would break our bond; that not only were we blood brothers, but from that day forward we considered each other to be brothers.

Jackie, Tiger and I would practice with Master Kim for three days each week, several hours each day. I began to spend more and more time at Tiger's house. Master Kim would take time outside our normally scheduled days to practice in order to work with me on my skills. My brother Jackie was much older than me; as well as more physically built for the strenuous training that we performed each day. However, that didn't deter me from achieving my ultimate goal of becoming a Black Belt in Tae Kwon Do. I knew that I just had to work harder than my brother at achieving that goal.

BLACK BELT CEREMONY

The day had finally come. August 12, 1995 would be a day that I would never forget. It was hard to believe that three years had already gone by. Not only was I about to start sixth grade in a couple of weeks, but I was taller, stronger and about to receive my first Black Belt in Tae Kwon Do. I was so excited that I could hardly sleep the night prior to the Black Belt Ceremony. The next day my entire family attended the Black Belt Ceremony at the training facility. The only two people taking the Black Belt Tests were Jackie and me. Prior to starting the ceremony, Master Kim stated, "I would like to take the time to say that Jackie and Jefferson worked extremely hard over the past three years in order to get to this point. They have gone over and above what was asked as well as what was expected of them. They started off as my students; however, now I consider them as family. Jefferson is here so much I consider him a son. Okay, with that being said, good luck and let's get started."

Master Kim first had us do our regular warm-up/stretching exercises in order to get loose. It is extremely important to properly stretch and warm-up prior to training. He said, "Okay, let's begin. You have to do as many push-ups as possible within one minute; however, the least amount you must do is 50 push-ups in order to pass."

Next we had to do 75 jumping jacks within a minute, then sit-ups; then chin-ups on a bar; then we had to run three miles in under 25 minutes. The next phase of the test was to perform our different Kicking Combinations/Basic Movements, which consisted of walking stances, front stances, low blocks, high blocks, middle blocks, kicking and punching, etc. The next and most important phase of the Black Belt Testing is the Poomses, our Taegeuk Forms. We had to do each form twice without making any mistakes. The forms were as follows:

Taegeuk Il Jang- This is the first Taegeuk, which is the beginning of all Poomses. It means the **Heaven**. It represents Yang (Heaven, light); therefore this Poomse should be performed with the greatness of Heaven.

Taegeuk Ee Jang- It means the Lake. In the depths of the lake are treasures and mysteries. The movements of this Taegeuk/Palgwe should be performed knowing that man has limitations, but that we can overcome these limitations. This should lead to a feeling of joy in knowing that we can control our future.

Taegeuk Sam Jang- This means Fire. Fire contains a lot of energy. Fire helped man to survive, but on the other hand had some catastrophic results. This form should be performed rhythmically, with some outbursts of energy.

Taegeuk Sa Jang- This means Thunder. Thunder comes from the sky and is absorbed by the earth. Thunder is one of the most powerful natural forces, circling, gyrating. This Taegeuk/Palgwe should be performed with this in mind.

Taegeuk Oh Jang- This means Wind. Wind is a gentle force, but can sometimes be furious, destroying everything in its path. Taegeuk Oh Jang should be performed like the wind, gently but knowing the ability of mass destruction with a single movement.

Taegeuk Yook Jang- This means like the Water. Water can move a mountain. The movements of this Poomse should be performed like water, sometimes standing still like water in a lake, sometimes striving as a river.

Taegeuk Chil Jang- It means like the Mountain. Mountains will always look majestic, no matter the size. This Poomse should be performed with the feeling that all movements are this majestic and deserve to be praised.

Taegeuk Pal Jang- It means the Earth. The associated trigram of this Poomse is Yin. The end of the beginning, the evil part of all that is good. Even in this darkness, there is still some light. Performing this Taegeuk/Palgwe one should be aware that while this is the last Taegeuk/Palgwe to be learned, it is also is the end of a circle, and therefore it is also the first, the second, etc.

Man, we finally did the last of the Poomse. What a grueling exercise. Not only did we perform all of the Basic Movements and Poomses twice, but Master Kim had us do them a third time.

"Great job," said Master Kim. "Okay everyone, we are moving on to the final phase of Black Belt testing, board breaking."

We had to break boards by way of side kick, round-house kick, Front Kick, Back Kick, Tornado Kick, Spinning Hook Kick, as well as punching directly to the board, then finally using our elbow to break the board. Everything was going well until I got to the tornado kick to break the board. When I had done the spin in order to break the board, it didn't break.

"Jefferson, please concentrate," said Master Kim. I took a deep breath, closed my eyes and did the move again, but the board still didn't break. Master Kim said, "Jefferson, please step aside so that Jackie can have a turn at breaking the board." Sure enough Jackie did everything perfect and broke the board on his first try. "Okay Jefferson, let's try again," said Master Kim.

I stepped up and closed my eyes, except this time I visualized myself breaking the board. I visualized my foot going directly through the board. Prior to me moving forward to break the board, Master Kim stopped me. "Jefferson, please wait. Tiger, please bring me another board," said Master Kim.

I was dumbfounded; I could also hear a gasp from my family in the audience. I could see the expressions on their faces, as if I couldn't break one board; now I'm being asked to break two boards. Master Kim said, "Jefferson, close your eyes, concentrate. I want you to visualize your movement from start to finish breaking these boards. Don't start until you clearly picture it for yourself. Now take a deep breath and focus. I want you to give a big KIHOP once you break them," said Master Kim.

I took a deep breath. Once I completely visualized me breaking the boards, I started the movement. I put everything I had into the kick. Once my foot touched the board, I could feel my momentum going through the first, then the second board. As my foot was passing through the second board, I let out the loudest KIHOP ever. I felt great; my family was yelling and jumping up and down. I immediately thought about how I used to wonder why the New York Yankees would be so excited after winning the World Series; now I knew because if winning the World Series felt anything like I was feeling, I knew it was magical. This was my World Series.

The final test was the elbow board breaking. Jackie went first and broke his board with ease. Then it was my turn. Master Kim had one board in his hand. I asked, "Sir I would like to break two boards."

Master Kim looked shocked. He said, "Why sure, Jefferson. Young Jae, please bring me another board."

I then closed my eyes and visualized me breaking both boards. Then I started and felt my elbow go through one, then both boards and let out a loud KIHOP. It was finally official. I knew that I had earned my First Black Belt.

Master Kim then said, "Jackie and Jefferson, please line up."

First up was Jackie. "Please remove your old belt," said Master Kim. Jackie did so and laid the old belt carefully on the floor. Then Young Jae gave Master Kim the Black Belt. Master Kim tied the belt around Jackie's waist and gave him a diploma signed and sealed by Kukkiwon University. Master Kim then shook Jackie's hand and they bowed gracefully.

Then Master Kim moved down in front of me. "Jefferson, please remove your old belt," asked Master Kim. I quickly untied and laid the old belt on the floor. Tiger then handed the Black Belt to Master Kim. Master Kim tied the belt around my waist, then gave me a diploma signed and sealed by Kukkiwon University. Master Kim then shook my hand and we gracefully bowed.

Master Kim then went in front of the room. He began to speak. "I would like to say that I'm proud of you both. You have worked extremely hard over the past three years to get to this point. You have gone over and above what was required to get here. I must say that out of all my years of teaching, of all the students that I have taught, I couldn't be more proud than I am today of you two students. You both came into my facility with no prior training, no skill-set, and no coordination; however, you have shown that with determination, desire, and discipline, anything is possible. Your family should be proud of you, but most important, you should be proud of yourselves. Obtaining a Black Belt is no easy task. There have been a many people who started the journey that you both have just completed, but they didn't finish. Now for whatever reason they didn't finish, you two have taken your reasons and completed the task. I say thank you for allowing me to go on as well as complete this journey with you. The Black Belt Ceremony is officially over. You are now Black Belts."

I yelled, "Yes sir, buddy."

The family quickly came over and gave Jackie and me a big hug. They also went up and shook Young Jae, Tiger and Master Kim's hands.

Grandfather Thomas said, "Damn boys, so you guys can actually do like Bruce Lee now."

I said, "Not quite as well as Bruce Lee, Grandpa."

As we were walking to the vehicles Dad said, "we are going out to eat today. We are going to Jackson to Willie's Steakhouse." He didn't have to tell me twice. After my Mom's and Grandma's cooking, Willie's was next in line.

The first day of school was finally here. I was starting the sixth grade this year. I was so excited because not only was I a Black Belt, but I was starting junior high. Tiger and I were in the same class; so was Olivia Jacobs, the love of my life, she just didn't know it yet.

The first day of school was going great until Tiger told me that he overheard some girls saying that Olivia and Gregory Richardson were now dating. I asked, "How did that happen?"

"Evidently it took place over the summer, when Greg's dad invited

Olivia's dad and family out to their annual Fourth of July cookout at their Lake House," said Tiger.

I said, "Tiger, how can I compete with a guy who comes from one of the richest families in Washington County? Greg's family is richer than Olivia's family."

"Jefferson, you have a shot," said Tiger. "Dad always says that money can't buy happiness; besides, you need to have your sights on baseball tryouts for Dixie Mills in Jackson over the next few weeks."

"Yeah Tiger, you're right," I said. "So are you going to go out this year as well?"

"Yeah, I will be there," said Tiger.

Tiger and I were walking to the front to meet our moms after the school bell rang at the end of the day. Olivia and her friends were walking behind us. Olivia called my name. Tiger and I stopped. She said, "What, you can't speak this school year, Jefferson?"

I said, "Well, I don't want to get beat up or anything."

She said, "What do you mean by that, Jefferson?"

I responded, "Well, with you having an older boyfriend, an eighth grader and all…"

Olivia responded, "Well, you and I are friends and there isn't anything wrong with friends being cordial with one another."

I said, "I guess you are correct, Ms. Jacobs." Then I said, "Well, enjoy the rest of your day." Tiger and I then continued to go meet our moms.

I had now been in school for a month. Tiger and I had baseball tryouts in Jackson after school. My mom and Tiger's mom would rotate days taking Tiger and me to tryouts. My mom was taking us today. When we got in the car she handed us two homemade turkey and cheese sandwiches, chips, and some of Grandma's famous lemonade. She said, "I knew that you two growing boys would probably be hungry."

We both said, "Yeah Mom, you are right." We both called each other's mom "Mom."

When we arrived at baseball tryouts, the first person that I saw was Olivia standing behind home plate batting cage. I wondered why she was here at the tryouts. I knew that with Greg being in the eighth grade, he would probably be playing for the school's baseball team because he was just that good. As Tiger and I were walking by her, she spoke then struck up a conversation.

"So what are y'all doing here?" she asked.

I said, "We are here for tryouts."

I asked, "So why are you here?"

She stated, "My younger brother Jason is here for tryouts."

I said, "That sounds good. Well, Tiger and I have to go sign up."

She said, "Good luck."

Tiger and I went and signed in, then they gave us a number to put on the backs of our shirts. Thirty minutes later one of the coaches told Tiger and me to grab our gloves and get ready to field some balls. Tiger went first; he played first base, then second, then third, then right field, center field, and left field. He did well at second base, third base, and shortstop. He didn't do so well at any of the other positions. Tiger was about five feet, five inches tall and weighed about 75 pounds.

Then next it was my turn. I was about five-eight and weighed about 100 pounds, not bad for an 11-year-old. I did well at all of the positions with the exception of shortstop. I dropped two balls that were hit to me. One took an unexpected bounce; the other went under my glove.

Next it was time for batting drills. Tiger was a good hitter; his only problem was that he didn't have much power. I, on the other hand, hit several balls out of the park and several off the right and left field walls. I could hit or catch with either hand. I guess you could say that playing baseball was in my genes. My Grandpa Thomas played in the Negro Baseball League. He had photos of him with Satchel Page and Jackie Robinson prior to Jackie Robinson going to the Brooklyn Dodgers. They both were playing for the Kansas City Monarchs in the Negro League. My Father was also an awesome baseball player. He had several high profile scholarships when he graduated from high school. Some folks say that he was a natural at first base. They say he had the talent to play pro baseball right after high school. He was even invited to Winter League Baseball program his junior year in high school. He played against professional baseball and college players. He did well; he had several homeruns and batted 348 during those two weeks that he played. My father batted right but threw left. He gave my older brother Abraham his middle name of Jackie out of respect for Jackie Robinson. My grandpa always tells us that Jackie Robinson was our distant cousin.

After tryouts as we were leaving, I looked over my shoulder and I could see Olivia waving at me. I waved back.

A few weeks passed by, then Tiger and I found out that we both had made the Willie Steakhouse Gravy Train Baseball team. We were so excited. Our first game was this coming Saturday. The Friday before the big game, while Tiger, Maurice, and I were sitting on the bleachers during recess, Olivia walked up. She spoke then asked, 'So which team are you playing on, Jefferson?" I told her which team that I was playing for. Olivia responded, "Wow, my brother Jason is playing on the same team."

Around that time the bell rang to end recess. I said, "I guess I will see you at the game on Saturday."

She said, "You bet; I will be there." She went back down where her girlfriends and Gregory were sitting. I spoke to all of them as Tiger, Maurice and I were walking back to our class.

When I got home that afternoon, my grandpa and Dad couldn't wait to see me. They wanted to talk. So I hurried to change out of my school clothes into my work clothes in order to take care of my daily chores. Once I got changed, I met them at the barn. They asked how I felt and if I was ready for the big game tomorrow. I said, "Yeah, of course."

Dad then pulled this old faded scarf out of his pocket. He said, "Here you go, son; this was given to me by your Grandpa Thomas when I was playing baseball. It will bring you good luck. I used to have it in my front pocket for every game the entire time I played baseball. I would only wash it once a year because I didn't want to damage it."

Grandpa Thomas then said, "Well, it was given to me by my father, your Grandpa Henry. He was the first one in our family to play baseball." Grandpa Thomas went on to say, "It just means so much to your dad and me that you love the game. I know your brothers Jackie and Antoine don't like the game. Jackie plays and love football and Antoine loves studying and working on the farm."

Dad chimed in, "I guess you can't win them all." He was referring to Jackie and Antoine not playing baseball. "We just wanted you to know how baseball and our family are connected."

I said, "Grandpa, Dad, I won't let you or this family down. I will do you proud. But right now, I have chores to do."

The next morning I was up bright and early. I hurried out the door to do my chores, then I arrived back in the house just in time for breakfast. After breakfast, I quickly went to my room to change into my uniform. As I was putting on my uniform, I thought about what my Grandpa and Dad had said. I couldn't have been more proud to be their grandson and son. However, now I was getting a little nervous. I quickly kneeled down beside my bed to pray. "Oh heavenly Father, please give me the strength today to play to the best of my ability; give me the strength today to will a victory for my team; give me the strength today to make my family proud. I thank you, oh Heavenly Father. In Jesus' name, I pray. Amen." I then jumped to my feet, opened my drawer and delicately pulled out the scarf that my father had given me. I placed the scarf in my front right pocket. I then picked up my glove, socks, shoes and hat and proceeded to the front porch.

All of my family was on the front porch waiting on me when I arrived. I quickly put on my socks, shoes and ball cap. My Mom said, "Jefferson, stand next to the door; I want to take a picture of you by yourself." Then she said, "Now I would like to take a photo of you, your grandpa and your dad." I also got a photo of me with the entire family. After taking the photos we all jumped in the family Suburban and headed to Jackson for the game.

When we got there I saw Olivia and her family in the stands. She waved at me and I waved back. Tiger was waiting for me in the dugout. The Coach called out the starting lineup. Tiger was starting at shortstop and I was starting in right field. Olivia's brother Jason was starting on second base. We took to the field while the opposing team was at bat. The first pitch of the game was a fly ball to me; I quickly ran and caught the ball for the first out. Then I looked over in the stands; I saw Olivia and her family as well as my family cheering. The next hit was a foul ball toward the outside fence, which I ran down for the second out of the game. The next batter got a hit past the third baseman. The next bat hit another line drive past the third baseman for a hit. The next batter hit a line drive directly past the first baseman, which he missed. I quickly ran to scoop the ball up. I then threw the ball to the cutoff man in order to hold the runners. The person from second base scored on that play. The next batter hit a ball toward Tiger. Tiger quickly scooped the ball up and threw it underhanded to Jason at second base in order to end the inning. We quickly trotted off the field to end the inning.

Our first two hitters each got on base. Then it was Tiger's turn at bat. He too hit a single. I was up next, batting in the clean-up position. The first pitch was a strike, right down the middle; the second pitch I fouled off the right field wall. The third pitch I fouled off the right field wall again. I asked the umpire for a time out, so I backed away from the plate in order to compose myself. I pulled my glove tighter; I closed my eyes briefly, envisioning me hitting the ball. Then I stepped back up to plate, waiting on the next pitch. The pitcher threw it directly down the center of the plate; I connected and the ball sailed about 30 feet over the right field wall for my first-ever homerun and grand slam. I couldn't believe it as I was trotting around the bases. As I crossed home plate I touched my pocket, kissed my hand and with one hand over my heart, I pointed at Grandpa and Dad with my finger. Not only were they up cheering; so were Olivia and her family.

That day was a great day; I ended up hitting two more homeruns and a double. I needed every hit that I had because it was a tough game. We won the game 11 to 9. Grandpa and Dad were so proud. After the game they gave me a big bear hug. Olivia's dad even came over and shook my hand after the game, telling me how well I had played and how much he enjoyed the game. Tiger and I both were happy that we won as well as elated that we played so well. He went three for four with three singles and a fly-out. We would go on to win the championship that year, with me being named the Most Valuable Player.

I would go on to make varsity my seventh eighth grade years for Leroy. Coach Jenkins would only use me sparingly because he had sophomore, junior and senior players that he would let play first. Grandpa and Dad were highly upset after attending my games during those years. They would always gripe and say, "Hell, Jefferson is better than the majority of the players on the team, with the exception of maybe three or four players."

I had grown a couple of inches over the past two summers. I was five feet, ten-and-a-half inches and weighed 155 pounds. I prayed on the matter; in so many ways God would always send a sign that it wasn't my time yet. I wasn't ready for all the responsibilities that came with playing at that level. Well, my time came during the last three games of my eighth grade year. I guess to teach a junior, Chip Jackson, a lesson for not attending practice, Coach Jenkins benched him right before one of our biggest games of the year. Chip was a decent player. He didn't run and chase down balls in right field very well, but he was a good hitter. We were tied with Millry High School for the best record in our conference. Right before the game was to start, Coach Jenkins looked at me and said, "Robinson, get your glove. You are starting today." (He always called me by my last name. Dad said that he called him by his last name also when he was in high school.) I could hear my family cheering as I got my glove and trotted out to right field.

When I looked over in the stands, I could see the confusion on a lot of people's faces as to who was I and why I was starting in Chip's position. I also saw Olivia in the stands. She waved at me, I waved back. She was there cheering on her boyfriend Greg. Well, I helped to ease a lot of their worries on the first play of the game. The batter hit a huge shot that flew over my head; it was going toward the fence, which would have surely been a homerun if Chip was playing. However, I jumped up and reached over the fence and pulled a homerun from the belly of the dragon. Our fans went wild.

Well, I guess you can say the rest was history. I cemented my position as a starter for Leroy with that play. I further helped my cause by going four for four with two homeruns, a single and a double on that day. Even the principal, Mr. Reynolds, came up to congratulate me after the games. We went on to win Regionals that year but lost in our State Championship game.

Once the season finished up, Tiger and I were training even harder for the Tae Kwon Do Championships in Dallas, Texas. We would practice six days a week with his dad, as well as Tiger and me one on one. My brother Jackie came home to train as well once college was out for the summer. He had just completed his first year of college playing football for the University of Alabama. Jackie had gotten a scholarship to the

University of Alabama. He was only the second player in Leroy history to get a football scholarship to a Division I school from Leroy. The other player was Emanuel King, who received a football scholarship to the University of Alabama in 1981. Paul "Bear" Bryant came to Leroy himself to sign Emanuel. Emanuel went on to play several years of professional football as well. The only other player to play professional sports from Leroy was Kelvin Orlando Moore. He received a scholarship to Jackson State University in 1975 and played professional baseball for the Oakland A's for three years. Kelvin Moore was the best baseball player to ever play for Leroy. We both had something in common; we both grew up working hard on a farm.

My brother Jackie is the starting middle linebacker for the Tide. He stands at six-foot-three, 225 pounds of solid muscle. He is also a Third Degree Black Belt in Tae Kwon Do. People always tell him that he looks like Michael Jai White, who used to play professional football; however, now he is an actor. Michael Jai White is a martial artist as well.

The Tae Kwon Do tournament was June 3. I felt like we were ready. I felt that I was ready for my age/weight category. However, I lost my second match and was eliminated from the tournament. Tiger, who is five feet, eight inches, 120 pounds won his Division as well as a trophy and gold medal. So did my brother. I was the only one who went back a loser that day. That was a long drive back with Master Kim, my brother, and Tiger that day. Even though I was happy that they had won, I was disappointed in myself because I knew that I could have done better, a lot better. I made a promise to myself that day that I would never be a position like that again. I had no problem with losing, especially if I knew that I gave my all or if I knew that the other individual was a lot better than me. But in this instance neither were the case. I knew that the person that I was fighting wasn't better than me; I just didn't give it my all. I wasn't in the best sparring shape, I got tired too quickly and I wasn't as crisp with my kicks and punches. I knew that during baseball season, I didn't stay in the best shape I possibly could have. I didn't spend enough time sparring, practicing and running.

When Master Kim pulled in front of our house to let us out, Jackie and I thanked him for allowing us to experience the tournament environment. He said, "Jackie, you did a great job today." He told me, "Jefferson, keep your head up; you will get it done the next time."

I said, "Thank you, sir. Good night."

When we walked through the door everyone rushed to congratulate us. I explained to them that I had lost but they didn't care; they still included me in the Robinson group hug. Grandmother had baked our favorite desserts: peach cobbler for Jackie and chocolate pound cake for me. After dinner, I had a big ol' slice of that cake and a bowl of homemade vanilla ice cream. Grandpa made the best ice cream in Leroy. Everyone loved coming by our house to our annual Mother's Day cookout just for his ice cream, as well as Dad's special barbecue.

After dessert, Jackie and I sat up explaining to everyone how great the experience of the National Tournament was. Sure, we had attended local Tae Kwon Tournaments, but nothing like the tournament that we had just completed. Jackie was telling everyone about life on the University of Alabama campus. He had just finished an unbelievable freshman year, where he led the team in sacks and tackles. He won the Dick Butkus and several other awards, as well as made the All-Defensive team. I was extremely proud of my Jackie. He had set the bar extremely high.

I'm also proud of my brother Antoine (but we call him Isiah); he is a senior at Leroy this year. He is extremely smart. He scored off the charts on all of his SAT and ACT scores. He has scholarship offers from several schools across the country: Harvard, Stanford, Alabama, Springhill, South Alabama, Yale and Ole Mississippi. Need I say which school he is leaning towards? Yes, you guessed it Alabama. My sister Aliyah (who we call Eve) is a year younger than me. She is very athletic as well as smart. She plays basketball and softball for Leroy.

While we were sitting having a weekly family quorum, I said, "Mom and Dad…"

They said, "Yes, Jefferson."

I said, "Can I ask you a question?"

They said, "Sure."

I said, "Why in the world would y'all give us all first names but you call us by our middle name except when you're upset with us? Abraham's name is Abraham Jackie Robinson, but you call him Jackie. Antoine's name is Antoine Isiah Robinson, but you call him Isiah. Eve's name is

Aliyah Eve Robinson, but we call her Eve. My name is Thomas Jefferson Robinson III, but you call me Jefferson. Please, I need to know."

Dad said, "I'm going to let your mom answer this one."

Mom started, "Well son, we had it all planned out. I wanted everyone's name to start with the letter A, and I also wanted everyone's name to be in the Bible, but we kept running into roadblocks. As it relates to your name, the minute you were born we immediately knew what your name would be. You were the spitting image of your dad and grandpa. Sure, the first two boys looked like your dad, but we knew the name Thomas wouldn't work well for them. Now you, on the other hand, we knew you were a Thomas. We call you by your middle name because it is the easiest thing to do to avoid confusion. Your grandparents call Dad Junior and his friends call him T.J. and your grandpa Big Tom. I wanted to have the other kids' first names start with the letter A and their middle name come from the Bible. But your father threw a wrench in those plans by making Abraham's middle name Jackie in honor of Jackie Robinson. Therefore, his biblical middle name Abraham became his first name."

Dad chimed in to say that everyone called us by our middle names because they were easier to pronounce. Everyone started laughing.

Then Grandpa changed the subject. He said, "We need to build a bigger and better barn."

My brother Isiah interrupted to say, "Not only do we need to build a better barn, but we need to build a state of the art and more efficient barn. If the barn is more efficient we can sell more products. I think that we need a barn that has A/C and heating, as well as a better cold storage and smokehouse to cure and smoke our meats a lot better than the current system. We also need better lighting."

Dad was a little hesitant because he is kind of tight and he doesn't want to spend the kind of money that my brother is talking about on a new barn. Dad and Grandpa ended the discussion by saying they would think it over and a decision on the new barn would be forthcoming.

On a different subject, I could tell by the looks on my parents' faces they were glad to have all of their children home again under one roof. I must admit, I was glad to have everyone home as well. My friend Maurice calls us the black Waltons. He said we were a close-knit family.

The remainder of the school year went by rather quickly. It was now summertime in Alabama. I enjoyed spending the summer on the farm. Even though I worked hard, I also played just as hard: riding horses, swimming in the pond, spending time in my tree house reading books. It was a great place to live.

It was finally official; Grandpa and Dad decided to build a new barn. They were moving forward with the process. Master Kim, who was the Chairman of E-room bank approved a $500,000 loan for Dad and Grandpa in order to build their state-of-the-art barn. That night at dinner, Dad stated, "Well, we are going to use Jacobs Construction to build the barn."

I asked, "Did you say Jacobs Construction, Dad?"

He responded, "Yes, Jefferson." He stated that he and Mr. Jacobs (Olivia's dad) had been talking during my baseball games.

I was shocked that a big company like Jacobs Construction would do such a small project. Mr. Jacobs stated that he would be honored to build the barn for Dad and Grandpa. I was kind of excited also; maybe just maybe, Olivia might stop by to look at the project.

Two weeks had passed before all of the paperwork and designs were approved. It was now official; they broke ground on the barn on June 15. It was estimated to take 60 days to complete, which meant that we would have a new barn prior to the beginning of my freshman school year. During the ground breaking, Mr. Jacobs pulled up to the jobsite. I was shocked to see Olivia and her brother in his truck when he pulled up. He got out of his truck and went to speak to Dad and Grandpa, who were standing near the area where the work was taking place.

Olivia and her brother Jason got out of the truck and were walking in my direction. My heart was beating about 200 miles per minute. Jason walked up and shook my hand and said, "What's up, Jefferson?"

I said, "Nothing much, just finished doing chores."

Olivia also said, "Hi," and I said hi back to her.

Jason asked, "Is it ok to go see the horses?"

I said, "Sure, we can go see the horses."

So we all started walking toward the corral that was holding the horses. My brother Isiah and sister Eve were talking about going riding earlier in the day; that is why the horses were in the corral instead of in the pasture grazing. Jason began running toward the horses, while Olivia and I were walking and talking.

I asked, "So what do you have planned for the summer?"

She said, "Well nothing much except we are going to our condo in Gulf Shores on the 25th of this month and returning the day before our annual Fourth of July celebration." Then she asked what I was going to do.

I replied, "Well, I have nothing planned except chores, Tae Kwon Do training, ride horses, fish and go swimming."

Jason asked, "Jefferson is it possible to ride the horses?"

I said, "Sure, why not?" Well Jason, prior to us riding, I need to know if you know how to ride a horse."

Jason responded, "Yeah Jefferson, I know how to ride a horse. We have horses at our grandparent's house that we ride at least twice a month."

There were only two horses out, Isiah and Eve's horses. Two-Tone and Star were their names. Isiah's horse, named Two-Tone, was a gorgeous American Indian Horse; he was brown with white spots. He was gorgeous. My sister Eve's horse Star was a beautiful female Tennessee Walker; she could run. I quickly got the bridles and saddles from the barn to get both horses ready. I went back in the barn to get an extra saddle for my horse, Storm, which was a beautiful Black Arabian Thoroughbred. Storm is a great horse. Dad brought her for me when I was ten years old. She is very high-spirited. She will only let certain people ride her. I named her personally because she is a quiet, mild-mannered horse unless she doesn't like you. Once you get her started running, Storm doesn't like to stop.

I asked Olivia if it would be ok to catch a ride with her in order to go get my horse. She said, "Of course." I picked up my saddle and placed it on the fence, then I had her jump onto Star, then I jumped on the back of the horse behind her. I held the reins and went by the fence to grab the saddle. Then we were off to find Storm. As I figured, she was out underneath the trees next to the pond. I quickly jumped off the horse with my saddle and bridle and called her name. She came running toward me. She knew two things, one she knew that I had her favorite snack, carrot sticks and two, she knew that we were about to go riding.

Once I quickly got her saddled; we were off. I took them down a trail that led to a different pond on the property. That was our swim-hole. It had a big rope hanging from a great big old oak tree. We use the rope to swing out into the middle of the pond.

Then I took them by our cabin just off the trail. I explained to them that Dad and Grandpa use it as their place to get away from Mom and Grandma. They also use it as a place to gather and drink when their male friends and male cousins come to town. All of the men would leave the women in the house and go out to the cabin. During deer season they come out to the cabin and spend the night after a day of hunting. We got off the horses and walked over to the cabin. I used my keys to open the door and showed them the inside. There were two bedrooms, a kitchen, a bathroom, living room, TV and a bar over in the corner. Dad kept his favorite drink, Tanqueray Gin, and other assortments of liqueurs on the bar. I explained, "Well, in the refrigerator you have the other beverage of choice by my Grandpa, Coors Light." Everyone laughed.

After leaving the cabin, I told them to follow me to my favorite place. It was probably about a thousand feet away. It was a great big old tree house. It was equipped with three windows a roof, with shingles, and a door. It actually looked like a small house perched up on the limb of a big old oak tree. Dad and Grandpa built it for my brothers many years ago. They stopped coming years ago, so this is my place of refuge. Whenever I have a bad day this is where I migrate to. This is where I come to think and get away from everything.

Jason was like, "This is so cool, Jefferson."

Olivia was like, "I would like to come back here some time."

I said, "Sure, whenever you are ready; just let me know."

Then she was like, "Jason, we better be getting back; Dad is probably looking for us."

So we walked back through the woods to the horses. Well, Jason ran, but we walked. Olivia was like, "Jason wait up." But he was gone; he ran to Two-Tone, climbed on him and was gone. Then when we got to the horses; Olivia asked, "Jefferson could you give me a hand on getting on Star?"

I said, "Sure, I will give you a hand."

She placed one foot in the stirrup and one arm around my neck. As she was about to lift up, her foot slipped and we both fell. She landed on top of me. We both started laughing; then we looked in each other's eyes. Before I knew it, we kissed. It seemed like that kiss must have lasted forever. Her lips tasted so good. They sort of tasted like strawberries. I asked, "So what do you have on your lips?"

She replied, "Lip gloss."

I asked, "What flavor?"

She said, "Well, it is Strawberry Passion. So is the Strawberry Passion a problem?"

I said, "No, the Strawberry Passion tasted very good." As we were getting up, I said, "Let's try this again; that is, you getting on your horse."

She said, "Ok."

This time she was able to get on her horse with no problem. Then I got on Storm. We were side by side. I asked her, "So what just happened?"

She replied, "Well Jefferson, we have just finished kissing."

I responded, "I know what we just finished doing, Olivia. But aren't you involved with Gregory?"

She said, "Yes, I am; is there a problem?"

I said, "Well, there is. I know Greg; he and I play on varsity baseball together. It just doesn't feel right."

"Well Jefferson, aren't you glad it happened?" asked Olivia.

I responded, "Of course, you just don't know how often I have daydreamed about doing just that—kissing you. However, I can't let it happen again because it goes against everything that I have been taught by Dad. He always tells me about the Golden Rules of Being a Man. The First Golden Rule is a man provides for his family; the second Golden Rule is that a man takes care of his responsibility, the third Golden Rule is that a man always tells the truth; at the time telling the truth may not seem like the right thing to do, but in the end telling truth will always make things right; the Fourth Golden Rule is a man always has his own, which means a man should own his own home, own his own car, have his own money, and most importantly have his own woman. Dad says that a man should never go after another man's woman; get your own. He always says that no good that comes out of a man having relations with another man's woman and/or wife."

"Well, I'm sorry, Jefferson, if I offended you or anything," said Olivia.

I responded, "Everything is ok. Olivia, as much as I want you, I can't have a relationship with you while you have a boyfriend; regardless if he is Greg or anyone else. I would much rather be your friend.

Olivia responded, "Jefferson, I can respect your decision." All of sudden, I saw her make a face as if something was wrong. She said, "Jefferson, I believe my foot is stuck; can you help me?"

As I got off my horse and was about to walk over to her, she immediately kicked Star in the side and told her to get going. They were off like a bolt of lightning. I quickly jumped back on Storm. I said, "Let's get them, girl; let's show them what we are made of."

She probably had about a sixty yard lead on me at the time. We were probably about a good three football fields in length from the barn. As I turned the corner of the pasture, I could see that she had Star stretched out. I was amazed how good a rider Olivia was. I could also see everyone in the front of the barn looking our way. Storm was just getting in stride; those big legs of hers were just getting going. This is what she lived for; I hadn't ridden her like this in a long time. She was really a thoroughbred. We were now about 10 yards from Olivia, approaching 60 yards to the barn. All of sudden we were even and about 25 yards from the barn, now 15 yards, now 10 yards. Storm and I ended up beating Olivia by three horse lengths.

Dad said, "Olivia, you sure can ride a horse."

Olivia's father was like, "She better; she has been riding since she was three years old. She has also has ridden in the Equestrians Horse Shows in Tennessee," said Mr. Jacobs.

My brother Isiah and sister Eve were also waiting at the gate for us. Olivia's dad said, "Well Jason and Olivia, it is time to go." Olivia got off the horse and gave the reins to my sister; then she walked over to me and stretched out her hand to me and I reached down and shook her hand and said goodbye.

Olivia said, "Maybe I will stop by with Dad later in the week and we can finish our race."

I said, "Sure."

My siblings and I quickly turned away and went racing back out across the pastures with our horses. The whole time I was racing across the field, I was like, *Wow, what an amazing day. It has to be ranked up there with one of the best days of my life.*

Later in the week Olivia and her brother stopped by to go horseback riding again. Once again we had a great time. Prior to them leaving, Olivia said, "Jefferson, is it ok to have your phone number? I might want to stop by next week prior to me going out of town to go riding again."

I said, "Sure, my home number is (205)246-2793."

She said, "Thanks."

Several days passed and it was now Saturday. Dad, Grandpa, Isiah and I had been working all day installing a new fence on the south part of the pasture in order to keep the horses, cows, and goats from getting out. We had noticed that during the previous night the rain and wind had knocked down a tree across the fence. We were fortunate that none of the animals got out.

While working on the fence, Grandpa asked, "So Jefferson, are you and that Jacobs girl courting?"

I said, "No Grandpa, we are just friends."

He then said, "It seems like more than friends to me, because now all of sudden she wants to stop by every day to go horseback riding." He went on to say, "I can remember not so long ago that a black man would get lynched for just looking at a white woman; now I have my grandson going off in the woods horseback riding with one every day. Well, you be careful."

Dad then said to my grandpa, "Yeah Dad, you even have white folks building you a new barn."

We all started laughing. Then my grandpa said, "I bet you never thought that would ever happen."

My brother Isiah then said, "Well Jefferson, you just need to be careful."

I asked, "So what do you mean by that, Isiah?"

He stated, "Well, the word around the school is that she is a little fast girl. She goes from one boy to another."

I then stated, "Well Isiah, that isn't true; those are just rumors."

Grandpa said, "Well Jefferson, the old saying is wherever there is smoke, there is usually a fire."

I said, "She has a boyfriend. She has been dating Gregory Richardson for the past three years."

Grandpa then said, "So is that Jethro Richardson's grandson?"

I said, "Yes, sir."

He said, "Well, you be extremely careful because some of those Richardsons aren't too friendly toward us black folks." He said, "Now Jethro has always been a good old fellow; he and I grew up together. But his brother Wayne Richardson and his uncle Jason Richardson damn near beat this black boy from Jackson to death back in the sixties because Wayne's girlfriend said that the black boy blew a kiss at her. After it all was said and done, it came to light that the girl had lied."

"Greg isn't like that, Grandpa; he and I play on the varsity baseball team together."

My grandpa then said, "Yeah, you both are ok right now, but I'm willing to bet that his feelings will change once he knows that his girlfriend likes you."

Dad then said, "Well son, don't forget about one of the Golden Rules."

I said, "Don't worry, Dad, I haven't forgotten about the Golden Rule that a man should have his own, own money, own home, and most importantly own woman. Dad, I even explained that to her the other day when she kissed me."

"So you both kissed?" Dad asked. I said.

"Yes, sir we did. It was the first time that I ever had kissed a girl."

Dad said, "From now on, I don't want you going riding off in the pasture by yourself with her. You be sure to have someone go riding with y'all at all times. I don't want any problems down the road."

I said, "Don't worry, Dad. I explained to her that we could be nothing more than friends."

When we arrived back home later that day, Mom, Grandma, and Eve had prepared a meal fit for a king—well, in our case, kings. They had prepared collard greens, black-eyed peas, fried chicken, pork chops, rice and gravy, macaroni and cheese, candied yams, and cornbread. I was glad that they had prepared that meal, because I was starved. I sure did stuff myself.

Mom said, "Jefferson, slow down; the food isn't going anywhere."

I said, "I know, Mom, but it is going somewhere."

She asked, "Where?"

I then pointed toward my stomach. Everyone laughed. As I finished eating my last piece of chicken, I said, "So what is for dessert?"

Grandma said, "We have banana pudding (which is my favorite), and we have Seven-up Pound cake."

I said, "Well, I will start with some of this good banana pudding."

After dinner, we all went and sat on the porch. We were at my grandparents' house, so I knew what was coming next. My grandpa brought his stereo on the porch, hooked up his speakers, and then he put on some blues. We played blues every Friday and Saturday evening at our house. Yeah, the blues played a major part in my upbringing. My grandpa loved Johnny Taylor. Dad loves Bobby Rush. Well, as for me I was and still am a Marvin Sease fan. My favorite Marvin Sease song is "Candy Licker". My older brother Jackie likes Clarence Carter; his favorite song is "Stroking". I love sitting on the porch watching Grandpa grab Grandma by the hand as they do the two-step to Johnny Taylor. Grandpa always says, "You youngsters don't know anything about that right there."

Once he says that, I know what is next. Dad jumps up and grabs Mom by the hand and says "Well, old timer, we are going to show y'all a thing or two," then they start doing their moves. My siblings and I always sit back and laugh.

I also used to love and listen to Grandpa and Dad tells stories about years past. One story that I enjoy in particular is about my grandma, Abigail Everett Robinson. My grandma is a sweet and kind woman. She only stands about five feet, five inches tall and weighs about 135 pounds, but don't cross her. Dad started to tell the story about when this one lady insulted Grandma in church. It all started when the Sunday collections came up short one Sunday. My Grandma was the treasurer so she stayed behind every Sunday to help count money and have it ready for the deposit at the bank on Monday. Well, anyway Ms. Wilson and Ms. King would always stay back and help count the money with her on Sundays. This one particular Monday, the money came up short $1200.00. Ms. Wilson immediately accused Grandma of stealing the money prior to investigating to determine what had happened to the money. Pastor Riley then called a meeting with Grandma, Ms. Wilson and Ms. King to discuss the events of last Sunday. Grandma explained that after all three of them counted the money twice to ensure that it was correct, they placed the money into the small lockbox and placed the lockbox in the closet in the Pastor's office like they always do. It was a total of $3500 from the Sunday offering. Well, someone went into the lockbox and stole $1200.

Ms. Wilson immediately stated, "I believe Abigail took the money because she is the treasurer."

My Grandma's response was, "How could you say that I took the money? If that is the case, you could have taken the money also."

Pastor Riley was like, "Ms. Wilson, now don't go accusing anyone of taking the money, especially if you don't have any evidence to prove it." Ms. Wilson kept talking on and on about how Grandma had taken the money.

At the time they were sitting in the Pastor's office because Bible study was taking place in the main part of the church. Well, Grandma stood up and said, "I don't have to take this kind of talk from you or anyone else."

As Grandma stood up Ms. Wilson grabbed her by the arm and said, "No thief, you sit your butt back down." Now why did she grab Grandma by the arm? My grandma hit her in the face so hard that Ms. Wilson fell backwards in the chair that she was sitting in. When she got up her wig was halfway coming off her head. My grandma was walking toward her to finish the job. Ms. Wilson was quickly running toward the part of the church where Bible study was taking place. She was yelling, "somebody please help me."

Right about the time she arrived in the front of the first pew my grandma caught her by her hair but Ms. Wilson's wig came off in my grandma's hand. So then my grandma grabbed Ms. Wilson and they both went flying over the first row of pews. By the time the men of the church were able to get to them, Grandma was sitting on top of Ms. Wilson, beating her in the face with her fist.

They say my grandma was yelling, "Heifer, so who did you say stole the money from the church?"

Ms. Wilson's response was, "I'm sorry, Abigail, it wasn't you. I'm sorry, Abigail, please don't hit me again. Please let me up."

Once they were separated they took my grandma to the back of the church in order to try and calm her down. About 10 minutes later Dad said that he and Grandpa had arrived at the church. They had received a phone call from Deacon Moore saying that Grandma was tearing the church down with Ms. Wilson. Once the commotion had calmed down, this 13-year-old kid came forward and stated that when he was leaving the church on Sunday afternoon he had seen Deacon Jenkins leaving the Pastor's office putting some money in his coat pocket. Everyone then looked at Deacon Jenkins at the time and questioned him about was being said about him.

Pastor Riley stated, "Deacon Jenkins, if you would confess up to this crime and pay the money back, the church won't press charges."

Deacon Jenkins confessed, "I stole the money, Pastor. I'm truly sorry."

Pastor Riley replied, "Deacon Jenkins, you're dismissed from the board as well as your duties of handing any money associated with the church. Please turn in your keys."

He was dismissed from serving on the board and eventually left the church as well as he agreed to pay the money back. It was later discovered that Deacon Jenkins was on drugs. He had to be admitted to a drug rehabilitation program. Ms. Wilson then came up to apologize to Grandma but Grandma was like, "I'm too damn upset to accept your apology right now."

Grandma also resigned from the church board as Treasurer at that time. She stated that from now on, "I will just be a member of the church and leave it at that." She told Dad and Grandpa that it was time for them to leave.

We were all in amazement, like, "Grandma, you were fighting in church."

My grandma then said "Hell yeah!" She was like, "Your grandpa and dad aren't saints either, you know."

Dad then said, "Yeah, your grandpa doesn't mind fighting either." He began to tell the story about when he, Grandpa and one of Grandpa's friends, Larry Sullivan (a Caucasian farmer who grew up with my grandpa), were on their way back from Waynesboro, Mississippi after taking cows there to sell at the auction. Well anyway, on their way back they had stopped by a bar in Mobile, Alabama to have a few drinks. Dad said he had just turned 21 years old so he was excited about being able to drink. Well anyway, they went to sit at the bar to order a round of drinks. While they were drinking their beers two Caucasian guys walked in and asked the bartender if he knew who was driving the dually truck with the long trailer attached to it. My grandpa overheard the conversation and said, "Yes, I'm driving the truck. Is there a problem?"

The guy said, "Yeah, there is a problem; you are taking up my parking spot, along with several other spots." The guy then said, "You need to move your truck right now."

My grandpa's response was, "There are 20 other spots in that parking lot for you to park."

The guy was like, "No, I want my spot."

My grandpa then replied, "You can have the spot once we leave."

The bartender was like, "Jerry (which was the guy's name), we don't need any trouble."

Around this time my Grandpa stood up. Jerry was like, "Yeah old man, stand up and go move your fucking truck."

My grandpa responded, "Son, you need to watch your mouth."

Then Jerry pressed one finger on my grandpa and said, "Nigger, you don't tell me what to do."

My grandpa quickly punched Jerry in the face. Jerry fell to the floor, then Jerry's friend came after Grandpa and Grandpa picked him up and threw him across the table. Dad said about this time he stood up to help my grandpa but my grandpa's friend Larry told him to sit back down. Dad sat back down. Dad said, "Mr. Larry, I need to help Dad."

Larry said, "There are only two men your dad is fighting. Your dad will take care of them."

He was correct; my grandpa beat the hell out of Jerry and his friend, then he came and turned up his beer and chugged it down and paid for their drinks. While they were on their way out the bartender asked Grandpa if he wanted to press charges against the two guys. My grandpa said no. Dad said that when they got to the truck my grandpa asked him and Larry why they didn't help him. Dad said, "Well Dad, Mr. Larry said that you could handle it."

Then Grandpa said, "Larry, you're an asshole."

Then they all started laughing. Then Mr. Larry stated, "Well hell,

T.J., I've seen you beat three guys twice as big as those guys and didn't have any problems."

My grandpa's response was, "Yeah, I was 20 years younger."

After Dad finished telling that story my grandpa started to tell a story about Dad. He was like, "I got your Dad back several years later for not helping me that day." Once again, my grandpa stated, "Well, it was your Dad, Larry Sullivan and me. We had gone to Montgomery, Alabama earlier that day to look at some tractors and cotton pickers. Well, on our way back we decided to stop at Willie G's Steakhouse in Jackson for a few drinks. We walked in and sat at the bar. Willie G, the owner, came over and spoke to us. Larry and I have known Willie since we were teenagers. Several guys from Jackson came by the bar. Well, your dad had busted one of the guys up pretty good in high school after they had gotten into a fight after a baseball game. To this day, he still didn't like your dad. Well he came by the bar to ensure my your dad saw him.

"He stated, 'Well, if it isn't Thomas Robinson Jr. It has been ages since I've seen you. So what do you do now, boy? I hear you didn't take that scholarship to the University of Alabama. So what do you do now, clean floors?'

"Your dad didn't answer. Willie was like, 'Bobby Joe, you and your goons need to go sit down or get the hell out of my business.'

"Bobby Joe was like, 'Hell Willie, all I was doing was trying to see what this boy has been up to.'

"Your dad put down his beer, stood up, and said, 'That is the last time that you call me boy.'

"Billy Joe looked at your dad and said, 'Boy, I owe you an ass whooping.' He then swung at your dad. T.J. ducked and picked up Bobby Joe and threw him up against a pole in the middle of the room. About this time the other two guys with Bobby Joe ran toward T.J. Your dad dove toward them and knocked both of the guys down.

"Larry looked at me and was like, 'Thomas, do you think we need to help T.J.?'

"My response was, 'No Larry, there are only three of them. T.J. will be ok.' Then I turned around and finished drinking my Coors Light. Sure enough, your dad beat all three of those guys' asses that day.

"After Willie and his bartenders broke up the fight your dad looked at Larry and me and said, 'Well guys, thanks for the help.'

"Larry replied, 'I was about to help you, T.J., but your Pa said there were only three guys.'"

My grandpa finished off the story by saying, "We all laughed on our way back to Leroy."

After Grandpa finished telling that story I was like, "All of you Robinsons sure do love to fight."

Grandma's response was, "Hell yeah."

Well, after sitting on the porch we all went inside. Normally I would watch a little TV but I was tired. I immediately told everyone good night. Then I went and took a shower and went to bed.

The following week I received a phone call from Olivia. She asked, "Jefferson, is it ok if Jason and come over and ride the horses on Wednesday?"

I said, "Sure, it won't be a problem."

Sure enough, that Wednesday morning she and her dad and brother pulled up in front of the house around 8 a.m. I was already standing out front with Dad and Grandpa as we were observing the work taking place on the new barn. Olivia's dad came over and was talking to Dad and Grandpa. I already had the horses saddled up and ready to go. On this day, I decided to take them to one of my favorite places. There was a trail that led through the woods about a mile away from the pastures. Once we got to the edge of the woods we came into an open field of the most beautiful green grass you ever did want to see. The property was owned by my grandpa. It was about 20 acres. We never planted anything on this property because the place was so beautiful. My grandpa always used to tell me that he had been coming there since he was a kid. There was a nice stream that ran down through the property. It had some of the purest and coldest water that you ever did want to taste. We all got down off our horses and took a sip of water.

I said, "Well guys, let's get back on the horses and go down to the sand pits."

We must have ridden for three hours. We rode down by the sand pits, and then up on this huge hill. Once we got to the top of the hill, we could look down into the valley and see for miles around. It was a beautiful sight. Each time I would go to the top of the hill, I would see Leroy in a totally different way.

Olivia said, "Jefferson, I like this place. Where are we going to go next?"

I replied, "We are going to go back to the field where we were earlier. It is time for lunch."

She said, "Lunch?"

I said, "Yeah, lunch."

When we got to the field we got down off the horses. I pulled out my lunch bag, which was on ice packs. Inside the lunch bag, I had three sandwiches, three Coca-Colas, three bags of Golden Flake potato chips, three slices of my grandma's homemade pie and small portable radio. I laid all of these items on my mom's red and white lunch blanket that I had brought with me. We all sat down, ate lunch and talked.

Olivia stated, "Jefferson, this was so wonderful thing to do, preparing lunch for us and all."

I replied, "It wasn't a problem because I love to eat." Then I said, "Well guys, please excuse me. I'm going to take a nap."

Olivia was like, "You are going to take a nap?"

I said, "Yes ma'am, a nap. I have good music playing, I've just finished a good meal, I'm in the presence of good company, and it's a gorgeous day. I can't think of a better time and place to take a nap." I lay down, placed my hands behind my neck and closed my eyes. I could hear Olivia and her brother talking. She even changed my radio station from 93 WBLX FM and moved it to some country station on an AM channel. Well, she better be glad that I listened to country also, or there would have been trouble that day.

After my 30 minute nap we got back on our horses and headed back toward the barn. Olivia said, "Jefferson, I've really had a great time today."

I said, "Thanks so, did I."

She stated, "I'm leaving for Gulf Shores in a couple of days and won't return until July third."

I said, "That sounds like fun."

She responded, "Yeah, it is a lot of fun. Jefferson, would you like to come to our annual Fourth of July celebration?"

I said, "I would love to come; however, I can't come over because we are having a lot of family in town during that time as well."

Before I knew it we were at the barn. We all got down off the horses. I quickly unsaddled the horses and took the saddles and bridles to the rack-room. We said our goodbyes, then they left with their dad. It was time for me to do the chores. I would normally have my brother Isiah helping me; however, he had the afternoon off since he covered for me earlier while I was out riding horses with Olivia and her brother.

The next couple of weeks went by rather quickly. It was the day before the Fourth of July and Tiger and I were in the gym sparring. We had already finished practice with Master Kim. I was telling Tiger about how I had been spending time with Olivia. Tiger said, "Jefferson, it sounds like Olivia likes you."

Then I threw a roundhouse kick and punch at him. I said, "No, we are just friends."

Tiger then threw a back kick that caught me directly in the chest. Tiger said, "See, she has you all messed up. You're not even concentrating. Any other time when we were sparring I never would have caught you with that move."

I then said, "Yeah, I know. So Tiger, are you and your family coming by my house for our Fourth of July Celebration tomorrow?"

He said, "Yes, we will be there."

The next day was great. We had a lot of family that came to town for the Fourth of July this year. I had on my new Fourth of July outfit that my Mom had brought me. I was out front playing around with my cousins when Tiger and his family arrived. I immediately ran up to greet Master and Mrs. Kim. I did my bow and formal Korean handshake to Master Kim. Every action that we do is a form of respect.

Tiger saw the new barn and was like, "That is a huge barn, Jefferson."

I replied, "I know, Dad and Grandpa went all out on the creation of this new barn."

After we played football and basketball it was time to eat. Tiger and I had large appetites. While I was sitting at the table my sister Eve came over and said, "Jefferson, you have a phone call."

I asked, "So do you know who it is calling?"

She replied, "It is Olivia."

I was thinking to myself, *What does she want?* When I got to the phone I said, "Hello."

She said, "Hi, this is Olivia."

I said, "Hey, what's up?"

She replied, "Greg and I called everything off yesterday."

I asked, "So what caused you and Greg to break up?"

She replied, "It is a long story."

I replied, "Well Olivia, I have time, so what happened?"

She started by saying, "Greg and his family were in Gulf Shores during the time that we there. Greg and I were spending a lot of time together; however, he got jealous of another friend of mine that was hanging out with us."

I asked, "So Olivia was this other friend a boy?"

She replied, "Yes, the friend was a boy."

I said, "Ok, now continue."

She went on to say, "I used to date this boy in question, whose name was Jeremy Bosch. I had already told Greg that Jeremy and I used to date as well."

I responded, "I can understand why Greg was upset. You had your ex-boyfriend hanging around you guys all day every day."

"Well Jefferson, I tried to explain to Greg that Jeremy Bosch's mom and my mom were best friends. But Greg didn't want to hear any of it. So Greg took it into his own hands and told Jeremy to stop hanging around us so much," said Olivia. "Then Jeremy responded by telling Greg that he could hang around as long as he liked. The next thing I knew Jeremy and Greg were fighting. Greg broke Jeremy's nose it was just a big mess."

I then asked whether she was ok she said, "Yes." She stated, "Jefferson, I want to see you. You're the only person that I've been thinking about. Can I stop by to see you next week?"

I said, "Olivia, I don't think that would be a good idea. I think that you need to clear your mind and get yourself together emotionally." I went on to say, "Olivia, before there can ever be a you and me, you need tie up whatever loose ends that you have with Greg, because I don't want to be caught in the middle of your lovers' quarrel."

Olivia stated, "Greg and I are over."

I replied, "I don't think that is the case. You need to take care of your unfinished business with Greg."

"Okay, Jefferson," said Olivia. "I will resolve all issues with Greg in order to ensure that things are over in the correct manner."

"Olivia, I want you to know that I'm your friend and that I truly care for you. However, at the present time, I think that it is best that we not see each other. I think that you really need to finish everything that you have going on in your life and get yourself together. I don't want to complicate the situation. If it is meant to be between you and me then it will be. However, I want to have a clear conscience going into a relationship with no regrets. Therefore, I hope that you enjoy the rest of your Fourth of July and we will talk soon."

Then we both said goodbye and hung up the phone. I went back outside and told Tiger everything that had happened. He was like, "Jefferson, I told you that she wants you." He went on to say, "I bet you Olivia set up that whole deal relating to Greg and this Jeremy guy in Gulf Shores in order to break up with Greg."

I said, "Tiger, you don't know Olivia. She wouldn't do something as cruel as what you are saying."

Tiger's response was, "Well, my friend, be careful."

I said, "I will."

The next week passed by and Olivia and I didn't speak over the phone or see other. Two weeks passed by, and we still didn't speak over the phone or see other. During that time Olivia's father was coming by to monitor the barn project nearly every day. I heard Grandpa and Olivia's father talking one day. Mr. Jacobs said, "Mr. Thomas, the barn is near completion. We are slated to finish on time and within budget."

My grandpa was excited because the barn was really nice. It was state of the art. I didn't see Olivia again until our new barn was completed. The barn was completed several days prior to the due date. I had already done my morning chores and decided to take Storm out for a ride. I had already put the saddle and bridle on her and walked her up and tied her to the front gate. Then I walked over to the front of the new barn where Dad, Grandpa, my brother Isiah and Jacobs Construction Project Manager Darryl Batley were standing. He said, "Everyone, as soon as Mr. Jacobs arrives we can begin the walk-through."

All of sudden I look up and see Olivia and her brother Jason pulling up in front of the barn in the truck with their father. Mr. Jacobs jumped out of the truck and came over and shook everybody's hand. He said, "Good morning, everybody. Let's get started." I believe he was more excited than Dad and Grandpa were.

While everyone else was walking in the barn Olivia and I gave each other a long embrace and said hi. I said, "Summer is almost over."

She replied, "Yes, it sure is. Jefferson, I'm sorry for not contacting you but I needed time to get my thoughts together to determine what I really want." Then she asked, "Jefferson, do you know what I want?"

I responded, "No."

She said, "I want you." She stated that she had never missed anyone more than she had not talking or seeing me over the past three weeks.

I said, "I have missed you also."

She said, "I see you have Storm out ready for a ride."

I asked, "So would you like to go for a ride with me?"

She replied, "I would love to go for a ride."

I said, "Once we finish walking through the barn, I will go get Star ready for you."

She said, "Ok."

We began walking through the barn. It was huge. One side of the barn had 16 insulated stalls, an insulated tack room, and an insulated wash room; on the other side of the barn there was a place to store the tractors and cotton picker. There was also an office, as well as living quarters equipped with three bedrooms and a kitchen. This barn had a state-of-the-art electrical and lighting system. In the back of the barn they had the stalls set up so that we could load the cows and pigs directly onto the trailer to ship them out. There was a loft that would be used to store hay and feed a large conveyor belt system that traveled from the bottom of the barn to the top and service elevator. The barn also had an A/C and heating system. They even had two stalls set up for animals to give birth. I must admit I was really impressed. Dad and Grandpa went all out. Everyone was excited about the barn.

Mr. Jacobs said, "I may have to build me a barn like this one."

Olivia asked Jason if he was ready to go riding. He replied, "Not today." He was all excited about looking over every inch of the barn.

I asked Isiah if he would like to go, he said, "No."

I said, "Well Olivia, we won't be able to go very far without someone else with us because Dad doesn't want us riding off by ourselves."

She said, "Ok."

We walked over to the fence then I walked in the old barn and got an additional saddle and bridle for Star. I told Olivia to get on Storm to ride while I went out back to get Star. However, Storm started acting crazy she wouldn't let Olivia ride her. So I got Olivia back down off Storm, held her reins and allowed her to walk behind Olivia and me while we were going to get Star. We didn't have to walk very far. Star was already walking toward the barn, I guess because she knew it was feeding time. Once I got Star all ready to ride I helped Olivia get on her, and then we were off. We didn't go too far away. We both stopped and got off the horses and started walking with the horses following us. We were just talking about life in general.

I said, "It is hard to believe that we will be sophomores this year. I can remember when we were in the third grade together. I also remember the first day that you started school at Leroy."

She said, "No way."

I said, "I can remember that you were wearing a little blue dress. You had two little ponytails with a blue ribbon on each."

Olivia was like, "Jefferson, you can still remember all of that?"

"I sure can."

I said, "The moment I saw you with those beautiful blue eyes, I said there sits the love of my life."

She stopped walking and said, "Really Jefferson?"

I said, "Yes." Then we looked into each other's eyes prior to me giving her a soft, passionate kiss. Her lips tasted like that Strawberry Passion lip gloss. We kissed again; this time as I was kissing her, I placed both of my hands on her butt and squeezed ever so gently (I got that move from the movie *Weird Science*—remember the scene when the kid kissed Kelly Lebrock then squeezed her buttocks?) She loved the way I held her. I said, "We better get on the horses and head back to the barn before, they send a search party out looking for us."

Olivia said, "I can't wait for school to start in two weeks."

I said, "I know, this has been a short summer. However, it has been my best summer yet."

When we arrived back at the barn everyone was just walking out by the gate. We quickly got off the horses and walked over to meet them. I stayed there talking with everyone for several more minutes, then Mr. Jacobs, Olivia and her brother said goodbye, got in their truck and left. Then I walked over and took the saddles and bridles off the horses and took them inside the old barn. When I came back out my grandpa told my brother and me that we would start moving some of the old items into the new barn once all of the animals were fed. We said, "Yes sir" and started the task of feeding the animals.

Once we were done feeding the animals we walked back to the front of the new barn. There was a large trailer unloading a brand new diesel tractor and two new all-terrain vehicles that looked like small trucks. Dad said, "Yeah, these vehicles will help y'all feed up a lot quicker than using the truck."

The next two weeks passed by in a blink of the eye. The new barn, tractor, and all-terrain vehicles helped make our jobs even easier. It eliminated a lot of redundancy around the farm.

My sophomore year was one of my best years in school. Olivia and I became an item. We dated each other exclusively from the beginning of tenth grade through high school. Leroy won the State Championship in baseball my tenth and eleventh grade years. I was named the MVP of the tournament both years. Going into my senior year in high school I had several colleges as well as some professional scouts looking at me. My baseball coach told me that the University of Alabama, University of Auburn, LSU, and South Carolina were interested. He also told me that there were scouts from the Baltimore Orioles, Los Angeles Dodgers, Houston Astros and New York Yankees who were at some of my baseball games the previous year.

MY SENIOR YEAR OF HIGH SCHOOL

It was the first day of my final year of high school. I was all pumped up. I arrived in the student parking lot one hour prior to the start of school. I pulled up in my new 2000 Chevy 2500 Twin-Cab Black pickup truck. My parents had brought it for me a couple of days before school started. Tiger pulled up in his new 2000 Toyota Supra. It was real nice. His parents had purchased it for him during the summer. It was candy apple red with chrome wheels.

I said, "Tiger, are you ready for the final year of high school?"

He said, "Hell yeah" as we jumped in mid-air and did a chest pump. He said, "Don't forget we have practice today. Dad wants to go over some moves prior to the tournament in Tennessee this Saturday."

I said, "No problem, you know I will be there."

Tiger said, "I'm just making sure; you know how Olivia gets sometimes."

Twenty minutes later Olivia, her baby sister and her friend Cindy pulled up in the parking lot. Olivia's parents had bought her a new convertible Ford Cobra Mustang about a week ago. It was yellow around the bottom with a black convertible top. It was sweet. She got out of her car and ran up to me and gave me a big kiss. She said, "Good morning, sweetie."

I said, "Hi gorgeous."

She said, "Hi Tiger."

He responded, "Hi."

Olivia looked at me and asked, "So is this your new truck?"

I said, "It sure is."

She responded, "It is really nice. So are we going out in it Friday night?"

I said, "No, I will be headed to Tennessee on Friday evening."

She asked, "Why are you going to Tennessee?"

I said, "Did you forget? Tiger and I have a Tae Kwon Do Tournament on Saturday in Tennessee."

She said, "Oh, I did forget. What about the remainder of the week?"

I said, "Sorry gorgeous, but I have training all week. However, I promise all next week I belong to you."

She was like, "I hate it when you are too busy to spend time with me. If you aren't practicing Tae Kwon Do, you're working on the farm. If you're not working on the farm you're playing baseball."

I said, "Yes, I may be doing all of those things, but I always make time for you. We see each almost every day with the exception of the past week. You were off on a trip with your family."

She was like, "I know, Jefferson, but I like being with my little munchkin." Then we started kissing.

Tiger was like, "Enough already; it is time to head to homeroom. Therefore, you guys can save that for later."

So Olivia and I kissed one last time then we headed in separate directions. During homeroom Tiger and I got our class schedules. Our senior homeroom teacher was Coach Sullivan. Yeah, my grandpa's friend Larry Sullivan's nephew. Coach Sullivan was the basketball coach for the boys' team. He was pretty cool. Tiger and I had every class together.

After homeroom we headed to our first class, English IV. Well, to my surprise, sitting across the room was my gorgeous girlfriend talking to her best friend Lindsay Jefferson. I waved to her as Tiger and sat in the back of the room. We had a great English teacher named Ms. Carolyn Garris. She was one of my favorite teachers.

The first week of school breezed by rather quickly. Before, I knew it Tiger, Master Kim and I were loaded into his Honda Odyssey minivan on our way to the Tae Kwon Do Tournament in Nashville, Tennessee. We stayed at the Marriott hotel. Tiger and I shared a room with double beds. We all went downstairs and ate at the hotel restaurant, then Master Kim said, "Tiger and Jefferson, it is time for you two to go upstairs and get some rest. You both have a busy day tomorrow." He said he had to go to the business center to work on the computer in order to finish several financial reports for work. Tiger and I were scheduled to meet him in the hotel lobby at 6 AM the next morning.

When we got to the room I quickly phoned my parents to let them know that we had arrived safely. Then I phoned Olivia to say good night. She stated that she was getting ready to go to Jackson to hang out with Cindy and a couple of other girls. I said, "Well, it is almost 11 PM and you are just leaving to go out."

She replied, "Well, there isn't anything else to do. You're not here."

I replied, "Well, you be careful and try not to have too much fun without me. I have a busy day tomorrow. Tiger and I probably won't be home until late tomorrow night."

Olivia responded, "Good night" and then she hung up the phone.

After I got off the phone Tiger asked, "So she is going out 11 o'clock at night?"

I responded, "Yes, she is going to hang out with her girls."

Tiger responded, "The girls that Olivia hangs out with love chasing boys."

I said, "Well Tiger, I know that my girl only has her eyes on one boy and you're looking at him right now." I already had my shirt off so I jumped up and flexed real quick. Then I cocked my leg and farted.

Tiger said, "You are super nasty. Open a window or something."

The next day when we arrived at the tournament I was ready. I was well rested. Master Kim told us to stretch. After we stretched, he came over and had a pep talk with us. He said, "You both know what needs to happen. You're both ready. You understand?"

We both said, "Yes, sir."

Then I felt someone lift me up from behind. To my surprise, it was my oldest brother Jackie. Jackie had graduated from the University of Alabama. He was drafted by the New Orleans Saints as the eighth overall pick as their starting linebacker. He said, "Well little brother, go out there and handle your business."

I said, "Thanks Jackie, but what are you doing here?"

He replied, "I had to come see my little brother kick some butt." He stated that he had flown in last night.

I said, "Don't y'all have a game tomorrow?"

He said, "Yeah, we have a pre-season game against the Tennessee Titans here in Tennessee."

He also had brought his girlfriend with him. Her name was Suzette Boudreaux. She was gorgeous. I pulled my brother to the side and asked, "What color is she?"

He responded, "Little brother, she is what Louisiana folks call Creole."

I said, "So she is Creole like Mom."

He said, "Yes."

I said, "Not bad, big brother, not bad."

He stated, "I told Master Kim to keep it a secret that I was coming to the tournament."

Now I felt really pumped up because my brother Jackie was here to watch the tournament. Tiger and I both won first place in our respective divisions. After the tournament my brother took us all of us out for dinner. Tiger and I ate real well.

Jackie stated, "Good thing I don't have to feed you two every day."

Then Master Kim said, "Yes, you should be glad because they eat like that every day."

Jackie asked, "So Tiger and Jefferson, would you two be interested in coming to New Orleans to visit and watch one of my games during one of your breaks from school?"

Tiger quickly said, "I sure would be interested in coming down." Then he looked at Master Kim and asked if it would be ok.

Master Kim responded, "Sure, I don't see a problem with you going down to visit Jackie."

I also quickly said, "Yes, big brother, I would love to come down to visit."

"Sounds great," said Jackie. "I need you two to check your schedules and let me know what works for you. Then I will check the schedule to see if we have a game during that weekend."

Tiger and I both agreed that we would let him know within the next couple of weeks. After dinner, my brother Jackie gave me a hug and congratulated Tiger and me once again, then his driver took him and his girlfriend to the hotel. I must admit that this had been a great trip even though I was missing Olivia. Tiger and I were so tired that as soon as we were in the minivan we both were fast asleep. He was on the front row of the minivan, and I was on the very last row. We didn't awake until Master Kim yelled out that we were arriving at my house.

Tiger got out of the van with me, shook my hand, and then got in the front seat with his dad. I then picked up my large trophy and went inside my house. Mom and Dad were still up in the living room watching TV. Dad said, "I take it you from the size of the trophy that you are holding that you won your division."

I responded, "Yes, sir, I sure did. Tiger and I both won for our respective weight classes."

Mom then asked, "So were you surprised to see your brother?"

I said, "Yes ma'am, I was surprised to see Jackie." I went on to say that seeing Jackie there really made my trip. I then asked her and Dad if it would be o.k. to go see Jackie during our break from school. They replied that Jackie had already informed them about the trip and that it would be ok for me to go visit. I then asked, "Did y'all know that Jackie has a girlfriend?"

They both said, "Yes we did know."

I said, "Well, she is a hottie."

Dad then said, "She better be because I raised you boys not to date any ugly women."

We all laughed. Mom then replied, "The way that a person looks shouldn't have anything to do with whether or not you like that person." She continued by saying it should be whether or not they are a good person and/or whether or not they treat you like you are supposed to be treated.

I said, "Mom, yes, that sounds good and all but there has to be some kind of physical attraction, 'cause in the beginning that is what going to catch your eye, their appearance. Now whether or not their looks keep your attention is an entirely different matter."

Dad then told Mom, "Yeah sweetie, I fell in love with you because of your inner beauty." He leaned over her and gave her a kiss. Then he was like, "I'm off to the kitchen for a little snack; do you want anything?"

I said, "Now Dad, you should know better to ask that question."

Dad then made us both a ham, turkey and cheese sandwich. We sat down and enjoyed our sandwiches over a cold glass of lemonade. Then I ate a slice of the leftover pecan pie before saying goodnight to my parents and going upstairs to bed. Prior to going to bed, I had to give my sweetie a call. When I called her house her dad answered the phone. I said, "Good evening, Mr. Jacobs, is Olivia home?"

He responded, "No Jefferson, she is staying the night at Cindy's house."

I said, "Ok, thank you, sir."

He asked, "Have you tried reaching her on her cell phone?"

I said, "Yes sir, I did, but I got her voice mail."

Then he asked, "So how did you do in the tournament?"

I said, "Well sir, I won first place in my weight class."

He said, "Well, that is great, Jefferson. I will tell Olivia that you called."

I said, "Thank you, sir. Goodnight." I then turned over in my bed and went to sleep.

I was up bright and early the next morning to start my daily chores. I met Dad and Grandpa, who were sitting on the porch sipping on a cup of coffee. It had just been us three doing the chores since my brothers left. My oldest brother Jackie has been gone for over five years now. Then it was my next-oldest brother Isiah, who has been away at college at the University of Alabama for his second year now. Isiah calls home almost every day. He is the one who is more likely to be a farmer as compared to my brother Jackie and me.

As I was taking a bale of hay off the truck while we were feeding the cows I asked, "So Dad, what are you and Grandpa going to do once I leave for college?"

He said, "Don't worry about us, son; your grandpa and I will manage. You see, your grandpa and I maintained the farm for a long time by ourselves before you and your brothers were even thought of being born. If we need to hire additional employees besides the three that we currently have in order to maintain the regular duties such as feeding and maintaining the animals on a daily basis, then we will do it. Therefore, don't worry about your Grandpa and me; we will be ok."

Before heading back home Grandpa told Dad and me that he wanted to go the south field to check on the watermelon crop. We would have normally only planted five acres of watermelons during this time of year because our peak season is during the summer months. However, at the request of several of our clients, we planted 20 acres of watermelons this year in order for these clients to complete additional orders. Grandpa had some of the sweetest watermelons in the state of Alabama. People would come from miles around to buy his watermelons. We also sold them to the local stores and markets. My brother Isiah was looking at ways to market the produce grown on our farm even more. He was always calling home from college with new ideas.

When we arrived at the field my grandpa picked out a watermelon and sat it on the tailgate of the pickup truck. When he cut it open, juice popped everywhere. The inner part of the watermelon was bright red.

I knew it was going to be sweet. My grandpa then cut Dad and me a piece. Boy, was that watermelon good. We sat there and ate half of that watermelon. My grandpa then said, "We better save room for breakfast." So we headed back to the house, ate breakfast and went to church.

After church, I came home and tried calling Olivia's cell phone but I got her voicemail again. The next day at school, she hadn't arrived by the time school had started. She came rolling into our first period class 30 minutes late.

After first period, Tiger and I were walking down the hall headed to our next class when I felt someone tap me on my shoulder. I turned around and it was Olivia. I said, "Well hey, stranger. You are a hard person to get in contact with."

She responded, "My cell phone battery had died and I didn't have my cell phone charger with me at Cindy's house."

I said, "Well, you could have used Cindy's cell or house phone to contact me."

She responded, "I tried calling your house phone but the line was busy. Jefferson, you need to invest in a cellphone."

I said, "You already know Dad's rules; we can't have a cell phone until we leave home for college."

She then replied, "That is a crazy rule."

I replied, "It is a rule that I'm ok with; it makes perfectly good sense to me."

She then asked, "so how was the tournament?"

I replied, "The tournament was great. Tiger and I both won first place in our respective weight class."

"Oh sweetie, that is awesome," she replied.

I then asked, "So how was your weekend?"

She replied, "Well, Cindy and me and a couple other girls had a blast. We hung out in Jackson in the Winn Dixie parking lot on Friday evening for a couple of hours, then we went to the bowling alley. We went to a house party in Palmer Circle on Saturday."

I asked, "So who gave the house party?"

She replied, "Chad Bell and his brother gave the party while their parents were out of town."

I said, "Well it sounds like y'all had a blast."

She said, "Yes, we had a great time. Cindy and I slept all day yesterday."

I said, "Well, I've been back in town since about 10:30 Saturday night."

She then apologized for not trying harder to reach me. I said, "Don't worry, it is ok." Then we walked to class.

During recess that day Tiger came up and said, "Jefferson, we need to talk." He started by saying, "You and I are best friends, blood brothers."

I responded, "Yes, we are Tiger."

He went on to say, "Jefferson, I would never do anything to hurt you. Therefore, don't get offended by what I'm about to tell you. Olivia can't be trusted and that she is a liar."

I said, "Now Tiger, she is my girlfriend and I love her."

"Jefferson, the things that she was telling you earlier were a lot of crap. She was lying. I've just found out from a credible source that Olivia got with someone else over the weekend."

I said, "So who did she get with?"

Tiger then made me promise that I wouldn't do anything crazy. I said, "Ok I promise."

He said, "Olivia got with Chad Bell on Saturday, and Cindy was with his younger brother John Bell."

I said, "I don't believe it."

He said, "Well Jefferson, I wouldn't lie to you. It was brought to my attention by several credible sources."

I was furious at this point. There were so many things going through my mind. I wanted to break Chad Bell's neck. However, after talking to Tiger, I calmed down. During the remainder of the day I was walking around in a daze. It seemed like everyone that I passed was snickering and pointing at me. Well, at least that is what I was thinking. I was so paranoid. I was thinking to myself, *This is the only woman that I have ever been intimate with. She is who I lost my virginity to.* It was just heart breaking. I was really at a loss for words.

After school Tiger and I were heading to our vehicles in the student parking lot when Olivia came running up to me. She asked, "Sweetie, what is wrong? I haven't seen you all day. It seems like you have been avoiding me all day."

I said, "Well, I have to go."

When I was getting in my truck, Tiger said, "Jefferson, give me a call, bro, if you need to talk. Don't forget that we have practice today."

I didn't say anything; I just left. I left Olivia standing in the parking lot. She then ran up to Tiger and asked him what was wrong with me. Tiger responded, "What is wrong with him? You need to look in the mirror and ask yourself that question. No, better yet, why don't you call up Chad Bell? He has a cell phone. I hear he is very accessible."

Olivia then responded, "Oh my God, oh my God! It isn't like that." She kept saying, "It isn't like that." She then ran and got in her car. She was saying to herself, "I need to talk to Jefferson. I need to talk to him."

While I was driving home, I was saying to myself, "How Olivia could do this to me?" I couldn't believe it. I needed to talk to Dad. When I got home, I immediately went inside the house and took my books to my room. When I walked through the door I could hear Mom ask if it was me. I didn't even respond. I just went straight to my room put my books on my desk and went outside to find Dad. He and Grandpa were underneath the shed. They were changing the tire on one of the tractor front wheels. I said, "Dad, can I speak to you for a minute?"

Grandpa said, "First your ass better speak. We didn't sleep with you last night."

I said, "Sorry Grandpa. Good evening. I didn't mean to be rude I just had a bad day."

Grandpa said, "I bet you are having girl problems. I told you to leave that white girl alone. I told you they can't be trusted. Once they get that alcohol in their system all bets are off. They are the devil, I tell you. They are the devil."

Dad and I then went inside the barn into his office. He said, "Sit down, son."

He sat on the top of his desk. He then asked, "So what it the problem?"

"Well Dad, I found out that Olivia was with another boy while I was out of town this weekend."

Dad responded, "So how do you know this is true?"

I then said, "Well, there were some individuals at school who told Tiger, then Tiger told me."

Dad asked, "So what did Olivia have to say about all of this?"

I said, "Well, I haven't spoken to her."

Dad asked "Why not?"

I said, "I was just upset. So I left her standing in the parking lot after school."

He then said, "Well son, you need to talk to her in order to find out what really happened." My father went on to say, "I know that your grandpa, grandma, mom, and siblings are teasing you about dating a white girl. But I'm here to tell you it doesn't matter what color a woman is as long as she loves you. It doesn't matter if she is purple or blue. Take, for instance, your mom," he said. "She has been by my side since we were 17 years old. It hasn't always been great. We had just gotten married after graduating college and were living in an apartment in Jackson. I had just started working with the Department of Transportation as well as working here on the farm. Well your grandpa and I had a very bad year. I mean a very bad year. It took the Good Lord's help as well as your grandma and mom to help us pull through. I was away traveling a lot with work. Everyone was working around the clock to ensure it was a success. I'm here to tell you not once did I ever hear your mother complain. Whenever I used to get down and start to doubt myself she would be right there to lift me back up. She used to always say, 'Thomas Jefferson Robinson Jr., I wouldn't care if we had to sleep outside underneath the stars; I will be ok as long as I am with you.' I say to you Jefferson, that if I have taught you about the Golden Rules, you must have someone invested in those same rules as you in order for any relationship to work. You must have someone that is willing to be by your side through good times and bad times." Dad then went on to say, "Now you are still young; you will make mistakes. But you have to learn from those mistakes. Don't be no fool." He stated that it was time for me to talk to Olivia to hear what really happened.

We then began to leave the barn and walk back underneath shed where Grandpa was standing. While we were walking underneath the shed I saw Olivia pulling up in front of our house. She saw me standing underneath the shed so she walked over. She said good afternoon to Dad and Grandpa. Then she looked at me and asked, "Jefferson, can we go somewhere and talk?"

I said, "Sure." So we started walking down the road that leads to our house.

She started by saying, "Jefferson, you have every reason to be upset with me. Those rumors that are being spread around school are just that—rumors. I didn't have sex with Chad. Sure, Cindy and I were at Chad and his brother's house party. Cindy and I got drunk and passed out. When we woke up the next day she and I were in the bed asleep. We both had our clothes on. I'm not sure why Chad and his brothers would spread those rumors. Chad had tried talking to me Friday night but I explained to him that you and I were going steady."

I replied, "I hear what you are saying, Olivia, but what would you think if the shoe was on the other foot? If you couldn't reach me the entire weekend, then when you arrive at school someone came up to you and told you those rumors about me?"

She replied, "I know I would suspect the worst. However, if you told me that nothing happened, I would believe you."

I replied, "I do believe you. Because like I've always said, you have no reason to lie to me. One of the Golden Rules is to always tell the truth even though at the time telling the truth may not seem like the right thing to do. However, in the end, telling the truth is the only thing to do. However, Olivia, I want you to know if I ever find out that you have lied to me there can be no trust, there can be no forgiving, there can be no us."

Then Olivia and I kissed and hugged each other then walked back toward her car. We kissed again, then she got in her car and left.

Later that night while having dinner with my parents, grandparents, and sister the topic of Olivia came up. My sister Eve began to say, "Jefferson, how can you continue to see a girl like Olivia?"

I replied, "What you are talking about? Olivia stated that nothing happened between her and Chad and I believe her."

"Well Jefferson," said Eve, "some of my friends were at the same party and they saw her and Chad kissing and holding hands."

I said, "I don't believe it. Olivia has no reason to lie to me."

Grandma said, "Jefferson, I don't trust that heifer."

Mom chimed in also and stated, "No self-respecting person would put themselves in that kind of predicament anyway."

I stated, "Olivia and I have resolved matter and we have put it all behind us." I then finished my dinner and asked to be excused.

I went upstairs to my room and called Tiger. Master Kim answered the phone. I said, "Good evening sir! I would like to apologize for not coming to practice today; however, I will be there to make it up tomorrow."

Master Kim said, "Ok Jefferson, I will see you tomorrow. Let me get Tiger for you."

"Hey Jefferson," said Tiger. He asked, "So what happened, bro?"

I replied, "Olivia told me that nothing happened between her and Chad."

Tiger said, "She is lying, Jefferson. She is lying to you."

"I told her that I believe her. Therefore, I'm asking you as my brother to be happy for me and let's move on."

Tiger stated, "We can move on but I'm not happy about it."

I asked him, "So what do you think about going to visit my brother Jackie in New Orleans on Labor Day weekend?" (Which was a couple of weeks away.)

He said, "Sounds good."

I said, "Ok I will call my brother and get everything set up."

I told Tiger that we would talk further tomorrow at school. I then hung up the phone with Tiger and called my brother. "Hey Jackie, it's Jefferson."

He responded, "What's up, little brother?"

I said, "Tiger and I would like to come down Labor Day Weekend."

He quickly checked his schedule. "Ok little brother," he responded, "that is a good weekend. We play the Miami Dolphins that week."

I said, "Sounds great."

I said, "Tiger and I are going to drive down. I'm going to drive my truck."

Jackie responded, "That sounds great. I will wire you some traveling money. Now go get a pen and paper so that I can give you my address."

"Ok, I have pen and paper."

Jackie then said, "My address is 384 Ormond Drive, Destrehan, Louisiana."

I said, "I got it."

"Well, little brother," said Jackie, "I will wire you the money next week. I'll see y'all in a couple of weeks."

I said, "Sounds great, Jackie. I will see you in a couple of weeks."

The next day I waited for Tiger in the parking lot. When he arrived 10 minutes later I was already hugged up with Olivia leaning on my truck. He got out of his car and walked over and shook my hand and gave me a man-hug. He barely spoke to Olivia standing next to me. He asked, "So Jefferson, did you speak to your brother last night?"

I said, "Yes, I sure did. We are all set. He will send us traveling money next week, so we can head to New Orleans the following week."

Tiger yelled out, "Oh yeah!"

Olivia was like, "So y'all are going to New Orleans? When did this happen?"

I said, "It happened last weekend when I couldn't get in contact with you. My brother Jackie and his girlfriend surprised me by flying to Tennessee to watch my tournament."

Her response was "Oh!" She asked, "So do you two need any company?"

Tiger said, "Hell no!"

I replied, "No sweetie, this is a fellow's trip. It is time to bond with my boy Tiger and see my brother."

The homeroom bell began to ring. I gave Olivia a kiss and told her that I would see her later. While Tiger and I were walking toward homeroom he was like, "I'm glad that you got some balls on that one, Jefferson. For a minute, I thought that you were going to tell her she could come with us."

The next week of school went by rather quickly. Finally, it was the day before Tiger and I were scheduled to go to New Orleans to see my brother. The entire day at school Olivia was very frisky. She kept telling me that she was horny. She was rubbing on me in class. I told her that I knew it difficult to control herself around a stud like me however, we couldn't be doing those things in public.

Finally the bell rang to dismiss school. When Tiger and I arrived in the parking lot, Olivia was waiting by my truck when I got there. She gave me a big hug and then a kiss. She then said, "Jefferson, let's go horseback riding today."

I said, "That sounds great. I should be done with my chores around 5:30, and then we could go afterwards."

She said, "Ok, I will be by your house around 5:30 today."

I said, "Ok gorgeous, see you then."

Tiger said, "I will see you tomorrow. Dad said that since we will be missing practice on Saturday and Monday that we have to practice Tuesday through Saturday the following week"

I said, "Ok." I rushed home and quickly changed out of my school clothes into my work clothes. Then I went out and began my daily chores. Once I was done with my chores I went to the barn and got two bridles and went out to the pasture to get Storm and Star. About the time I was walking back with the horses Olivia was pulling up in front of my house. She parked beside my truck. I tied the horses near the front gate near the barn then I walked inside the tack room to get the saddles. When I came back out, Olivia was standing next to the horses rubbing Star on the head. I said, "I like the way you are rubbing Star on the head."

She replied, "Are you jealous?"

I said, "I sure am." I quickly put the saddles on both horses and got them both ready to ride then we were off.

Olivia asked, "So where do you want to go?"

I said, "We can go to my place of refuge, my tree house."

She responded, "Ok."

We rode the horses about 300 yards past the tree house. I took them farther in the woods past the tree house. Just in case someone came looking for us, they wouldn't see the horses tied there in front of the tree house. We got off the horses and tied them up to a tree. I had brought a half bale of hay with me to feed them while we were gone. Then Olivia and I hurried back to the tree house. We quickly went in the tree house. I got a blanket down that I had stored away on the shelves. I also got out a box of condoms that I had stored away as well. Olivia was quick to say that I was prepared. My response was that I always aimed to deliver.

She then said, "Well, you don't need those condoms. I am on the pill."

I replied, "Dad told me to always use a condom. He always tells me that I better use the condom up until the day I get married because you don't want have any babies until you are sure that this is the person that you want to spend the rest of your life with."

We made love for what seemed like hours that day. After we were done, Olivia and I were lying on the covers naked. I was like, "What got into you? You were like a mad woman."

Her response was, "I just wanted to let you know what you have at home waiting on you once you get to New Orleans. So don't go off to New Orleans and get wild hanging with Tiger and your brother."

I said, "Now that is one thing you don't have to worry about, my love. First off, my brother Jackie has a girlfriend."

Olivia was lying with her head on my chest when she said, "Jefferson, I am madly in love with you." She went on to say that she wanted to spend the rest of her life with me.

I responded, "Olivia, you are the love of my life. I can't imagine spending the rest of my life with anyone else. Olivia Elizabeth Jacobs, you are my Wonder Woman."

She replied, "You are just saying that because I look like Lynda Carter."

I responded, "Well, yeah, you do look like Lynda Carter with your fine, sexy, self. But you are my Wonder Woman."

She punched me in the arm. I said, "Seriously, this is it. Within the next several months we will be graduating high school and off to college. Therefore, it is time to think about what you really want in life." I went on to say, "You see, I already know what I want in life. First thing is to attend the University of Alabama, then get drafted by the New York Yankees, then make you, Olivia Elizabeth Jacobs, my wife."

She responded, "So you already have everything figured out."

I said, "Sure, don't you?"

She was like, "Not really." She went on to say, "I know that I want to attend college, and I know that I want to be with you, Jefferson."

I replied, "Well, start thinking about life after high school, gorgeous, because it is rapidly approaching."

We quickly went another round in the sack, then we got up and got dressed and went back to get the horses. While on our way back to the barn Olivia asked, "Jefferson, how much do you love me?"

My response was, "Olivia, I love you more than just one lifetime because just one lifetime of loving you could never be enough."

She looked at me and started crying. She said, "Thank you, Jefferson, for making me the happiest girl in the world."

We got off the horses at the front gate, then I walked Olivia to her car. We kissed, then we embraced each other for what seemed like hours. Then we gave each other one last kiss. She told me to be careful on my trip, then she got in her car and left. When I got back over to the horses Dad and Grandpa were already taking the saddles and bridles off the horses. I said, "you old-timers better be careful and don't hurt your backs lifting those saddles."

My grandpa responded, "You better worry about your back, you little young whippersnapper. You will need it for that little young tender-roni that you have." My grandpa then said, "All I have to do is lie there now. Your grandma does all the work."

I tried not to visualize that picture. I quickly responded, "Grandpa, that is a little too much information about you and Grandma.

Dad was like, "Boy, you are using condoms."

I played dumb. I was like, "What are you talking about, Dad?"

He said, "You know what I'm talking about."

I said, "Yes sir, I use condoms. I will always remember what you and Grandpa have taught me; it will stay with me always." I went on to say, "A man always remembers!"

My Grandpa was like, "Well, you make sure you take some protection with you tomorrow, when you and Tiger go to New Orleans."

I said, "Grandpa, I won't need any."

He said, "You just might because there isn't anything like a Louisiana woman." He went on to say, "I should know, because I married a Louisiana woman."

I said, "I know, Grandpa." I then went in the house and washed up for dinner.

The next morning when I was having breakfast prior to going to school Mom said, "Jefferson, now you and Tiger be careful on that road while traveling to New Orleans."

I said, "I will, Mom, don't worry. I will call you when we get there. I have the directions; all I have to do is put them in my GPS system and it will take me directly there. Jackie stated that they will be done with practice around 4 p.m., so he will be home way before we arrive."

After breakfast she and Grandma gave me a hug. Then I picked up my suitcase and went out the front door. Dad and Grandpa were sitting on the front porch drinking a cup of coffee. I went and gave both of them a hug. Grandpa said, "Don't forget what we talked about yesterday."

I said "I won't forget, Grandpa."

Dad then said, "Well, you boys be careful. Do you have enough money?"

I told him that Jackie had wired me $2000.00 dollars for traveling last week.

When I arrived at school Olivia was already in the parking lot waiting on me. My sister, who rides to school with me, quipped, "I'm shocked to see Ms. Prissy is at school already," referring to Olivia.

When I parked and got out of the truck, Olivia came running up and gave me a kiss. She said, "Hi Eve." My sister Eve barely spoke back to her.

Several minutes later Tiger pulled into the parking lot. He walked up and shook my hand and gave me a man-hug. He then asked Olivia if she was feeling ok. She replied, "Yes, I am feeling just fine; why would you ask?"

Tiger responded, "I ask because you are at school prior to the homeroom bell ringing."

She replied, "Oh, you are trying to be a smart ass."

Then the homeroom bell began to ring so off to homeroom we went. When Tiger and I arrived at homeroom all the guys were like, "Can we come to New Orleans with you and Tiger?"

I said, "Sorry, but no clowns allowed."

They were like, "Jefferson, I know your brother is going to have some girls waiting on y'all and all."

I said, "No, my brother has a girlfriend."

They were like, "Dude, he is a professional football player; they have tons of women. They have girls in every state."

It seemed like in every class, everyone was talking about the trip that Tiger and I were going to be embarking on later that day. I could tell from her facial expression that all the talk about the trip by other students was getting to Olivia. During recess, I reassured her that everything was going to be ok. Her response was that I needed to call her every hour. My response was that I would do no such thing. I explained to her that I loved her and only her. I continued that there had to be a trust factor. Then I joked, "I don't have a cell phone anyway."

Then one of the guys named Maurice yelled, "Jefferson, you and Tiger are geniuses, man."

I asked, "So what do you mean by that?"

Maurice replied, "Well, you don't have cell phones, which means you aren't easily accessible."

My response was, "I never thought of it like that—that is, not having a cell phone."

Finally, the bell rang to dismiss school for our Labor Day break. Tiger and I yelled, "Oh, yeah." We basically ran to the school parking lot. Tiger's parents met us in the parking lot in order to get Tiger's car. Tiger got his suitcase out of his trunk and placed it on the back seat of my truck. I hugged Tiger's mom then I gave Master Kim a man-hug. Tiger hugged his parents, then his parents left with his car. Olivia came up to give me one last hug and goodbye kiss. She asked, "So do you have to take your sister home today?"

I said, "No, not today. My sister rode home with one of her friends."

Tiger and I then jumped in my truck and we were off. We stopped at the Texaco station in Wagarville to gas up. Then I got a bag of barbecue chips and a Gatorade and we hit Interstate 43. Tiger and I both looked at each other then we said, "Oh hell yeah! New Orleans, here we come!"

It took us about three hours to arrive at my brother's house. He had a nice house in a gated community. His girlfriend met us at the door. She said that Jackie was in the shower. She then showed us to our room upstairs in order to put up our bags. When we arrived back downstairs my brother Jackie was in the kitchen drinking a bottle of water. He gave Tiger and me both a man-hug. I was like, "Dang, you are swollen, Jackie. So how much do you bench press now?"

He responded, "I can lift 520 pounds."

Tiger asked, "Jackie, so where are all of the cool whips (cars)? I didn't see any in the driveway."

Jackie replied, "I don't need all those expensive cars. I'm ok with my Chevy 2500 King Cab pickup truck." Jackie went on to say, "My truck is paid for, as well as my house. All the money that I earn goes toward investments and into my bank accounts." Jackie went onto to say, "There are guys who play on my team who wear a lot of bling, drive expensive cars, have big houses and spend a lot of money. They also live from paycheck to paycheck. That is also their prerogative, but it's not me."

My brother's girlfriend Suzette was like, "Please don't get Jackie started about wasting money."

I was like, "Jackie, can I use your house phone? I need to call and let Mom know that we made it safely."

Tiger quipped, "Jefferson also needs to check in with Olivia."

I said, "Well, yes, that too." After I finished calling Mom and Olivia, Tiger also phoned his parents. I asked "So where are we going for dinner?"

Jackie replied, "We are having dinner at Katie's Restaurant downtown." He said that was his favorite restaurant. So we all jumped into my brother's truck and went off to dinner. When we walked in the restaurant they already had our table ready. The owner/chef came over and greeted Jackie. Jackie said, "Chef, I would like you to meet my two brothers, Tiger and Jackie."

The chef responded, "It is nice to meet you two young men. I will have a couple dozen of my famous smoked oysters sent out to y'all shortly."

While we were waiting on the oysters to come out I ordered a fried shrimp and catfish platter. Tiger ordered the same entrée. My brother Jackie quipped, "That is a large platter; do you think you guys will be able to handle it?"

Tiger and I grinned and looked at each other and said, "Yep."

A few moments later the oyster appetizer came out. The oysters were great. There was an assortment of oysters on the trays. They had Oyster Rockefeller, oysters with shrimp, and oysters with creamed spinach. The oysters were great. Not long after we had finished the oyster appetizer, our main entrees arrived. Tiger and I were starved. We quickly devoured the massive plate of fried catfish, fried shrimp and French fries before us. We not only ate the fried catfish and fried shrimp but we also had dessert.

My brother Jackie said, "When it comes to eating, you two always amaze me." Once we had finished dinner he said, "I'm going to take you down to the famous Bourbon Street aka the French Quarter." He was like, "Everything goes on down in the Quarter. Y'all are too young to go in the bars but we can walk down Bourbon Street so that you can enjoy the scenery."

Boy, did they have some sights to see on Bourbon Street. There were half-naked women on almost every corner. There was this one place in particular that had a woman on a swing with her feet coming out the side of the building. We only stayed on Bourbon Street for about an hour before leaving to go back to my brother's house. Once we were back at my brother's house we played Monopoly until about two in the morning, then we went to bed.

I was up by six o'clock the next morning. When I made it downstairs my brother already had breakfast prepared. He was like, "I know this breakfast isn't like Mom and Grandma's, but you won't be hungry."

We both had to laugh. I was like, "I thought you would be sleeping and/or having someone prepare your meals."

He was like, "Jefferson, listen to what I have to say. Please don't ever forget, because you are going to travel down the same road that I traveled one day." He went on to say that he had seen me play baseball and there was no doubt in his mind that I had what it takes to go to the next level. He said, "Please never forget where you come from. Never forget the values that were instilled in you by our parents and grandparents. But most importantly, once you do start making money, don't go spend it all on all the flashy things. When you get that nice signing bonus, go buy you a house and a vehicle and pay cash for them both. Then invest a portion of the money then the remaining portion that you have left, place in a bank account. You see, Jefferson, I have no debt, no credit card debt—I'm debt free. I don't own a credit card. I use my debit card and/or cash to pay for everything. I refuse to be a hostage to anyone."

I said, "Don't worry, big brother, I'm taking in everything that you are saying."

He said, "Now go upstairs and wake Tiger and Suzette up for breakfast."

After we ate breakfast, my brother took Tiger and me to football practice with him. While we were on our way to the Saints training facility Tiger asked Jackie if he still practiced Tae Kwon Do. Jackie responded, "Hell yeah!" He stated that he practiced Tae Kwon Do every day in his garage.

We had a blast that Saturday. We had the opportunity to meet the entire Saints team. We even got an autographed football and jersey. After football practice Jackie was rushing to take us to a different restaurant before it closed. I asked, "So why are we rushing? It is only two o'clock in the afternoon?"

Jackie responded, "This place only stays open until 3 pm every day."

Tiger asked, "So why do they close so early?"

Jackie replied, "They only serve breakfast. He said, "They serve the best chicken and waffles in the country."

When we arrived at the restaurant Tiger and I ordered the same thing that Jackie had ordered: chicken and waffles. I have to admit they were good. Tiger and I ordered two orders of Chicken and Waffles to go.

The next day was Jackie's game. They were playing the Miami Dolphins. We went to the stadium with Jackie and hung out in the locker room with the players until the game started. Once the game started Tiger and I went to our seats, which were on the 50 yard line. They were perfect seats. My brother had an awesome game. He had 14 tackles that day as well as three sacks.

Once the game was over we went back to my brother's house, where we had a cookout. We didn't have that many people over. Suzette had invited some of her family members over. Her parents, younger sister and several of her cousins came over. She had also invited several of her co-workers. Suzette was born and raised in New Orleans. She graduated from Xavier University with a degree in Journalism. She is currently a news anchor for one of the local news stations. Well, she had some beautiful women in her family, and they could also cook. They had made gumbo, crab cakes, fried shrimp, boiled shrimp, broiled crawfish, baked beans, and potato salad. My brother prepared barbecue chicken, pork chops, steaks, hamburgers, and hot dogs.

While I had a minute to myself I went and called Olivia. She was like, "Hey stranger, I haven't spoken to you since the first night that you arrived there."

I responded, "I'm sorry, gorgeous, but my brother and I have been catching up on a lot of things." I told her all the things that I had done since Tiger and I had been there. Then one of Suzette's cousins came and told me that the food was ready. I told her thanks.

Olivia asked, "So who was that?"

I told her that it was my brother's girlfriend's cousin. She then asked how old the girl was. I responded, "How I would know? I just met the girl." I told Olivia that I would talk to her later; I was about to eat. "I love you, Ms. Jacobs."

She replied, "I love you too!"

I made sure that my plate had everything on it. Everyone was like, "Are you going to eat all that food?"

My brother Jackie responded, "He is a bottomless pit."

I asked Jackie, "Where is Tiger?"

He replied, "I believe Tiger has found him a girlfriend."

I looked up and Tiger was over in the corner talking to one of Suzette's cousins. The girl looked nice. She was Creole with light brown eyes, and she had her hair cut short, like Halle Berry. I walked over to see if Tiger was having anything to eat. He already had a plate with food sitting next to him. I was shocked to see the food was still on the plate. He only had one barbecue chicken breast, a small portion of baked beans, salad, and a piece of toast. I asked, "Tiger, is that all you are going to eat?"

His response was yes, he had to get back on his training regimen. Then the girl said how amazed she was to be sitting next to a National Martial Arts Champion. I said "Well, let me let Tiger finish telling you about all the tournaments that he has won."

I went back on the back patio by the pool where my brother was sitting. Jim Boudereaux, a local sports broadcaster, was sitting there talking to my brother. He was like, "You had a hell of game today, Jackie." The broadcaster turned to me and said, "I hear you are a good baseball player, Jefferson."

I said, "Yes sir, I guess you can say that."

He asked, "So what colleges are looking at you?"

I said, "Pretty much all the colleges in the South Eastern Conference. However, I'm only interested in one college, and that is the University of Alabama."

Mr. Boudereaux replied, "Well, that is a fine University indeed; you can ask your brother Jackie all about that."

I replied, "I also have another brother who attends the University of Alabama. His name is Isiah."

"So does Isiah play any sports?"

I said, "No sir, he doesn't. Isiah is all about the books. He is a Business and Finance major."

I then left to go grab a bottle of water. When I went inside, Suzette's cousin Leah came over to speak to me. She was a freshman at Southern University in Baton Rouge, Louisiana. She asked, "So Jefferson, how are you enjoying New Orleans?"

I replied, "From what I've seen thus far it is a very interesting place, Leah. So what is your major at Southern University?"

She replied, "I'm majoring in Criminal Justice because one day I would like to be a lawyer."

I asked, "So what kind of law do you want to practice?"

She responded, "I want to practice Corporate Law."

I said, "Well, I'm looking at attending the University of Alabama. I want to study Accounting and Business."

She said, "Well, you can't go wrong in Accounting; everyone needs someone to count their money. So do you have a girlfriend, Jefferson?"

I said, "Yes, her name is Olivia. We have been dating for three years now."

"Olivia is a very lucky girl," responded Leah, "because you would be a great catch for any woman."

I responded, "Thanks. So do you have a boyfriend or husband?"

She replied, "No, I have neither."

I said, "I'm shocked that a beautiful girl such as yourself doesn't have a significant other."

She responded, "It is by choice that I don't have anyone." She went on to say that she hadn't met anyone worthy of being in the position to be her number one—that is, until now. She said, "I think you are the total package, Jefferson: tall, strong, handsome, and intelligent and know what you want in life."

I said, "Well thank you, Leah. I'm very flattered but my heart belongs to someone else."

Leah responded, "It isn't your heart that I want" as she gently rubbed her hands across my chest. She then said, "Ooh, what a nice muscular chest and big arms you have."

It was getting hot in that kitchen, and I'm not talking about the heat from the oven either. I quickly wiped my forehead with a napkin and said, "It is getting a little hot in here. I need to go outside and get a little fresh air."

She said, "Ok, but don't stay too long."

I went outside and sat by the pool. I stayed away from Leah the rest of the day until the barbecue was over. Prior to Leah leaving, she came up to me and gave me a piece of paper with her phone number. She said, "If you ever need someone to talk to, please don't hesitate to give me a call."

I said, "Thanks, I will keep that in mind."

As my brother and I were standing in front of his house after the last guest had already left, I explained to him what Leah had done. He seemed shocked that Leah would be so aggressive toward me. Then he said, "I find it shocking that Leah was so aggressive, little brother, but women do have a way of gravitating toward us Robinson men."

We both laughed and went back inside his house. He, Tiger and I sat up that night talking until about one in the morning. We talked about everything from Tae Kwon Do to girls to college to sports. The next morning Tiger and I ate breakfast, said our goodbyes and hit the road on our way back to Leroy. We left about 10 that morning. I told Jackie not to contact Mom to let her know that we had left because I didn't want her to worry.

I asked Tiger about the new girl that he had met.

He said, "Her name is Sarah Batiste. She is currently a sophomore at Southern University in New Orleans, majoring in Finance." He said, "I told her that is what I wanted to major in— Finance."

I asked, "So was she a nice girl?"

Tiger responded, "Yes, she was very nice." He then asked, "So how was that little hottie, Leah, that you were talking to?"

I responded, "She was a little too hot for me."

We both laughed. Tiger asked, "So are you going to tell Olivia about what happened?"

I said, "Sure."

Tiger and I arrived back home around 1:30 that afternoon. I dropped Tiger off at his home then I went by Olivia's house to see her. She was so happy to see me. She ran outside and gave me a big hug and kiss. We then sat on her porch. She asked, "How was the trip?"

I responded, "Tiger and I had a great time. I did have the college girl who made a pass at me."

Olivia got upset but I told her nothing happened. Olivia asked, "So what did you do with her phone number?"

I replied, "I threw her number in the trash."

She then replied, "You better have thrown her number away, because she didn't want this country white girl to come to Louisiana and kick her ass."

After staying at Olivia's house for about an hour I told her that I had to go home, so we kissed and then I left. When I arrived home a little while later my parents and grandparents were happy to see me. I believe that my sister had missed me a little also. They asked me how my trip was. I told him it was great. Dad teased me by saying, "I hear you have a Louisiana girlfriend."

I laughed and then replied, "No, that's not the case."

My grandpa chimed in, "There isn't anything wrong with a Louisiana woman" as he looked over and winked at Grandma.

My senior year in high school was going by so fast. I couldn't believe that it was baseball season already. I knew that once baseball season arrived, the school year was almost over. I'd already taken and passed the Alabama High School Graduation Exam. I also scored high on the ACT and SAT exams. It was now the first game of the season. We were playing in Fruitdale, Alabama against our division rival Fruitdale High. Fruitdale always had a good team; however, I felt that we had the better team this year. Fruitdale scored first off a sacrifice fly ball to left field. That was the score until the fifth inning, when I hit a solo homerun off the center field wall. I had been batting right-handed the entire game; however, I decided to bat left-handed this time at bat. I hit a double at the top of the ninth inning in order to score Jason from second base. It was just what we needed to win the game because our defense held Fruitdale to three up and three down during the bottom of the ninth. It wasn't a pretty win; however, a win is a win. We will take it any way that we can get it.

Over the next six weeks we plowed through a grueling and difficult schedule. Our record was 16-4. We had a tough non-divisional game coming up against Jackson High School. They were a much larger school located just 15 miles from Leroy in Jackson, Alabama. I was having an awesome season. I had 37 homeruns, 81 RBIs, a .312 batting average, 426 on-base percentage and a Slugging Percentage of 1.07. I led the state in all categories. There were college and pro scouts from across the nation at all of our games.

Jackson was always considered our cross-town rival. We hadn't beaten them in a baseball game in over ten years. The game was to be held at our stadium this year. When I walked on the field to warm up before the game, you could tell that there was magic in the air. The stadium was filled to capacity. There were people standing up all around the batting cages and fence. There wasn't anywhere to park at the school. People were parking along the highway in order to see the games. There were cars parked for miles and miles along the highway. Everybody was there: Tiger, Master Kim, my parents, my grandparents, my sister, Olivia and Olivia's parents in the stands.

The game started off with the first batter up from Jackson hitting a single to left field, then the next batter hitting a single down the first base line, then the next hit a homerun to center field. After the homerun I ran up to talk to Bobby Johnson, the pitcher, at the pitcher mound. I said, "Bobby, calm down; you got this. Just take your time. These guys can't hit you."

Coach Jenkins also came up to the pitching mound to talk with Bobby. Afterwards, Bobby calmed down and we were able to retire the next several batters to get out of the inning. We were able to get one of the runs back that inning when I drove in Jason from third base on a single to right field. The next several innings weren't too kind to us. Jackson scored two additional runs to take a commanding 5 to 1 lead going into the seventh inning.

There were currently two runners on base when I came up to bat. There were two outs. The first pitch that came my way was a low fast ball. I connected and the ball soared over the center field wall for a three-run shot. The fans went crazy. I took in all the energy as I was rounding the bases. When I crossed home plate I put my left arm across my chest and pointed at Dad and Grandpa with my right index finger, as I always did after I hit a homerun. Then I ran and sat in the dugout. The crowd starting chanting my name, "Jefferson, Jefferson" so I walked out of the dugout and waved my hat.

We ended the inning when Bobby, our pitcher, hit a fly ball to center field for the final out of the inning. Coach Jenkins replaced our starting pitcher with Jonathan Reed to start the eighth inning. Jonathan was a hell of pitcher; he threw smoke. He had pro scouts looking at him already and he was only a sophomore. He came out and struck out the first two to start the inning. The next batter hit a shallow fly ball toward center field. Ben was playing too deep, and I knew that he was too slow and didn't have any chance of getting to the ball to get the batter out. So I shouted that I had it and ran for the ball at full speed. I had to make a diving effort with my glove and my entire body stretched in order to have any chance at getting the out. I hit the ground extremely hard but I came up with the ball and out going into the bottom of the eighth inning.

We were able to get one run during the eighth inning to tie the game going into the top of the ninth inning. As usual Jonathan was pitching shutout baseball. He retired the entire side on strikes. Now, going in the bottom of the ninth inning, we were only one run away from beating our arch-nemesis the Jackson Aggies. The first two batters each got out. One hit a pop-up behind home plate so the catcher was able to get an out, then the other batter hit a fly ball to center field for an out. It was now up to me to keep the inning going in order for us to have any chance of winning this game. The first two pitches I had fouled out of play. The third pitch I fouled back and out of play. I had fouled off seven straight pitches back and out of play.

I then asked the umpire for a timeout. I then backed away from the plate, pulled up the gloves one at a time on each hand then closed my eyes and envisioned me just making contact with the ball. Then I clapped my hands together, grasped my bat and went back to the plate. The next pitch was a curve ball that found its way to the bottom right corner of the plate. I connected and the ball soared over the right field wall for my second homerun of the day in order to win the game.

The crowd went crazy as they ran onto the field. You would have thought that we had won the State Championship the way they were acting. I guess it had been a long time coming. We had finally ended the 10-year drought in baseball as it related to beating Jackson. Everybody came over and congratulated me. Then I laid eyes on my gorgeous girlfriend and gave her a tremendous hug. She was like, "It is time for a celebration."

This was my championship. We may not have won a trophy but Leroy had bragging rights for the next year, until the next game. We went on to win the next game against Silas to bring our record to 18-4 before starting the playoffs against Cottonwood, located in Cottonwood, Alabama. We went on to win the Alabama State 2-A Championship against Choctaw in Birmingham, Alabama. What a way to end my high school career—on a winning note.

I ended up accepting a baseball scholarship to the University of Alabama. We had the scholarship signing in the school's cafeteria two weeks prior to graduation. There were a lot of people there that day as I sat at the table next to the Alabama baseball coach with my parents, grandparents, brothers Jackie and Isiah and sister standing behind us. Then Tiger, Master Kim, Dad, Grandpa and I took photos with the coach. Yes, of course, this was one of the greatest days in my life. I was proud to wear the Alabama ball cap that day. Afterwards Olivia and I took pictures with Coach Foster, the Alabama baseball coach.

I could tell that Dad and Grandpa were so proud of me that day. I could tell that they were living their dreams through my eyes. I knew that my great-grandpa Henry, the man who started all of us playing baseball, was looking down from heaven smiling. I knew that this was just the start of the long journey that I had in front of me; however, it was a journey that I was prepared to make. I took in all the excitement of that day. I didn't want it to end.

We had the local news, radio, and newspaper outlets there that day. The reporters were over asking Dad and Grandpa questions. Even though it was my time it was their day. It was a day that was long overdue. I went and sat at a table by myself that day and just said a prayer. I said, "Oh heavenly Father, I would like to thank you for blessing me with the ability and the desire to play the game of baseball in a way that makes Dad and Grandpa proud. I want to thank you, heavenly Father, for allowing me the opportunity to play the game that I love. But most importantly, heavenly Father, I want to thank you for this wonderful day that I'm now witnessing and all of the wonderful days that has yet to come. Amen."

Then my mother walked over sat, beside me and put her arms around me. She said, "Son, I'm so proud of you."

I said, "Thanks Mom."

She said, "There are so many reasons that I'm proud of you. You are a wonderful, strong, intelligent, kind, and caring young man. I'm so proud of you for allowing your dad and grandpa to share in your glory, your day. Now look at them over there answering questions as if they were receiving the scholarship." She went on to say, "I know your father would never admit it but sometimes I used to think that in some ways he resented not accepting the scholarship from the University of Alabama to play baseball."

When the event was over I told Olivia that I would call her later; I was going home to hang out with the family. She said, "Ok." We kissed and said goodbye.

My brothers and I followed the rest of the family home in my truck. Jackie and Isiah both told me how proud they were of me. They went on to say, "Well, little brother, you're going to keep the Roll Tide tradition moving forward."

I said, "Hell yeah."

When we got home everyone else was already inside the house. My brothers went inside but I had to get some things off the back of my truck. Dad came out to the truck and gave me a big hug—no, not a man-hug but father-to-son hug. Then he said, "Son, I'm so proud of you." He went on to say, "Words can't explain how special this day has been. Do you know that your grandpa cried earlier?"

I responded, "I had no idea that Grandpa had cried."

He said, "Your grandpa and I are living our baseball dreams through you. Please continue to do your best and make us proud. I love you son."

We hugged once again then we went inside the house. My family and I sat up talking and laughing until midnight.

Finally, graduation day arrived. Tiger and I were pumped up. While we were behind the stage waiting for the rest of the graduates Tiger broke down and said, "Jefferson, I don't want this to end. I'm not ready to move on and go to college."

I said, "Tiger, if anybody is ready to move on, it's you. You're smart, intelligent and plus you can kick probably 95% of the population's ass if you wanted. You have a full scholarship to one of the best universities in the country—well, it is nowhere close to University of Alabama."

Tiger responded, "I still can't figure out why out of all the scholarships that you were offered, you chose the University of Alabama. You know, during the short period that my family lived in San Francisco I enjoyed every minute of my time there. I just felt home when we visited the University of San Francisco campus."

About this time all of the graduates had arrived—all 60 of us. Olivia came over and gave me a hug. She said, "Jefferson, I'm nervous."

I said, "You have nothing to be nervous about. It will be over before you know it." Then I jokingly said, "I take that back; you have everything to be nervous about."

She said, "What do you mean?"

I said, "You're going to the school at Auburn University. Your stomach should be in knots."

She jokingly punched me in the arm and said, "Thanks for making me feel better."

I said, "Don't worry about it."

Sure enough, the graduation went great. Once they said, "Congratulations to the Class of 2002, we all begin to hug each other. Tiger and I gave each other a hug—no, not a man-hug but an I-love-you-my-brother hug. I said, "I love you, man."

Then my beautiful girlfriend (my Lynda Carter, Wonder Woman) came over and hugged me. She melted and melted in my arms. She said, "Thomas Jefferson Robinson, I love you. I love you more than life itself."

I said, "I love you also, gorgeous." I held her in my arms for what seemed like forever.

She was crying. "I don't want this night to end."

I said, "Everything will be ok."

She then said, "Jefferson, things will never be the same because I won't see you every day."

I then explained, "You will only be a couple of hours down the road at Au-bum—I mean Auburn—University. We may not see each other every day but we will definitely see each over every weekend."

She then told me that she was going home because she had a lot of family in town for her graduation.

I told her that I was going home as well. We kissed and said goodbye. My family came over and gave me hugs and kisses. Then we took a lot of photos and went home. While I was driving home it finally hit me that this was it. I was closing one chapter of my life; now it was time to move on to the next chapter.

CHAPTER TWO

The Turning Point

"Jefferson are you ready yet?"

"Yes, Mom, I'm ready. Well, I will be by the truck. Please be sure that you have everything."

I sat on my bed and looked around my bedroom for one last time. I still found it hard to believe that I'd graduated high school and was now on my way to start college at the University of Alabama. I'd dreamed of this day as far back as I could remember. Now that the day had finally arrived I was sad, scared, and excited all rolled up into one.

When I got downstairs by my truck Dad, Mom, Grandpa, Grandma,

Sister, and both my brothers and Olivia were all lined up waiting for me. I was shocked to see Olivia there because we had said our goodbyes the night before. They all gave me a big group hug. There were also some of the members from our church and some next door neighbors, as well as my grandpa's best friend Mr. Lionel Jacobs. He and my grandpa had been friends since they were knee high to a toad frog. They acted just alike. They worked together for years at the Department of Transportation. They both were instrumental in bringing my father aboard there as well.

There was also my crazy Uncle Abraham. His name was Samuel Abraham Robinson. Everybody in our town would sometimes call him Samuel L. Jackson, since every other word out of his mouth was "fuck" or "mother fucker." He would curse around everybody except my grandmother. She didn't play. She would smack the taste out of his mouth.

Tiger and his parents had shown up as well. He was leaving in a couple of days to attend the University of San Francisco, located in San Francisco, California. He was majoring in Finance. I said my goodbyes to everyone, then I gave Olivia a kiss and hug. She was crying hard. I told her that I would drive down next week, once she arrived at Auburn, then I jumped in my truck, ready to leave. My parents, grandparents and sister were leading the way in the Chevy Tahoe, my brothers Jackie and Isiah were behind them in Jackie's Chevy Silverado 2500, then there was me on the tail end driving my Chevy Silverado. My brother Isiah was headed back to school as well. He was starting his senior year at the University of Alabama, majoring in Finance and Business. I was glad that he was going to be there for my initial year. We were on the road. We had a two and a half hour drive ahead of us. I couldn't wait.

Once we arrived at the University of Alabama, Isiah showed my parents and me where to register as well as pick up my dorm room key and school instruction. Then my entire family and I walked up to my dorm room. My grandma and mom began to cry once again. I hugged them both and told them that everything was going to be ok. I do believe that my grandfather was the proudest out of everyone there. He said, "Isn't it ironic that 40 years ago it wasn't heard of black folks to attend the University of Alabama. The majority of white folks in Alabama as well as the governor of the great state of Alabama tried to stop it from happening.

Fast forward to today and I've already had one grandson to graduate and two additional grandsons now attending the University of Alabama. I am one proud grandfather." He then said, "Don't ever forget this country's past. Don't ever forget where y'all come from, your family's name/legacy but most importantly, don't ever forget who y'all are and the men that you were raised to be. Because I don't want to have to drive back up here and put my foot in your asses if you mess up."

Isiah said, "don't worry, Grandpa, we are going to continue to make you proud as well as not tarnish the family name, because we have one more person, Ms. Eve, we have to get here in three more years."

My brother Jackie then asked, "So is anybody here hungry?"

Everybody said yes, of course; we Robinsons love to eat. He then stated, "I know this great country/soul food restaurant where we could go have dinner."

Sure enough, the food was great at Sugar Ray's Soul Food Restaurant. After dinner, we all went back to the hotel and sat around and talked and laughed until well after midnight. The next morning Isiah and I saw our family off on the road headed back home. He said, "Little brother, let me show you around the campus."

The campus was huge, especially coming from a small town like Leroy. Our high school was kindergarten through twelfth grade. My graduating class only had 60 students. However, if both of my brothers could make it here at the University of Alabama I knew that I could. The next week I drove down to the University of Auburn to see my sweetie pie. Olivia was happy to see me. She ran up and jumped in my arms and gave me a big ol' sloppy wet kiss.

I asked, "So are you hungry?"

She said "Yeah, but eating food can wait. So where are you staying?

I said, "The Marriott."

She said, "Let's go there now."

She could barely keep her hands off me in the truck on our way to the hotel. When we did get to the hotel room she practically tore my clothes off me. We made passionately love it seemed like for hours. Instead of going out we ordered room service. After we ate we made love again and again and again. Then we woke up and ordered breakfast in our room; after breakfast, you guessed it: we made love again and again.

We did have the opportunity to ask each other how we were enjoying school thus far. She stated that she had met Susan Johnson and Tracy Wiggins from Leroy, who were starting their junior year at Auburn.

I said, "It must be pretty cool having someone from your hometown to show you around the campus."

She responded, "It can't be any cooler than you having your brother Isiah to show you around campus."

I said, "Yeah, it is pretty cool. I wish he was there longer but I'm grateful I get to hang around with him for his senior year."

We then went downstairs and had lunch at the restaurant, then we checked out of the hotel. I dropped Olivia back off at her dorm room and she introduced me to Susan and Tracy, who I kind of knew from Leroy. Both of them were known for being party girls. I told Olivia to be careful and not party too much. Then I gave Olivia a big kiss and I was on my way back to Tuscaloosa. On my drive back, I spoke to Tiger over the phone. He was loving San Francisco as well as the girls in San Francisco. He was like, "Jefferson, you have got to come visit me. There are so many beautiful girls."

I said, "Tiger, don't forget why you are there. You better get your studying done first, then the girls."

The semester was finally over. I felt like that I had done well on my final exams. I waited on Isiah to complete his exams, then we were on our way back to Leroy to see our family for the holidays. During my drive, I spoke to Olivia. She stated that she wasn't going to come home today but instead she, Susan and Tracy were going to drive home the following day. I then asked why she wasn't coming home today she stated that they were going to attend an end of semester party. I told her ok, to just be safe and that I would see her when she got home. After I got off the phone Isiah said, "Let me guess. Olivia is staying back to attend a party."

I said, "Yes, she, Susan Johnson and Tracy Wiggins are going to attend a party tonight and drive back tomorrow."

My brother was like, "Susan Johnson and Tracy Wiggins?"

I said, "Yes."

He was like, "Those girls have a bad reputation. They had a bad reputation as sophomores in high school at Leroy, and I know some guys at Alabama who know them as well. Just tell Olivia to watch herself."

I said, "Not to worry; she will. I have a good girl." I asked, "So what are you going to do once you graduate?"

Isiah responded, "I'm going to go back to Leroy and help Dad and Grandpa with the farm."

I said, "What? You're going to graduate from the University of Alabama only to come back to Leroy?"

He said, "Yes, little brother. I love our small town as well as I love farming. There isn't anything like rubbing your fingers through freshly tilled soil or planting seeds and watching them grow into beautiful ears of corn, or tomatoes or watermelons. There is no other feeling like the feeling I get when I'm farming. I have so many great ideas on how we can expand the farm and produce extra income."

I said, "That sounds great! However, I want to experience the world first before I ever think about settling down in Leroy again."

When we arrived home everyone was happy to see us. They had a million questions to ask. However, I was glad to answer every last one of them. I know that I had told Isiah that I wasn't ready to settle down back in Leroy just yet; however, it was great to be home. As usual, Mom and Grandma had cooked a feast for our arrival: candied yams, black-eyed peas, fried chicken, baked chicken, smothered okra, sausage, rice, corn on the cob, fried corn, corn bread, and for dessert, chocolate pound cake, carrot cake, red velvet cake, sweet potato pie, pecan pie and apple pie. To wash it all down, we had lemonade, ice tea and Kool-Aid. Of course the majority of the desserts were for Christmas dinner.

My brother Isiah and I stuffed ourselves. Dad was like, "Do I have to carry you boys from the table?"

We were like, "No sir. We have just been eating so much fast food lately. It makes you appreciate this good cooking even more."

The next week flew by. It was now Christmas Day. I had Christmas dinner with Olivia's family first because they always ate around 1 p.m. Why they ate so early, I'm not sure. Olivia's father asked me if I was ready for baseball season. I said, "Yes sir."

He was like, "Jefferson, I know that you are going to do quite well for the University of Alabama. However, as always, Auburn will be kicking Alabama's ass again in baseball this year, as we always do."

"Well sir," I replied, "not if I can help it. My goal is for Alabama to win the Southeastern Championship this year, as well as the College World Series."

Mr. Jacobs kind of chuckled. "Well Jefferson, I think you're a hell of a player but you're not that good. I don't think that if y'all had Barry Bonds and Mark McGuire on your team this year that winning the College World Series would be possible."

I said, "Mr. Jacobs, let's revisit this conversation in July."

After we had dinner we sat around and watched my favorite NFL football team, the Dallas Cowboys, beat up on the Detroit Lions. Then around 5:30 p.m. we headed to my house.

My family's Christmas dinner didn't start until 6pm. When we arrived I saw my brother Jackie's vehicle parked in the front as well. My brothers Jackie and Isiah, as well as Mr. Lionel, Grandpa, Dad, Uncle Abraham, my older cousins Willie and Jeremiah (who were Dad's age, Grandma's sister's kids) and my cousin Dewayne (who was my Grandma's brother's son) and my Uncle Billy (Dewayne's dad) were all sitting underneath the barn drinking beer and liquor. I knew only one thing: they were telling a lot of lies and joking. Olivia walked over and spoke to everyone and hugged Jackie and Isiah. Then she walked into the house to be around the women.

Uncle Abraham started it off. "Jefferson, what did I tell you about them white women? Boy, they are the devil with a pussy. But damn, she is fine. If you got to sleep with the devil, damn sure make sure she looks like that one, nephew."

Everybody started laughing. Jackie asked, "So are you ready for baseball season, little brother?"

I responded, "Yes, I'm ready. We have this one freshmen pitcher on campus from Huntington Beach, California and a couple of other top recruits coming aboard as well."

Uncle Abraham asked, "Damn all that, nephew, are you going to start?"

I said, "Uncle Abraham, those are my intentions. I'm not there to sit on the bench."

Grandpa said, "That is my boy. That's a Robinson right there."

My sister Eve came on the porch and rang the chow bell. She said, "Come and get it; dinner is now ready."

As I was on my way inside, Tiger called me on my cell. Yeah, I finally got a cell phone. Dad gave it to me a few days prior to me leaving for college. He said, "I'm in town and I will see you tomorrow."

I said, "That is cool. I will stop by your house tomorrow so that I could see your parents and your brother Rabbit."

I could tell that Olivia was glad to see me when I came into the house. She quickly made her way over to me. My cousins Victoria and Trina and my sister Eve had her hemmed up in the living room talking. I could only imagine how that conversation went. As always, dinner was great. I could barely walk after eating all of that food. I definitely enjoyed my Mom's collard greens.

Grandpa stated, "The majority of the items that you see here on this table were home grown here on the Robinsons farm. It starts from corn to the potatoes all the way down to the chicken and ham. Hell, we even raised the cow, as well, that produced the roast. The cows and pigs were taken to the cold storage then brought back here and smoked in our smokehouse. The turkey you ate was raised right here as well. We are proud of these accomplishments for several reasons. One reason is that we can feed and provide for our families. But the most important reasons is that we know what chemicals were used to fertilize and grow our crops. We know what was fed to our animals in order to produce that meat that we have eaten here today. There were no steroids and/or poisonous chemicals used. Hell yeah, I approve this message."

After dinner, Olivia and I walked outside. I whispered in her ear and asked if she was ready to go to our love shack. She said, "Not today, Jefferson, it has been a long day and I am tired."

So I took her home. I was kind of curious because she is always ready to go to the love shack. I didn't see her the next day. I stopped by Tiger's house to see his family, as well as so he and I could catch up. He and his brother were at the gym practicing. Their parents were in the gym as well. I ran up and hugged Ms. Kim first, then I hugged Master Kim. The first words out of his mouth were "When was the last time you practiced?"

I said, "Two weeks ago."

Before, I could say anything else he said, "Go get changed into your Gee, then we will practice." (A Gee is a uniform used by martial artists to practice. It consists of bottoms/pants and then a top that wraps around. Your belt is used to hold the top together.) He always kept extra Gees for me to practice in, just in case I left mine at home.

I gave Tiger and his brother Rabbit a quick hug, then Master Kim put us through a two- hour practice that included three-minute rounds of sparring. After we had finished sparring Ms. Kim had prepared us some shrimp fried rice and vegetables for lunch. Then Tiger and I went out front on the porch and talked. He told me about how much he loved San Francisco. I told him I would come up and visit for about a week during the summer before he headed home for summer break. He said, "That sounds great."

I also told him about how Olivia had been acting earlier. He was like, "Jefferson, I know that you love her and all. But something just isn't right."

I said I could understand that she was tired and didn't want to do anything on Christmas because we had been up all day dealing with our families.

Tiger responded, "No matter what, I'm here for you, my friend."

We hung out for the rest of the day, then I went home.

The holidays were now over and it was now time for my brother and me to go back to school. Olivia and I had only seen each other a total of three times during the entire time that we were home for Christmas holidays. We were only intimate once during that time frame. On the way back to Tuscaloosa, my brother Isiah could tell that something was wrong. I told him everything that had been happening.

He said, "Jefferson, what does your gut say?"

I said, "My gut?"

He said, "Yes, that little voice inside that talks to you. Everybody has that little voice."

I said, "The little voice is telling me that she isn't acting like herself and that something seems wrong."

"Well, there you have it," said Isiah. "Something is wrong. So you need to have a talk with Olivia and see what is wrong."

I said, "Sure thing, brother. I will do just that over the next couple of days. Thanks for the advice, Isiah."

He said "No problem, little brother."

The next day Olivia and I spoke over the phone. I had asked her what was going on. She stated that she just needed some space. I had asked her what she meant by needing space. I said, "It isn't like we see each other every day. We are miles and miles apart."

She stated, "That's the problem—we are miles and miles apart."

Then I heard a knock at the door. I asked, "Who is it?"

It was my brother Isiah. He stated that he needed to talk to me. I told Olivia that I would give her a call right back. She said, "Ok."

I opened the door and let my brother Isiah into my dorm. He said, "Jefferson, sit down." He then proceeded to tell me that some of his friends on campus told him that Olivia had a guy that she was dealing with at Auburn.

I asked, "How do you know this is true?"

He stated these same friends were mutual acquaintances with Susan and Tracy. They were introduced by Susan to Olivia as well as the boy she had been seeing for the past month. Isiah said, "Jefferson, this is the reason Olivia stayed back, to attend the party that his fraternity was having."

I asked, "What is his name?"

"His name is Jeremy Bosch," said Isiah. "His father is this bigwig in Montgomery that owns Bosch Engineering Firm. He is a big-time donor for Auburn University." Isiah said, "I'm sorry to have to tell you this, bro, but you're my brother and I love you."

I said, "Thanks for the information. I have a phone call to make. I will see you at the cafeteria for dinner later." I then called Olivia and asked her about Jeremy Bosch.

She broke down crying. She asked, "How did you find out?"

I told her that people that care about me told me.

She said, "I am so sorry, Jefferson I wanted to tell you about the entire situation."

I asked, "Olivia, how could you do this to me?"

She said, "One night Susan, Tracy and I were at a party. I had had too much to drink and Jeremy and I made out."

I said, "Olivia, I would have never done anything like that to you."

Her response was, "Jefferson, I was lonely and it just happened." She begged, "Jefferson, please forgive me."

I said, "Olivia, don't you think that I get lonely? Don't you think that I miss you as well? If you love someone you don't continue to do things to hurt that person. We were talking on the phone every day and saw each other almost every weekend with the exception of three weekends because of testing. Olivia, it is best that we call it quits and go our separate ways."

She started crying even harder and asked for my forgiveness.

I responded, "I have no forgiveness to give. I wish you and Jeremy Bosch the best." Then I hung up the telephone.

Over the course of the next couple of weeks, Olivia called me daily; however, I would not answer her calls. Then finally the calls stopped. Tiger and I had talked daily. He said, "Jefferson, you were too good for her anyway. Do you need me to come down and kick this guy Jeremy's ass?"

I said, "No, I'm ok."

I was glad that it was time for Spring Training. Baseball season was finally here. I finally had something to do besides practice Tae Kwon Do every day to keep my mind off Olivia.

The first day of Spring Training was here, and boy, was I pumped. I had my blue scarf, my good luck charm, in my front right pocket. I loved to pick up the red clay and let the dirt run through my fingers, then wipe the dirt on my pants. There is nothing like the smell of fresh-cut grass. Yes, baseball season was upon us.

Coach Barry Foster was the head coach of the University Of Alabama. He was the coach who recruited me on many occasions to attend this great university. However, he ran us like there was no tomorrow for the first day of practice. Then after practice he asked each player what they wanted to accomplish this year. Jamie Rollins, the freshman pitcher from Huntington Beach, California stated that he wanted to pitch a no hitter. Center fielder Phillip Jenkins from Marietta, Georgia wanted to hit at least 18 homeruns this year, breaking his previous record of 15. Right fielder, Team Captain and senior on the team Butch Sullivan stated he wanted to lead the nation in batting averages, homeruns and on base percentage. Pedro the shortstop stated that he wanted to earn Golden Glove and steal 40 bases.

He posed the same question to me next. I said I wanted us to win the SEC Championship and the College World Series. Coach Foster asked me why. He also asked why I didn't have any personal goals. I said, "Sir, there is no I in team. I was taught that it is always we and the team comes first. Yes, I have personal goals; however, I know that if we achieve the ultimate goals, which are to win our conference and win the College World Series, that somewhere along the way I would have achieved my personal goals in order to have helped us get to that point."

Coach Foster said, "Great answer, Jefferson. I knew there was a reason I recruited you."

When I was leaving practice that day Butch Sullivan came up to me and said, "That was a lot of bullshit. You're nothing but a brown-nose warming up to Coach Foster. I know you play right field as well, and there is no way a snotty-nosed punk from Leroy, Alabama is coming here to take my starting position."

My response was, "Yes, I'm from Leroy and yes, I do play right field. But I also play every other position on the field. I will play any position that my coaches want me to play in order to help the team." I said, "Let's not get it twisted. I'm not going to be too many more snotty-nosed punks."

No sooner had I had said that, first baseman Ricky Williams was walking up and he could see it was getting heated. He said, "Now Butch, if you don't want any broken bones and want to at least have a chance at keeping your position this year I think you better keep it moving. Because I've seen Jefferson sparring in the gym and he will definitely break some bones."

Butch then walked off. Ricky walked over and officially introduced himself. He was a senior on the team. He said, "I'm Ricky Williams. I'm from Coffeeville, Alabama. I have heard nothing but great things about you, Jefferson."

I said, "Well thanks. It is good to have someone who doesn't live that far from Leroy."

He then said, "Now they have some other town to make fun of besides Coffeeville." We both laughed and headed to the cafeteria to eat.

Spring Training went great for me. I hit the ball well. The coaches pretty much had me play every position on the field except pitcher and catcher. I really excelled at all of the positions. After the final practice Coach Foster called me into his office. Coach Phillips (First Base Coach) and Coach Dubose (Assistant Head Coach) were also in his office. Coach Foster was like, "Jefferson, you're damn good enough to take Butch's position in right field and I know that is the position that you're accustomed to playing. However, if we give you that position, hell, Butch sucks at playing any other position. We can't bench him because we need his bat in the lineup. On the other hand, you're good at pretty much any other position on the field."

Coach Phillips chimed in and said, "Hell, you're a natural at first base. Where did you learn to play first base like that?"

I said, "Sir, my cousin Kelvin Moore played first base at Leroy. He went on to play professional baseball for the Oakland Athletics."

He then said, "You can start on first base as well if you want."

I said, "Sir, I just want to play baseball. I'm not that good at pitching; however, if you want me to pitch, I will pitch. Whatever position that you want me to play, I will play. I just want to play."

Coach Foster then stated "Ok, we want you to be our starting shortstop. You will take Pedro's place."

I hated to take Pedro's place because he and I had become close during Spring Training. The coaches told me that I could leave. Then they called Pedro into the office and delivered the news to him.

Later that day Pedro and I met outside the cafeteria. I begin to explain my side of the story. He said, "Jefferson, there is nothing to explain. The coaches wanted you because you're good and they need your bat in the lineup. I'm here to help you any way that I can."

I said, "Well, I need some pointers on playing shortstop."

Pedro said, "From now on we will stay 30 minutes after each practice and a couple of hours on Saturdays and Sundays."

Then I said, "Sounds good."

He said, "Now let's go get something to eat."

Sure enough, the next day after practice and every day after that we would stay and work on my eye and hand coordination. Coach Foster and the rest of the coaches loved it. Then Butch came up to Pedro one day after practice and said, "Why in the hell would you help someone that is taking your position?"

Pedro's response was, "There is no I in team. Maybe one day you will learn that, Butch." He proceeded to hit balls in my direction and give me pointers on what I was doing wrong.

Finally, the opening day of baseball season was here. My parents, grandparents, brothers and sister were all in attendance at our opener against Ole Miss. It was a conference game as well as we were playing in Mississippi. I was excited as I trotted out onto the field in order to start the game. I felt sorry for Pedro because his family had already purchased tickets and had come up from Miami to watch the game. However, I had a job to do. The first pitch of the game was a line drive in my direction. I quickly scooped up the ball and threw to first base just in time to get the runner out. It appeared that Ole Miss wanted to test me to start the game because every ball was hit in my direction and I got all three Ole Miss players out.

While running to the dugout Ricky, our first baseman, said, "Great job."

The coaches and everyone else gave me props as well, except Butch. In the lineup I batted fifth, directly after Butch. He was the cleanup hitter. Well, we went down the first three batters. So it was time to go back outfield. During Ole Miss's next bat up they scored three runs prior to us retiring their side for the inning. One of their runs was scored because of an error made by Butch. Butch was our next batter up. He hit a single into right field.

Then it was my turn. The first pitch that came up I hit a foul ball to left field. The next two pitches were ball. The next pitch I fouled directly back behind home plate. The next pitch was a ball. It was now a full count, 3-2. The next pitch I was swinging regardless. It was a little low but I pulled it and got all of my body into it. The ball went sailing over the left field wall for my first college homerun. My family was going crazy in the stands. My teammates congratulated me as I crossed home plate.

My homerun was the fire that my team needed. We won the game 5 to 3. After the game Grandpa and Dad ran up to congratulate me. They were extremely proud. My entire family was proud.

This was the beginning of a great season for our baseball team. Our young freshman pitcher Jamie Rollins from Huntington Beach, California or as we called him, the Huntington Beach Stud, was lights out when he was on the mound pitching. We were 6-1 heading into SEC play against our heated rival Auburn University. We were 2-0 in conference play with Auburn beginning our 24 games straight of conference play. The entire country was talking about the University of Alabama one-two punch with Jamie Rollins on the mound and Jefferson Robinson playing shortstop as well as hitting over .500 behind the plate. There were a lot of magazines and newspaper editors going to talk to my parents and grandparents. There was a lot of buzz about both Alabama teams. We were 6-1 and Auburn was undefeated at 8-0.

I had this date, March 6, circled on my calendar for months because I knew that I would get the opportunity to see Olivia at the game (or at least I thought she would be there). My gut feeling was telling me that she would be there. The day of the game, as we were on the field stretching and warming up, I heard someone call my name. I looked up and it was Olivia waving from the Auburn section. I quickly waved at her as well, no smile or anything else, just a quick flip of the hand to say hi.

Then I looked to the right in the Alabama section and I spotted a huge sign that said "Leroy, Alabama is in the house. We support #40 from University of Alabama." I had never been so nervous in my life. I had serious butterflies. I thought that I was going to have an anxiety attack. I felt in my right pocket to make sure that I had my good luck charm.

Ricky and I were playing catch. I kept throwing the ball in the dirt and/or over his head. I guess Ricky could tell that I wasn't my normal self. He walked up to me and said, "Jefferson, you've got this. I know this is a huge game. I know your ex-girlfriend is in the stands; however, you've got this. Just calm down and take a few deep breaths. We need you to be the normal Jefferson Robinson for this game, ok?"

I said, "Sure Ricky, I'm ready." Then I heard another familiar voice walk up behind me on the field. It was my main man Tiger. We gave each other a hug. I said, "Man, first off, what the hell are you doing here? Second, what the hell are you doing out here on the field? Do you want to go to jail?"

Tiger's response was, "Did you think that I would let my brother play one of the most important games of his career without his main man here? Plus Coach Foster said it was ok to come out and say hi."

That was just what I needed. I was glad to see Tiger. Let's play ball.

The first play of the game was a line drive toward first base. Ricky quickly scooped up the ball and threw it to Jamie, who was running toward the bag in order to get the Auburn player out. It was a close call; however, Jamie made it to first base in time for the out. The next two batters Jamie struck out in order to retire the side for Auburn. Our first batter hit a fly ball to center field for our first out. Then Jamie, who not only was a great pitcher but also a solid hitter, hit a line drive down the third base line for single. The next batter up was Ricky. Ricky was an all around good player. The first two balls were strikes, then the third ball thrown to him he smacked for a long drive off the left field wall.

Jamie was rounding the bases headed toward third base, where he was told to hold up. Ricky was a big, solid guy and he was headed toward second. The Auburn player had a shot to get Ricky out at second base as well. He took the shot and Ricky slid feet first. The slide didn't go well. Ricky's right foot got twisted and bent backwards. It wasn't a pretty sight. Coach Foster and the rest of the coaches quickly ran onto the field. Ricky was in serious pain. The paramedics quickly came onto the field in order to escort Ricky to the waiting ambulance. Players from both teams came up to wish Ricky well. As I touched Ricky on the shoulder and told him that everything was going to be ok, he stated, "Go kick Auburn's ass. I want you to take my spot on first, Jefferson."

I said, "Sure, if the coach gives me the nod. But you just need to worry about getting better."

Coach Foster quickly put a pitch runner on second to take Ricky's place. Then Butch was at bat and I was in the batter's box. Butch hit a double off the centerfield wall, which drove in Jamie and Phillip. We now had a 2-0 lead.

I was at bat and was extremely nervous. The first pitch was low but I swung anyway. I could hear the umpire say "strike one." The next pitch was low and inside. I swung again. I could hear the umpire say "strike two." I then asked the umpire for a timeout. I quickly stepped outside the batter's box, took a deep breath, reached down and picked up dirt and rubbed between my hands, then I gripped my bat and walked back up to home plate. I pushed my helmet down with my right hand and gave the umpire the sign that I was ready.

The umpire then said, "Let's play ball." The next ball was down and inward but I didn't swing. It was a ball. The next ball was down and inward, another ball. The third ball was a good pitch but I barely tipped the ball to stay alive. The next ball I fouled away. The next ball thrown was a ball. Now it was a full count, 3-2. My favorite count. The next ball was directly down the middle. I connected and the ball went soaring over the centerfield wall for a homerun. We now led 4-0.

Our next batter struck out in order to retire the inning. Prior to me going back onto the field, Coach Foster told me that Pedro would be playing shortstop and that he would like me to take Ricky's position and play first base. I said, "Sure thing, coach." I quickly got a first base mitt from the dugout and ran over to first base.

We ended up beating Auburn 7-1 to win the game that day. It was great. I had a single, double, and homerun for the game and I made several plays at first base. I hated to see Ricky get hurt; however, I was glad to have Pedro back in his original spot at shortstop.

After the game I was over talking to my family and Tiger when Olivia walked over to ask if she could speak to me. I could see the eyes rolling when she walked over. My sister, Eve said, "Now what does she want?"

I asked my family to excuse me while I walked over to talk to Olivia. Olivia said, "Great game, Jefferson; you played great. You looked really hot out there playing. A lot of my girlfriends were asking, 'How did you let that hot stud get away?' They're all ready to jump your bones."

I said, "Tell them thanks for the compliments."

Olivia said, "Jefferson, these past three months have been difficult without having you in my life. I made a huge mistake, Jefferson. I miss you and I want us to be together again." said Olivia.

I said, "I miss you also."

She asked, "So how may girlfriends do you have now?"

I replied, "I don't have any girlfriends. I just have the game of baseball and Tae Kwon Do. So what about you and Jeremy?"

She responded, "Jeremy and I broke it off two weeks ago. Jefferson, I really find it hard to believe that you don't have a girlfriend. I mean you're hot; you're on TV as well as in every sports magazine in the country."

"I just haven't had time to get involved with someone else because I've been so zoned in, concentrating on my studies, baseball and martial arts."

She asked whether or not I had been intimate with anyone else besides her. I told her I hadn't. She then started crying and said that she was truly sorry. I gave her a hug to console her, then I told her that I had to go back to my family. "Jefferson, can I call you later?"

I said, "Sure." Before I walked away I said, "Tell Mr. Jacobs that this is only the beginning for Auburn this season."

When I walked back over to my family my sister Eve said, "Jefferson, I hope that you don't go down that road again."

My grandma responded, "Well, Jefferson is an adult and he can make his own decisions."

I quickly agreed. My family stated that they were getting on the road to head back home. Tiger stated that he was headed back to the airport; he had exams coming up in two days. I gave him a hug and thanked him for coming down for the game. He said, "I will call you later, bro. We need to talk."

The next day we were headed to Starksville, Mississippi for a four-game series against Mississippi State. Olivia called me that night and we talked for hours over the phone.

She asked, "Jefferson can I come down and watch your game in Starksville?"

I said sure.

She said, "Jefferson, I want you back. Please tell me what I can do in order to make things right. I love you so much and I'm finding it difficult to cope without you."

I said, "I love you too, Olivia. I'm willing to give us another chance. You're my soul mate."

She was so excited. She said, "Jefferson, you make me so happy."

Sure enough, Olivia came down to watch two of our games against Mississippi State. We won three of the four-game series and were headed to LSU to play a four-game stretch as well.

Olivia said, "Jefferson, I have to go back to Montgomery to take exams; however, some of my friends and I will be in Baton Rouge, Louisiana to watch your Thursday afternoon game."

We and LSU split the first two games, one each. Our next games were Thursday and Friday. We won the Thursday game and lost the Friday games to split the series 2 to 2. We were then off to Gainesville, Florida to meet the Florida Gators for a four-game set.

Before we left Baton Rouge, Oliva and I were kissing outside the stadium. She said, "Jefferson, I want you so bad. I'm so damn horny."

I said, "After this four-game series, we will be back in Tuscaloosa on Tuesday. Why don't you drive up that Tuesday afternoon? I will reserve us a room at the Marriott downtown."

She replied, "I will see you in Tuscaloosa on Tuesday. Good Luck and hit a homerun for me against Florida."

I said, "No problem, I got you covered on the homerun."

On the bus ride to Gainesville Pedro and I sat on the same seat together, as we did on all the road trips. He was excited that his family was going to be at the game. He said, "Jefferson, you will finally have a chance to meet my family, my parents and my sisters Sophia and Manuela. I think that my sister Sophia would be a perfect match for you."

Jokingly, I said, "I think the name Manuela Robinson sounds a lot better."

He said, "No hombre, she is only 16."

I said, "I'm just kidding, Pedro. I have a girlfriend."

He replied, "Your current girlfriend is no good for you. She doesn't treat you good, my friend."

I said, "I'm ok, my friend."

We ended up winning the first doubleheader to lead the series 2-0. Pedro played great. He even had a leadoff homerun in the top of the eighth inning of the second game to give us the go-ahead lead of 5-4 for the victory. I had two homeruns for the first game and one homerun for the second game.

After the second game Pedro introduced me to his parents Mr. and Mrs. Santiago, his sisters Sophia and Manuela, and his cousin Eduardo. Mr. Santiago said, "Great game, Jefferson. You're a hell of player." He went on to say, "Good thing your first baseman got hurt or Pedro would have never gotten his position back."

Mrs. Santiago said, "Constantine, what a cruel thing to say."

Mr. Santiago responded, "Well, it's true Alejandra."

Pedro said, "Sophia and Manuela, this is my friend Jefferson. He is the best baseball player in the entire country."

Manuela said, "Hi, nice to meet you."

Sophia said, "Hi Jefferson, Pedro has said nothing but nice things about you."

Pedro said, "Jefferson, this is my cousin Eduardo, who is a big time baseball fan."

I said, "What's up, Eduardo?"

He said, "Great game."

I said, "thanks."

Mr. Santiago said, "Once y'all get washed up we will all go out to have dinner. We will be to pick y'all up from your hotel around 7 p.m."

Pedro and I said, "Sounds great!"

As we were leaving on the team bus I saw two Chevrolet Suburbans out front with bodyguards and personal drivers escorting the Santiago family into the waiting vehicles. I jokingly asked, "Pedro, is your father the President of the United States or something?"

Pedro responded, "No, he owns several companies. One of the companies is Sanchez Holdings Company. He has offices in Miami, Venezuela, New York, Los Angeles, Mobile, New Orleans and Cuba."

I said, "I didn't know you were rich."

He said, "We do ok" with a grin.

We hurried back to our hotel room and showered. After showering we got dressed and met Pedro's family downstairs at 7 o'clock. The first Suburban had the driver and two bodyguards. It was the vehicle for Pedro and me. Then Manuela and Sophia stated that they wanted to ride in the same vehicle with us instead of in the vehicle with their parents. Their father stated that it was ok. In Mr. and Mrs. Santiago's Suburban it only left them, the driver and Carlos, who is in charge of security (Carlos had been friends with Mr. Santiago since they were young boys running the streets in Venezuela).

Now we were off to the Dragon Fly Sushi & Sake Restaurant. Once we got there and were seated Pedro asked, "Jefferson, have you ever tried Sushi?"

I said, "No, I haven't. Grandpa always says that if it hasn't been cooked then don't eat it."

Mr. Santiago asked, "Jefferson, what is your field of study at the University of Alabama?" (It sounded funny when he pronounced Alabama with his Venezuelan accent.)

"Well sir, I'm majoring in Accounting with a Minor in Business."

Pedro chimed in, "Father, Jefferson isn't going to need a major after all the money he will be making in the pros."

I quickly responded, "My education comes first, over anything else. I'm committed to earning my degree first, prior to anything else."

Mr. Santiago said, "Smart man. I like you, Jefferson Robinson, I like you. There might be a job opportunity for you at my company once your baseball playing days are over."

Sophia asked, "I hear that you are a martial artist?"

I said, "Yes, I have a Fourth Degree Black Belt in Tae Kwon Do."

Ms. Santiago said, "How impressive. How long have you been taking Tae Kwon Do?"

I responded, "I have been studying Tae Kwon Do for almost 12 years."

"I'm liking you more and more, Jefferson," said Mr. Santiago.

Then young Manuela chimed in, "So do you have a girlfriend?"

Ms. Santiago said, "Manuela that isn't any of your business."

I said, "That's ok, Ms. Santiago. Yes Manuela, I do have a girlfriend. We had broken up for about three months and just recently got back together."

Then we all ordered dinner. I ordered Shrimp Stir Fry. After dinner, Pedro's parents dropped us back off at our hotel. They were staying at the Wild Flower condos. I said, "Pedro, you have a beautiful family."

He replied, "Thanks. I believe both of my sisters and my father like you. My father was ready to hire you tonight."

We ended up splitting the next series 1-1 with Florida. We won the head-to-head series 3 to 1, then we were back off to Tuscaloosa. After the last game, prior to us leaving I said goodbye to Pedro's family. His parents had invited me to visit during the summer. I said sure.

Our record was now 15-5 headed back home for two days, then we were off to Vanderbilt, Georgia and Arkansas. I hit five homeruns during the Florida series to bring my total to nine homeruns for the season.

After we arrived back in Tuscaloosa I quickly dropped my things off at the dorm and drove to meet Olivia at the hotel. When I got there she was downstairs in the lobby. I quickly paid for the room. Once we got into the room it was crazy. We were like wild animals, tearing our clothes off each other. We made hot, passionate love from one in the afternoon until seven that night. Then we got up, took a shower, got dressed and walked down to Avenue Pub restaurant to grab a bite to eat.

When I walked in Chrissy, the waiter, walked me over to my favorite table in the corner next to the wall by the last window next to the entrance. She then gave us our menus. "Jefferson, are you having your regular chicken club and fries with a sweet ice tea?" asked Chrissy.

I said, "Yes ma'am, you read my mind."

Olivia stated, "I would like to try your nachos."

There were several patrons who noticed me and walked over and stated that I had a great game. One older gentleman stated, "Jefferson, you're the best damn ball player that I've seen come out of Alabama." He said, "Please excuse my manners; my name is Jimmy Mosley. I was born and raised in Leroy and my family knows your family quite well."

I asked, "So are you related to Bedsole and Rosa Mosley of Leroy?"

He said, "Yes, Bedsole is my second cousin." (The Mosley family were big time farmers in our town.) He said, "You're even a better ballplayer than your cousin Kelvin Moore that went on to play professional baseball for the Oakland Athletics."

I said, "I don't know about that, Mr. Mosley, but I thank you for the compliment anyway."

"Well Jefferson, I'm going to let you and your lady friend eat your dinner. You boys keep up the good work and bring us back a title because we damn sure need one. Our damn football team hasn't done anything in years."

After Mr. Mosley had gone back to his table Olivia asked, "Does everybody in the place know who you are, Jefferson?"

I responded, "I wouldn't say that. They just love their sports teams here in Tuscaloosa."

After dinner we went back to the hotel room and picked up where we had left off. Then the next day, I saw her back off to Montgomery.

We went on to win our next series and complete our season with a 48-12 regular season record, which had us not only leading the SEC but also the country in wins. I was leading the country in Homeruns, On Base Percentage and Batting Average. We were now heading into the Regionals, where we were the #1 seed set to face #4 seed Rice University from Houston, Texas. We beat Rice University and Georgia Tech in straight sets in order to advance and play Stanford in the first round of the College World Series in Omaha, Nebraska. Our entire team was excited about the opportunity to play Stanford in the first round of the College World Series.

My entire family as well as Olivia's and Pedro's family and Tiger were in attendance at the game. Prior to the game Pedro and I introduced our two families to each other. They all seemed to get along well, especially our mothers. Pedro's mom reminded me a lot of my mom. They were both beautiful, intelligent, strong-willed and strong minded women who didn't take any bull-crap off anybody, not even their husbands.

Well, it was time to play ball. Ricky walked up to greet the team and give us a pep talk prior to us going onto the field. It was great seeing Ricky walking again, especially after that horrific accident that he had in the beginning of the season. Even Butch had warmed up to me over the course of the season. I bet you never thought that would have happened; at least I never thought that it would have.

I couldn't believe how nervous I was once the game had started. However, all of that was gone once the first pitch of game was hit and a blistering line drive was headed my way down the first base line. I had to dive and get the ball and quickly toss it to Jamie, running over to first base in order to get the first out. I'm thankful that Jamie got there in time. I quickly got up and dusted the dirt off of my uniform. I ran over to first and yelled over to Pedro, "Let's play ball" as I punched my fist into my glove. Jamie struck out the next two batters. Then we all trotted into the dugout.

The first batter struck out and the next batter walked. Then it was time for Pedro. Pedro hit the first pitch thrown to him for a single straight down third base line. Both of our families went crazy. Then Butch came up and hit a double off the centerfield wall, which scored the first runner, and Pedro was told by our third base coach to hold up at third base; however, he had a full head of steam turning the corner at third base with no chance of slowing down. Pedro had his mind made up that he was going to score. The centerfielder threw the ball to their second basement. The second baseman then turned around to throw the ball toward home plate. It was going to be close. Pedro started sliding three feet out from home plate. The throw was a little high so it took the catcher off the plate to get the ball; by the time the catcher had tagged Pedro, Pedro's left hand had already touched home plate.

Our fans were pumped. The entire stands were rocking. I gave Pedro a high-five. It was my turn to hit. Butch was on second base. The pitcher threw the first pitch in the dirt for Ball 1; the second pitch was a little high for Ball 2; the next pitch was a little low but close in the strike zone, but the umpire said Ball 3. It didn't matter what the next pitch was going to be because I was swinging. (When I'm ahead in the ball count 3 balls to no strikes or even 3 balls to 2 strikes, it is always my favorite spot to be.) The next pitch was straight down the middle and I swung hard and connected. The ball kept soaring and soaring over the centerfield wall and into the parking lot. (I was told after the game that I had broken someone's car window.) It was my first homerun in the College World Series. I was pumped as I rounded the bases.

My team was waiting to congratulate me as I crossed home plate. We now led 4-0. The Stanford team begin to settle down. They struck out our next two batters. We didn't score anymore. I'm grateful that we had a great pitching staff because we needed an all-hands effort in order to win the game 4 to 3. We went on to win the next game as well. Our next opponent was Florida State in the College World Series Championship game in the best two out of three series. We lost the first game 2-0 to Florida State. We won the second game on a leadoff homerun by Butch in the top of the ninth. Our pitching bullpen shut down Florida State's side to end the ninth and secure the win for us.

The Championship game had Jamie, our ace pitcher going up against their ace Billy (The Kid) Applegate. It was a battle. We were scoreless through the first six innings. Then we began to catch fire. We now had bases loaded and I was at the plate. I was already 0-2 for the game. Therefore, Billy The Kid was gunning for me. He wasn't trying to pitch around me. He was coming straight down the middle. I was swinging; however, The Kid was throwing smoke. We now had a full-count 3 balls, 2 strikes (my favorite count). The next pitch I swung and connected. The moment my bat connected with the ball I knew that it was going to leave the ball park. I quickly flipped my bat and trotted toward first base. The ball sailed over the right field wall. It was my second Grand Slam of the season. It was just what we needed in order to put the nail in the coffin for Florida State. We won the Championship game 4-2.

Once the final out was over, our fans rushed the field. We were all hugging each other, yelling and singing 'Yellow Hammer, Roll Tide Roll." Then Olivia ran up and gave me a big hug and kiss. Then her parents walked over. Her mom gave me a hug and her dad gave me a handshake and said, "Great game, Jefferson."

I responded, "Well Mr. Jacobs, we didn't need Barry Bonds and Mark McGuire after all."

He gave me a little smirk and walked off.

Tiger was walking up, yelling, "MVP, MVP." He gave me a hug and said, "Great series, my brother, great series. Now where are all of the Alabama girls."

My entire family walked over. It looked like Dad and Grandpa had tears in their eyes as they gave me a hug. Mom and Grandma were excited also. My brothers just took me by the head in a headlock and rubbed their knuckles across my head saying, "Great game." My sister Eve ran up and gave me a big hug.

As we were leaving the field we stopped by Pedro and his family, who were next to the entrance on the field. Mr. Santiago said, "Great game, Jefferson."

Pedro's mother gave me a hug and kiss on both cheeks. She said, "You played wonderful, Jefferson." Pedro's sisters Sophia and Manuela both congratulated me as well.

Then Mr. Santiago asked Dad, "Senor Jefferson, if it is ok with you and your family, I would like to invite you all out for a celebratory dinner."

Dad said, "Sure Constantine, that sounds great!"

However, before we could go anywhere Pedro and I had to go back to the locker room to shower and change. Before we could go to the locker room Coach Foster walked over and greeted both of our families. He said, "Y'all should be proud of both of these young men. Not only are they great ball players, they are great students and role models for our other students and players. They are also great ambassadors for the great

University of Alabama." Coach Foster ended by saying, "Y'all did a hell of job raising these young men."

Then Coach Foster, Pedro and I walked back to the locker room, where Coach Foster gave his speech to the team. He started by saying, "Thomas Jefferson Robinson was named the MVP of the Tournament. Jefferson, come on up and say something to your teammates."

I said, "Sure, coach. First off, I would like to say that there is no I in team. This was a team effort in what we did here in Omaha but most importantly what we have done all season. We aren't just a team; we are a family. Now all of us are champions. The headlines tomorrow will not say 'Jefferson Robinson College World Series Champions,' they will say the 'University of Alabama Baseball College World Series Champions.' I would like to close by saying Roll Tide."

Then everyone started yelling and we got in a big circle, said our prayers and then closed by saying Roll Tide.

After we had finished showering and got dressed Pedro and I met our families so that we could go have dinner. We ate at Chophouse at The Paxton, which served steaks and seafood. The food as well as the service was great. I'm not a big steak eater; however, the filet mignon was great. Our families got along great. Even Grandpa liked the Santiagos.

After dinner Mr. Santiago, while sitting at the table, asked Dad, Grandpa and my brothers if any of them would like a cigar. They all said sure. He then had Carlos bring over his cigar box. Then he pulled out five cigars and gave each of them a cigar. He then said, "Everyone raves about how good Cuban cigars are; however, they have never had a cigar from Venezuela."

Then the five of them walked outside to smoke their cigars. Pedro and I sat at the table and entertained everybody about the game. Tiger was trying to talk to one of the cute waitresses. I saw them exchanged phone numbers. After dinner, we all thanked Mr. Santiago for dinner, then I went and met Olivia at their hotel pool in order to have our own celebration.

There were some Alabama fans at the pool as well, who were excited when they saw me. They were all coming up to me and saying, "Great game." Olivia was jealous and didn't like all of the attention that I was getting so we decided to take a walk.

The next day I met Tiger in the hotel lobby for breakfast. He was telling me about how much fun he had last night hanging out with the waitress from Chophouse and her friends. He was telling me about how one of the waitress's friends wanted to meet me and that he had tried calling me last night but my phone went to voicemail.

I said, "I was spending time with Oliva last night."

He said, "I'm not surprised."

My family later came down and we were off to Leroy. Tiger and I rode home with my brothers Jackie and Isiah. My brother Jackie asked Tiger and me, "So how are you enjoying your first year of college."

We both said college was great.

He then replied, "Enjoy every hour, minute and second of college because before you know it, you will be graduating."

Tiger responded, "We have three years left and that's a long time."

My brother Isiah then chimed in, "It may seem long but it really isn't."

I began to reflect on what a great year I had after completing my first year of college at the University of Alabama (the best college in the land); also we had just won the College World Series where I was voted MVP. I had also won Dick Houser Trophy for Most Outstanding Player in the Country, Golden Spikes Award and Rotary Smith Award Notary. I'd also made some great friends: Pedro and his family, Ricky, Jamie and other players on the baseball team. What a great way to finish my Freshman Year.

CHAPTER THREE

The Big Leagues/The Wedding

H ere I was standing in the batting box, about ready to go bat. I was now a senior and we are now playing in our Second College World Series Finals. Who would have thought that after winning our first College World Series my freshman year that it would be so difficult to make it back here to Omaha? Everyone on our team thought that teams would lie down to us and we would make it here every year; however, that hadn't been the case. The previous two years we lost each time in the Super Regionals tournaments, cutting our dream short of making it back to Omaha.

I stood here reminiscing about when we had won our first College

World Series and I was driving back to Leroy with my brothers and Tiger and we were talking about how three years were a long time. However, after thinking back to that day my brother Jackie was correct. Time does pass quickly. You must cherish every hour, every minute, and every second. This time around, I'd definitely been cherishing everything about this experience.

I was thinking about how I'd been picked by the New York Yankees as their first overall pick in this year's Major League Baseball Draft. I was selected tenth overall. I was selected early in the season to go first to the Kansas City Royals; however, I had hit a minor slump midway through the season. My family and friends attributed it to Olivia and me having personal issues again.

Olivia was jealous of me spending too much time with Pedro's family, hanging around Pedro's sisters. Olivia and I didn't break up this time; however, we did come close to it. She finally began to settle down; however, it wasn't until after I told her that if she left this time, if we broke up there was no coming back—once we were done, we were done. So we have been good the past two months.

I told my family that God has a way of working things out because if I didn't have issues with Olivia and experience the slump, I would have gone first to the Kansas City Royals and not the Yankees (the team that I wanted to go to). I have been a New York Yankees fan as long as I can remember. Dad and Grandpa have been Yankees fans since the Billy Martin and Reggie Jackson days. They love the owner George Steinbrenner (the Boss).

Yes, I was thinking about a lot that day. Now I was up to the plate. We had two people on bases, with two outs and we were down by one in the bottom of the ninth. I felt good I was in a good place. I was planning on proposing to Olivia after the game. I was ready. I was talking to myself as I gripped the bat waiting on the first pitch. The ball zipped by my bat for strike one. The next ball zipped by as well for strike two. I asked the umpire for a timeout. I stepped out of the batter's box, leaned down and picked up a handful of dirt and rubbed my hands together. I looked over my shoulders and could see my family patiently looking on. I picked up my bat and gripped it tightly and took a deep breath and walked back up to the plate.

The umpire asked if I was ready. I said, "Yes."

He then said, "Let's play ball."

The pitcher threw another ball. This time he had switched it up and threw a fast ball, my favorite. I connected with the ball. It sailed toward the center field wall and hit the fence and fell back down onto the field. It wasn't a home run, but it was good enough to score two runs and make us College World Series Champions again.

As the fans were bombarding the field again I couldn't believe it. I just dropped to my knees as I was rounding second base. Then all of my teammates ran and knocked me over, yelling that we had done it once again. I had tears in my eyes; this was so sweet.

Pedro yelled, "Jefferson, we have done it again."

I responded, "Yes, we have."

After the game Dad invited Pedro and his family to dinner, this time his treat. So we all went to the Chophouse once again for dinner. What a way to close out a college career. While we were waiting for dessert to come, I told Dad that I wanted to speak to him. He said, "Sure, son," so we walked onto the balcony.

I pulled the ring out of my pocket and showed him. He was like, "Whoa, that is a nice rock you have there, son. Jefferson, are you sure about this?"

"Yes, Dad I'm sure. I have already spoken to Olivia's father. Olivia's father said I had his blessing."

Dad said, "Jefferson, I'm ok with you marrying Olivia on one condition."

I asked, "What is that condition, Dad?"

He replied, "You must get a prenuptial agreement."

I asked, "why would I need a pre-nup? Olivia loves me and I love her."

Dad then said, "What makes her not get upset and leave you once again and take all of your damn money, the money that you have worked hard to get? You've just graduated from the University of Alabama, you won your second College World Series, and you've just signed a three-year, $15 million contract with the New York Yankees, $6 million guaranteed. Lord knows how much your next contract will be. So therefore, you have to get a prenuptial agreement and have our family attorney and your brother Isiah look over everything."

I said, "Ok, Dad."

He said, "Fine. Now come over here and give your Dad a hug."

I said, "Dad, please don't tell the rest of the family until later tonight."

He agreed. When Dad and I walked back to the table everyone was asking where we had gone. Dad replied, "We had to talk about manly business."

My sister Eve blurted out, "Jefferson was probably telling Dad about the engagement ring that he brought for Olivia."

Mom and Grandma asked, "What engagement ring?"

Eve replied, "I saw him showing an engagement ring to Tiger earlier, saying that he was going to propose to Olivia." My

Grandma said, "Oh hell no, you're not marrying that heifer."

Pedro asked, "Are you sure, Jefferson?"

I said, "Yes, I'm sure."

I could tell that Manuela wasn't excited about the whole engagement thing. She excused herself and went to the restroom. Sophia came up and gave me a congratulatory hug, as did her mother. Mr. Santiago said, "Salut to Jefferson and his upcoming wedding."

I thanked everyone for their well wishes, then I told them that I was off to propose. Tiger came along with me to meet Olivia and her parents at their hotel. As I was about to exit the restaurant, Manuela ran up to me and gave me a hug and a big kiss on my lips. After kissing me she said, "Thomas, I want to wish you well on your marriage to Olivia. However, she doesn't love you like you need to be loved. I love you, Thomas." Then she ran back into the restaurant.

I looked at Tiger with amazement. I was like, "What the hell just happened?"

Tiger responded, "I'm not sure but I believe that Manuela is in love with you."

"I never noticed. I always looked at her as Pedro's little sister. However, after she kissed me just now, I just don't know. All I can say is wow!"

Tiger and I then walked over to Olivia's hotel. We caught the elevator up to their floor. When we walked into their hotel room Olivia, her parents, her sister, her brother, her grandparents and some of her friends were all sitting in the living room part of the hotel room. The hotel room was a large suite. I then grabbed her by the hand and got down on one knee. She asked, "What are you doing, Jefferson?"

I said, "Olivia Newton Jacobs, will you marry me?"

She started crying and said, "Yes, yes, I will marry you, Jefferson."

Then all of her family congratulated me. Olivia's mom pulled her away. I asked, "Where are y'all going?"

Her mom started laughing and said, "Well, we have a wedding to start planning."

Olivia's father said, "You better make my daughter happy."

I said, "Mr. Jacobs, I will do my best to make her happy."

After about an hour Olivia and her mom came back out of the room. She then gave me a kiss and I told everyone goodnight. Tiger and I then walked next door to the hotel where my family were.

Pedro called me later that night and told me that his sister Manuela was taking it hard that I was getting married. I said, "Pedro, I had no idea that Manuela felt that way about me."

He said, "Yeah, my friend, she has had a crush on you since the first time I introduced you to her."

I responded, "Well, she is only 18 years old. She will forget about me once she starts college."

Pedro responded, "I would rather see her with you as opposed to being with Escobar."

I said, "Who is Escobar, Pedro?"

He explained, "Escobar is the son of my father's business associate, Pablo Medina." Pedro went on to say that Escobar had asked his father to take Manuela out on a date. His father stated that it was up to Manuela. However, Manuela had been putting him off. "Jefferson, I think that Manuela will start dating Escobar now that you proposed to Olivia."

I responded, "Pedro, I don't think this Escobar guy can be as bad as you say he is."

Pedro responded, "Escobar is a rich, spoiled, young creep." He was about to tell me something else; however, he said that he would tell me later in person.

The next day Olivia stopped by our hotel before she and her family left for home. She and I met in the hotel lobby. She was all excited. She said, "We have our date planned already."

I said, "What date?"

Her response was, "Our wedding date, silly."

I asked, "So what is the date?"

She said, "August 18."

I said, "That is kind of soon."

She was like, "I know but we need to go to New York and find a place and get settled."

I said, "I have a week off then I have to report to the Yankees Triple A team for practice. The Yankees are in contention for the playoffs and they want to use me as a designated hitter." I said, "Olivia, I'm not sure if August 18 will be a good date because I'm not sure what days we will have games if and when I'm called up to the big leagues."

Olivia's response was, "I'm one step ahead of you. Mom and I have already checked; the Yankees are off the eighteenth, nineteenth, twentieth, twenty-first and twenty-second." She continued, "We can get married on the eighteenth and fly to the Bahamas for our honeymoon on the nineteenth and return on the twenty-second in time for the game."

I said, "Well, ok. You and your mom have less than two months to plan a wedding."

She said, "Don't worry; we will have everything worked out within the next couple of weeks." Olivia then added, "I will also need your Platinum American Express card and I'm all set."

I said jokingly, "Aren't your parents by tradition supposed to pay for the wedding?"

She said, "Well yeah, they are going to cover some of the cost; however, since you are a multi-millionaire, I think that it is only fair that we pay for the bulk of the wedding."

I said, "Ok, so what is the budget?"

She responded, "I haven't quite put one in place yet but I promise not to go over $100,000."

I said, "$ 100,000? Are you crazy? We aren't spending that kind of money on a wedding. We need to bring that sum down tremendously."

Olivia then replied, "This is my day and I want it to be perfect."

I said, "I agree, our day can be perfect without breaking the bank."

Her response was, "Well we will try."

I then reluctantly gave her my American Express card. "Well sweetie,

I will see you when you arrive back in Leroy," said Olivia. Olivia then kissed me and left with her parents, who were waiting out front in the car.

When Dad came downstairs I said, "Dad, can we talk?"

He said, "Sure, son."

My brothers Jackie and Isiah sat in on the meeting with Dad and me. We all went and grabbed a table in the bar area of the hotel. I told them about what had just transpired between Olivia and me. Dad then stated, "Once again, that is why I told you that you need a prenuptial agreement in place."

I said, "I totally agree because spending all of this money on a wedding is ridiculous."

My brother Jackie chimed in, "Once you get married join a credit monitoring agency so you can have your credit profile monitored where no one can open a credit card and/or anything else on credit in your name without your permission." He went on to say, "By doing this your credit is protected. Little brother, you need to have credit limits placed on all of your credit cards where they can't be raised without direct authorization from you. Because being a former professional athlete myself, I have seen players' lives ruined by spouses, family members, and friends by not monitoring their finances." He stated, "Since you will need a place to stay in New York, I have a friend who is a realtor there who is already currently looking for you and Olivia a nice but modest place to live."

I said, "Jackie, that is great. Thanks a lot, bro." I personally trusted my brother Jackie because he played professional football in the NFL for 13 years before retiring. My other brother Isiah, who also graduated from the University of Alabama in Finance, is the financial guru. He currently had our family farm almost doubling its yearly revenue in the three short years since he graduated and had been back home running the farm.

Isiah stated, "I know you graduated in accounting, little brother, but I will help you create a monthly budget to live on while you play out the years of your first contract. I will tell you some good options on how to invest your $6 million signing bonus. You can take $5 million of that $6 million and invest in stocks, money market accounts and CDs because the $5 million investment won't be a joint account; it will only be for you. Olivia doesn't need to know about this account, nor should she have access to it unless you decide to tell her about it. The $1 million you take and place a portion in a joint checking, savings, and money market account for you and your wife. You can use a portion of that money as a down payment for a place for you two to live. Once you start playing and receiving your $3,000,000 annual salary, have 50% of that money from each game go toward your $5million investment portfolio and 25% goes towards your real estate portfolio. The remaining 25% can go toward your joint account."

Dad said at the end of the day it is their job to ensure that I didn't get caught up in this lavish spending lifestyle which bankrupts the majority of the athletes today. I felt pleased with the system that Dad and my brothers were putting in place for me. They were helping me secure my future. I was just hoping that Olivia was on board with the prenuptial agreement.

After we had arrived home from Omaha, the week flew by rather quickly. It was time for me to report to the Yankees Triple A Team, the Scranton Rail Raiders in Scranton, Pennsylvania. Dad, Grandpa and my brothers drove me up to Pennsylvania to begin my professional career.

After I had arrived at the stadium the Head Coach said, "Jefferson, I need you to suit up."

I responded, "You need me to suit up?"

The coach said, "Yeah, because you are starting tonight. The Yankees were hoping to call you up to the majors in time for the playoff push."

I was nervous and excited all at the same time. My family decided to stay overnight and watch me play. I was on fire that night. I hit two homeruns and had two doubles. After the game Dad and Grandpa came up and gave me a hug and said, "Great game." My brothers even congratulated me as well.

Grandpa said, "You're one step closer to making your dream a reality so keep your foot on the damn gas and don't take it off for nothing or no one."

I replied, "There is no need to worry, Grandpa."

We then went and ate dinner and checked into the hotel. The next day I saw them leave, headed back to Alabama, and I went back to the stadium to get ready for practice.

I only played Triple A ball for a month before the Yankees called me up to the majors on July 15, 2006. During that month's time with Scranton I was hitting over .478 with nine homeruns. It was like a man playing against boys.

When I called home to tell my family that the Yankees had called me up, they wanted to come up for the next day for my first game. I told them that there was no need because I wasn't sure if I would even play. Once I arrived in New York, I was told that I would be a designated hitter that night for our games against the Kansas City Royals. The Royals were the team that would have selected me if I hadn't gone into a minor slump prior to the draft. I believed this was why the coach inserted me into the lineup.

When I was walking up to the batter's box my knees were shaking. I was trembling. I was nervous, excited and scared all rolled into one. I wasn't this scared when I first played Triple A ball. I missed the first pitch and fouled the second pitch back. I asked the umpire for a timeout. I stepped away from the plate, picked up a handful of dirt and then rubbed my hands together, then I gripped my bat and took a deep breath. I said to myself, "Jefferson you've got this. You're living your dream as well as the dream of your father, grandpa and your grandpa's father." I took another deep breath, then I walked back to the plate. I gave the umpire the signal that I was ready.

The next pitch came straight down the middle and I connected. I automatically knew that it was gone. I flipped my bat as I ran toward first base. When I crossed home plate some of the Yankees players came up to greet me. When I made it to the dugout the fans started chanting my name. A-Rod said, "You need to go back out and acknowledge them," which I did to a cheering crowd.

Then as I sat on the bench it finally hit me that I was in the Majors. Here I was sitting next to my childhood idols Derek Jeter, Alex Rodriguez Mariano Rivera and Jorge Posada. I was literally floating on cloud nine. We ended up winning the game 4-3. When I got back to my hotel room that night I called my family. Everyone was excited and screaming through the phone. They told me that they were yelling at the television when I hit that homerun.

I said, "I knew the ball was gone the moment my bat connected with the ball."

After 20 minutes on the phone with my family I said, "Goodnight, because I have an early day tomorrow."

I called Olivia and she was all excited. She said, "You had a great game."

I said, "Well, thank you, gorgeous."

She said, "We are almost complete with the wedding arrangements."

I said, "That sounds great."

Olivia asked, "So who do you want your groomsmen to be, as well as your Best Man?"

I said, "Tiger is my Best Man and Pedro, Jackie, Isiah, Ricky Williams and your brother, Jason."

She said, "The wedding invitations will be going out next week."

I told her that I loved her and that I would call her tomorrow after practice. After Olivia and I had hung up the phone, Pedro called to congratulate me. I said, "Pedro, I already have you down as a groomsman for my wedding."

Pedro replied, "No problem, my friend, I will be there."

I asked, "So how is Manuela?"

He replied, "Manuela is doing ok. She has gone on several dates with Escobar."

I said, "Well, that sounds great. I will talk to you later in the week. I have a busy day tomorrow." I didn't know why but all of sudden that bothered me for some reason. I often thought about the night that Manuela had kissed me. She was the first girl other than Olivia that I had ever kissed. I wasn't having second thoughts about marrying Olivia because I truly loved her; however, I had caught myself thinking about Manuela more often than I would have liked.

The next morning I had a meeting with my agent about several endorsements. One opportunity was with Nike and another with Smoothie King. Nike and Smoothie King were two of my favorite companies, one because all of my sports shorts, gear, and shoes were Nike, as well as Michael Jordan, one of my favorite athletes, had a great shoe and clothing line with Nike. I also like Smoothie King because I always had at least two Power Punch Plus smoothies each day. I told my agent that I would love the opportunity to represent both companies and that I needed him to close the deal. He stated that he already had contract offers and all I needed to do was look over the contracts along with my attorneys. I told him to email a copy of the contracts to my brother Isiah as well as to me.

After I left the meeting I went and ate lunch, then I went back to my hotel room. I then looked over both contracts prior to me going to practice. I called my brother Isiah to see if he had received copies of the contracts. He said that he had. Isiah stated, "Jefferson, I will give you a call later in the evening to discuss."

I replied, "Isiah, that will be great!" I then left for practice.

When I had arrived at the clubhouse there were several reporters waiting to talk to me about my performance the night before. They were asking me all kinds of questions. They even asked about whether I was excited about my upcoming wedding. I explained to them, "Yes, I'm very excited to be marrying my high school sweetheart."

After practice, just as I was settling in at my hotel room after eating dinner, my brother Isiah called. He said, "Jefferson, your attorney and I have gone over the contracts with Nike and Smoothie King and everything looks great." He also stated, "Jefferson, once you sign the contracts they are ready to shoot commercials immediately." Isiah went on to say, "Jefferson, these contracts will add an additional $6 million over the next two years to your investment portfolio."

I replied, "Isiah, this is wonderful news." While I was on the phone with Isiah my oldest brother Jackie beeped in, so I put him on three-way with Isiah and me. I said, "Hey Jackie, what's up? I have you on three-way with me and Isiah."

Jackie replied, "What's up, little brothers?" He then stated, "I have great news: My realtor friend has found a house in Greenwich, Connecticut for under $600,000, which is a steal." He went on to say the homes in this neighborhood were appraised at $1.3 million to $1.8 million. Jackie stated, "The current home owners died and their children live out of state so they are trying to offload the house as quickly as possible."

I asked, "Jackie, so what are your thoughts on me buying this house?"

He replied, "I think it is a great deal for this house. You can't lose. However, I would make an offer of $565,000 cash because the house needs some work. Then once you purchase the home, put some money toward the renovations and watch the price of the house go through the roof. I will email you and Isiah a copy of the link to your phones," said Jackie.

Once I had received the links I scrolled through the photos. I loved the house even though it needed some work. It was a beautiful home. I said, "Isiah, I will be out of town starting tomorrow for a three-game road trip, returning on Sunday. Therefore, if you could make the offer on the home and close the deal, then we can go look at the home on Sunday when I'm back in town."

Isiah asked, "Jefferson, you don't at least want to physically look at the home prior to purchasing it?"

I responded, "No, not really. The numbers make sense. The home is selling for $600,000 and based on the current home values of over a million dollars that points towards at least $300,000 to $400,000 worth of equity. The photos of the home show it as being well cared for. Although there are several items that are outdated, it isn't a deal breaker."

Prior to getting off the phone we all agreed on me purchasing the house. Isiah stated, "I will fly to New York on Sunday and we could then go see the house in person if they accept your offer, Jefferson."

I said, "That sounds great. I will talk to y'all later." After I had gotten off the phone I emailed Olivia a link of the house then I gave her a call over the phone.

She said, "Hi sweetheart, I've just received a link of a house. What is that all about?"

I said, "You are looking at our future home."

She said, "What, our new house?"

I said, "Yes, our new house. I'm putting an offer in on the house tomorrow."

Olivia replied, "I thought that we would at least look at homes together." Olivia went on to say, "I thought that we would purchase a home in the heart of New York."

I replied, "Do you know how much a condo and/or a home like that would cost in New York City? It would be way too expensive."

Olivia replied, "I at least wanted to have some kind of input on where we live."

I said, "The house is roughly 45 minutes to an hour from New York.

We can go visit New York anytime we like. Gorgeous, you can help with the designing of our new home. Why don't you fly up on this Sunday so we can go look at the house?"

She said, "I'm sorry, Jefferson, but I can't. Mom and I are making the final arrangements for our wedding, which is less than three weeks away." She then said, "I can come up the following weekend."

I said, "I will be out of town next Thursday through Monday, returning on Tuesday morning."

She said, "Well, I will fly up when you get back."

I said, "I have something that I wanted to discuss with you in person."

She said, "Well Jefferson, what is it?"

I said, "I don't want to discuss it over the phone; however, I don't want it to wait another week either." I asked, "Do you remember that I had started to discuss with you about a prenuptial agreement the last time that we saw each other? However, you didn't want to discuss it at the time. Well, Isiah and my attorney have the agreement drawn up. I was going to give it to you this week; however, since you aren't coming, I will send it to you via email."

Olivia became heated. "What is this about Isiah and your attorney drawing up a prenuptial agreement for us? What does Isiah have to do with our personal life and finances?"

I responded, "Well, first off, Isiah is my brother; secondly, he is my financial advisor and helps me make well-informed decisions when it comes to my finances and wellbeing."

Olivia asked, "Jefferson, why do we need a prenuptial agreement?"

I responded, "Olivia, a lot of times money changes people and makes them do things that they wouldn't otherwise normally do. I'm not saying that you would change and do these things, Olivia; however, in order to protect myself I have to have this agreement in place prior to us getting married."

Olivia responded, "Jefferson, I don't need your money. My family has money and I have a trust fund."

I responded, "My thoughts exactly—you don't need my money and I don't need yours. Therefore, this prenuptial agreement will protect both of us. It states that what is yours prior to our marriage remains yours and what's mine remains mine. It also states that what we accumulate when we get married will become community property. I also added that you will get an extra $200,000 for each year that we are married and an extra $100,000 for each child per year that we have while we are married."

Olivia's response was, "I'm not trying to have any children anytime soon."

I responded, "Well, I'm not talking about right now; however, I'm saying maybe two to three years down the road."

She responded, "Maybe six to seven years down the road."

I said, "We will discuss that later. Please check your email. You will find a copy of the agreement attached. Please take a look at the agreement as well as have your parents and attorney look over the agreement. We can discuss the agreement over the next couple of days." I said, "You can either sign it in the presence of your attorney or wait to sign it when you visit me."

"Sure thing, Jefferson," Olivia replied. "I will talk to you later." She didn't even say that she loved me. She hung up in the middle of me saying "I love you."

I felt bad about having to give her the prenuptial agreement; however, the way that she was acting reinforced that I needed to have something in place to protect me.

We finished our road trip and my brothers were waiting on me when I arrived back in New York. We left New York that Sunday afternoon and drove to Connecticut to see the house. The pictures didn't do the house justice. The house had its own private driveway, which led to a large circle-shaped driveway in the front of the home. It was a large Victorian-style home with five bedrooms and seven bathrooms. It also had a two-bedroom, two-bathroom guest house in the back. It sat on 2.75 acres. I fell in love with the house the moment that I laid eyes on it.

When we walked up to the door my brother Isiah said, "Here you go, little brother, keys to your new home." Isiah then showed me the paperwork where he had used the Limited Liability Company (LLC) that he, Jackie and I had started earlier in the year to purchase the home. The name of the company was Triple A Holdings. The name was a play on words. Me being a baseball player the T stands for Thomas, as well as it is a play on my profession—at the time I was in Triple AAA Baseball League—and then the first letter of each of my siblings' first names: Abraham Jackie Robinson, Antoine Isiah Robinson and Aaliyah Eve Robinson.

Isiah then said, "You pay Triple A Holdings each month, which will be a write off for you as well as the company. The good side of this is that if things don't go well with you and your new wife, which I hope it goes well, then you will still have the house," said Isiah.

I then said, "Funny you should mention that, because when I told Olivia about the prenuptial agreement again she flipped out." I went on to tell them how I had emailed the agreement over to her and told her either she could sign it in front of her attorney back home or sign it in front of an attorney here in New York when she came to visit me. "She then hung up the phone on me."

Jackie stated, "Well, aren't you glad that you're at least getting this agreement in place prior to you marrying her?"

Isiah chimed in, "Well, at least now you see what you are up against. Money has destroyed a lot of relationships."

I said, "I love Olivia and I know that she will sign the prenuptial agreement." I also told my brothers about Pedro's sister Manuela and how she had a crush on me for the past several years and that she was highly upset when she had found out that I was going to marry Olivia. I explained to them that I had never looked at her that way until she had made a scene at the hotel that night and after she had hugged and kissed me. "It seems like since that night she has been in my thoughts quite often."

Jackie then responded, "Well little brother, it appears that you're having second thoughts about marrying Olivia."

I quickly responded, "No I'm not having second thoughts. It was just that Manuela had been on my mind."

Isiah then stated, "I think that Manuela is a beautiful, funny, and attractive young lady."

I said, "Well, let's drop the subject and go find a bite to eat and grab a few beers."

We then left the house. Our driver took us to Blackstone Steakhouse in Greenwich. The food was great. My brothers and I had a great time talking about old times while having dinner. They left the next day, heading back home.

I still hadn't heard from Olivia since the last time that we had spoken, and she had not returned any of my calls. So I gave her a call. This time Olivia answered the phone. I said, "Well hello, stranger."

She replied, "Hi Jefferson."

I asked, "Why haven't you answered or returned any of my calls?"

She replied, "I needed time to think. Jefferson, I felt hurt. When I told my parents they couldn't believe that you would ask me to sign a prenuptial agreement." However, before I could respond she stated, "I love you, Jefferson, and I want to marry you. Therefore, I will sign the prenuptial agreement when I come to New York next week."

I replied, "Olivia, that is wonderful news."

"My flight arrives at JFK Airport in New York at 2 PM next Tuesday afternoon. I will only be able to stay in town two days because I have to finish making last-minute arrangements for the wedding."

I said, "I love you, Olivia Newton Jacobs, and I can't wait to see you." Pedro was beeping in while I was on the phone with Olivia; however, I ignored his call. Olivia and I talked on the phone for the next hour as she laid out all of the details for our wedding.

"I have to go eat dinner," said Olivia."

I said, "Ok sweetheart, please text me your itinerary and I will be waiting at the baggage claim for you when your flight arrives."

After we got off the phone I returned Pedro's phone call. He answered, "What's up Jefferson?" in his deep Spanish accent.

I said, "Nothing much, Pedro. What is going on with you down in South Beach?" I see you were called up to the Florida Marlins last week. Congratulations."

Pedro said, "Thanks. Thank you for sending the congratulatory text as well as the case of champagne."

I said, "No problem, South Beach."

He said, "I look forward to attending your wedding in a little over a week. We have a night game that Friday in Los Angeles; however, I will be catching a red eye over to Mobile, Alabama."

I said, "Don't worry, Pedro, I will personally be there to pick you up at the airport."

Pedro responded, "I hate that I'm going to miss the bachelor party."

I said, "Don't worry, we will find something to get into after you arrive."

"My parents and sisters will be flying on their private plane into Mobile on Friday morning," said Pedro. "They will be there for the rehearsal dinner."

I said, "That is awesome news. I can't wait to see everyone."

"Manuela will be bringing Escobar with her," replied Pedro. "She and Escobar have been spending a lot of time together."

I replied, "I'm glad to hear that she is moving forward with her life. I wish them well."

Pedro replied, "I wish it was you marrying Manuela instead of you marrying this girl Olivia. I hate the fact that Manuela dating Escobar. Escobar is no good for her, just like Olivia isn't the right person for you, my friend. Well, enough talk about that. How is everything with you, my friend?" asked Pedro.

I responded, "Everything is going great."

"I see that you're a movie star now," said Pedro.

I said, "What are you talking about?"

He said, "I saw your new Nike commercial today, and I saw your Smoothie King commercial a few days ago."

I was like, "I didn't know they were released yet."

"Yes, they are released," said Pedro.

"I taped the commercials a little over a week ago."

Pedro then said, "The only way that I saw it was Manuela sent me the link to your Nike commercial. The commercial was pretty cool with you in your Nike gear hitting homers out of the park. I like the cutie serving you that smoothie in the Smoothie King commercial. I would definitely like to get her number."

I responded, "It was pretty cool shooting those commercials. I had the opportunity to meet some great people."

As soon as I got off the phone with Pedro Tiger called. "What's up, Jefferson?" he asked in his loud voice, as always.

I responded, "Nothing much. So how is San Francisco?"

He said, "San Francisco is great, man. But I will be moving back to Leroy next month to help Dad and my brother manage the bank."

I said, "That will be great. I know your dad is excited about you coming home."

"He is very excited. He told me that you called him on the phone the other day."

I said, "Yeah, I try to call him at least two to three times per month."

"Well Jefferson, you know my parents consider you their adopted son, right?"

I replied, "I can't wait to get home and eat some of your mom's steak stir fry."

"Well, she is going to have some ready for you as soon as you get there. Are you nervous about your big day in a couple of weeks?"

I said, "Yeah, the closer the date gets the more nervous I am." Tiger and I hadn't spoken in a couple of weeks. I brought him up to date about me and Olivia and my new house, as well as me constantly thinking about Manuela.

Tiger responded, "Jefferson, look, you're my best friend; you're my brother from another mother. I'm telling you that if you're having second thoughts about marrying Olivia then don't go forward with the wedding. You already know how I feel about Olivia. If she cheated once, then she will do it again."

"Tiger, I understand what you're saying. But I trust Olivia. I don't think that Olivia will cheat on me again. I just need you to be happy for me as well as be my best man, bro."

"Don't worry, I'm going to throw the greatest bachelor party ever. I have reserved two huge suites next to each other at the Marriot in Mobile," said Tiger. "I have 12 strippers flying in from San Francisco to perform at the party. I already have food and drinks set up for the event."

I asked, "Tiger, what are you doing? This is crazy; it is going to cost a fortune."

"Don't worry about that. A couple of these girls owe me big time so they are going to come down to Mobile for half price. I'm putting them up in five hotel rooms and covering their expenses."

I said, "At least let me cover some of the costs for the party."

"No way," said Tiger. "Your brothers have already donated money to the cause, as well as my brother and members of your Alabama Crimson

Tide Baseball Team, including Pedro. Therefore, we have everything covered."

I said, "Ok, let's do this." We then hung up and I went to bed.

The team and I were now on our way back from an exhausting six-game road trip. I couldn't wait to get back New York to pick up Olivia from the airport at 2 PM. We hadn't seen each other in almost a month. When I got off the plane I received a text from Manuela congratulating me on how well I had been playing as well as a link to my Nike and Smoothie King commercials. I responded, thanking her as well as explaining that I didn't think she would be sitting down watching our boring games. She immediately replied, "I have watched every game that you have played in since you were called up to play for the Yankees."

I responded, "Wow, I never would have thought that you would be watching."

She then responded, "You need to loosen up a little when you're behind the plate. You look too tense."

I said, "Thanks for the tip. I will be sure to take that into consideration the next time I'm at bat."

Manuela then said, "Goodbye and have a great day."

I replied, "You have a great day as well, Ms. Santiago."

When I walked outside the clubhouse my regular driver James was there to pick me up. "Good morning, Mr. Robinson," said James.

"Good morning to you also, James."

On our way back to the hotel I had James stop by the flower shop. While at the flower shop I picked up six dozen roses: three dozen pink roses and three dozen yellow roses. I also stopped at the local wine store and picked up two bottles of Merlot wine and a box of candy from the store next to the wine store. James dropped me back off at my hotel. I said, "James, please be back to pick me up at noon in order for us to pick my fiancée up from JFK Airport by 2 PM." I quickly went up to my room to take the wine, candy and roses.

A little while later I received a text from James at 11:45 AM stating that he was downstairs. I went downstairs, then we were off to JFK Airport. Good thing that we left a little early, because the traffic was hectic. One thing that I'd learned since I'd been here in the Big Apple was that you never knew when the traffic was going to be smooth sailing or bad. Traffic was one thing that I never had to worry about while growing up in Leroy, Alabama.

When we arrived at the airport James dropped me off at the baggage claim for American Airlines. I was about 30 minutes early; however, I couldn't wait to see Olivia. Sure enough, about 45 minutes later I saw this gorgeous brunette girl from Leroy, Alabama strolling down toward the American Airlines baggage claim. As soon as our eyes met we started running toward each other. As she jumped in my arms I gave her a passionate kiss and said, "Girl, I have really missed you." After we had finally come up for air, I said, "Let's get your bag and go grab something to eat."

Olivia's response was, "We can order room service. The only course that I want is Thomas Jefferson Robinson III."

I replied, "Sounds great to me."

We quickly jumped in the car and headed back toward the hotel. I said, "James, I would like to introduce you to my future wife, Olivia."

James replied, "Nice to meet you, ma'am. Mr. Robinson talks about you all the time."

Olivia's said, "He better talk about me."

Olivia and I couldn't keep our hands off each other while we were in the car. As soon as we got in front of the hotel we quickly got out of the car. We waited as James got Olivia's bag out of the trunk of the car. I quickly grabbed the bag and said, "James, if I need you later I will give you a call."

Olivia quickly turned and said, "James, you can have the night off. Mr. Robinson is going to be occupied the remainder of the day."

James gave me a salute as he headed back toward the car. Olivia and I quickly entered the hotel and headed toward the elevator. Once we were on the elevator, there was an elderly couple on the elevator as well. Olivia turned around and gave me a long kiss. I jokingly said, "You better stop; there are other people on the elevator with us."

The elderly lady asked, "So you two are newlyweds?"

"No ma'am, we are scheduled to be married next Saturday," said Olivia.

The elderly lady responded, "How sweet." They got off on the next floor.

We were the only people remaining on the elevator and we had seven floors to go. As the elevator doors closed I quickly grabbed Oliva and threw her against the elevator wall and began to passionately kiss and caress her. She was getting so turned on she began to take off her top but I quickly stopped her. Good thing the doors opened, because it was about to become x-rated on that elevator.

We quickly hurried to my suite. As soon as I closed the door Olivia was already out of her clothes, with the exception of her panties. Her body was gorgeous. It had been so long I had forgotten just how beautiful her body was. I quickly grabbed her in my arms as I passionately kissed her. I reached down and pulled her panties off. I noticed how extremely wet her panties were. I then ran my fingers between her legs until I had reached her sweet mound of joy. She was so wet. I gently placed one finger inside, then another. She was panting uncontrollably. I then picked her up and carried her to the bedroom. She laid me on my back as she climbed on my lovejoy. She began to move slowly, up and down. She was so good. We made love for the next several hours. It seemed like an eternity. Then we ordered room service and lay in the bed talking for what seemed like hours.

I said, "After practice tomorrow morning we can go see the house in Greenwich tomorrow afternoon."

Olivia said, "That would be great."

Olivia woke me up about six in the morning with her mouth on my lovejoy. She said, "It is time for round three; let's get back in there, champ."

I said, "Don't you worry, the champ is ready. In other words, as the Greatest of All Time would say, the Champ is here." What a great way to start off my morning.

As soon as we had finished making love and I had my shower James called to let me know that he was downstairs. I told him that I would be there shortly. "Sweetheart, if you need anything just call room service. I should be back around 2 PM, then you can meet me downstairs and we will go to see the house." I then gave Olivia a kiss. I grabbed a bagel with cream cheese, a banana and a bottle of water from the buffet in the hotel restaurant prior to getting in the car with James.

James saw me eating in the backseat. He jokingly asked, "So you didn't have a chance to eat breakfast this morning, Mr. Robinson?"

I said, "No, I was preoccupied. I had to go a few additional rounds."

He responded, "There isn't anything wrong with doing that, sir."

Practice that day went great. We only had five games left to play prior to our several days off. James picked me up from practice and we were off, back to hotel to pick up Olivia. Once we were in the front of the hotel I called Olivia and told her that I was downstairs. I was checking messages when Oliva tapped on the window to enter. James quickly got out of the car and opened the door for her.

"Hi dear," said Olivia as she gave me a big kiss.

I said, "Sweetheart, you're going to love this house."

Once we got to the entrance of the property, Olivia said, "I love the entrance. It gives you the impression that it is secluded."

I responded, "Well, actually it is secluded. The hedges and trees block the house from the street. The property sits about 500 yards back from the trees. The trees and hedges sit about 30 feet deep from the street. The house sits on 2.75 acres. The trees separate us from our neighbors on each side of the house as well as in the back of the house."

She was in shock when I opened the front door. Her response was, "What a magnificent entry way."

"That leads to the stairs, then there is a study on one side of the room and on the other side there is a large dining room."

"Jefferson, I would like it more open. There is a wall separating the dining room from the kitchen area."

"My dear, you can make whatever changes you want made to the house. I've already hired a contractor; therefore, once we get married and we move in we can begin the renovation."

"Oh no, Jefferson," said Olivia. "I'm not moving in here until all of the renovations inside the house are complete."

I asked, "What are you talking about? Do you want me to continue to pay for us to stay in the hotel until all the renovations are done?"

Her response was, "Well yeah, either the hotel or find us a fully furnished condo to rent downtown."

I said, "That is just a waste of money."

"Jefferson, I have already gone through renovating a home with my parents while we were still living there. It was a disaster." She replied that she didn't want to go through that again.

I thought about it for a moment. That was the least I could do because after all, I did purchase a home without her input. So I conceded and said, "Ok my love, I will have the realtor start looking for a furnished condo right away."

While we were looking through the rest of the house I called Jane Johnson, who was our realtor, and put her on notice to select some fully furnished condos for us to rent. Jane stated that she had roughly 10-15 properties that she could send over right way. I told her that the property would only be short term until our home was renovated. She stated that it wouldn't be a problem.

Olivia stopped in the kitchen. "Oh no, we have definitely got to do something with this," she said, pointing toward the laminate countertops and the white stove, white oven and white microwave.

I said, "Well sweetheart, this house was probably built in the 70s."

She then said, "I want new ceramic countertops, new dark hardwood floors and stainless steel appliances. I want to have this current island ripped out and replaced with a new one. I want to have a gas stove put in the center of the island."

I knew right away the $200,000 budget that I had for the renovation of our new home wasn't going to be enough. We then stopped by one of the guest bathrooms and she stated that the brass shower doors and brass knobs from the sink weren't going to work. The next stop was the master bedroom. She was very pleased with the size of the bedroom and she liked the separate sitting area with the television directly over the gas fireplace. However, she wanted crown molding around the entire bedroom as well as new carpet installed. Once we walked into the master bathroom I thought that she was going to have a heart attack.

"Oh no, Jefferson, this bathroom is a travesty. I have never seen so much brass in my life. These floors are terrible. Jefferson, I want to replace the entire shower and make the shower bigger, with ceramic tile backsplash and the rain shower heads coming from the ceiling. I want one on each side. I want it where water comes out different sides of the wall if I want to hit my body."

I said, "What we need is to get a home decorator."

Olivia said, "Fine."

I said, "Jane had already referred one to me so when we talk with Jane about the condo we can get the decorator's phone number."

Olivia said, "Sounds great."

We then went out the backdoor onto the patio. She was like, "The yard is nice but there is no pool."

I said, "I know. We can have one installed."

She said, "With a property like this we will need a nice pool with decking, a spa and a nice outdoor kitchen."

All I could do was agree. Our next stop was the guest house, which was off about 50 feet to the right of where we were planning on installing the pool. The guesthouse had two bedrooms, two bathrooms, a living room and a kitchen. The total square footage was about 1200.

"Well honey," said Olivia, "we need to update this kitchen and both bathrooms and install new flooring throughout."

I said, "Ok, now can we go get dinner? I'm starving." I asked, "So where would you like to eat dinner, here in Greenwich or go somewhere in New York?"

She replied, "I would prefer to have dinner in New York and go out for cocktails."

I said, "I can arrange that." So we got in the car with James and headed back to New York. I said, "We can have dinner at Delmonico's Restaurant. They serve great food."

Once we got back to the hotel I told James to wait for us downstairs while we went up to the room to shower and get dressed. I said, "James, we will be about an hour or so; therefore, if you want to go grab a bite to eat that would be great."

"Sure Mr. Robinson," said James. "Just let me know when you and Ms. Olivia are ready to go to dinner."

I said, "Sure."

We hopped out of the car and walked toward the elevator. The older couple that we had seen on the elevator the day before was waiting at the elevator to get on as well. Olivia and I said, "Good evening."

They spoke back as well. The older lady said, "So you've out sightseeing?"

Olivia said, "No, we went to look at our new home in Greenwich, Connecticut."

The older lady said, "Oh how wonderful." She said, "My name is Tammy and this is my husband Jonathan."

Olivia responded, "My name is Olivia and this is my soon-to-be husband Thomas, but everyone calls him Jefferson."

We all shook hands and exchanged our pleasantries. "We are getting ready to go have dinner at Delmonico's," said Olivia.

Ms. Tammy said, "I heard that they serve great food there. I'm not sure where we are going to have for dinner."

Without hesitating, Olivia asked, "So would y'all like to have dinner with us?"

Mr. Jonathon responded, "Oh no, we couldn't impose on you two young people. You need some time alone."

I quickly chimed in, "Sir, y'all wouldn't be imposing. We would enjoy your company."

The couple agreed to have dinner with us. I said, "Well, our driver will be meeting us downstairs in about an hour in order to take us to dinner." So we all agreed to meet in the lobby by 7 PM. Mr. and Mrs. Montana got off the elevator onto their floor. While heading up to our room I gave Olivia a kiss and said, "What a nice thing to do, inviting that old couple out to dinner."

She replied, "So you're not upset? I know you wanted to spend some time alone."

My response was, "How could I ever get upset at you? I love you. I love you even more for doing the things like you just did."

We got off the elevator and went into our room so we could get ready to dinner. We both got undressed and headed toward the bathroom for a shower. "We haven't showered together in a long time," said Olivia.

After looking at the water glisten on her gorgeous body my nature began to rise. I hugged her as the water glistened over both of our bodies. She said, "I can tell somebody is happy to see me." I started to kiss her and she said, "Jefferson, stop. You know we have to get ready for dinner."

I replied, "We can get a quickie in, can't we?"

We made love in the shower then we finished our shower and walked into the bedroom to get dressed. While I was getting dressed, Olivia was blow-drying her hair. I wore a navy blue sports coat with a light blue shirt and gray slacks and black shoes. After I had gotten dressed I went to the living room to watch Sports Center. A little while later Olivia walked in wearing a nice-fitting v-neck blue dress that highlighted her bosom. The dress was the same color as her eyes. She had on a nice diamond bracelet and necklace that I had brought her as well as diamond earrings. She had on a nice diamond-encrusted Movada watch with a royal blue setting. Her hair was combed backwards and almost midways her back. When I saw her my mouth dropped. I turned off the television and walked up to her and grabbed her by the waist.

I said, "You are so gorgeous." I gave her a kiss on her forehead. I said, "Are you ready to go?"

She said, "Yes."

I said, "James just texted and he is downstairs. I told James earlier that we were going to have an additional couple with us so he went back and exchanged vehicles. He exchanged the Town Car for the Chevy Suburban so we will have lots of room."

When we went downstairs Mr. and Mrs. Montana were already there waiting. I said, "you look quite lovely, Ms. Montana."

She said, "Well, thank you."

She said, "You two make a great-looking couple."

Olivia and I both said, "Thank you, ma'am."

Mr. Montana told Olivia that she was beautiful. He then said, "You clean up quite well also, Thomas."

It took a moment for me to answer because I'm not used to people calling me by my first name. I said, "Thank you, sir. Our driver is out front waiting on us."

Olivia and I got in on the last row of seats and Mr. and Mrs. Montana got in on the second row.

When we had arrived at Delmonico's, the maitre d' said, "Hi Mr. Robinson, we have your table ready." She then escorted us to our table. She said, "You had a great game the other day."

I said, "Thank you."

Once we were all seated at the table Mr. Montana asked, "So what is it that you do, Thomas?"

I replied, "I play baseball for the New York Yankees."

Ms. Montana said, "Oh, how impressive. Jonathon is a retired Supreme Court Judge from the state of New Hampshire and I'm a retired lawyer with one of the largest firms in New Hampshire."

I said, "Very impressive."

Mr. Montana stated, "We have three children and four grandchildren. We have two boys, Jason and David. Jason has a set of twins, a boy and girl. David has one three-year-old girl and our daughter Mary has a teenage boy."

Olivia said, "Well, I graduated in May from the University of Auburn with a degree in Engineering. I'm currently taking time off to get ready for our wedding."

"So the big day is quickly approaching," said Ms. Montana.

"Yes, that is correct," said Olivia. "We get married next Saturday."

"That sounds wonderful," said Mr. Montana.

"Well, I get to go look at condos tomorrow, while Jefferson is at practice," said Olivia.

"That sounds like fun," said Ms. Montana.

"So would you like to go with me?" asked Olivia.

"Thank you for the invite," said Ms. Montana, "however, Jonathon and I are seeing two shows tomorrow as well as having dinner with our friends tomorrow evening our last night in town."

"So y'all are leaving on Thursday as well?," asked Olivia.

"Yes, we fly out Thursday morning," said Ms. Montana.

"Well, I fly out Thursday morning as well, so at least ride to the airport with me on Thursday morning," said Olivia.

"Sounds great," said Ms. Montana. "We will gladly ride to the airport with you.

After dinner we all went back to our hotel. Mr. and Mrs. Montana said good night as they left to go upstairs to their room. Olivia and I went to the bar downstairs for cocktails. We sat at the bar and waited for the bartender to serve us. I said, "I would like a Tanqueray and tonic." Olivia ordered a Dewars on rocks. I said, "That is a strong drink, missy."

She said, "Well, I like my drinks strong just like my men."

I then asked her, "so have you been watching any of my games?"

She replied, "Well, I have been busy getting ready for our wedding, sweetheart. However, Dad has been watching your games."

I replied, "Well, I'm not marrying your father, I'm marrying you."
Olivia responded, "I love you, Jefferson."
I then asked, "So have you watched any of my commercials?"
Olivia's response was, "Yes, I've seen both commercials."
I said, "I'll let you have a pass this time for not watching any of my games thus far."
"I will make it up to you later tonight," said Olivia.
I quickly said, "Bartender, can I get another round, please?"
"So are you trying to get me drunk, Jefferson Robinson?" asked Olivia.
I responded, while laughing, "No, I'm just thirsty."
She hit me on the shoulder and said, "Yeah, I bet you are."
Once we had finished our final drink I closed out our tab and we went upstairs to our room. Olivia went to the bedroom once we were in the room. I went to the kitchen to grab a bottle of water then I went to the bedroom. As I walked into the bedroom Olivia was walking out of the bathroom in a sexy two-piece blue lingerie. I quickly got undressed. I was walking over to grab her when she said, "No, Mr. Robinson. I need you to sit in the chair next to the desk."
I said, "Yes ma'am."
She then took out this blindfold and put it over my eyes. I couldn't see anything. The next thing, I felt these feathers go across my chest and then across my ears. Then she kissed me from my ears all the way down to my neck. I tried to grab her but she pushed my hands down. She continued to tease me over the next 10 minutes, which seemed like an eternity. I said, "The hell with this."
I took off the blindfold and laid her down on the bed. We made love into the early hours of the morning. The next morning I was up bright and early getting ready for practice. I gave Olivia a kiss on the forehead as she lay in bed sleeping. I said, "Sweetie, here is my Platinum American Express and a couple hundred dollars for spending."
She woke up and said "Thanks, sweetheart."
I said, "James will be here at 11AM to pick you up to go look at condos."
She said, "Thanks and have a great practice."
I said, "I will call you later." I quickly ran downstairs and grabbed a

banana and jumped in the car with James. I said, "James, don't forget to come back and pick Oliva up to go look at condos today."

James said, "I will be here on time, sir, at 11 AM."

I said, "I will be done with practice around 1 PM but don't worry about coming back to pick me up. I will catch a cab back to the hotel."

"No problem, Mr. Robinson," said James.

I had a great practice and I called Olivia as I was on my way to the hotel. "Hi sweetheart. So how is the condo shopping going?" I asked.

She said, "Everything is great. I've already seen four properties. Jane and I are currently having lunch."

I said, "Well, tell Jane I said hi. So have you decided which property you like thus far?" I asked. She replied, "I like all the properties; however, I know that I have to make a decision."

I said, "Please be mindful of cost."

She didn't reply. She said, "Well sweetheart, Jane and I are finishing up our lunch. I will contact you when I'm on my way back to the hotel."

I said, "Sounds great. I will see you later."

Once I got back to the hotel I went to the hotel restaurant and grabbed lunch. After lunch, I went back up to my room and took a nap. Later that afternoon, Olivia came back to the hotel. I said, "So how did everything go today with the condo shopping?"

She replied, "I have found the perfect place."

I asked, "So what is the cost?"

Olivia responded, "Well, it's not that far from here."

I was still asking, "So how much does it cost?"

She responded, "It has three bedrooms and five bathrooms."

I said, "For the last time, how much?"

She responded, "$15,000 per month."

I said, "$15,000 dollars per month—are you serious?"

She responded, "Yes, I'm serious."

I said, "Olivia, that is a lot of money to be staying somewhere temporarily until our house is completed."

Her response was, "Jefferson, I need somewhere where I will be comfortable as well as feel safe, because you're going to be on the road a lot playing baseball and I'm going to be here by myself. The new place has a doorman, private maid, gym, restaurant, and laundry service.

I said, "Well, we have to be mindful of the cost."

Olivia responded, "The condo is also fully furnished."

I said, "It is what is." I then gave Jane a call and told her to send me over a copy of the contract. I told her that I would stop by tomorrow morning after I dropped Oliva at the airport to sign the contracts. I then told Jane to email a copy of the contract over to my brother Isiah so he and my attorney could look over it as well.

Jane said, "That sounds great. I have your brother's email address so I will forward him a copy right away."

I said, "Sounds great. I will see you tomorrow morning."

I then called Isiah and told him to be expecting an email from Jane concerning the condo contract. He said, "Ok." He said he would contact me later this afternoon to discuss the contract. I then told Olivia that we would go ahead and sign contract for this condo; however, we must be mindful of our spending habits moving forward.

She responded, "Well, my mom likes the condo and she doesn't think that is too much to pay."

I said, "Your mom? Well, your Mom isn't going to be paying the $15,000 per month." I said, "Well Olivia, I'm not going to discuss this anymore; we are going to get the condo." I then asked, "So where would you like to go for dinner tonight?"

She responded, "I'm not that hungry."

I responded, "Well, you're not hungry now but you probably will be when it's time for dinner."

She replied, "Why don't we just order room service for dinner tonight?"

I said, "No problem." That night for dinner we ordered room service as well as watched movies in our room the remainder of the evening.

We were both up bright and early the next morning for Olivia's flight departure. We both showered and met Mr. and Mrs. Montana downstairs, who were waiting to ride to airport with us. On our way to the airport we exchanged our contact information with the Montanas. We dropped them off at the terminal for JetBlue. Then our next stop was American Airlines for Olivia. After we had checked her bag Olivia and I kissed and I watched as she walked through the doors headed toward her terminal. I told her to give me a call once she arrived home.

While I was on my way to Jane's office to sign the contract my brother Isiah called me. He stated that everything with the contract looked good with the exception of the price. I told him that I knew the price is ridiculous; however, I let Olivia keep the condo because I felt guilty because she didn't have any input on the purchase of the house. Isiah responded, "Jefferson, you're spending too much money for this unit. Hopefully your renovation at your house won't last longer than four months. Well, little brother, I will see you in a few days. I have a call coming in."

I said, "Sounds great. I will see you soon." I went to Jane's office and signed the contract as well as received the keys, security passcode and details about the condo. Later that afternoon, I flew out with the team to start our road trip.

The road trip went great. We went 5-0 for the trip. I hit four homeruns and had 12 runs batted in (RBIs). Our team flight got in that morning at eleven. James was there to pick me up from the from the team facility around 11:15 and my flight to Alabama was leaving at 1:30 PM.

"Hey Mr. Robinson," said James. "Great to see you. So are you ready for your big day in a few days?"

I replied, "I sure am. James, do you have the exact date to pick me and my soon-to-be wife up from the airport?"

He said, "I sure do, sir."

I said, "sounds great." My phone began ringing and it was Tiger. He said, "Hey Jeff, what's up? So are you on your way to the airport?"

I said, "Yes."

He said, "Well, I will be at the airport to pick you up at 5 PM. So get ready; your bachelor's party is tomorrow night after we finish the rehearsal dinner."

I said, "Well my friend, I will see you at 5 PM."

James dropped me off at American Airlines for my flight. He then said, "Mr. Robinson, have a great trip and congratulations on your wedding."

I responded, "Thank you, James."

THE WEDDING

It was a great feeling heading back home. It was an even better feeling getting ready to marry the only girl that I had ever loved. However, I couldn't get Manuela out of my head. I knew that it would be awkward, seeing her and Escobar at my wedding rehearsal dinner and wedding. I wasn't having second thoughts about marrying Olivia; however, it was that little voice inside that kept telling me to wait a little longer to marry her. Finally my plane landed in Mobile. As I was walking through the concourse at the airport I heard someone call my name. It was Tiger running up to me. We gave each other a hug.

He asked, "Are you ready, my friend?"

I said, "Yes, I am."

He said, "Well let's head to your parents' house so that you can wash up prior to going to Olivia's house for the wedding rehearsal and dinner."

My family was happy to see me when we drove up. They all came running out and giving me a hug. I said, "I need to hurry up and shower and get dressed because our wedding rehearsal starts at 7 PM at Olivia's parents' house."

It was 6:40 and Tiger and the limousine driver were outside waiting on me and my brothers in order to take us to Olivia's for the rehearsal dinner. Olivia's parents' house is the same place where we were going to have the wedding rehearsal dinner as well as our wedding. I was kind of nervous about having everything outside, especially in the middle of August, dealing with the Alabama heat and humidity. However, I was pleasantly surprised when the limousine turned into Olivia's parents' ranch. I saw several enormous tents strategically placed on the property. When we arrived Olivia came running out and jumped in my arms and gave me a big kiss. She then hugged Tiger and my brothers. I said, "These are some huge tents."

She said, "Yes, the smallest of the three tents is for our wedding rehearsal and wedding rehearsal dinner. The other big tent is for our wedding. Then the biggest of the three tents is where we will have our wedding reception."

She escorted me to our wedding rehearsal tent. Inside, you would have never thought that it was actually a tent. It was very well lit as well as had tables neatly arranged for the dinner. The temperature inside the tent was very cool. She then took me to the tent where we were having our wedding. I was floored by all of the cool decorations and how all of the chairs were arranged. The main attraction was the gazebo in the front of the tent where we were going to be married. Everything was just so tastefully done. I was very impressed. Then we went into the remaining tent, which was gigantic. It was arranged with tables and chairs that could seat comfortably three hundred people. It also had a huge dance floor. I was about to ask Olivia how much all of this cost; however, I didn't want to ruin the glow that she had on her face. She seemed so happy. I knew deep down that this cost far exceeded the $100,000 that she and I had initially discussed for our wedding.

I then felt someone tap me on my shoulder. I turned around and it was Pedro Santiago. I said, "Pedro, my friend," as I gave him a hug. I said, "I thought that you wouldn't be able to leave until on a redeye later tonight because of your game."

Pedro said, "Hey, I lied. We did have two games today; however, my coach let me leave during the fourth inning of our last game. We were winning 4-0, ha-ha. So I jumped on a plane and flew directly to Mobile. You didn't think that I would miss your bachelor party, did you?"

I said, "Well, of course not."

Then we looked at each other and proceeded to say, "Roll Tide."

Then Olivia said, "Oh no, there will be no 'Roll Tide' at my house and not at my wedding rehearsal dinner." She then said, "War Damn Eagle."

Olivia's sister Jessica then walked into the tent and yelled for us to get moving unless we both wanted to be late for our own wedding rehearsal. We all then walked over to the wedding rehearsal tent. Everything went as planned with the wedding rehearsal. We started about 7:10 PM with the wedding rehearsal. We were done with the wedding rehearsal by 8 PM. By the time we had completed our wedding rehearsal everyone was coming in and getting ready for the wedding rehearsal dinner. We had on the list a total of about 80 guests for the dinner. I was outside talking to my brothers, Tiger, and Pedro when my parents and grandparents and sister pulled up. They were followed by Pedro's parents and his sisters, as well as Escobar, in a limousine that followed. Pedro's parents came up and gave me a hug. His mother and sister Sophia gave me a kiss on the cheek. When I saw Manuela my heart dropped. She looked stunning. She came up and gave me a warm hug. It felt so good. She also gave me a kiss on the cheek. Her lips felt so soft. She then introduced me to Escobar. He and I shook hands. I could tell that he didn't really care for me too much. Mr. Santiago then came up and shook my hand. He said, "Jefferson are your ready for your big day?" in his thick Spanish accent.

I responded, "yes sir, I sure am."

We all then proceeded to go inside the tent and sit at our assigned seats. Pedro and his family sat at the table with my parents and grandparents, Tiger's parents and my crazy Uncle Abraham. My brothers, Tiger, Pedro and my sister Eve sat at the table with Olivia and me and the rest of the wedding party.

The wedding rehearsal dinner went great. The food was great, the music was great and it appeared that everyone had a great time. We talked and danced until 11 PM. Then Tiger stood up and made a speech, then after his speech he said, "As much as we would love to stay and congregate with everyone here, I must complete my duties as best man and take the groom and the rest of the male participants to the bachelor party in Mobile. Therefore, if you would excuse me, we must say our goodbyes and then be off."

Everyone laughed and gave Tiger a round of applause. I then gave Olivia a big kiss and told her that I would see her tomorrow at 5 PM.

She said, "You better be good and don't be late, Jefferson Robinson."

I said, "Don't worry, I'm always good."

As we were leaving, I said, my goodbyes to everyone and thanked them for coming out to the wedding rehearsal dinner tonight. I then felt someone tap me on the shoulder. When I turned around I was shocked to see that it was Manuela. She said, "Thomas, let me be the first to congratulate you on your wedding tomorrow just in case I don't get the opportunity to see you."

I said, "Well thank you, Ms. Santiago." I then asked, "So do you have any cash on you?"

She said, "No, I don't. Why would I need cash?"

I said, "It is an American tradition that people at the wedding pay to dance with the bride and groom. The men pay money to dance with the bride and the women pay money to dance with the groom. I was just asking because I was going to save a money dance for you tomorrow if you wanted one."

Manuela responded, "I will make it a point to have cash with me tomorrow, Thomas Jefferson Robinson."

I asked "So how did you know my full name?"

She responded, "I have my way of finding things out."

I responded, "Well, you forgot something."

She said, "What did I forget?"

I said, "My full name is Thomas Jefferson Robinson III." I then gave her a kiss on the cheek and said, "I will be waiting on my dance tomorrow."

As I was walking away I saw Escobar come up to Manuela. I could tell that he was questioning her about what she and I were talking about. Manuela's response to Escobar was that our conversation didn't concern him. I then saw Pedro go up to Escobar and ask him if he wanted to go to the bachelor party. Escobar's response was no. "I don't get entertained by seeing strippers. Those type of women don't excite me."

Pedro's response was, "Well, I hear that you're a regular at Scarlett's Cabaret and Eleven in Miami, so don't play that 'I don't entertain strippers' to me. We are going to go have good, clean fun." Pedro then kissed his sister Manuela on the cheek and we then jumped into the limousine.

It was my brothers Jackie and Isiah, Tiger, Pedro, and Jamie my other teammates Butch and Ricky who played with me on the University of Alabama Baseball team. Olivia's brother Jason also rode with us. When we arrived at the hotel it was almost midnight. I went up to my room, then Tiger went and gathered the girls. Then we all met at the two suites that Tiger had reserved for the entertainment. The room was already stocked with alcohol and food, plus we had two servers along with the bartender that served the beverages. Then a few moments after we arrived in the suite, Tiger arrived with the strippers. I have to admit Tiger had selected some gorgeous strippers from Las Vegas. Then there was a knock at the door and there were some of my friends from high school and additional members from my baseball team in college. There were also some members from the Yankees there as well.

"Yo Pedro," I asked, "so why didn't Escobar come to the bachelor party?"

Pedro's response was, "Escobar is a buster. He tried to pretend like strippers were beneath him. However, I told him in front of Manuela that this isn't the case. I was told that his second home is in two of the top strip clubs in Miami."

I asked, "So what did he have to say?"

Pedro responded, "What could he say?" We both laughed.

He then said, "Escobar is jealous of you. I guess that he can sense that Manuela likes you."

I then said, "I wish them the best. So let's enjoy the night and have fun."

The party went on until about five in the morning. I left at 4:30 AM and went to my room. By the time that I had left the majority of the guys had left as well. I slept until about 10 AM, then I went by and knocked on my brothers' door to see if they wanted to go get breakfast. Then we went and stopped by Tiger's room. He was still sleep with two strippers in bed with him. We then proceeded to stop by Pedro's room. Pedro was still preoccupied as well. Jackie, Isiah and I went down and had breakfast.

Jackie asked, "So are you nervous, little brother?"

I responded, "I was a little nervous earlier but I'm better now."

My brother Isiah started going over the numbers about renovation of the house in Connecticut as well as the prenuptial agreement. He stated, "You are in pretty good shape financially, little brother. The house is yours even if things don't work out, and I hope everything does work out." Isiah also said, "I don't agree with you renting that pricey condo for the amount of money that you will be paying until your house is renovated." He said, "Jefferson, it doesn't make sense to pay $15,000 per month to rent a place for three to four months. That is $45-$60000 out the window."

I responded "I know it is a waste of money; however, I felt guilty because she didn't select the house in Connecticut for us to live in. I just wanted to make her happy."

Isiah was about to say something else until Jackie interrupted. Jackie said, "Hey little brother, it is your wedding day, so what time would you like to leave heading back to Leroy?"

I responded "Let's leave around 3 PM."

"That sounds good to me," said Jackie. He asked, "So how did you enjoy your bachelor party?"

I responded, "Everything was great."

"It appeared that your soon-to-be brother-in-law (Jason) enjoyed himself as well," said Isiah.

"Yeah," said Jackie, "he was making out with one of the strippers in the bathroom."

I said, "Really?"

"Yeah, he was getting it in," said Isiah. All three of us started laughing.

We were still sitting at the table drinking coffee when Tiger and Pedro came down about an hour later. I asked, "So Tiger and Pedro, did you two have a good time last night?"

Tiger responded, "I'm not sure about Pedro but I had an unbelievable night."

I said "I bet you did with two women."

Tiger responded, "I couldn't decide whether or not I wanted to take the blonde or the brunette back to the room with me so I took them both."

A little later Olivia's brother Jason came down to the area where we were sitting. He was still hung over. I said, "Jason you need to get something to eat and try to sober up. You need to be dressed by 2:30 PM and downstairs with your things so that we can leave."

"No problem, Jefferson," said Jason.

Next thing I knew, I felt arms wrapped around my neck from behind. I turned around and it was one of the strippers named Cindy. She was the leader of the group. She gave me a peck on the cheek. She said, "Not only were you a gentleman, Jefferson, but so were all the guys who took part in your bachelor party." She went on to say how impressed she was with everything. "I just want y'all to know that the girls and I had a wonderful time," said Cindy.

I asked, "So is everything ok?"

She replied, "Yes, everything is fine."

I replied, "That is good to know."

She replied, "There is only one small problem."

I asked, "So what would that be?"

She replied, "The girls and I need a ride to the airport."

I said, "That is not a problem whatsoever." I paid our limousine driver $200 to drop Cindy and her party off at the airport. They were very gracious and wished me well with my marriage. I gave each one of them a hug and thanked them for coming. I then thanked Tiger for doing such a wonderful job. I also thanked my brothers and Pedro for pitching in as well and covering the cost of the bachelor party. We all then proceeded to go upstairs and get ready for the wedding.

It was around 2:30 PM when I received a phone call from the limousine driver saying that he was downstairs. I said, "We will be downstairs in 15 minutes."

While I was putting on my tuxedo my hands started trembling when I was fastening up my shirt. I was getting more and more nervous as the time crept closer and closer to 5 PM. I was able to finished getting dressed and then met the rest of the party downstairs in the lobby. I said, "Hey guys, y'all are looking dapper."

My brother Jackie responded, "Well little brother, you clean up rather nicely yourself." We all were dressed in black tuxedos with pink cummerbunds and I wore a regular pink tie while they wore pink bowties.

We loaded into the limousine and were then off to Leroy, Alabama to my wedding. It was only about a 45-minute drive.

Olivia's brother Jason said, "The girls had strippers at their bachelorette party also."

I was like, "Oh really? So where did they have their party?"

"They had party at the new barn that we had never used out near the main house," said Jason. "There were about 40 girls and 10 male strippers. Olivia asked me whether or not you were good. I told her you were," said Jason.

I said, "Well, thank you very much for doing such a noble thing. Although you were telling the truth."

"Well, she said that she was a good girl as well and that she went to bed by 3:30 this morning," said Jason.

We finally arrived at Olivia's parents' for the wedding. Olivia's cousin Helen escorted all of the groomsmen as well as me into the living room of the main house. She said, "All of you need to stay downstairs only."

They had everything well thought out. They had laid this green carpet that looked like Astroturf grass throughout the property, so wherever you walked you walked on this carpet. You didn't have to worry about getting your shoes dirty on the dirt and/or grass. We were sitting around in the living room eating a lot of finger foods and drinking. Tiger was cutting jokes. My brother Isiah asked him, "So how was your night? I bet you were a real Tiger last night."

All Tiger could do was laugh. Tiger responded, "Let's just say they know how I got my nickname."

Olivia's cousin Helen came downstairs at 4:30 PM and told us to make our way to the tent where the wedding was to be held. We all jumped and saluted her and said, "Yes ma'am."

When I stood up my knees started trembling; however, I didn't let anyone else know about it. We all then walked into the tent where the wedding was to be held. I started shaking friends' and family members' hands as I walked toward the front by the gazebo. I saw my parents and grandparents sitting up toward the front. Manuela and her parents were sitting on the row directly behind my parents. I spoke to the Santiagos as I walked by them. Manuela's and my eyes briefly connected. Escobar was looking directly at me to see if I was looking at Manuela. I quickly turned away from her and acted as if I didn't see her. I then hugged Grandmother and Mom. My grandfather and Dad stood up and I hugged them. My Uncle Abraham then said, "You can still turn back. son. You don't have to move forward with this wedding. You have time." He was laughing the entire time.

You could hear people in the audience chuckle and start laughing. I said, "I'm moving forward, Uncle Abraham."

Uncle Abraham then looked back at Manuela and said, "You passing up on that pretty Santiago girl?"

Everyone turned around and looked shocked. Manuela's dad, said, "What is he talking about?"

Ms. Santiago said, "Jefferson's uncle was just playing around." However, she and Manuela's sister Sophie knew that it was the truth.

My grandmother had to tell Uncle Abraham to keep his mouth closed. Manuela and I looked at each other and both of our faces turned red. I looked over at Escobar; he was fuming. He gave me a look as if he wanted to take me out right there in front of everyone. I'm thankful that Olivia's uncle and her other family members didn't hear my Uncle Abraham because they were sitting on the opposite side of the tent.

I had finally made it in front of the gazebo prior to the bridal party and groomsmen beginning their walk down toward me. As each member of the party walked down the aisle I seemed to become more and more nervous. My brother Jackie noticed it as he hugged me as he stood next me. He said, "Are you ok, little brother?"

I said, "Yes, I'm fine, just a little nervous."

My brother Isiah came down and gave me a hug, then Pedro as he walked down the aisle with Olivia's cousin Helen, then came Tiger as he walked down the aisle with the Matron of Honor. He stopped and gave me hug. He said, "Jefferson, this is it. I'm the last person to walk down the aisle prior to the bride coming out. Therefore, if you want to get the hell out of here, we can. I see you shaking worse than a scalded dog."

I said, "Tiger, I got this" as we both started laughing."

Then I heard the wedding music begin to play. Then the Pastor said let everyone stand for the entrance of the bride. Then as the tent doors opened I could see Olivia and her father make the long walk down the aisle toward me. She was truly beautiful. I was a lucky man. As they made their way in front of me her father shook my hand and then he gave me Olivia's hand. We proceeded to say our vows and 10 minutes later I heard the Pastor say, "You may kiss the bride." Olivia and I kissed. The Pastor then said, "I now pronounce you man and wife."

Then we proceeded to leave the facility. Everyone was cheering and throwing rice as we walked down the aisle. I said, "Are you ready, Ms. Thomas Jefferson Robinson?"

Olivia said, yes, Mr. Robinson."

We walked out the door and proceeded to meet the photographer and bridal party so that we could began to take our photos. While Olivia and the bridesmaids were taking their photos, Tiger asked, "Jefferson, so how does it feel to be a married man?"

I replied, "It feels the same. I don't feel any difference. I was nervous at first; however, now all of that is gone. I'm just happy to have my new bride, the only girl that I have ever loved. I fell in love with her the first time that I saw her."

Tiger then said, "Congratulations, my brother from another mother. I'm proud of you."

I said, "Thanks, bro."

My parents and grandparents came out so that they could take the photos with us also. I also told Pedro to tell his family to come out and take the group family photo with the groom, then with bride and groom. Tiger, his parents and his brother also were in the family photo. Escobar decided to not be in the photo, and I'm glad that he didn't.

Afterwards everyone went over to the reception tent. It was time for the bride and groom's first dance. Olivia and I danced to Lionel Richie's "Truly." As we were dancing she said, "Thank you for not asking how much all of this cost."

I said, "You're the woman that I love. I have loved you since the moment that I first saw you. Everything was so beautifully done. You and your mom did a wonderful job. Let's not talk about the cost right now. Let's enjoy our day, Mrs. Robinson."

Olivia said, "Thank you, Jefferson" as she placed her head on my shoulder and we completed our first dance as husband and wife.

The next dance was the father and bride and groom and mother dance, which was a wonderful dance. My mother and I had a wonderful dance. We danced to Billy Ocean's "Suddenly." The final dance prior to us opening up the dance floor was the money dance. All of my groomsmen as well as a line of about 15 other men had lined up with money to dance with my beautiful wife. I had a line of about 10 girls, including some of the bridesmaids. After I had finished dancing with almost the last of the girls the first song had just gone off. I was looking for Manuela; however, I didn't see her. The next song had just started, which was "I'll Make Love To You" by Boyz II Men. I don't know who in the hell requested that song for a money dance song anyway. I was dancing with the final girl when Manuela walked up and tapped the girl on the shoulder to cut in on the dance. She must have placed about $3,000 in the money bag. All I could see was a roll of money being placed into the bag.

I said, "So you finally got some cash."

She said, "I wouldn't miss this dance for anything in the world." She smelled so good. It felt so good dancing with her. She said, "Thomas, I would like to wish you and your bride a wonderful life together. I just want you to know that the entire time during the ceremony, I was wishing that it was me you were marrying instead of her. I was saying to myself that she doesn't deserve you." Manuela went on to say, "I hope I find a man who will be as loyal, faithful and loving to me as you are to Olivia. She just doesn't realize how lucky she is. I also said to myself," said Manuela, "even if it was me that you were marrying that it wouldn't feel right because I knew that I wouldn't have your heart. I know that your heart belongs to Olivia and I'm finally ok with that. I don't like it but I can learn to live with it. I will now move on with my life," said Manuela.

The final money dance song was over so the DJ played another song, this one by Marvin Gaye, "I Heard It Through The Grapevine." I said, "Manuela, there is something in me that cares deeply about you. I didn't realize it until the night after the Championship game and I was about to propose to Olivia. It was the night that you walked up to me and kissed me. It was even more prevalent when I saw you walk in with Escobar last night. However, I'm married now and I must give this marriage my all because I do love Olivia. I wish you and Escobar the best even though deep down I know that he doesn't deserve you." Then we kissed each other on the cheek left the dance floor.

I went to find my bride. As I was walking off the floor, Tiger ran up to me and said, "What the hell was that?"

I said, "What do you mean?"

He said, "You and Manuela danced for like two songs straight, the entire time looking at each other all serious. Escobar just walked out the facility looking all pissed. Mr. Santiago, I believe, after looking at you two and after you telling me what Uncle Abraham said earlier today, has put two and two together. Anybody that really sat and watched you tonight probably could have sensed some kind of chemistry."

I said, "I understand, my friend. However, I'm looking for my wife."

"Well, that is what I was coming to tell you," said Tiger. "The guy, Jeremy Bosch, who she cheated on you with, was here as well."

I said, "What?"

Tiger said, "Yeah, he even danced with her during the money dance. I didn't know who the hell he was. I thought that he was just the average Joe until I heard one of your brother Isiah's friends tell him who the guy was. Then I saw Olivia and her sister Jessica leave the tent. I then asked her cousin Helen where she was going and she said that Olivia was going to change out of her wedding gown. I followed her," said Tiger.

"Olivia went inside the house. But Jeremy was inside the house also, along with Olivia, Olivia's sister and Olivia's mother. All four of them were in the kitchen. I could hear Jeremy tell Olivia that he loved her and that he knew that she loved him as well. Olivia, then said, that she loved him also but she loved you more. Jeremy said that he didn't know about the wedding until less than five hours ago. Jeremy went on to say that if he had had arrived prior to the ceremony he damn sure would have stopped the wedding." He asked Olivia, 'So if you love him so much, why did you cheat on him with me?'

"About this time I could hear Olivia's mother tell Jeremy that he had to leave, that it was too late because Olivia was now a married woman. Before they could all leave the kitchen I walked in. I said, 'Hey, what's going on here? Your husband is looking for you, Olivia.' I asked, 'What was all the yelling going on in here?' Then they lied and said Jessica and her ex-boyfriend had a disagreement; however, everything was ok now.

"The guy Jeremy then left the house, got in his car and left. Olivia and her mom and sister then went upstairs for Olivia to change into another outfit besides her wedding gown. I'm telling you this because you're my brother from another mother and because I love you."

I said, "Thanks Tiger. I love you too, brother. I'm quite sure that my wife will tell me all about this." I said, "It sounds like this Jeremy guy was pulling for straws because Olivia loves me and she wouldn't dare cheat on me again."

Around five minutes later my brother Isiah walked over. I quickly said, "There is no need to say anything. Tiger already informed me of what transpired." I said, "Thanks, y'all, for caring." I then saw my beautiful wife walk through the crowd. She came to me and gave me a big kiss. We danced the rest of the night away and departed for our flight to the Bahamas the next day. I was expecting my wife during our honeymoon to tell me about the incident with Jeremy at our wedding, but she never did.

CHAPTER FOUR

Marriage Isn't Easy

After our honeymoon, Olivia and I flew to New York. It would be a few weeks before our condo would be available to move in. Therefore, we would be staying at the hotel for another couple of weeks. James was at the airport waiting on us once we got back from our honeymoon.

"Welcome back, Mr. and Mrs. Robinson. Congratulations on your wedding." Olivia and I both thanked him. "Do you'll need to make any stops prior to going back to your hotel?"

"No James, we will be going straight back to the hotel," I said. "We will be eating in today."

It was still early however, I had a game tomorrow. We were currently in the middle of a pennant race. Once we arrived back at our hotel, we were both tired. We both took a shower and went to sleep. We woke up around 7 PM and ordered room service. While waiting on our food to arrive, I leaned over and kissed my beautiful wife. She said, "What was that for?"

I said, "It was because I love you and I'm so glad that you're my wife."

We ate dinner and went to bed. The next morning, I kissed her as I was about to go out the door for practice. I gave her an American Express Platinum and a Visa Black card with her name on them. She said, "What are these?"

I said, "They are credit cards. You need to buy groceries and clothes, don't you?"

She said, "Yes."

I said, "Ok then. We can go to the bank tomorrow afternoon so that I can add you to my checking and savings accounts."

She said, "Thanks, sweetie."

I said, "There is no need to thank me. You're my wife. While I'm at practice if you need to go anywhere James can stop by and take you."

The next two weeks went by rather quickly. We were now moving into our condo. The only thing we had to bring were our clothes and personal items because the condo was fully furnished. We were staying in one of the penthouse suites. The owner of the building gave us a deal for $15,000 per month. I didn't think it was that great of a deal personally. I told my brother that I had added Olivia to my checking and savings account. He quickly asked, "Jefferson, tell me you didn't add her to your main accounts."

"No Isiah, I didn't add her to the main accounts as of yet. I added her to my Wells Fargo checking and savings accounts, which have a total of $400,000 in checking and $250,000 in savings, respectively. I didn't add her to the Merrill Lynch investment account, nor did I add her to my Branch Banking & Trust checking and savings that has the large amounts." I said, "My Merrill Lynch account has the balance of my $5,000,000 in stocks and bonds and annuities and $1,500,000 CD. I want to invest $2,000,000 of the $3,500,000 in my BB&T accounts, which comes from my endorsements with Smoothie King and Nike, in real estate. Please look into the cost of building a house on five acres that Dad gave me there in Leroy. I want to build a house so that Olivia and I will have somewhere to stay when I come home. I will overnight you a set of plans tomorrow of the house that I want to build. It is 5,000 square feet and I want a pool and guest house in the back. Olivia doesn't know about these plans. This house will go under our LLC."

"Sounds great, little Brother I see you have everything under control."

"I also will be going up to Connecticut next week to check on the status of the renovation for our house. I'm being told that everything should be ready before Christmas."

We were in the thick of the pennant race coming into second week of September. I was lighting them up behind the plate. I was happy. My wife was happy; she had made new friends with some of the female tenants in our building. Some of them were around her age. She had met them at the gym in our building as well as at our community pool on the eleventh floor. My life was going great. "Olivia, so where do you want to go eat tonight?" I asked.

"How about let's eat in the restaurant in the building tonight," said Olivia.

"Sounds good to me, Mrs. Robinson." So we got dressed and went to dinner downstairs. "So tell me, sweetheart, how do you like New York?"

She replied, "I'm beginning to like it. I'm supposed to be going out to a club with Emily Watson and Susan Rockefeller on Friday night."

"That's no problem," I replied. "We will be playing in Baltimore on Friday and Saturday and returning to New York on Saturday evening." I asked, "So what are some of your long-term goals?"

Olivia said, "What do you mean?"

I said, "you have an Engineering Degree from Auburn University, so do you see yourself working for someone in the next several years or owning your own business, etc.?"

"So are you trying to tell me to get a job, Jefferson?" asked Olivia.

"No that's not what I'm saying. You don't have to work if you don't want to," I said. "I'm just saying that you need to do something to occupy your time. I know you just don't want to sit around the house all day and do nothing. Maybe you can take some cooking lessons or something."

"Oh, you have jokes?" asked Olivia.

I said, "Let's go grocery shopping tomorrow. I will cook you dinner on Thursday before I go on my road trip."

"Well, that sounds so sweet, especially after you told me to go get a job," said Olivia. Then she reached across the table to give me a kiss. "The food at this restaurant is amazing," said Olivia.

I jokingly said, "Yeah, it tastes ok."

The next day after practice my beautiful wife and I went grocery shopping. Once James and I had loaded the groceries in the car, we headed back home. Olivia was in one of her quizzical moods. "So James, what part of town do you live in?" asked Olivia.

"I live in Queens, Mrs. Robinson," said James.

"Are you married?"

"Yes, ma'am, I've been married 15 years and my wife and I have three kids, two girls and a boy."

"That's wonderful," said Olivia. "My parents have two girls and a boy also."

I said, "Why are you asking James all of these questions?"

She replied "I'm just curious, Jefferson. It helps to know the people you are around the majority of the day." Olivia said, "I bet you don't even know James's last name, do you?"

I replied, "I bet you I do!"

"So what do you want to wager?" she asked.

I said, "How about whoever loses has to cook dinner for a week straight?"

She said, "You're on."

I said, "His name is James Bond."

She said, "Stop lying, Jefferson. Is he serious?" she asked, looking at James.

"Yes, ma'am, he is correct," said James. James pulled out his driver's license and passed it over the seat for her perusal.

I said, "Well Mrs. Robinson, I'll write down a menu of what I would like prepared over the course of the next week. I will keep it simple, especially me being a country boy and all."

I could see James up front laughing. He said, "I get that all the time when I tell people my name is James Bond. To be honest, that is how I met my wife. She was working as a bartender at a local pub while she was finishing up college. I walked up to her and asked her to make me an Apple Martini, shaken but not stirred. She then responded with a little attitude, 'Who do you think you are, James Bond?" I said, 'Well actually, I am James Bond. I'm the real James Bond.' She didn't believe me so I showed her my driver's license. We have been together ever since. That was almost 18 years ago."

"How sweet," said Olivia.

We were pulling up in front of our building. James helped me unload the groceries onto the Bellman's cart as the Bellman brought the groceries up to our penthouse. I told James that I would see him tomorrow. I prepared brown rice with broccoli and salmon and a salad for starters, then pecan pie for dessert. My wife really enjoyed the dinner. I also opened a nice bottle of Merlot. I said, "Sweetie, isn't having dinner in our own home great?"

She was like, "Yes, it is great; however, I don't want to cook and/or have dinner at home every day. I want to experience New York."

I said, "We can go to dinner sometimes but not all the time. However, I prefer a home-cooked, wholesome meal all day every day." After dinner, I grabbed all the dirty dishes and placed them in the dishwasher. Then I went to the bar and made me a Tanqueray and tonic cocktail and poured Olivia another glass of wine.

Olivia then said, "Mr. Robinson, you can do it all—cook, clean, bartend play baseball and act. I mean, you can do everything."

I said, "Well, it is Mr. Robinson's neighborhood." I then walked up to her and kissed her on her neck, then I moved up to her ear, then I kissed her cheek, then her nose, then her forehead.

Olivia then said, "Mr. Robinson, you're being a bad boy."

I said, "Don't you like when I'm naughty?" I took her glass out of her hand and placed her on the island in the kitchen. I gently pulled up the nice. tight-fitting blue dress that she was wearing and pulled off her panties. I then proceeded to caress her feet, then I kissed her feet, then made my way up her leg, kissing every part of her. Once I got to her knee she started to moan. Then as I kissed her inner thigh she begin to moan even louder.

She said, "Oh Mr. Robinson, you're being a very, very bad boy."

I asked, "Do you want me to stop?"

She said, "Oh, please don't stop."

My wife and I made passionate love in our kitchen that night on every counter top, on the chair on the table, and on the kitchen counter looking out over the beautiful New York City nightline. It was wonderful.

The next morning I kissed Olivia on her forehead as she was sleeping. I told her that I would see her tomorrow night, which was Saturday night. We were flying out to Baltimore that morning for a game that night, as well as an afternoon game on Saturday.

She said, "I love you, Jefferson."

I said if she needed James to drive her and your friends around later that night when they went out, she needed to contact him early enough to let him know.

She replied, "Emily already has a driver that is going to drive us around."

I said, "Well that sounds great. You be careful." I kissed her and headed downstairs to meet James.

"Good morning, Mr. Robinson," said James.

"Good morning to you as well, James." While we were on our way to the stadium I said, "James, do you have any plans tonight?"

He said, "No Mr. Robinson, other than staying at home relaxing with the wife and kids. My son has a baseball game tomorrow afternoon and my daughter has a soccer game tomorrow morning. Did you need me for anything, sir?"

"No, I was just checking just in case Olivia and her friends needed a driver to drive them around later tonight. She has made some new friends and they were supposed to go around to bars later tonight."

"Well sir, if she needs me to drive her and her friends around, just let me know," said James.

I said, "No problem."

As he was dropping me off in front of the Stadium James said, "Good luck in the game tonight."

I said, "Thanks."

That night our game started at 6 PM. We beat the Orioles 8 to 2. Our game the next day versus the Orioles started at 3 PM.

After the game I went back to my hotel room. I ordered room service, then I called my wife around 10 PM. The phone went to her voicemail so I left her a message. I then received a phone call from Pedro. I said, "What's up, Pedro Santiago. So are we having dinner for one of the nights that you're in town?"

He responded, "Sure, the loser is buying because we are going to beat the Yankees' ass all over New York."

I said, "You fail to realize that we don't lose at home."

He asked, "So how is married life?"

I said, "So far, so good, other than my wife wanting to go out and eat each night and not cook. Married life is great."

He said, "Well, we can go on a double date when I get there. I want you to meet this girl that I have been seeing for the past month. Her name is Maria Sanchez." So

I asked, "Where did you meet her?"

Pedro responded, "I met her in Miami at a Salsa Club. She was in town on business and had gone out with several of her friends. She lives in Old Greenwich and works for the Federal Government in New York. She is truly amazing."

"So how old is she?"

"She is 26 years old."

I said, "Sounds like this young lady has your nose wide open, my friend."

Pedro's response was, "She does. I have let all of my other girls go and have gotten rid of the additional cell phones. I only have this cell phone, my main cell phone number, remaining."

I said, "Pedro, we have a game against y'all on Tuesday at 3 PM and a noon game on Wednesday. What night do you want to have dinner?"

Pedro said, "How about both nights? We can have dinner in the city on Tuesday and then y'all can come to Old Greenwich to her parents' house to have dinner on Wednesday."

"What do you mean her parent's house?"

"Yes, she still lives with her parents. They have a guest house in the back of their main house. She is trying to save money because the cost of having a place in New York is way too expensive."

I said, "Trust me I know how much it costs to live in New York."

"I can also get a chance to see your house in Old Greenwich as well," said Pedro.

I said, "Sure, that sounds like a plan. We can eat at Dick Anthony Steakhouse in our building; the food is great. Let's meet at 8 PM on Tuesday."

"Sounds great," said Pedro.

I said, "I look forward to seeing you on Tuesday."

Then Pedro and I hung up the phone. I tried calling my wife again; however, it went straight to voicemail again. I was tired so I went to bed. The next morning I awoke and checked my phone, however, still no call from Olivia. I tried calling her phone again but the call went straight to voicemail. I was beginning to get worried. I got up and got dressed and went downstairs to grab breakfast.

After breakfast I met the rest of the team in the lobby so we could head to the stadium to get ready for our second game against the Baltimore Orioles, which was at 3 PM. We won the game 5-4; however, I played terrible. I struck out twice and flied out twice. This was the worst game that I'd had since I had been in the Majors. I had never struck out twice in a game before. After the game, we boarded the plane and flew back to New York. When we touched down I was about to call a cab to take me home because James was off this weekend. However, there James was out front waiting on me. I said, "James, I thought that you were off today."

He said, "I was, sir, but my kids finished all their games earlier today and my wife is off to take the girls to a sleepover. So I decided to come take you home since I didn't have anything else to do."

I said, "That was very nice of you, James."

He said, "I hope you don't mind but I have my son in the car with me. He is a big fan of yours."

I replied, "No, I don't mind."

When I got in the car James introduced me to his son James Jr. I said, "What, another James Bond?" with a smile. I said, "Well, it is nice to meet you, James Jr."

He responded, "Nice to meet you, sir."

I asked, "James, would you and your son like tickets to the game on Wednesday to watch us play the Florida Marlins?"

He said, "Sure, but I work on Wednesday."

I said, "Don't worry about that; you can have the day off."

He said, "That is awesome. Thanks for your generosity, sir."

I said, "No, thank you for your generosity because you didn't have to come pick me up on your day off." I had several of my baseball cards in my jacket pocket so I autographed them and gave them to James Jr. as I was exiting the car. He was extremely happy. James once again thanked me as I grabbed my bag and headed into my building.

Once I walked into the penthouse it was very dark. I called Olivia's name but didn't get a response. I went to the bedroom but she wasn't there either. It appeared that the bed wasn't even slept in the night before. So I tried calling Olivia again on her cell phone. This time she did answer. I said, "Thank God, you're alive. So where are you?"

Her response was, "I'm at Emily's house. Samantha, Emily and I are eating dinner."

I said, "How inconsiderate of you not to answer your phone for two days, then not be home when I come back from my road trip."

She replied, "Oh Jefferson, stop complaining. I was so hung over from hanging out last night, I stayed over at Emily's house. We all just woke up around 6 PM and I knew that you were probably finishing your game, so that is why I didn't call."

I said, "Olivia, that is a sorry excuse from not calling me. It sounds like a lot of bullshit to me."

"There is no need for you to take that tone with me, Jefferson," said Olivia. "I sit around that damn penthouse all day doing nothing and it is boring."

I replied, "Like I told you before, Olivia, if you're bored either get a job or take up a hobby, preferably cooking. Whatever you do, please do something constructive with your time."

"Well, I don't have time to listen to your criticism, Jefferson," said Olivia. "I'm going to finish my dinner. I will be home shortly. Bye." Olivia hung up the phone. I was pissed.

Olivia went back to talking to her friends. She said, "Can you believe the nerve that he has questioning my whereabouts? I'm a grown-ass woman."

"Yes, you're grown," said Samantha, "however, you're very married. I tried to talk to you last night about not drinking so heavily and dancing so flirtatiously with those guys. It wasn't cool."

"Why don't you calm down with your motherly advice?" said Emily. "Olivia just needed to let her hair down a little. She had cabin fever from being locked up in that penthouse all those weeks."

"Emily," said Samantha, "you need to be a better friend. She has only been married for a month. I'm not trying to be her mother I'm just stating facts."

"Hey girls, that is enough about me," said Olivia. "I know how to deal with my husband. I have him wrapped around my little baby finger."

"Well, since we have just finished dinner," said Samantha, "don't you think you should go home to be with your husband?"

"No, not right now," said Olivia. "He needs to cool down before I go home. So let's go to the little bar where we were at last night around the corner."

"Sounds like a plan to me," said Emily. "Let's go."

I was so upset after getting off the phone with Olivia that I almost punched the wall but I caught myself. I decided to call my brother Isiah. "Hey little brother," said Isiah.

"Hey," I said.

"I guess you knew I was about to call you about that horrible game that you had earlier today," said Isiah. "It appeared that your mind was thousand miles away. Is everything all right, little brother.

I replied, "Yes, everything is fine." Then I said, "No, everything isn't all right. I left yesterday morning going to Baltimore to play for our two-game matchup with the Orioles and Olivia didn't answer her phone last night nor earlier today. When I got home tonight she wasn't home. She finally answered my call tonight, only to say that she was out with friends. I knew that she was going out last night with two girls that she had met in our building but I didn't think that she would stay out all night and not come home."

"Well, little brother," said Isiah, "you two need to put rules or boundaries in place. It appears that Olivia thinks that she is still single. When she gets home you two need to have a long talk. Ask her how she would feel if you went out and partied all night and didn't answer her call until the next night. Hopefully that will let Olivia see things through your eyes, little brother. Although if she doesn't see things from that perspective then there may be some hidden motives. On another note, little brother," said Isiah, "I have found a contractor who is ready to break ground on your new house here in Leroy. The name of the company is TMG Industrial Inc. They have many years of experience working in the construction industry. The total cost to build your house is $325,000 plus another $85,000 to build your swimming pool and outdoor kitchen and cabana. Since we are allowing TMG to perform turnkey services (do everything), we are saving about $25,000. We are still $90,000 under the $500,000 budget."

I said, "That is great news, Isiah. You sure have brightened my day with this news about the house."

"Well, little brother, there is more," said Isiah. "I have given TMG Industrial a 25% deposit ($102,500) earlier today. They are currently pulling the permits and getting with the architects on the plans. Per my conversation with the owner, Herbert Moore, they will start next Monday with the land clearing. He gave me a target date of the second week in December for having everything complete."

"Wow, so you mean to tell me that this house will be ready before Christmas?"

"Yes, that is correct, Jefferson, your house will be ready before Christmas."

I said, "Thanks Isiah. I don't know what I would do without you."

Isiah replied, "We are family, little brother. I will always be there for you. I will give you an update next week. Talk to you later."

I was very tired and didn't feel like going out to eat dinner so I ordered room service from the restaurant downstairs. I ate then went to bed. It was around two in the morning when Olivia came walking through the door, making all kinds of loud noises. She started calling my name. "Jefferson, Jefferson." She came in the bedroom and pounced on me, kissing me on the cheek and trying to kiss me on the lips.

I pushed her to the other side of the bed. I said, "I'm tired and not in the mood. Olivia, we need to talk but not right now. We can talk later in the day when you are sober."

Olivia got upset, got out of bed and went to the other bedroom. I didn't think twice about what had just happened. I turned over and went to sleep.

I was up bright and early the next morning. I went to the bathroom and washed my face and brushed my teeth, then I peeped in at Olivia in the other bedroom. She was half dressed, with her bra on and her pants halfway off as she lay across the bed. I finished taking her pants off and placed her correctly in the bed on the pillows and gently pulled the covers up to her chin. I then kissed her on her forehead and set the clock to alarm for 11 AM, which gave Olivia four more hours to sleep.

I then went downstairs for a workout and then swam several laps in the pool. I finished my workout around 9 AM, then went downstairs to the restaurant and ordered breakfast for Olivia and me. When I walked back into the penthouse I went in the kitchen and broke out the plates and silverware and made a pot of coffee. A few moments later I saw Olivia walking in the kitchen in her panties and bra. I asked, "So are you hungry, party animal?"

She replied, "Yes, I'm very hungry. Oh, that coffee smells so good. The smell of coffee is what woke me up."

I poured her a big cup of coffee. Then we sat down and ate breakfast. During breakfast not one word was spoken. I was flipping between the Sunday morning news shows and Sports Center. After breakfast I gathered the dirty dishes and placed them in the dishwasher. I then went back and sat at the table near Olivia. I said, "Sweetheart, have I done something to you that I don't know about?"

Her reply was, "No Jefferson, you haven't done anything to me."

I replied, "So why would you go a day and a half without accepting my calls, as well as stay out all night and away from home? Picture yourself in my situation. What if I went out with my friends on a Friday night and didn't come back home until two on a Sunday morning? What would you think? What if I didn't answer your phone calls while I was out?"

Olivia responded, "I'm sorry, I never thought about it that way. I get what you're trying to say, Jefferson. I should have at least called you back and let you know that I was ok."

I said, "You're damn right, you should have contacted me. There is too much going on for a woman to be out until three or four in the morning. Like my mother always used to say, nobody has any business being out in the streets till three or four in the morning, because nothing good ever happens after midnight."

Olivia responded, "Jefferson, I sometimes just need to unwind. I just felt so cooped up being here in the penthouse and in a strange city. I have to be able to roam be free."

I said, "You act like you want to be single again. Olivia, you're married now; it isn't just about you anymore. When I call you for whatever reason, you need to answer my call. Because it doesn't matter what I'm doing, if I see a call coming over from you, Olivia, I'm going to answer the call."

Olivia then walked over to me and said, "Fair enough, sweetie." She then gave me a big kiss. She asked, "So did you miss me?"

I responded, "Of course I missed you."

She then said, "Well, show me how much you have missed me."

I quickly picked her up in my arms and carried her toward our bedroom. We made love for what seemed like all afternoon. Then we got up and took a shower together and walked around the corner to Delmonico's to have dinner. While we were having dinner I said, "So do you remember my friend Pedro?"

She said, "Sure, I remember him; he is the Mexican kid that played on your college baseball team."

I said, "He isn't Mexican; he is Venezuelan. Anyway, he will be in town Tuesday and Wednesday. We play his team, the Florida Marlins, on Tuesday and Wednesday. Both are day games. He currently has this girl that he has been seeing for the past month that he wants me to meet. So I told him the four of us can have dinner at Dick Anthony's downstairs at 7:30 PM on Tuesday. He also wants us to come to Greenwich on Wednesday and have dinner at his girlfriend's parents' house. I told him both dates would be fine."

Olivia then said, "How could you commit me for a dinner date prior to talking to me?"

I responded, "I tried calling you several times but you didn't answer my call."

She replied, "Well Jefferson, I had plans already. I was having dinner with Emily and Samantha on Tuesday."

I said, "So you are going out with your girls again? Why so soon?"

She didn't respond. I said, "Well, you can invite your girls to come have dinner with us at Dick Anthony's on Tuesday night."

Olivia replied, "I don't think that will be a good idea. Why don't you have dinner with your friend Pedro on Tuesday? I will go with you to Greenwich instead."

I replied, "You make it seem as if going out to dinner with your friends is more important than spending time with me and bonding with my friends."

"It isn't that it is more important, it's just that I had already made plans," said Olivia.

I asked, "So at least are you going to come to either one of the games to watch me play?"

Olivia responded, "Well, I wasn't planning on coming because Emily and I are taking this Art and Wine class every Wednesday afternoon."

I said, "Ok, you have a class on Wednesday, but what about Tuesday?"

"Well Tuesday, I'm going shopping as well as getting my hair and nails done, so the day is pretty much shot," said Olivia. "The girls and I are also going out for dinner that night."

I responded, "You are truly unbelievable. I mean, you haven't watched any of my games since we have been married. The game on Wednesday is the final game of the season prior to playoffs starting."

Olivia then stated, "Well, I will be there for the playoffs."

I said, "No further comment." I then asked the waiter for the check, paid the bill, and we went home. Olivia and I didn't really speak the rest of the night. When I went to bed she was sitting at the island in the kitchen on her cell phone.

James picked me up at 8 AM Tuesday to take me to the stadium in time for the noon game. I gave him tickets and VIP passes for him and his son to attend today's game as well as the game on Wednesday. I said, "After the game you can use these passes to come to our clubhouse. I will introduce James Jr. to Derek Jeter, Alex Rodriguez, Johnny Damon, Mariano Rivera and some of the other players so that he can get their autographs."

"Thanks Mr. Robinson, my son will be very excited when I tell him about the passes to meet the players."

I was determined that moving forward, I wasn't going to let Olivia's actions get to me anymore. I had a great game. I went three for four and had two homeruns. We won the game 7-5. Pedro also had a great game as well.

After the game, I introduced James and his son to some of the Yankee players for autographs and photos. They both had a wonderful time. Then as I was walking over to see Pedro I met his parents and both sisters, Manuela and Sophia. I said, "I wasn't aware that y'all were going to be in town" as I shook Mr. Santiago's hand and kissed Mrs. Santiago. Then I hugged and kissed Sophia and Manuela on the cheek as well.

Mr. Santiago responded, "You didn't think I would miss both of my boys' final regular season game of the year, did you?"

I said, "Well of course not, sir." Then Pedro introduced me to his girlfriend, Maria. I said, "Well hi, Ms. Sanchez" as I gave her a big ol' Alabama hug. She was a beautiful girl with long black hair and beautiful brown eyes. She looked a lot like Jennifer Lopez.

I asked, "So Mr. Santiago, where are y'all going for dinner?"

He replied, "We are going downtown to this steakhouse."

I said, "No sir, you will do no such thing. You must join us tonight for dinner at the best steakhouse in the city, which is located in my building."

"We don't want to intrude on your and Pedro's double date tonight," said Mr. Santiago.

I replied, "Well, as you can see, I don't have a date. My wife had already made plans to have dinner with her friends."

Mrs. Santiago responded, "I'm sorry to hear about that, Jefferson."

I replied, "It's no problem. I will call the restaurant and let them know that we will need a table for eight as opposed to four people. I will also get us a quiet location in the back of the restaurant for privacy."

I saw Mr. Carlos, Mr. Santiago's Head of Security. It doesn't matter what part of the world that Mr. Santiago goes, Carlos is there. They both grew up in Venezuela. Mr. Santiago's parents took Carlos in when he was six years old. Carlos' father, who was the Chief Financial Officer for Pablo Medina's father, was killed in an explosion along with Carlos' mother and older sister. Carlos is more like Mr. Santiago's brother than Head of Security. Manuela, Sophia and Pedro all call him Uncle Carlos. He heads Mr. Santiago's security detail for his family as well as for his business. Mr. Carlos said, "It is nice to see you again, Senor Jefferson."

I said, "Welcome to New York, sir."

I then gave them the restaurant name and address. I told them that I would meet them at the restaurant at 7:30 tonight. I then said goodbye and jumped in the car with James and went home. On my way home I called Dick and Anthony's and changed the reservation from four people to eight people. I also told them to put us in the back of the restaurant in a private room. I didn't realize how tired I was until I had gotten home and sat down on the sofa watching CNN.

The next thing I knew, I felt Olivia waking me up about 6 PM. She said, "Jefferson, I'm on my way out."

I said, "I didn't hear you when you came in."

She responded, "You were in a deep sleep. You were snoring kind of loud." She gave me a kiss and said, "I will see you later."

I'm glad that she did wake me up or I would have overslept. I got up, brushed my teeth, shaved, took a shower and selected an outfit to wear to dinner. Tonight, I decided to wear a navy blue suit with a nice, crisp starched white shirt, black belt and a brand new pair of black Cole Haan shoes. I combed my hair. Then I topped all of that off by putting on Dolce & Gabbana Light Blue cologne and aftershave. Like Deion Sanders, pro football player once said, "If you look good you feel good. If you feel good you play good. If you play good you get paid good." I then went downstairs to the restaurant. I went into the restaurant to talk to Tony, the General Manager, to ensure everything was in order.

Tony said, "Yes, Mr. Robinson, everything is ready." He took me to the private room in order to show me the setup.

I said, "Thanks Tony, everything looks great."

When I walked back in the front of the hotel I could see Pedro and his family entering the front. I quickly walked up and greeted everyone. Then Tony escorted us to our table. Manuela and I were at the end of the line. I said, "Manuela, you look stunning."

She said, "Well thank you, Thomas, you look very handsome yourself."

I asked, "So where is Escobar?"

She replied, "He is out of town on business. So where is Olethia?"

I said, "Her name is Olivia. She is out with her friends."

We were finally at our table. I ended up sitting next to Manuela on the opposite side of the table from Pedro, his girlfriend, Carlos and Sophia. Manuela sat next to her mom, then her father, and I was on her other side. We quickly ordered appetizers as well as the main course because everyone was starving.

Mr. Santiago started off conversation by saying, "Jefferson, you had a great game."

I said, "Thank you, sir. My friend Pedro had a great game as well."

"So who are y'all playing in the first round of the playoffs?" asked Mr. Santiago.

I responded, "More than likely we will be playing the Detroit Tigers."

He responded, "The Tigers have a good team this year."

I said, "Yes, they do. They also have a great group of pitchers."

"Jefferson, I think that you're going to do quite well," said Mr. Santiago.

Manuela chimed in, "Just as long as you don't play like you did last week against the Baltimore Orioles."

I asked, "Manuela, so how did I play?"

She responded, "You played terrible."

I asked, "So did you actually watch the game or did you hear this from someone else?"

"Manuela watches all of your games," said Sophia. "She probably knows your stats better than you do."

I said, "Oh really?"

Manuela replied, "Thomas, let's just say you played like your normal self today. It appeared that you had something on your mind last week."

I said, "You're actually correct, I did have a lot on my mind last week. So how is business, Mr. Santiago?

"Well Jefferson, thanks for asking. Business is going great. So when are you going to come work for me?" asked Mr. Santiago.

I replied, "I still have some years to go doing my current full-time job."

Mr. Santiago replied, "Why don't you come work for me a couple of months during this off season? I really think that you will like it."

I said, "Let me talk to my wife first. I don't think that she will mind coming to South Beach to hang out during the winter months."

"Well ok, then it is settled," said Mr. Santiago. "Once you get a confirmation let me know. I will have everything ready for you once you get there."

"That sounds good, Dad, but I don't think Eduardo is going to like you training someone in his area of expertise," said Pedro jokingly.

Mr. Santiago replied, "I think Eduardo is going to be ok. He is a little bullheaded at times but he is good at what he does."

I then asked Maria, "What have you done to make Pedro settle down?"

She jokingly said, "He only likes me for my cooking."

I said, "so you can cook." Then Pedro quickly answered, "Yes, she is a wonderful cook."

I then said, "There is nothing like a woman who can cook."

Mrs. Santiago asked, "Jefferson, can your wife cook?"

I said, "No Mrs. Santiago, she can't cook. I have told my wife that since she complains about being bored why not take some cooking lessons. She became offended. I believe that she is the only woman in the state of Alabama who can't cook."

Everyone started laughing. After we had completed dinner Mr. Santiago pushed back from the table. He said, "You know, Jefferson, I have to admit that was a wonderful steak."

Mr. Carlos chimed in as well. "Yes, it was, Constantine. It was quite tasty."

As they were bringing out dessert Maria stated, "I look forward to providing dinner for all of you tomorrow evening."

I asked, "So is everyone coming to Greenwich tomorrow?"

Manuela said, "Yes, we will be at Maria's house for dinner."

I said, "That sounds great. If y'all come up early enough, I can show you the house that I purchased."

Mrs. Santiago said, "That would be wonderful." "o

"So when will your house be ready?" asked Pedro.

I responded, "My contractor said that the house should be ready a few weeks prior to Christmas. I'm also getting a house built in Alabama on some of my parents' property. My father had given each one of his kids five acres of land to build a home."

"So you're building a house there for you and your wife, as well?" asked Mrs. Santiago.

"Well, sort of, kind of—the house is being built under a company that my brothers and I formed. The same goes for the house being renovated in Greenwich. I purchased the property back in July, prior to me getting married."

"That was very smart of you, Jefferson," said Mr. Santiago. "I'm beginning to like you more and more."

I said, "As much as I would like to take the credit for purchasing the property that way, Mr. Santiago, it was my brother Isiah's idea. He is the financial wizard."

Sophie then asked, "So will your wife be at the game tomorrow?"

I responded, "No, she and her friend Emily will be at Art and Wine Class."

"What exactly is that?" asked Maria.

I said, "Well, it is a class where people learn how to draw and drink wine while they are doing it."

"So has she gone to any of your games this year?" asked Sophia.

I responded, "Well, she went to one back in July while she was here; that's about it."

Tony the General Manager came to table to inquire whether or not we enjoyed our dinner. Everyone gave a thumbs-up and said how much they had enjoyed their dinner. Mr. Santiago reached for his wallet in order to pay for the dinner, however, Tony responded, "Mr. Robinson has already paid for the meal, sir."

"Mr. Santiago, you and your family are like my family. You are in my City, therefore, it is only right that I pay for the meal. I would like to add that if my memory serves me correctly you paid for the last meal that we all had in Nebraska for the College World Series."

Everyone thanked me for the dinner. We all said our goodbyes then I went upstairs to the penthouse.

During their ride back to their hotel Ms. Santiago said, "It doesn't sound like Jefferson is happy right now."

Mr. Santiago responded, "I don't think she is the right girl for him. She doesn't cook and she isn't there to support him on fulfilling his dream."

Sophia chimed in, "I'm willing to bet that she doesn't show up for dinner tomorrow."

Manuela responded, "That is enough of talking about Thomas and his wife. Thomas loves her very much. He has been with her since the third grade in school. I think somewhere deep down she loves him as well. I hope they work things out."

"Well, if they're starting off their marriage like this, where she would rather hang out with her girls as opposed to being with her husband, I think that it is already headed the wrong direction," said Sophia.

It was almost 10 PM when I arrived back at my penthouse. I was hoping to find Olivia at home. However, she wasn't home yet. I started to call her but I decided to give her space. I went and took a shower then lay in bed watching TV. I tried waiting up for her but I was tired, plus I wanted to be well rested for our season finale against the Marlins tomorrow.

When I awakened the next morning Olivia still wasn't home, at least not in the bed with me. I walked over to the guest room and there she lay, all snuggled in bed. Well, at least this time she didn't sleep in her clothes. I went over and gave her a kiss on her forehead. She suddenly awoke and said, "Good morning."

I said, "Good morning to you as well, night owl."

She said, "Well, I was in the house before 2 AM."

I said, "I have no clue what time you came home because I was out like a light. I just want to remind you to be ready around 4 PM today to head to Greenwich for dinner."

Olivia responded, "Oh yeah, about that, Jefferson—I was wandering if we could do that over the weekend because the art class isn't going to start until 3 PM and we are not going to be done until 5 PM or later."

I responded, "Not only are you going to miss my game, the final game of the season, but you're not going to make the dinner that we had already planned for as well as to check the status of our house. Olivia, I'm not going to even say anything. I have a game to prepare for, I guess I will see you later tonight. That is, if you come home."

"Jefferson, that isn't fair," said Olivia.

I just threw my hands up and walked out the door. I stopped downstairs and picked up my usual three egg whites, two slices of wheat toast and two slices of turkey bacon from the restaurant. I then walked outside and got into the car with James.

"Mr. Robinson, good morning," said James.

I said, "Good morning, James."

James then went on to thank me once again for what I had done for him and his son the day before with tickets and passes for the game. "Mr. Robinson, my son and I really enjoyed everything about yesterday. My son couldn't stop talking about meeting all of his heroes."

I said, "No problem. You deserved it."

We were soon in front of Yankee Stadium. I said, "James, don't forget that after the game we will be heading to Greenwich to check on the status of my house as well as have dinner with some friends."

"Mr. Robinson, don't worry," said James. "I will be here. We are all set for the journey, sir."

I then walked into the stadium and headed toward the locker room. It was a hard-fought game but we prevailed. We won the game 11-9. Pedro hit three homeruns during the game with five runs batted in. He was a one-man army. However, I came to play as well. I went four for four, with three homeruns.

After the game I quickly showered then briefly spoke to the reporters. One of the reporters asked, "So how did it feel playing against your former Alabama teammate Pedro Santiago?"

I responded, "It felt great playing against Pedro. Not only is Pedro a former teammate, he is also a great friend. Pedro really had a hell of game today. He was firing on all cylinders. It felt great seeing him have a game like the one that he had today."

The reporter went on to say, "Well Jefferson, you didn't have a bad game yourself."

"Yes, everything went great for me today. The stars aligned and I was able to get a good read of some of the balls that came my way. Guys, thanks for your time but I have a prior engagement that I have to attend."

Before, I could leave another reporter, Jake Reilly, asked me about how married life was treating me as well as how I felt about our chances entering into the playoffs. "Well Jake, I'm really enjoying being married thus far, although I must admit there is a learning curve. I feel really good about our chances in the post-season. If we continue to play good, sound, mistake-free baseball I think that we can beat any team out there, which includes the Detroit Tigers, who we play next week in the playoffs."

As I was making my way outside the stadium to meet James I received a text. I quickly looked at the text, thinking it was from Olivia saying 'Great game, congrats' or something. However, it wasn't a text from my Olivia. It was a text from Manuela saying what a great game I had played. She stated that the entire family was rooting for both Pedro and me. Even though one of us had to lose, they were proud of how well we played. She went on to say how proud she was of me and that she knew I would have a good game. I texted her back and said thanks for believing in me. I asked her if they had left for Greenwich yet. She said, no that they hadn't left yet. I told her that I was texting her the address to my house so that they could meet me there first, prior to going to Maria's house for dinner. She said that would be great since dinner didn't start until 8 PM anyway."

I then called Sandra Wilson, our home decorator for the house, to ensure that she would be meeting me at the house at 5 PM. She stated that she would be there. I arrived at my house in Greenwich about 15 minutes ahead of Manuela and her family. The navigation system in their vehicle had taken them the long route. Once they arrived we all went inside the house. Once we walked in I met Sandra Wilson, the home decorator. The realtor, Jane Johnson, was also there. I introduced them to Pedro and his family.

Sandra asked, "Mr. Robinson, will Mrs. Robinson be joining us today?"

I responded, "No, she had a prior engagement and will not be in attendance. We will be stopping by over the next week."

Once I told Sandra that Olivia wouldn't be in attendance, I could see the entire expression change on Manuela's and her family's faces. I said, "Jane, y'all are moving at a fantastic pace and the updates look wonderful."

Mrs. Santiago said, "What a wonderful home."

We all then walked into the kitchen, which was now huge because the dining room wall was taken down and the both rooms were completely open.

Manuela said, "I love the concept of this kitchen. It is really beautiful and everything flows."

Everyone else walked upstairs with the realtor Jane; however, Manuela and I walked in the backyard with Sandra, my home decorator.

Sandra said, "Mr. Robinson, I made a few changes to the layout of the pool. I had the contractor change the layout to an infinity pool, which means to someone sitting in the kitchen looking out the kitchen window at the pool the pool will appear as if it is never-ending. I also installed a swim-up bar and added stools in the pool for swimmers to sit while they drink their beverages."

"So how much extra will this cost?" I asked.

"It won't cost you anything extra, sir. It cost less money to tear down the wall, which turned out not to be a load-bearing wall. Therefore, we took the extra money and used it toward upgrades to the pool. Plus, since I referred this pool contractor for this project he gave me an extra 7% percent discount, which I used toward the upgrades as well."

I said, "Sounds great."

We then walked into the guest house, which was already completely upgraded. Manuela said, "Thomas, I love this space."

I said, "Manuela, your bedroom is probably larger than this entire house."

Her response was, "Yes, you may be correct about that; however, that is Dad's doing, not mine. I would perfectly be ok. with a smaller space." She went on to say, "This space has everything that you need, i.e., a place to sleep, a place to cook and eat, a place to bathe and a place to relax. It has everything. It just needs furniture."

Sandra said, "That was my exact reasoning for getting this space completed first, Mr. Robinson, because Jane told me that you and your wife were leasing a condo in the City."

I replied, "Yes, we are."

Her response was, "I know that isn't cheap."

I said, "Sandra, you're right again."

She said, "Well, you can save almost three months of rent by moving in here until your house is completed."

I said, "Sandra, yes, that would be the rational thing to do; however, my wife wouldn't be onboard to do such a thing."

Sandra replied, "Well, it would at least be worth a try."

I said, "What the hell." I called Olivia on her phone. I was surprised Olivia answered her phone. I said, "Hi sweetie, how is your art class going?"

She said, "It is going fine."

I said, "Well, I'm currently at the new house with Sandra, our home decorator, and everything is coming along great. I'm currently standing in the guest house and all of the upgrades are complete. It looks great and is currently move-in ready. I wanted to see if you were willing to move into the guest house until the main house is complete. We could save about $45,000 for the three months of rent."

"Oh hell no, Jefferson," said Olivia. "I'm not living in any guest house. Once the main house is complete I will move to boring-ass Greenwich, but not until then."

"Olivia, you're really not making any sense right now."

"Jefferson, I'm not moving into the guest house. Now if you want to move there you can, but I'm not moving there," said Olivia.

I said bye and that I would talk to her later.

A few moments later Sophia, Pedro, Maria and Mr. and Mrs. Santiago walked into the guest house. Mr. Carlos and two bodyguards stayed outside the door. Pedro said, "What a great place, my friend. So I can see where I will be staying when I visit."

I said, "Sure, no problem, Pedro, this will be your space."

Mrs. Santiago said, "I love this kitchen."

I said, "Thank you, ma'am."

Sandra said, "Jane, Mr. Robinson is onboard moving into guest house until the main house is complete; however, his wife isn't onboard with moving in until the main house is complete."

Jane said, "I'm sorry to hear that, Mr. Robinson, because you could have saved a lot of money from leasing that penthouse."

I replied, "I would like to thank you and Sandra for your kind gesture by renovating the guest house first. Sandra, why don't you go ahead and completely decorate and furnish the guest house? I may decide to stay out here a few nights after the season is over."

She replied, "That sounds great. I will get started right away."

It was now around 6:30 PM. Maria said, "Ok everyone, it is time to go over to my house because I have to finish helping Mom get dinner ready. I only live five minutes away on 25 Havenmeyer Lane."

I said, "That sounds great, because I am hungry."

Everyone told Jane and Sandra goodbye, then we headed toward the vehicles. Manuela asked, "Thomas, is it ok if I ride to Maria's house with you?"

I said, "Sure."

So we all jumped in the vehicles and left.

Once Sophia was in the Suburban with her parents she said, "I feel sorry for poor Jefferson. It appears that he is having difficulty with his marriage already."

"Sophia, marriage isn't easy," said Mrs. Santiago. "It takes a commitment on both parties. It appears that Jefferson's wife is young and really wasn't ready to get married."

Pedro said, "What wife would not want to save her husband money, which would benefit their overall life. I think that she is very selfish. Olivia is all about Olivia. I told Jefferson this a long time ago."

"I think in due time," said Mrs. Santiago, "a little switch will be turned on in Jefferson and he will realize that marriage isn't a one-way street."

"Thomas, I think that you purchased a wonderful property," said Manuela. "I truly love how the house is hidden from the main street. Your home decorator is really good also. I must come back and see the finished product," said Manuela.

I said, "Why sure, you are more than welcome to come back and visit anytime."

We soon arrived at Maria's house. We then got out of the car and congregated with the rest of her family in front of Maria's house before going in. Once inside, Maria introduced us to her parents, two younger sisters and her older brother. Her sister Selena was 22 years old, her sister Isabella was 24 years old and her brother Ricardo was 30 years old.

Pedro introduced everyone to Maria's family. Isabella said, "This person needs no introduction," pointing to me. "Mame and Pape, do you know who this is?"

"Why, of course," said her father. "He is Jefferson Robinson with the New York Yankees. You played a hell of game today, by the way.

Pedro started clearing his throat. Mr. Sanchez responded, "You played a great game today also, Pedro."

Everyone started laughing. Mr. Sanchez then escorted us to the family room. His wife brought out refreshments. Sanchez, Maria and the other two daughters went to the kitchen to finish dinner.

Finally dinner was ready. Isabella came to the family room and told everyone to come to the dining room to eat. Once again, when we were seated, Manuela and I were sitting next to each other. Mr. Sanchez asked, "I thought Maria had said that your wife was coming to dinner as well, Jefferson?"

I responded, "I thought the same thing, sir; however, she had a prior engagement to attend."

"Well, you're a newlywed, Jefferson. It will take a little time for you two to get adjusted to each other," said Mr. Sanchez. "I hear you're to be our neighbor."

I responded, "Yes sir, I purchased a home on Greenwich Court."

"So when will your home be ready?" asked Isabella.

I replied, "I was told the second week of December."

"Pedro, how was it going to the great University of Alabama?" asked Mr. Sanchez.

Pedro responded, "It was a tremendous experience, I made a lot of good friends, Jefferson being one of them. Jefferson, who do y'all play in the first round of the playoffs?" asked Pedro.

I said, "We play the Detroit Tigers. The Tigers were a Wild Card with a record of 95-67. We finished the season with 97-65 record. The first game is Tuesday, October 3, which is only a few days away." I asked, "So does anyone want tickets?"

Mr. Sanchez, his son Ricardo, his daughters and Pedro all said that they wanted tickets. Mr. Santiago, his wife, Sophia and Manuela stated that they wouldn't be able to attend because they were headed back to Miami tomorrow. During dinner we talked about a lot of things, from investments to politics to real estate. I also told everyone about how I had just broken ground on a new home in my hometown of Leroy, Alabama. They were all fascinated by that, especially Manuela.

I said, "The house is in my business name, Triple AAA, an LLC formed by me and my two brothers. I'm also looking to invest in some other properties, whether they are residential or commercial."

I really enjoyed myself at dinner. It is always great to be around wonderful people. Pedro and I were alone briefly while walking out to the cars. I said, "Pedro, you have found yourself a keeper. She has a wonderful family and to top it off, she is a great cook."

Pedro said, "Thank you, my friend."

I said goodbye to everyone. Manuela pulled me to the side and said, "Thomas, I know things aren't the best between you and your wife right now but don't give up. If you love her you will fight for her. Just give it all you've got, then if that isn't enough, at least you know that you tried."

I said, "Thanks Manuela. It really means a lot hearing those words from you. What is this I hear that you are in the process of transferring from the University of Miami to the University of Alabama?"

She replied, "Well, they have a better Finance program at the University of Alabama, as well as a better golf team."

I said, "Yes, their Business and Finance programs are some of the best in the country. Pedro told me that you haven't told your father yet."

"No," she replied, "I've told my mother but not my father. I will probably tell him later this evening on our way back to our hotel."

I said, "Welcome to the Tide family." I gave her a kiss on her cheek and walked her back to the Suburban. I told everyone goodbye and went and got in my vehicle. It was almost 11:30 PM but there was no word from my wife. James dropped me off at my building around 12:15 AM. I was expecting to see my wife when I walked in penthouse; however, Olivia still wasn't home. I went and took a shower and brushed my teeth. I then put on a tank top t-shirt and my pajama bottoms. I went and grabbed a bottle of Ozarka water out of the refrigerator and sat on the sofa and turned on CNN.

It was around 1:30 AM when Olivia arrived home. She was shocked to see me still up when she arrived home. When she came in she said, "Hi." She reeked of alcohol.

I said, "Olivia, we need to talk."

She replied, "Talk about what?"

I said, "Talk about us; talk about our marriage. It seems that you would rather spend time with these new friends of yours as opposed to spending time with me. I've been bending over backwards to ensure you are happy but it appears the only time that you are happy is when you are out with these girls. I had a great time tonight with Pedro and his family, as well as his girlfriend's family, but it didn't seem right because you weren't there. I went and saw our house, which is coming along great, but it didn't feel right because you weren't there."

Olivia replied, "It felt great when you bought the house when I wasn't there."

"Olivia, I thought that we were past that stage. You were given complete authority to design the house as you would like. I even arranged it where you would have your own personal home decorator. However, you have not once contacted Sandra, our home decorator. Sandra and Jane arranged for the contractor to complete the renovation of the guest house first in order for us to move in the guest house and save money on leasing this penthouse. We could save roughly $45,000, but for some reason you don't want to move there. So I'm asking you right now, once the house is complete do you want to move to Greenwich, Connecticut?"

"Jefferson, to be honest, I don't want to move to Greenwich," said Olivia.

"So what it is that you want, Olivia?" I asked.

She replied, "I'm not sure, Jefferson, I'm not sure."

I replied, "I want you, Olivia. It is you I love; however, it just can't be a one-way street as it relates to this commitment, as it relates to this marriage."

"Jefferson, I love you," said Olivia. "I want to make this marriage work."

"Olivia, I'm tired of you talking about how much you love me. You have to start showing me with your actions."

Olivia and I then kissed and promised to give our marriage everything that we had.

CHAPTER FIVE

The Injury

The next morning I gave Olivia a kiss on her forehead as she lay sleeping in bed.

She asked, "Where are you off to so early in the morning?"

I responded, "I'm on my way to practice."

She replied, "I thought the season was over."

I said, "Yes, the regular season is over but the playoffs are about to start. We play the Detroit Tigers Tuesday at 7 PM in the first round of the playoffs."

She responded, "Well sweetheart, have a good practice. I will see you later this afternoon."

So I gave her another kiss. I stopped downstairs and got my regular breakfast from the restaurant. Then I got in the car with James, who was waiting out front of the building. Everything went well at practice. All of the players were pumped and ready to play ball; after all, we were the Eastern Division Champs. The skipper spoke to us after the practice and stated that Detroit was a tough opponent that shouldn't be taken lightly. We were given the next two days off from practice and had to report back to the stadium at 10:00 on Monday morning.

When I arrived back home Olivia wasn't there. She had sent me a text earlier that she was having lunch with Emily, but it was now 5 PM. I put my bag in the closet and went and got me a cold bottle of Ozarka water. I was always drinking Ozarka water because it was so good. I had to bring Ozarka water with me to New York because they didn't sell Ozarka at the stores here. Ozarka is a Texas-owned company. I had just ordered 20 cases of Ozarka a few weeks ago, directly from their facility. My agent was currently in negotiations to land me an endorsement deal with Ozarka. It should be going through any day now. Once the deal went through I would get all the Ozarka that I wanted for free.

Olivia arrived home a couple of hours later. She didn't tell me where she had been, nor did I inquire about where she was. I asked, "So are you hungry?"

She replied, "No, not really."

I said, "Well, I'm going to order Chinese food because I'm starving."

I ordered enough for her just in case she got hungry later.

"Jefferson, I need tickets for the playoff game on Tuesday," asked Olivia.

I said, "How many do you need?"

She replied, "I need eight."

I asked, "Why so many tickets?"

She replied, "Emily and Samantha want to bring a couple of their friends to the game as well."

I said, "I will leave the tickets at will call. Well, I'm all yours this weekend, so what would you like to do?"

She replied, "Nothing, really."

I said, "Let's go up and take a look at the progress of the house on

Saturday. Jane should have the guest house fully decorated and furnished by now."

"I forgot, Emily and I are supposed to go out Saturday night."

"I thought you didn't have anything planned."

"Well, I do," she replied.

I said, "So is this going to be an every weekend thing, going out with these girls?"

"No, it isn't. We just made plans to go out on Saturday."

I said, "Well, I'm not going to argue with you. I'm going to catch the train to Greenwich on Saturday morning. I will be back Sunday afternoon."

The doorbell rang. It was the Chinese food delivery. I paid the delivery man and set the food on the table. I said, "I ordered enough food for you if you like."

She replied, "I'm still not hungry."

My phone was ringing; it was my agent Jerry Reilly. He said, "Jefferson, I have great news. The deal is ready to sign with Ozarka Water. I will be emailing you and your brother a copy of the contract over shortly for your review."

I said, "Jerry, that is great news. You may not be Jerry Maguire but you are Jerry Reilly, the best damn agent in the business."

He said, "It is a small deal, $400,000 per year for five years."

I responded, "Jerry, that is a great deal. Hell, I would have done it for free if I could have gotten a lifetime deal of free water."

Jerry replied, "We don't do anything for free, my friend."

After I got off the phone with Jerry I called my brother Isiah. I told him about the Ozarka contract coming over shortly. He was all excited. "Little brother, if we get another four or five endorsement deals like this one you can be set up for life." Then he said, "On another subject, they are moving rather quickly with your house. They have already poured the slab and they started framing the house today."

I said, "That is great news."

He said, "Dad, Grandpa and Jackie aren't going to be able to make any of the games in New York because they are going to be out of town on business."

I said, "Dad and Grandpa are both retired, so what kind of business will they be doing?"

"I don't know," said Isiah. "I don't know if I had told you or not, but Dad and Grandpa got Jackie on with their old department with the government."

I said, "You mean to tell me that they have Jackie working with the Department of Transportation?"

"Yes, that is correct," said Isiah. "Yeah little brother, I just found out about it last week. Jackie had been working there for several months. He had gone through training and everything."

I said, "Jackie must have really been bored after retiring from professional football."

"Well, he was bored," said Isiah. He said he might as well to put his criminal justice degree to work."

I responded, "Master Kim had mentioned to me that Jackie had been back training with him over the past year and a half since he retired."

"Yes, little brother, Jackie is in awesome shape," said Isiah. "Well little brother, we will see you in Detroit on Thursday. The entire family is driving down for your two games," said Isiah.

"Sounds great, I will see y'all there." After I got off the phone with Isiah I said, "Sweetie, I got the endorsement deal with Ozarka water."

She replied, "That is wonderful news, Jefferson. So does that mean we get a free supply of Ozarka water?"

I said, "I'm not sure. I will know more when the email comes over with the contract." I asked, "Do you want to watch *Underworld Evolution*, which is now on Showtime?"

She said, "Sure, we can watch it."

So I ordered the movie then made some popcorn. Olivia yelled, "Jefferson, since you're in the kitchen, could you bring me a glass of tea?"

I responded, "Sure, sweetheart." I grabbed a bottle of tea and a bottle of Ozarka water and headed back to the living room with the popcorn and beverages.

"Wow, what a great movie," said Olivia.

I said, "I believe that was the best Underworld movie yet. My agent has extra tickets to *The Wedding Singer* on Broadway for tomorrow evening. Would you like to go?"

"I don't feel like going to a Broadway show," replied Olivia. "I would much rather go grab dinner at Delmonico's and then drinks afterwards."

I replied, "Well, if that is what you really want to do, I guess we could have dinner and drinks. Let me text Jerry and tell him thanks for the offer of the tickets but maybe next time." I reached over to kiss Olivia but she stated that it was that time of the month and that her stomach was cramping. I said, "I understand," so I kissed her on her forehead and went to bed.

The next day I went to the gym and worked out, then came back home and checked my emails. Sure enough, the email that I was expecting from Jerry concerning the Ozarka Water endorsement contract was attached. I called my brother Isiah. He stated, "Little brother, I have already sent a copy to your attorney and he will be calling us back later."

I said, "Sounds great."

Isiah said, "I went over the contract thoroughly several times. It appeared to be ok to me. However, it always helps to have an extra set of eyes looking over the contract."

A couple of hours later Isiah called me back. He said, "Little brother, everything looks good. You have the green light to sign the contract."

I said, "Thanks Isiah. I had been looking over the contract myself all afternoon and everything looked in order to me as well." So I signed the contract and sent it back to my attorney to notarize and email to my agent.

While I was in my office working on the computer, to my surprise, Olivia had brought me a chicken sandwich, French fries and a bottle of Ozarka water from the restaurant downstairs. She also gave me a kiss. I said, "Thanks for the lunch, gorgeous."

She asked, "So what time would you like to leave for dinner tonight?"

I replied, "Let's leave around 5 PM."

She asked, "Why so early?"

I responded, "The sooner we go out the sooner we can come back home, because I will be leaving around 8:00 tomorrow morning going to Greenwich."

She replied, "Ok. So will James be picking us up for dinner?"

I said, "No, not today. I told James that he could have today, as well as the weekend off."

Olivia replied, "How considerate of you. So how are we supposed to travel?"

I asked, "Why are you being so sarcastic? We can either catch a cab to Delmonico's for dinner or I can call a car service to come pick us up for dinner. Personally, I thought that it would be kind of cool to catch a cab around New York or either walk and enjoy the fall weather since Delmonico's is less than five blocks away."

She replied, "I guess the car service it will be" as she walked out the room. Olivia came back into the room a few moments later. "Well, I've called a car service and the driver will be here to pick us up at 4: 30 PM."

I said, "No problem, I will be ready."

I then picked up the phone and called Tiger. Tiger answered, "Hey, what's up, Jefferson?"

I said, "What's up with you, Jin Ho?"

He replied, "I got your Jin Ho."

I said, "Well, that is the name that your parents gave you, so don't get mad at me; blame your parents." I was laughing uncontrollably. I then said, "Well, at least they got part of your name correct; you're a Ho. So how is the big City of Leroy treating you?"

"Everything is going great working here at the bank with Dad and my brother," said Tiger. "We have been very busy lately." Tiger went on to say the area was booming. They had just finished building one steel plant in Jackson and they broke ground on a new chemical plant down near Boise Paper.

I said, "Wow, that sure is going to bring some much-needed jobs to the area."

He replied, "Sure is."

I said, "I have to call your father, because I need to find a place to practice Tae Kwon Do here in New York. He had mentioned a place to me before but I didn't write it down."

"Yeah, you better get back to practicing because your brother Jackie has been practicing nonstop with Dad as well as Master Yu."

I asked, "Who is Master Yu?"

Tiger replied, "Master Yu is Dad's good friend from South Korea. Master Yu and his family moved here to the U.S several months ago. He runs Dad's martial arts center full time now. We currently have roughly 100 students and growing."

I said, "That is awesome. I wonder why my brother Jackie is practicing so hard now?"

"Maybe because he needs something to keep him motivated," said Tiger, "now that he is retired from football and all. How is married life treating you, bro?"

I responded, "Well, it has its challenges." I explained to Tiger everything that had been going on with Olivia and me.

He said, "Jefferson, there is something going on, man. I think she may be messing around again."

I said, "I don't believe that, Tiger. I think she is just not used to being married and having me around all the time."

"Well Jefferson, you can tell yourself that if you want to but I think that it is more than what she is telling you," said Tiger.

"Enough talk about that, Tiger; did Jackie tell you that I'm having a house built there in Leroy?"

"No, he hasn't mentioned anything to me about it," said Tiger.

"Yeah, Dad had given each of us five acres several years ago, so I decided to build a house. It should be ready before Christmas. It is going to be 5,000 square feet with a guest house in the back, swimming pool and outdoor cabana with a kitchen."

"That is awesome," said Tiger. "Tell me you don't have your wife's name on the paperwork."

"No, the house is in the company name that my brothers and I had formed."

"Jefferson, I'm glad that you were smart enough to set everything up that way," said Tiger. "My parents, my brother and I are going to follow your parents to Detroit for your game on Friday."

"That is awesome news, Tiger. I look forward to seeing everyone."

"We will be there for both games Friday and Saturday night."

"Sounds great, Tiger, I will see you next week." Tiger and I then said goodbye and hung up.

I went into our bedroom and began to get undressed and placed my clothes in the dirty clothes hamper. I then walked into the bathroom to shave and brush my teeth prior to taking a shower. I saw Olivia getting out of the shower. The water was glistening off her gorgeous body. She was totally beautiful. When she saw me she stopped and tried to cover up. I asked, "What are you ashamed of? You have a beautiful body? I have seen your body before; you have never tried to cover yourself before."

Olivia replied, "I'm sorry, dear, I just feel bloated."

I didn't respond. I finished shaving and brushed my teeth. I then jumped in the shower. I had so many thoughts running through my mind. A lot of what I was thinking about was going back to what Tiger had said earlier during our phone conversation. I was thinking about Tiger's words and then Olivia's actions lately. But then I thought about how much she and I loved each other, all of our previous conversations, and all of the years we had been together. When I looked at it that way, all of the positives outweighed the negatives. When I thought about it that way, I knew that Olivia and I were meant to be together.

After I got out of the shower I got dressed and was ready to go to dinner. I decided to wear jeans, a blue designer shirt I had purchased in Miami and my brown crocodile cowboy boots. When I walked into the living room Olivia was wearing a white blouse and jeans and had her hair combed back like I like it. I said, "Hi Mrs. Robinson, you look stunning."

She replied, "You look handsome yourself."

I then walked up to her and gave her a long, passionate kiss. She asked, "What was that for?"

I responded, "It has been a long time since we actually kissed. I miss you."

She replied, "It hasn't been that long, only a little over a week since we have been intimate." Then her phone started ringing. It was the driver saying that he was downstairs waiting on us.

When we arrived at Delmonico's there was a long waiting list. However, General Manager Jimmy was up front. He came over and said, "Mr. Robinson, your table is ready." He walked us to an available table in the back. I shook his hand and places 3 $100 bills into his hand. He said, "Thank you, Mr. Robinson."

I said, "No, thank you for taking care of my wife and me, Jimmy."

I hadn't made reservations because I didn't think it would be this busy at 5:00 in the afternoon. Along the way I had stopped and signed several autographs for fans. They also wished me good luck for our game on Tuesday. Once we were at the table the waiter came and we ordered drinks. I grabbed Olivia's hand as I looked into her eyes and said, "It is great to finally have you to myself."

Then her phone rang. I could hear her say, "Hey, yes, we are here. If you come to the back of the restaurant we are at the table to the right."

After she had gotten off the phone I asked, "Who was that?"

She replied, "Oh that was Emily, Suzanne and Melissa."

I asked, "So how did they know that we were going to be here?"

Olivia responded, "Well, Emily had called me earlier and asked what I was doing tonight, so I told her that we were coming here for dinner and drinks. Emily then said that they would meet us here because they wanted to meet you."

I responded, "You should have told Emily that they could meet me on another occasion because you were going to spend quality time with your husband tonight."

Before Olivia could answer her friends arrived at our table. Olivia introduced me to Emily, a blonde with fake boobs and a dark tan. She was very attractive; she looked like a younger version of Pamela Anderson. Then there was Susan, who also was a blonde; however, she was very tall, around 5'10", with a slender build and also very attractive. She resembled Britney Spears. And finally there was Melissa; she was Hispanic. She was about 5'9" and had a very nice body. Melissa had dark hair and kind of resembled Jessica Alba. I said hi to each one of them and when the waitress came back I ordered drinks for them as well.

Susan said, "Jefferson, thanks for getting us tickets for the game on Tuesday."

I replied, "No problem. I have tickets for y'all for both Tuesday's and Wednesday's games."

She replied, "That is awesome."

Emily and Melissa thanked me for the tickets as well. I said, "There are only four of you so where are your other four friends? I have eight tickets reserved."

Everyone was silent. Then Emily said, "They may be out later tonight."

I said, "That sounds cool. Maybe I might be able to meet them."

Their drinks came and I ordered another Tanqueray and tonic for me and a Dewars on the rocks for Olivia. Then everyone ordered dinner. Then I excused myself as I left to go to the bathroom. I had only walked about five feet away from our table when a girl in her mid-twenties asked for my autograph. Then, as I was signing her autograph, the next thing I knew there were about seven girls and two guys crowding around me, asking for my autograph and asking to take photos with me. After I had finished signing their autographs I made my way through the large crowd at Delmonico's to their restroom.

"Olivia, your husband is extremely hot," said Susan.

Melissa and Emily chimed in and said, "He sure is."

Olivia responded, "Yes, he is isn't he?"

Then Susan said, "I don't know why you love to be out drinking so much when you have someone who looks that good at home waiting on you."

"Then on top of that he is famous and rich," said Melissa.

Olivia chimed in, "But he travels a lot."

"Yeah, he is working while he is traveling," said Susan. "He appears to be the faithful type."

Emily whispered to Olivia, "Guess who is here right now?"

Olivia asked, "Who is here?"

Emily responded, "Jake Goldstein."

"What is he doing here?" asked Olivia.

"I told him that we all were going to be here," said Emily.

"Well, tell him not to come back here, because my husband is here," said Olivia.

Susan responded, "Girl, you're playing a very serious game. You know that old saying if you play with fire then eventually you're going to get burned."

A few moments later I walked back to the table from the restroom. I said, "It is an absolute madhouse in here." Then our food and drinks came. I said, "Perfect timing." I asked, "So what do you do for a living, Susan?"

"I'm an attorney for a big law firm here in New York."

I replied, "How fascinating. So what kind of law do you practice?"

"I practice civil law," said Susan.

"Well, in a city like New York practicing civil law can be quite lucrative," I replied. "So what about you, Emily, what kind of work do you do?"

"I graduated from St. John's University in Business Administration and I'm a Business Consultant at my father's engineering firm here in New York."

Before I could ask Melissa, she stated, "I just graduated from University of Connecticut in Drama and I'm here in New York going to acting school."

I said, "That is great; if you can make it in New York, you can make it anywhere." I said, "I can talk to my agent; he may know of some upcoming auditions."

She said, "That would be great."

I said, "No problem." I asked, "Do all of you'll live in our building?

"Yes," said Susan. "Emily and I have been living there for about four years. Melissa just moved there several months ago. Melissa, Emily and I are roommates."

After we finished our dinner, I asked, "So does anyone want dessert?"

Everyone said no.

"We just want more drinks," said Emily.

I ordered another round of drinks for everyone. "We have to go to the little girls room," said Olivia. Everyone went to the restroom except Susan. Once they were out of my sight Emily said, "Olivia, Jake and his friends are in the front of the restaurant at the bar. After we use the restroom we can go up front and say hi."

Olivia said, "That sounds great."

I asked Susan, "So are you originally from New York?"

She responded, "Yes, I was born and raised here in New York."

I said, "New York is an interesting city. New Yorkers can be some of the rudest people and at the same time a more liberal group of people than you ever did want to meet." I asked, "So Susan, how you fit in with this group of girls, my wife included?"

She responded, "What do you mean by that question?"

I replied, "You seem so much more mature and disciplined. You know where you're going and what you want out of life."

Susan replied, "Well, that is how I was raised. I come from a long line of influential New Yorkers. I was taught that we have to have targets and goals and each day strive to obtain those goals."

I said, "Well, I come from a family of farmers in a small rural town in Alabama. I was taught to work hard for what you want in life. I was also taught that I could become whatever I wanted to become in life, even the President of the United States if I wanted to." I said, "I tell Olivia that sometimes and she laughs and says, 'I don't think that there will ever be a black President.' I would always say, 'Never say never; you might just be looking at the first black President."

Susan responded, "I agree wholeheartedly with you, Jefferson. Our country has come so far compared to 200 hundred years ago. We have come so far compared to just 40 years ago."

I responded, "You are so right, Susan. I believe your friends and my wife have gotten lost. Let's go see if we can locate them." I said, "I knew Olivia wanted to go out for drinks but I'm not sure if she wanted to stay here or go somewhere else. I did tell Olivia that I won't be staying out late tonight because I am catching the train to Greenwich tomorrow morning to check the status of our house."

"How is the house coming along?" asked Susan.

I responded, "It is coming along great. I was there last week and the main house is still a couple of months from being completed. However, our guest house is currently ready. Our home decorator has it fully furnished and decorated. I'm going up and spend the night tomorrow. I wanted to give up our penthouse and stay there until our main house was ready but Olivia was against moving to Connecticut until the main house was ready."

"I don't know why she would want to continue to pay high rent when you have a house ready to move in," said Susan.

I responded, "Those were my thoughts exactly."

"So Olivia isn't going with you tomorrow?" asked Susan.

"No, she isn't going with me because she stated that she had plans with y'all tomorrow night."

"Well, it will probably be Emily and Melissa that she will be hanging out with tomorrow," replied Susan, "because I will be driving to Upstate New York to see my family tomorrow and won't be back until Sunday afternoon."

Once Susan and I walked up to the front of the restaurant I saw Emily, Melissa and Olivia standing around the bar talking to four guys and two girls. When Susan and I walked over to Emily, Melissa and Olivia I said, "We came looking for y'all because we thought that y'all had gone to the bathroom and fallen in."

Olivia became nervous and said, "We were just on our way back to the table."

I said, "No worries. Do y'all want to stay here for drinks or do you want to go somewhere else?"

I saw Jimmy the General Manager of Delmonico's and told him that I forgot to close my tab out for dinner and asked if he could transfer the tab up front to the bar. He said, "Mr. Robinson, I'm sorry but we will have to close your previous tab and have you reopen a new one."

I said that would be fine. I went to the bar and closed out the previous tab and opened a new tab. It appeared that Olivia, Susan and Melissa had full drinks, so I ordered drinks for just Susan and me. Emily then introduced me to her friends, the four guys and two girls. I didn't really pay any attention to their names. There was a new group of girls coming by the bar and I saw two of them whispering to each other, then one of the girls walked up to me and asked, "Are you Jefferson Robinson?"

I replied, "Yes, I am." Then I signed autographs and took several photos with them. This started a wave of people coming up to me for autographs. After about 10 minutes of signing autographs I asked, "Olivia, are y'all ready to leave?"

Olivia replied, "No, we aren't ready to leave just yet. We want to stay here a little while longer."

I replied, "No problem." It was only about 8:30 PM. I was giving myself till midnight before it would be time to leave.

A DJ started playing music around that time and one of my favorite songs came on. The song was "Let's Get It On" by Marvin Gaye. I grabbed Olivia and put our drinks down and went on the dance floor. She asked, "Jefferson, what are you doing?"

I responded, "I'm about to dance with my beautiful wife." Olivia smiled. As we were slow dancing I looked in her eyes and said, "You are the most beautiful girl in this place."

She said, "I couldn't tell after seeing you signing autographs for all of those girls."

I said, "Well sweetheart, I was only doing my job. Those individuals, my fans, pay my salary. If it wasn't for our fans there would be no New York Yankees. I only have eyes for you, Olivia Robinson; now you, on the other hand—that is a different story. I saw how those guys were looking at you when I walked up to you at the bar."

She asked, "What do you mean?"

I said, "You know what I mean. The guy with blonde hair and blue eyes is looking at you dance with me right now."

Olivia and I must have danced about four slow songs straight, with a couple of fast songs in between. Then as we were about to leave the dance floor the DJ played another oldie, "Make It Last Forever" by Keith Sweat. Olivia knew right away that we were going to dance to that song as well. We started laughing as we fell into each other's arms again. After about a minute into the song I felt someone tap me on the shoulder and ask if they could cut in and dance with Olivia. I turned around and it was the guy with blonde hair and blue eyes. I said, "No, my man, I'm dancing with my wife." I turned back around and continued dancing with Olivia.

Then he tapped me on the shoulder. "I would like to dance with her now."

Before I could say anything, Olivia said, "Jake I don't think that would be a good idea."

Jake replied, "You didn't say that all of the other nights that we were dancing together."

I asked, "What is your name? Jake?"

He said, "Yeah, it's Jake."

I replied, "It might be a good idea if you keep it moving because I don't want any trouble."

Jake replied, "Well, it's too late for that."

I replied, "Jake, you really don't want to go there with me."

Then I saw Susan get Jimmy the General Manager and Jimmy came running over. Jimmy asked, "Mr. Robinson, is there was a problem?"

I replied, "No Jimmy, there is no problem. My wife and I are about to leave, so please close out my tab."

"Sure thing, Mr. Robinson, let's close out your tab," said Jimmy.

Olivia grabbed and held onto my hand as we walked over to the bar. As I was signing the check and closing out my tab I could hear Olivia tell Emily, Susan and Melissa that we were leaving. The girls replied, "We are leaving also."

Jake just wouldn't give up; he and his three male friends walked up to me and asked if there was an issue.

I replied, "There is no problem. I just need y'all to please move out of the way and let us leave."

One of the guys with Jake yelled out, "Just because you're some kind of baseball star doesn't mean that we won't kick your ass."

I paid him no mind as I told, Susan, Emily and Melissa, "Head toward the door. We have a car outside."

I grabbed Olivia by the hand and began walking outside. Jimmy came running over and asked whether or not I needed some assistance. I said, "No Jimmy, my wife and I and her friends are trying to leave but, for some reason these guys have an issue with me."

Jimmy told the guys to back off. The girls and I made it outside and were waiting on the driver to make his way to us. Sure enough, Jake and his friends made their way outside to start trouble again. Emily was trying to tell them to leave but they wouldn't. Jake tried to reach around me and grab Olivia. This was the last straw. I quickly took his arm and flipped him over and punched him. His other three friends then charged me. I quickly moved to the side and gave a round house kick to the loudmouthed one and he fell face-first into the ground. I gave another one a side kick to his knee and a backhand punch to the side of the face. The last guy, who was about 6'5", grabbed me in a bear hug. I quickly gave him a double open hand slap to each side of his head simultaneously. Then once he let me go I gave him a front ax kick to the back of the head. He fell to the ground and then he was out. I then walked over to Jake, who had gotten up to his knees, and I quickly took him to the ground and gave him several punches to his face until Jimmy and Olivia pulled me off the guy.

We all then waited for the cops to come. The cops then took my statement, the girls' statements, Jimmy the General Manager from Delmonico's statement, as well as multiple witnesses statements, who stated that these guys started it with me first on several occasions. They then arrested all four guys and had them sitting in the back of their police cars.

The lead officer came over to me. He said, "Mr. Robinson, do you want to press charges against these guys?"

I said, "No Officer Johnson, I don't want to press charges. I think that they have learned their lessons."

Officer Johnson replied, "Yeah, it appears that you kicked their asses pretty good." Then he and his fellow officers asked for an autograph as well as a photo.

I said, "No problem."

Jimmy came over and asked, "Are you ok, Mr. Robinson?"

I replied, 'Yeah Jimmy, I'm fine."

I could overhear some of the witnesses say, "Damn, not only is he a great baseball player but he can fight as well."

One of them stated, "Yeah, I have the entire event on video."

Olivia and the girls were now sitting in the Suburban. When I got in the vehicle I told the driver to take us to our building. Susan asked, "Are you ok, Jefferson?"

I replied, "I'm ok, but thanks for asking, Susan."

She replied, "Yeah, but your hand is bleeding."

I replied, "Don't worry, it isn't my blood."

Once we got to our building it was about 12:30 a.m. I waited on Olivia as she signed the credit card receipt for the driver. As I was walking through the lobby the bellman Davey came running up. "Mr. Robinson, you're one bad man. They're showing on the news where you beat four guys by yourself." Davey saw the blood on my hand. He asked, "Mr. Robinson, are you ok?"

I said, "I'm just fine, Davey."

He said, "If you need anything, please let me know."

I replied, "Sure thing."

When we got on the elevator everyone was quiet. Emily, Melissa and Susan said goodnight when they got off the elevator on their floor. Olivia and I continued going up to the penthouse.

"Damn, Jefferson is a bad motherfucker," said Melissa as they were walking toward their condo.

"Yeah, he kicked four guys' asses all at once," said Emily. "Did you see how he took down that big Andre the Giant looking dude?"

Susan angrily said, "Do y'all think this is a game? How do you think Jefferson feels right now? He has to deal with a cheating wife as well as a blemish on his public image even though he didn't start the altercation."

"Well, I never thought about it that way," said Emily. "However," she said jokingly, "I know to never make him mad."

Susan responded, "You're a sad person, Emily. A lot of this is your fault."

Emily replied, "It isn't my fault because Olivia is a grown-ass woman and she knows right from wrong."

"I'm done with this," said Susan as they walked inside their condo. Susan went straight to her room and closed the door behind her.

Jefferson's phone was blowing up. First his agent Jerry called. "Hey Jeff, are you ok, buddy? I just saw everything on ESPN."

"Jerry, yes, I'm ok."

Jerry replied, "The cops and the press are saying that it wasn't your fault, that you were trying to leave the restaurant but these guys were constantly antagonizing you."

I replied, "Well, that is what actually happened."

"Jefferson, there are also reports coming out stating that your wife was having an affair with the lead instigator," said Jerry.

I responded, "Jerry, I currently don't know all of the details; however, I will update you tomorrow."

"Don't worry, kid," said Jerry. "I will put all kind of spins and twists on this and you will come out of this smelling like a rose."

I replied, "Jerry, I didn't do anything wrong."

"Yeah, that may be true but you have some evil and cruel people out here who will do anything for five minutes of fame," said Jerry. "Jefferson, I will have my guys start finding out the names of these guys and pull up any information on them that they can. I will touch base with you tomorrow. You might have to do an interview over the next day or two, but I will keep you posted."

"Jerry, I had already planned to be at my new house in Greenwich tomorrow."

"Well, keep your phone close to you," said Jerry. "Bye now."

Then there was a call coming in from Tiger. "Hey Tiger, what's up?"

"I just saw the news. Are you ok, Jeff?"

"Yes, I'm fine."

"I told you about her," said Tiger.

"Tiger, I don't want to hear that right now."

"Well, you need to hear it Jefferson. She is no good for you," said Tiger. "She is now causing trouble in your professional life. You need to make a decision or this girl can ruin your life."

I said, "Tiger, I have a call coming in from Isiah. I will call you tomorrow."

"Ok Jefferson, I will talk to you tomorrow."

"Hey Isiah, what's up?"

"No, what's up with you, little brother? I have Jackie on a three-way call."

I said, "Hey Jackie."

"Are you ok, little brother?" said Jackie. "What is going on?"

I went through the entire scenario of what happened. They both said, "Well, it sounds like that Olivia was having an affair with this dude."

"I don't have all the specifics yet but as soon as I do I will let y'all know. I want to thank both of you for calling but I'm ok. I'm going to have a talk with my wife, then I'm going to take a shower and go to bed." I said, "Oh, by the way, my guest house at the new house in Greenwich is ready. Sandra the home decorator had decorated and fully furnished the guest house. I had already planned to stay the night up there tomorrow prior to all of this happening so that is where I'll be tomorrow."

"Well, Mom and Dad and your grandparents are already in bed, but you already know that you will be hearing from them tomorrow," said Isiah.

I said, "I'm already aware of that, guys, so goodnight."

"Jefferson, wait a minute your little sister wants to speak to you."

"Hello Jefferson, are you ok?"

"Yes, little sister, I'm ok."

"Do you need me to come up there and kick Olivia's ass?" said Eve.

I replied, "No Eve, I don't need you to come up here and kick anybody's ass. Little sister, you need to go to bed sounding like your ma and grandma."

"Ok Jefferson, I love you," said Eve.

"I love you too, sis, goodnight."

The phone was ringing again. This time it was Pedro.

"Hey Jefferson," said Pedro, "are you ok, my friend?"

"Yes, I'm doing great, Pedro." I asked, "So are you still in Greenwich?"

Pedro replied, "Yes, I'm still in Greenwich."

I replied, "Well, that is great. I will be in Greenwich tomorrow. I'll be staying in my guest house. I'll give you a call when I get there."

"Sounds great, my friend," said Pedro.

After I got off the phone with Pedro I went in the living room where Olivia was sitting. I said, "Olivia, please tell me what have I done to deserve this kind of betrayal. I mean, not once but twice. All I have ever done was love you unconditionally. I have loved you since the first moment that I laid eyes on you in the third grade over 14 years ago."

"Jefferson, I don't know," said Olivia. "I mean I love you with all my heart and soul. But I don't know why I cheated," said Olivia. "I think that we are too young and we just need to experience life more."

I said, "I asked this same question after you cheated on me in college with Jeremy and you said that this wasn't the case. We broke up for several months and you came running to me, begging me to take you back. However, we are now married and what's so crazy is that we have been married less than two months." I said, "Before I gave you the benefit of the doubt. I said, 'Hey, we live several hours apart in different parts of the state and we only see each once or twice per month; maybe she was just vulnerable and Jeremy caught her at the wrong time.' I was making up all kinds of excuses in my head why you cheated on me. But fast forward to now. We are married. We live together. I travel out of town but my longest time apart from you has been three days during the past two months. However, you still go out and cheat with this Jake jerk who was at the restaurant tonight. I mean, how disrespectful can you be, having the guy you're having an affair with meet you at the same restaurant and on the same night and same time that your husband is there having dinner with you. I mean, you have some big cahunas. I mean, I know you don't have a set of balls down there but I haven't been down there in a couple of weeks, so I may need to check because you may have grown some."

I said, "Olivia, what else can you say besides, I'm sorry?"

"Well Jefferson, I was lonely," said Olivia.

I replied, "What do you mean lonely? The longest that we have been apart is three days." I said, "What, your ass is so hot that you can't wait three days for me to come home?

"Jefferson, why are you talking down to me," said Olivia. "I bet you have girls in every city like the rest of the single and married players."

I responded, "Damn it, Olivia, don't try and switch this thing around on me and blame me for your transgressions. I have always been loyal to you; there has never been another woman but you." I said, "Have you forgotten our wedding vows: one man, one woman, one lifetime, forever? Olivia, you're flesh of my flesh, the bone of my bone. So how long have you been seeing Jake?"

She replied, "I have been seeing him almost three weeks now."

I said, "You're truly unbelievable. You have been sleeping with us both during the same period. This is truly unsettling."

Olivia asked, "So where do we go from here, Jefferson? Do you think that we can work through all of this and make our marriage stronger?"

I said, "I don't know what else I can do on my behalf to show you that I love and adore only you. I don't know what else I can do to show you that I cherish and am committed to only you. Olivia, I don't know what else I can do. However, the answer to your question is I don't know. I first have to pray to God and ask him to make me stronger in every capacity. I need God to make me stronger mentally, physically and spiritually. So I say to you, Olivia, you need to get on your knees and ask God for his forgiveness first. Goodnight. I will be sleeping in the guest room. I will also be leaving for Greenwich tomorrow and arriving back Sunday afternoon."

That night prior to me going to bed, as I always do each night, I got on my knees and prayed to God, asking him to give me the strength to make the correct decisions not only in my marriage but in life itself. "Lord, I know that I'm not perfect even though I strive to be but help me to learn lessons from every tragedy and success that comes my way."

The next morning I was up and dressed by 7 AM, getting ready to go catch the train. I went and got my bag out of our bedroom closet that was already packed. Olivia was up sitting with her back against the bed talking on the phone. I told her that I was leaving.

When I went downstairs there was a whole group of reporters waiting to speak to me. They were asking all kinds of questions. I explained to them that at the present time that I was informed by my counsel not to discuss anything. Once I made my way outside I was surprised to see my driver James standing outside waiting on me. I said, "James, what are you doing here?"

"Please get in, sir," said James. "Mr. Robinson, after watching the news this morning on TV, I figured you would prefer to have a little privacy on your way to Greenwich as opposed to riding a public train."

I said, "Well thanks, James." I asked, "James, why are we going toward New Jersey?"

"Well sir, we have several reporters following us. I will make a few quick turns and lose them." James did his thing and we lost them, then we headed toward Greenwich.

"James, you really are the real James Bond." We both laughed. I said, "I'm hungry."

He said, "Don't worry, sir. Sarah from the restaurant downstairs already had your food ready: two pieces of turkey bacon, two slices of wheat toast and two egg whites and a bottle of orange juice."

I said, "Wow, how considerate."

James said, "Well Mr. Robinson, people really care about you. You take care of a lot people and you're a kind and generous man. When you do good, good comes back to you."

I said, "Well thanks, James. I wish I could say that about my marriage. Hell, I've never cheated on my wife and we have been together since third grade, but this is the second time that she has cheated on me."

James said, "Well Mr. Robinson, if you don't mind me saying, God is just showing you the kind of woman you don't need as a young man as opposed to having you be with the wrong woman your entire life and realize as an old man that you were with the wrong woman. Now it is up to you to decide which way you would like to go."

I said, "James, thank you for your words of wisdom."

I called Olivia and said, "I just want to give you a heads-up about all of the reporters in the lobby downstairs." I then called my General Manager and Coach to let them know what happened and that I was ok.

They said, "We're glad to hear that you're ok, Jefferson; however, your agent Jerry has already informed us that you were ok. We just need you to get your rest and be prepared for the game on Tuesday." I told them thanks and that I would see them on Monday morning for practice.

I had a call coming from Dad. I said, "Hey Dad, how are you doing?"

He replied, "We are doing great. How are you doing, son?"

I said, "I'm doing fine. Dad."

He said, "Hold on, Jefferson. I'm going to put you on speaker phone. I have your mom, grandma and grandpa here in the kitchen with me."

I said, "Good morning, everyone." Everyone then told me good morning.

Grandma said, "I told you about that little heifer. She now has your name across every damn news station in America."

I replied, "Well Grandma, I didn't do anything wrong. I tried to avoid these guys on several occasions. Olivia and I as well as her friends had already left the restaurant. We were waiting on our driver to pick us up when these guys came outside and the guy Jake who Olivia was cheating on me with reached over my shoulder and grabbed Olivia by her hair. Then at that point I had to defend my wife and myself."

Mom replied, "Well baby, you wouldn't have had to fight if your wife were doing right by you and obeying her wedding vows."

I said, "I know, Mom; however, that wasn't the case."

"Jefferson. you sure kicked those boys' asses," said Grandpa. "I mean, I enjoyed how you beat the hell out of that 6'11" fucker."

I said, "Well Grandpa, it wasn't easy."

Grandpa replied, "You made it look easy, son."

I replied, "Well, I'm on my way to my house in Connecticut. The guest house is ready and I was planning on staying there tonight. I will see y'all next week in Detroit."

"All right Jefferson, you be careful. We love you."

I then hung up the phone and called Pedro to let him know that I would be by his hotel in five minutes. When we arrived at Pedro's hotel he was already outside waiting on us. He said, "What's up, my friend? How are you doing?"

I said, "I'm doing ok. So how is Maria?"

"Oh, she is doing wonderful. She and her mom have been cooking for me every day," said Pedro.

I asked, "So how much longer are you going to be here?"

"Maybe another week or so," said Pedro, "then I will go home to Miami to visit my family."

We were then pulling up in front of my house. We got out of the car, then James got my bag out of the trunk. "Mr. Robinson, would you like me to pick you up tomorrow afternoon?" asked James.

I replied, "No thanks, James, you have really done enough."

"Well sir, if you change your mind please don't hesitate to call me."

I said, "James, thanks, now please go enjoy the remainder of your weekend with your family."

As James was leaving down the driveway Sandra Wilson, my home decorator, and Jane Johnson, the realtor, were coming up the driveway. They said, "Good morning, Jefferson and Pedro."

I replied, "What are y'all doing here?"

They replied, "We recalled you saying that you were coming down this morning so we decided to stop by to see how you like the guest house, which is furnished and decorated."

I picked up my bag and we all walked around to the guest house. When I walked through the front door I was literally floored. I had to give Sandra a hug. I said, "Sandra, you have really outdone yourself. Everything flows so well. I like how open everything is—the living room by the fireplace flows into the kitchen. I really love the long island with the granite countertops."

Pedro chimed in and said, "This is a wonderful living space."

I said, "I also like how you decorated the two bedrooms and two bathrooms as well. Everything was so tastefully done."

Both Jane and Sandra said, "Jefferson, we are pleased that you like the finished product. Your main house is coming along nicely as well. When you have a moment to walk through and see everything, please let us know what you think."

I said, "No problem. I will let y'all know what I think prior to leaving."

They said, "Well, we must be on our way. We have a busy day today."

So I walked them out to their car. Jane said, "Jefferson, I want you to know how sorry we are for what happened. I want you to know that we have got your back. We support you." Sandra chimed in and said the same thing.

I replied, "I thank y'all for your support. It is just a difficult time right now. Those guys took something that was personal and private and made it public."

Jane and Sandra both gave me a hug then got in the car and left. When I walked back inside Pedro said, "At least they could have stocked the refrigerator."

I laughed and replied, "I know, right."

Pedro said, "I can have Maria stop by and take us to pick up a few groceries later if you like."

I replied, "Sure, that sounds great. Pedro, you know that you can stay here next week if you like, because I'm not going to be here."

Pedro replied, "That is a nice gesture, Jefferson but I have already paid for the week."

I responded, "You can always have them put the funds back on your card."

Pedro replied, "Maybe next time I'm in town."

I said, "Sure thing, we can make an extra key when Maria stops by later."

Pedro asked, "So Jefferson, how are you really doing?"

I replied, "I'm doing as well as can be expected. I never would have thought that Olivia would cheat on me again. Pedro, I'm just at a loss for words."

Pedro replied, "Jefferson, sometimes you just have to cut your losses and move on."

"I know Pedro, but I've been married less than two months."

I said, "It is just difficult right now. Well, there is a bright side; your sister Manuela texted me earlier to see how I was doing. I told her that I was doing ok. Manuela told me that she was there if I needed someone to talk to. I told her thanks."

Pedro said, "Well my friend, my sister still loves you."

I replied, "I know, Pedro; however, I love my wife and I've never thought about nor have I ever cheated on her. On the other hand, Manuela had crossed my mind prior to me walking down the aisle to get married. Manuela is so young; she hasn't even experienced life yet. Plus she also dates Escobar."

Pedro replied, "Yeah, she does date Escobar but she doesn't love him. Escobar knows that she cares for you."

I said, "Pedro, I really don't feel like going out to the grocery store. Why don't I give you a list of some items for Maria to pick up from the grocery store and bring here."

Pedro said, "I agree. You know Alabama plays Ole Miss tonight at 7:30 in football."

I said, "The game sure is tonight. Pedro, here is the list for Maria. Please have her bring a bottle of wine and some beer as well."

Pedro called Maria and she stated that she would stop by the store to pick up the items and stop by afterwards. I then sat in the recliner and Pedro lay on the sofa as we watched the College Game Day Program.

Maria and her sisters Selena and Isabella stopped by around 7 PM. They said, "Jefferson, the place is beautiful. Your home decorator did an excellent job."

I said, "Thank you." Maria also brought dinner that her mom had cooked for us. Her mom had made homemade pizza and meatballs and spaghetti. Selena said, "Mom prepared the food for you to say thank you for providing tickets for both of the games this week."

I said, "She didn't have to do that but I thank her anyway."

Pedro and I both were starving. So the five of us sat at the island and ate dinner. The food was great. We had a great time talking that night, even though Alabama lost by three to Ole Miss. The girls and Pedro left around midnight. They stated that they would see me at the game on Tuesday.

I went and lay down on the sofa. Even though I was going through difficult trials in my life, God had a way of telling me that everything was going to be ok. I had so many things to be thankful for, such as a beautiful family that loves me, great trustworthy and loving friends, a wonderful career, I was a graduate from one of the best colleges in the country and the owner of my first home. Hell, I was a prize catch for any woman even though Olivia didn't appreciate me.

The next morning I woke up around 8 AM. I then called a taxi to come pick me up and take me to the train station. When I arrived home around 11 AM all of the paparazzi had gone. When I had walked through the door of the penthouse I found Emily and Melissa laid out asleep, one on the sofa and the other laid back in the recliner.

Olivia came running out of the bedroom calling my name when she heard the front door open. She came running up to me and gave me a hug, saying that she was sorry and how much she missed me. I told her that I had to go work on some things in my office. I went in my office and locked the door then lay on the sofa and picked up my Bible. I opened the Bible and it went to Corinthians 7:12-15: *to the rest I say (I, not the Lord) that if any brother has a wife who is an unbeliever, and she consents to live with him, he should not divorce her.* Then the last paragraph says, *But if the unbelieving partner separates, let it be so. In such cases the brother or sister is not enslaved. God has called you to peace.* After reading that scripture I closed the Bible. I then opened the door and called for Olivia to come to my office.

When she came in I closed the door. I said, "Olivia, I have prayed about our situation and our marriage. I have asked God to guide me in making the correct decision. My God is awesome and he has given me a sign." I said, "I love you and I'm not throwing the towel in just yet. We will work through this difficult situation. I'm not saying it will be easy but we will work through it as one, bone of my bone, flesh of my flesh. But moving forward there are no other chances. If you cross the line again, I'm done."

Olivia replied, "Oh Jefferson, thank you, thank you. I love you so much. I haven't been able to sleep at all since all of this happened."

The next day I got up early to get ready for practice. I looked over to see Olivia but she wasn't there. I then heard the door open and it was Olivia saying, "Jefferson, please come to the kitchen. The food is ready." When I went to the kitchen she said, "Sara from downstairs already had your food ready: two slices of turkey bacon, two egg whites and two slices of wheat toast."

I said, "Thank you, sweetheart, that was sweet of you."

Olivia replied "That is the least that I could do."

The phone rang and it was Jerry, my agent. "Hey Jefferson, I have an interview scheduled with Barbara Ellis from Sports Reel later today for 4 PM. You need to be over at their studio by 3:30 PM."

I said, "No problem, I'll be there."

Jerry said, "Hey kid, just tell the truth about how everything went down. Good Luck."

I said, "Thanks Jerry. Olivia, that was my agent Jerry. He has scheduled a prime time interview for me with Sports Reel today for 4 PM. Therefore, I will be going to the interview after I leave practice today."

Olivia asked, "So what are you going to say during the interview?"

I replied, "I'm not quite sure what I'm going to say." I quickly ate my breakfast, gave Olivia a kiss, grabbed a suit and placed it in my garment bag for the interview, and I was off to practice. Once I got to practice there were droves of reporters there to see me. I stopped and told them that I would be doing an interview today at 4 PM with Sports Reel and everyone would hear my side of the story.

When I walked in the locker room all of my teammates came and told me that they supported me. It felt great to hear them say that they had my back. We had a great practice. After practice I took a shower and got dressed for my interview.

Once I had arrived at the Sports Reel studio they took me directly to the dressing room for makeup, then it was time for the interview. Barbara got right down to business. I explained everything to her, exactly how it happened and exactly as the witnesses had explained it happening. She asked whether or not my wife had cheated on me and I said, "Yes, she did; however, I asked God to give me a sign whether I should stay married to my wife, and he did." I said, "It has been a very difficult past couple of days. I came here today to tell my side of the story and to ask for privacy for my wife and me at this difficult time in our lives. My wife and I have a difficult time ahead of us however, we are determined to move past this and hopefully for the better. Right now I just want to concentrate on being there for our team to help us advance in the playoffs."

After I finished the interview I received a phone call from Jerry stating that I had nailed the interview. When I had arrived home my wife came and gave me a big hug as I walked through the door. She said, "I'm so proud of you and I'm glad that you're my husband." Olivia said, "Jefferson, I won't be at the game tomorrow because you don't need that distraction."

I asked, "Are you sure?"

She responded, "Yes, I'm positive. You need to be focused on the game."

The next day we got off to a great start. During the game I went three for four and we beat the Tigers 8-4. I was pumped. The entire team was pumped after the game. The skipper told us to go home and get some rest, then come back and do it again tomorrow night.

The next game we lost a nail biter 4-3. Detroit won to even the series 1-1. We were now headed to Detroit for our game on Thursday. My parents, grandparents, siblings, Tiger and his parents and brother and Pedro all had stated that they were going to be at the game on Thursday night but the game was postponed until Friday night due to rain.

Since the game was postponed I took everyone out for dinner. I was surprised but no one brought up anything about Olivia. I guess they wanted me to keep my mind on the game and winning. We had a great dinner. I told everyone that I was really glad that they had come down for my games. The next night the rain held off and we had a terrible game. We couldn't get going. Not only did our pitching let us down but our bats did as well. We just couldn't get anything going at the plate nor on the mound. We really looked defeated after that game. We had elimination staring us right in our face.

The next night the skipper told us either we win or go home—it was just that simple. He told us to play our game so that we could take this puppy back to New York for game 5. The Tigers got hot in the third inning, bringing in five runs to our nothing. I was next at bat. There were two outs with two men on base when I took a fastball over the right field wall. During the bottom of the sixth inning they drove in three runs to take an 8 to 3 lead. We were getting desperate. I singled my next time up. Bobby Rush was the next batter up. He took two strikes. I had a huge lead off the bag. I had already made my mind up that I was going to steal second base. Once the pitcher wound up to throw I was gone.

After I slid into second base I knew something was wrong. I was in excruciating pain. When I looked down at my right foot it was bent backwards facing the opposite direction. I was rolling around on the field trying to grab my leg. The paramedics rushed on the field to stabilize my leg and loaded me on a stretcher. All the players from both teams came over to give me encouragement. I knew that it was very bad. As they were rolling me off the field I gave a thumbs-up and the fans gave me a standing ovation. My brothers came and met me at the locker room. They went and got all my things out of the locker to bring to the hospital. Tiger rode in the ambulance with me and everyone else followed the ambulance.

When I arrived at the hospital they immediately rushed me to surgery. I was in surgery for seven hours. After surgery, the Head Physician came out and told my family that I was resting fine in recovery. Olivia and her friends Emily, Melissa and Susan had just arrived. Olivia had received a lukewarm reception from my family, although they treated her with respect since she was my wife.

The surgeon stated that I had dislocated my ankle so severely that the bone had completely torn through my skin. He stated that I had destroyed the ligaments in my ankle. He said although it was an unusual injury, I should make a full recovery. However, it would be a slow and long recovery. He told us that he would send the nurse to get us once I had awakened from the anesthesia.

When I awakened, Olivia, my parents, grandparents, Tiger and his parents, Tiger's brother, Pedro, Mr. and Mrs. Santiago, Sophia, Manuela, my agent Jerry, James and the skipper were all either in my room around my hospital bed or outside the door. I said, "What's up with the gloomy faces? Did I die?"

Everyone started to cheer, "He is awake."

Dad said, "How do you feel, son?"

I looked down and saw my leg in a cast, then I wiggled my toes. I said, "As long as I have feeling in my foot and I can wiggle my toes, then I'm ok, Dad."

Olivia came and gave me a hug and kissed me on my forehead. I looked over at Mom and Grandma and I could tell it took everything within them to keep from beating Olivia's ass. You see, my family is a little cray-cray.

My brother Isiah said, "You scared us, little brother."

I said, "I'm sorry about that." I then asked, "So did we win the game, skipper?"

My Coach looked around and then said, "No Jefferson, we lost the game 8 to 3."

I said, "Don't worry Coach, we always have next year. We will get the job done."

He responded, "That's right, Jefferson, we will get them next year."

The nurse came in and told everyone that I needed to get my rest. Prior to leaving the room Mr. and Mrs. Santiago came over and gave me a hug. I said, "Y'all didn't have to come way down here to see me."

They responded, "Jefferson, you're like a son to us. It wasn't a problem."

Pedro's sister Sophia came up and gave me a hug as well. Then Pedro said, "Jefferson, I have to teach you how to slide" and everyone started laughing.

Manuela came up and gave me a hug. Then she playfully tapped me on the shoulder and told me, "Don't ever scare me like that again."

Tiger's parents Master Kim and Mrs. Kim came and gave me a hug afterwards. Master Kim said, "You're going to need to come back home in order to get better. I have some old ancient herbs and treatments that can help with the healing process."

I said, "Sure Master Kim, just as soon as I'm cleared by the doctors I will be home."

Rabbit, Tiger's brother, came up and shook my hand. He said, "You were always slower than me; now you're going to be even slower."

I replied, "Don't count on it, Rabbit. With the help of your father I'm going to be even faster."

Rabbit replied, "I know Jefferson, your competitive spirit is going to have you back working out in no time."

My sister Eve came and placed her head on my chest. I could see that she had been crying. I asked, "So why have you been crying. She replied that she was scared" I said, "Don't worry, you know that I'm too tough for anything to stop me." Then I said, "You wipe those tears away. You're a Robinson; you know that we Robinsons are fighters. I love you little sister."

I stayed in the hospital a week prior to being discharged. The Yankees sent a private plane to transport my parents, grandparents, Olivia and me back to New York. My parents and grandparents had booked rooms at the Marriott hotel next to our building. I said, "Y'all can cancel those reservations because we have a three bedrooms and four and a half baths at our condo."

Once we got to our penthouse they were saying how beautiful the penthouse was. I replied, "It cost enough."

Dad and Grandpa sat me on the sofa and elevated my foot on the foot on a pillow and sat it on the love chair. My grandma Abigail went and looked in the refrigerator. She said, "You'll need some real food in this refrigerator."

I responded, "I can have James take you and Mom shopping."

She responded, "Yes, that would be fine."

I called James to see what time he could stop by to pick Mom and Grandma up to go shopping.

James stated, "I can be there by 11:30 AM.

I had to forewarn my Mom and Grandma that they were not going to be able to find the same foods here in New York that they have in Alabama. I said, 'So I'm telling y'all now you're not going to find any Conecuh Sausage or White Lily flour."

My Grandpa Thomas said, "Well, we got to get the hell up out of here."

Everybody started laughing. Mom and Grandma left with James at 11:30 to go grocery shopping.

Olivia stated, "Jefferson, I'm going to go with Emily to work out and get my hair and nails done."

I said, "I'll be here when you get back."

After she had left my Grandpa Thomas said, "You need to put her sorry ass out. What's wrong with you, boy? I wonder sometimes whether or not you have my blood running through your veins. Thomas, are you sure that you and Anna Mae didn't adopt this damn boy?"

Dad responded, "Yes, I'm sure, Dad, he is your flesh and blood. Jefferson just has a certain way to do things. Trust me, when he has given it his all and still doesn't get any results, his decision will be swift and permanent." Dad went on to say, "I respect my son's beliefs and I have all the faith in the world that when the time is right he will make the right decision that is best for him and only him."

I replied, "Thanks Dad." My father didn't know it but he really made my day. For a brief moment, I didn't feel the pain and throbbing in my ankle. I then took a couple of pain pills and a sip of my Ozarka water. I said, "Before y'all leave, I want y'all to go see my house in Greenwich."

Dad replied, "That sounds good. They are really coming along with your house in Leroy. It is going to be a beautiful house. They have already gotten both the guest house and the main house framed."

I said, "That is awesome. I'm hoping to come down to Leroy in about eight weeks. I will be letting Isiah know to let the contractor know that I would like my guest house complete prior to then."

When James brought Mom and Grandma back he helped them, along with Davey the bellman, to bring up the groceries. When he came in he said, "How are you feeling, Mr. Robinson?"

I replied, "I'm feeling much better, James." I asked, "do you know of a company with those miniature RVs that can transport us to Greenwich so that I can show my parents and grandparents my new house?"

James replied, "Sure, sure, what day would y'all like to travel?"

I said, "Let's go Thursday morning at 9:30."

He said, "Great. I will get everything set up for y'all to travel." He said, "Enjoy the rest of your day" as he exited. Prior to James leaving I slipped him a $1500 check for all the extras that he had been doing for me and my family. He didn't want to take the check but I told him to go buy his wife something.

Mom and Grandma went to the kitchen and got started cooking dinner. They fried chicken, made sweet potatoes, rice and gravy, fried corn, homemade biscuits, string beans, and Grandma even baked a buttermilk pound cake.

I said, "How did you make a cake, Grandma?"

She replied, "I purchased a mixer and cake pans."

I said, "You didn't have to do that, Grandma, but I'm glad you did."

It was after 8 PM when Olivia had arrived back home. My parents, grandparents and I had already eaten dinner by the time. We were all sitting in the living room when she arrived home. She came in and spoke and then went straight to the bedroom. She didn't come back out of the room for the remainder of the night.

I got up on my crutches around 9 PM. and showed my parents and grandparents their bedroom, along with where the linen and bath and face towels were stored. I said, "The maid will be here around noon each day. She cleans the house, makes the beds, washes the laundry and will take any clothes that need cleaning to the cleaners."

Dad said, "Sounds great, son, now you go get some rest."

When I made it to the bedroom Olivia was sitting in the lounge area talking on her cell phone. I went to the bathroom and brushed my teeth. I then went to my drawers and got out my pajamas. I sat on the edge of the bed and removed my sweatpants and sweatshirt and threw them at the foot of the bed. Once I was lying in the bed comfortably Olivia asked, "You need anything, Jefferson?"

I replied, "No thank you, I'm good." I said, "My parents, grandparents, and I are going to Greenwich on Thursday to see the progress of the new house. Would you like to go as well?"

She replied, "No thank you, I have my art and painting class on Thursday."

I said, "That's fine. I just thought that you might want to see your new home since it has been a while since you have seen it." I said, "Once the doctor clears me to travel I want to go stay in Alabama for a couple of months to train."

She replied, "A couple of months? Why so long?"

I responded, "I want to finish my rehabilitation there as well as train with Tiger's father."

Olivia replied, "I will only stay for a month because I would go crazy in that little small town."

I replied, "You were born in a county even smaller than Leroy. However, it shouldn't be about whether or not you're bored; it should be 'as long as my husband is there I'm happy to be there as well.'"

Olivia didn't respond. She went into the bathroom to shower.

When Thursday arrived the weather was beautiful. James met us downstairs at 8:30 AM. We had just finished breakfast at the restaurant downstairs. James had rented a nice miniature RV in order to drive us to Greenwich. There was a nice comfortable chair for me to sit in as well as prop my leg. When we had arrived in front of my house in Greenwich Sandra, my home decorator, was already there waiting on us. When I had gotten outside the RV she said, "How are you doing, Jefferson?"

I replied, "I'm doing much better now. Please meet my parents and grandparents."

We all then went inside the main house. Mom and Grandma fell in love with the interior of the house. "This is a beautiful home," said Mom.

Grandma said, "Yes, it is a magnificent home."

Dad and Grandpa liked the house as well. Their favorite part of the house as well as mine was the kitchen. "The house has come a long way since the last time you saw it," said Sandra.

I replied, "It sure has come a very long way. Y'all can go upstairs. I'll wait downstairs until y'all come back."

They went upstairs to see the rooms, bathrooms and theatre room. I could hear all the ooh's and aah's all the way downstairs. When they came back downstairs they were very impressed with everything. I said, "We aren't done yet. Let's go out back."

Sandra opened the huge sliding doors, which opened into a dining and sitting area on the back deck, which led directly to the swimming pool.

"It is truly beautiful," said Mom.

We then walked to the guest house. When we walked into the guest house all of their mouths dropped. My grandpa said, "Hell, you can live in this house."

I knew what was coming next. Dad asked, "I know the penthouse is nice and all but why aren't you and Olivia staying here until your house is complete?"

I replied, "Those are my sentiments as well, Dad, but Olivia didn't want to stay here until the main house was completed."

Grandma said, "I could wring that little heifer's neck." Everybody started laughing.

Grandpa asked, "How much does it cost to stay at that penthouse?"

I replied, "$15,000 per month."

He replied, "Boy, you have lost your damn mind. I was just kidding earlier but now I'm sure that your ma and pa adopted your ass now. There is no way I would be wasting that kind of money on the penthouse when you have this wonderful place here."

I said, "Sandra, as you know I'm building a house in my hometown in Alabama as well. I was wondering if you would be interested in decorating and furnishing my main house and guest house there as well?"

She replied, "I would be delighted to decorate your homes, Jefferson."

I said, "Perfect, here is my brother Isiah's phone number. You can call him. He is managing the project." I said, "I will be going to Leroy in seven weeks to complete my rehab. They currently have both the main house and guest house framed and enclosed so if you could have the guest house completely decorated and furnished like this one before I arrive, that would be fantastic."

She said, "Don't worry, Jefferson, we will have everything ready to go when you arrive there."

I said, "That sounds great." I then gave Sandra a $40,000 check to cover her previous invoice for furnishing and decorating the guest house. We all walked her back out to her car then we loaded back up in the RV.

My parents and grandparents flew back to Alabama the following week. I really did enjoy their stay. I believe I gained about five pounds.

The next week I went to my doctor to have my cast taken off. After the doctor took my cast off he checked my ankle to see if everything was healing properly. He said, "Jefferson, it must be nice to be young and healthy. Everything is healing wonderfully. I'm going to write you a prescription for some ointment for you to use each time you get out of the shower."

I responded, "No problem, Doc."

He said, "I would like you to wear this protective boot over the next four weeks, then come back to see me."

I really felt great. Everything was coming along beautifully. Olivia and I stopped by Capital Grille to have lunch on our way home. I felt so good that I had a couple of Tanqueray and tonics cocktails with my meal.

"So how do you feel?" she asked.

I replied, "I feel great."

While we were finishing up dinner the restaurant General Manager stopped by and introduced himself. "Mr. Robinson, I'm a big fan of yours. I'm glad to see that you are doing better."

I replied, "Thank you." I even took a photo with him and several members of his wait staff.

We finished up our lunch and went home. I was feeling really frisky. As soon as we walked through the door I pulled Olivia close to me and passionately kissed her.

"Jefferson, are you healthy enough to do this?" she asked.

I said, "Oh yeah, I feel great."

We made love right there on our big white bearskin rug in front of the fireplace. It had been six weeks since we had been intimate. I still loved her but for some reason it just didn't feel right. It was as if she was just going through the motions but I didn't confront her about it.

The next day while Olivia was out with the girls I called Jerry, my agent. I said, "Hi Jerry."

He replied, "I saw your x-rays from the doctor. You are healing way ahead of schedule, my friend."

I replied, "Thanks, but I'm calling to see if you have a good private detective that you can refer to me."

He said, "Sure, here is my brother–in–law Ray's contact information. He has been a private detective for 25 years."

I thanked Jerry and hung up the phone. I then called his brother-in-law Ray and scheduled a meeting with him for lunch the next day. We met at Tony Dragonas restaurant for lunch. I explained to Ray about the two previous times before that she cheated on me as well as my current suspicions. I told him that she currently left every day around 11 AM going to work out and that she goes to this painting and wine class every Tuesday and Thursday evening at 6 PM. I gave him a photo of her. I then gave him a check for $ 2,000.

When I arrived home I sat down in the lobby in my building for about an hour prior to going up to the penthouse. I was on the phone with my brother Isiah getting updates about the status of my house. "Don't worry, Jefferson, everything looks great," said Isiah. He said, "I have already spoken to Sandra and she will be down the week prior to your arrival to furnish and decorate the guest house."

I said, "That sounds great." I said, "Isiah, I hired a private investigator today to follow Olivia." I said, "You know, we had sex for the first time in six weeks yesterday, and it just didn't feel right. I just don't want to go down the same road again. Isiah, I need you to find me a private investigator to follow her when we come home as well."

Isiah asked, "Jefferson, are you serious?"

I replied, "Yes, I'm serious. Please locate a private investigator from Mobile and have them sign a Non-Disclosure Agreement as well."

Isiah said, "Well Jefferson, if that's what you want, consider it done, little brother."

I said, "Thanks" and we hung up.

Olivia and I were only intimate one other time over the next four weeks. Each time that I wanted to make love she made an excuse. The four weeks in between my doctor visits passed by rather quickly. My doctor took x-rays of my ankle and said everything looked great. He said, "Jefferson, you are healing way ahead of schedule and you look great as well."

I said, "Doc I work out five days per week and ride the stationary three miles per day to try and build muscles in my ankle."

He replied, "Well, you're doing a great job. If you would like to take your rehab to a totally different level you can contact this guy out of Miami. I hear that he is a hell of trainer plus he has an awesome vitamins and supplement shop. His name is Presario Gonzales."

I replied, "Thanks Doc, but I will be training with my Tae Kwon Do instructor in Alabama for the next four months."

He replied, "Well, I'm just putting it out there in case you hit a rut."

I responded, "I will keep that in mind."

On my way home that day, I gave James a $1200 gift card for his kids and a $20,000 check.

He asked, "What is this for, Mr. Robinson?"

I said, "I will be gone for the next four or five months. I just want to say thanks for not only being a great driver but a good friend as well. From now on you can call me Jefferson."

He replied, "Thanks Mr. Robinson—I mean Jefferson."

I asked, "Could you pick us up at 7 AM tomorrow? Our flight leaves out of LaGuardia Airport for Mobile, Alabama at 10 AM tomorrow."

"Sure thing, sir," said James. "So what airline, sir?"

I responded, "We will be flying on JetBlue airlines."

When I got home Olivia was just getting back from shopping. I asked, "Are you ready to go to Alabama?"

She replied, "Not really."

I said, "You have been doing a lot of shopping lately. I also saw where you had wired $45,000 to an outside account. So what was the wire for?"

She replied, "Well, if you must know, I invested $45,000 into Emily's beauty and day salon."

I asked, "So why didn't you discuss this with me prior to investing that kind of money?"

She replied, "So what, it isn't my money too?"

I responded, "No, that isn't what I'm saying, Olivia. I'm just saying that $45,000 is no small sum of money, especially to invest in a friend's business. I would have preferred to see a business plan, then information on the company to send over to my brother Isiah as well as my attorney to look over." I said, "In the future before you take such a large sum of money out of the accounts, check with me first."

I asked, "So what is your ownership percentage in this business?"

She replied, " Twenty-five percent. The name of the spa is Unique Boutique Day Spa and Salon."

I asked, "Could you contact Emily and have her provide me with a business plan and financial information on this company? Because I would like to have my brother Isiah and my attorney look over everything."

Olivia replied, "There is no need for you to look over any of this information because you don't have any ownership in this business. Everything is under my name."

I responded, "I have no ownership but you can utilize my hard-earned money to invest."

While talking with Olivia I had a missed call from Ray Donovan, the private investigator. I called Ray back. He said, "Jefferson, can you talk right now?"

I said, "Sure" as I walked into my office.

He said, "All I can say is that your hunch was correct. I will have a complete listing, breakdown and photos available for you within the next two weeks. I have to finish compiling my reports as well as talk to witnesses."

I said, "Ray, thanks" and hung up the phone.

CHAPTER SIX

Going Home

When I awakened the next morning I was excited because I was going home. Olivia and I were dressed and waiting in the lobby by 6:30 AM. When I had gone into the restaurant Sara already had my usual breakfast ready to go. I took the food to go and gave Sarah a $1000 tip and stated that I would be out of town for the next couple of months. She said, "Take care, Mr. Robinson, and be safe."

James was waiting in the lobby when we walked out of the restaurant. He put our bags in the car and we were off to the airport. Once we were at the airport James pulled up curbside to JetBlue ticketing station and parked. He helped us give our bags to the JetBlue agent. He said, "Goodbye Mrs. Robinson, enjoy your trip."

Olivia said, "Goodbye, James."

I reached out to shake James' hand; instead of shaking my hand he gave me a hug and said, "Take care of yourself, Jefferson. If you need me just call me."

I replied, "James, take care and I will see you in several months."

Olivia and I checked in and got our tickets and went to the terminal to catch our flight. We were a couple of hours early so I pulled out a book and started reading. Olivia asked, "What was that all about?"

I replied, "What do you mean?"

She replied, "James barely told me goodbye but he gave you a hug."

I looked at her and said, "If you do good by people then good will come by you."

She then turned away and didn't say anything. I asked, "So are you going to stay by me at my parents or are you going to go to your parent's house?"

She replied, "Well, there isn't any privacy at your parents' house."

I said, "Yes, there will be privacy. There is a guest house already decorated and furnished just for us."

She replied, "I will be staying at my parents' house for the first couple of weeks, catching up with my family."

I replied, "I understand; however, the invitation still stands whenever you want to come over and stay."

Before I knew it we had boarded our plane and were on our way to "Sweet Home Alabama." Our plane touched down on time at 1 PM. My brother Isiah was there to pick us up from the airport. Once he had picked us up he asked where we were off to.

I said, "First we are going to go see Olivia's parents."

It was a beautiful fall day in Alabama. I loved this time of year. When we arrived at Olivia's parents' house some of her high school friends were already there waiting on her. We got out of the car and I grabbed her two bags and started toward the porch where everyone was sitting. Olivia's brother Jason said, "Let me get those bags, Jefferson; you shouldn't be carrying that much weight."

I said, "Thank you, Jason."

I gave Olivia's mom and grandma a hug and shook her dad and grandpa's hands. They asked, "How are you feeling, Jefferson?"

I replied, "I feel great. I've started back training and my rehab is way ahead of schedule." I stayed about another 30 minutes. I said, "Well everyone, I must go. My brother Isiah is waiting in the car."

They said, "Why don't you tell Isiah to get out and come over as well?"

I said, "I would but he has a busy day planned today."

They said, "Don't you be a stranger, Jefferson. Make sure you stop by over later."

I said, "I sure will." I went and got in the car with Isiah and we were off to our parents' house. Isiah asked, "Little brother, so was it awkward being around her family after everything that Olivia had done?"

I replied, "No, not really."

He said, "You're going to love your guest house. Sandra did a great job with the furnishings and decorations."

I said, "I already know that it looks great. Sandra is real good at what she does."

Isiah said, "Yeah, and it doesn't hurt that she is a cutie as well."

I was excited about being back home. There is just something about coming home that sends chills down my spine. Isiah and I stopped by my house and guest house first in order to drop off my bags. When we walked inside the guest house my parents, grandparents, Eve, Jackie, Uncle Abraham, Tiger, Rabbit and Tiger's parents were all sitting in the kitchen eating.

Everyone said, "Welcome home, Jefferson."

I said jokingly, "Thanks but what are all you folks doing in my house?"

My grandma replied, "Well, we had to test out your kitchen."

I said, "Well, y'all could have at least waited for me before you started eating."

Grandpa said, "Y'all's asses were taking too long and we were hungry."

My sister Eve asked, "So where is your sweet and wholesome wife?"

I said, "Why do you have to say it like that little sister? Isiah and I dropped her off by her parent's house."

"Why isn't she staying here with you?" asked Grandma.

I responded, "She hasn't seen her parents in a while so she is going to stay over there the next couple of weeks to catch up with them." I said, "Sandra really did do a great job with this place."

Everyone chimed in, "She sure did."

"Where did you get that girl?" asked Mom.

I replied, "Greenwich, Connecticut."

"Well, she is damn good. Is she going to decorate your house also?" asked Eve.

I said, "Yes, she is. Does anyone have any objections, ma'am?"

She replied, "no objections whatsoever."

I said, "Master Kim."

He replied, "Yes, Jefferson."

I asked, "When do we start training?"

He replied, "Jefferson, we can start Monday evening at 6 PM. We will train Monday, Wednesday and Friday evenings at 6 PM as well as Saturdays from 9 to 12 PM."

I replied, "I'm ready, sir. I feel stronger and stronger each day." I said, "I hear that you have another Robinson that took my place training."

He said, "Yes, Jackie has been training very hard."

I asked, "So why are you training so hard, Jackie?"

Jackie was caught off guard by my question. He responded, "Well little brother, I have to stay in shape."

I said, "Yeah, I forgot you're now a pencil pusher working at Grandpa and Dad's old job. So what is it exactly that you do?"

He responded, "It is a long story I will have sit down and tell you at a later date."

I replied, "I understand. Well, I'm ready to eat."

My grandma had already prepared a plate for Isiah and me. I was glad because I was starved. After we had finished eating we all sat around talking and having a good time.

I received a call from Ray, my private investigator from New York. He said, "Jefferson, I'm almost done putting all the information together as it relates to the investigation concerning your wife. Please provide me your address so that I can forward you the information via priority mail once everything is complete."

I said, "Sounds good" and gave him my home address.

After I got off the phone with Ray, Tiger, Isiah, Jackie, Rabbit and I walked over to look at the progress of the main house. Once we were inside the house Tiger said, "Jefferson this is a nice place. Who is the builder?"

I said, "It's a local builder named TMG Industrial."

He said, "Great, I might need to get their contact information because I think it is about time for me to move out of my parents' house."

I said, "Isiah can give you the information; he knows the builder. They are coming along very nicely with the project. I can't wait until everything is complete."

"So how are you really doing, Jefferson?" asked Tiger as we all stood in the kitchen of the main house.

I replied, "Considering everything that has happened over the past several weeks I'm doing fine. My ankle rehabilitation is way ahead of schedule. I currently can't make sharp cuts but I know once your father is done with me I will be back to my old self." Then I said, "Now as it relates to my marriage, I don't know. The next couple of weeks will determine a lot of things."

Tiger replied, "I personally don't think that she was ready, not only for marriage but a relationship in general. She loves to go out and party too much."

I responded, "Well, however, the wind blows I will be prepared. Once I complete my training here with Master Kim I decided to take my surgeon up on a referral and go to Miami for several weeks to train with Presario Gonzales, a fitness trainer/supplements guru. My surgeon, Dr. Dawson, referred this trainer to me. I have already spoken to Presario and I'm scheduled to be there on January 5, right after all of the holiday festivities. I've also been in communication with Mr. Santiago about working for his firm while I'm there. He has been trying to get me to come work for him over the past several months."

"I think you are going there to try and get closer to Manuela," said Tiger.

I replied, "If I was trying to get close to Manuela I wouldn't have to go to Miami."

Tiger asked, "Why not?"

I replied, "She transferred to the University of Alabama to take up

Finance at the Capstone College Of Business as well as their golfing program."

When we had finished walking through the entire house we all went back to the guest house. Everyone was on their way out. We all said our goodbyes as Tiger, Rabbit and their parents left to go home. My parents and grandparents jumped on their golf carts and drove home as well. My brothers and I sat in the living room in my guest house and talked a little while longer. Isiah said, "Jefferson, the private investigator is currently on duty. His name is Mickey Hammer from Mobile. He stated that if he comes across anything he will let me know."

I said, "Thanks Isiah, for your assistance, because I need to come to some kind of resolution with my marriage. I just noticed the other day where Olivia had taken $45,000 from our joint checking account. I asked her what the money was taken for. Guess what she had the nerve to say to me?"

"What did she say?" asked Jackie.

"She said, 'Why is it any concern of yours why I took the money out?' I was extremely upset," I said, "however, I didn't let her know that I was upset. She finally told me that the $45,000 investment was in her friend Emily's beauty salon and massage business. I said, 'Well, if you had discussed it with me I could have given the information to my brother Isiah and my attorney to see whether or not it was a good deal or not.' Her response was, 'Why would I do that? You don't have any ownership in the firm; it is really none of your business.' I said, 'It isn't any of my business but you used my money to make the investment.'"

My brothers were dumbfounded. Jackie said, "I hope that you don't have her on all of your accounts, little brother."

I replied, "No, I don't, and I have Isiah to thank for that. I currently only have her on one joint checking and savings account and one investment account. All of my other checking, savings and investment accounts are separate. I don't even have the statements and information pertaining to those accounts come to our address in New York; all of the mail comes here to Mom and Dad's address. However, I do have a substantial amount of money in those joint accounts. I'm currently waiting on the reports from the private investigators to come back before proceeding to remove her from my accounts."

Jackie replied, "Well, based on all her actions and what you have just told us it is time to talk to a divorce attorney. Little brother, I know you love her; however, she is a wild woman and doesn't have your best interest at heart. Do I need to mention that she cheated on you twice, had you get in a fight and invested money without discussing with you and not showing any kind of moral support or compassion as a devoted wife should have?"

Jackie and Isiah left around one in the morning and went home.

The next day I was up bright and early I felt like going jogging but I knew that my ankle would not allow me to do it so I ate the delicious breakfast that Mom had prepared for everybody. My family is a God-fearing Bible carrying, scripture reading, choir singing, church going type of family. So I got dressed and decided to go to church as well, because it had been a long time since I had attended anybody's church. I didn't even get married in a church. So once I got dressed I rode to church with my brother Isiah. I'm really glad that I attended church today. Reverend Juanita Johnson preached a beautiful sermon as it relates to marriage, commitment and knowing when to let go. I felt like she was talking directly to me.

I knew that after the announcements were read she was going to acknowledge that I was present and ask whether I wanted to stand up and say anything. Sure enough, like clockwork she called my name. I said, "I would first like to give God praise for waking me up this morning and blessing me with ability to come to church."

The congregation said, "Amen."

I said, "There is no place like home. It doesn't matter how far away you travel or how many homes you own, it is always a blessing to come home to God's house here at Good Stoney A.M.E. Church. It is always a blessing to have the opportunity to stand up and speak to the wonderful members and also the visitors of this wonderful church. I don't have too much more to say other than I know that the church is wanting to add some new classrooms and make some additional upgrades to the building. Therefore, I've scheduled a celebrity basketball game to be played at Leroy High School in three weeks on Friday November 17. All of the proceeds will go toward building those classrooms. I will also be calling on additional friends to make donations. In closing, I would like to start off the fundraising. I have a check in the amount of $15,000 to go toward those classrooms and upgrades."

Reverend Johnson stood up and started shouting, "Thank you, Jesus."

I said, "I would also would like to say that on my behalf UJ Chevrolet is donating a brand new 15-passenger van to replace the old van that is currently out of service. My good friend Paul Maye with UJ Chevrolet currently has the keys to that vehicle, which is parked outside."

Everyone was extremely happy. Reverend Johnson hurriedly dismissed the church and everyone went outside. She came up and gave me a big hug. She said, "Thomas Jefferson Robinson, thank you. You were heaven sent."

After church we all went back by my parents' house. My grandparents went home and changed first, then they came over afterwards.

"Jefferson, that was a wonderful thing that you did for the church," said Mom.

Dad said, "You kept everything a secret, didn't you, boy?"

I replied, "I didn't want to say anything about the van until I had all of the details worked out. All I have to do is an autograph session at that dealership." I said, "As it relates to the donation and the celebrity fundraiser, that came together over the past several days after learning about the classrooms and upgrades from Isiah." I said, "I'm really shocked that I had to hear about the church needing money for classrooms and repairs from Isiah, as opposed to Mom and Grandma."

Mom said, "Jefferson, we knew that you were already dealing with a lot and we didn't want to burden you with anything else."

I said, "Thanks, but you know I'm never too busy for God or for family." I then went next door and changed out of my suit. I called Olivia; she answered. I said, "I tried calling you several times but it went straight to voicemail."

She replied, "I didn't have my phone on me. I probably was out riding the four wheeler."

I said, "Would you like to go horseback riding as well as go out for a picnic later?"

She responded, "No, not today. I already made plans with my sister to hang out."

I said, "Ok. Just let me know when you want to go do something because I start my training tomorrow." Then I said, "I love you" but she had already hung up the phone.

Instead of going back to my parents' house I went and lay on the sofa. I was almost asleep when my phone rang. It was Manuela. I said, "Good afternoon, Senorita. How is T-Town treating you?"

She replied, "I love this University. I see why you and Pedro chose this school." She said, "So why didn't you tell me that you were going to be working for my father at the beginning of the year?"

I said, "I was meaning to but I have had a lot going on lately."

She asked, "Is there anything you would like to discuss?"

I responded, "Not right now. I'm still sorting out some things. As it relates to working for your dad, I figured that I would give it a shot since I was going to be there furthering my conditioning with Presario Gonzales in Miami."

Manuela asked, "Who is Presario Gonzales?"

I replied, "He is a fitness trainer referred by my surgeon, Dr. Dawson. I'm glad that you called because I'm putting together a fundraiser for my church. I'm needing to raise money for new classrooms plus the current building repairs, upgrades and appliances. Therefore, I was wondering if you could assist me in putting everything together as well as get some additional donors."

Manuela replied, "Sure, I can help you, Jefferson."

I said, "The fundraiser is Friday November 17. I'm putting together a celebrity basketball game. Pedro has already confirmed that he will be playing. He says that he currently has seven athletes/celebrities confirmed. I currently have three players confirmed. My brother Jackie has a couple as well. We have enough players; we just need to have additional donors."

She replied, "I can contact Dad and some of his friends."

I replied, "That would be totally awesome. I will email you the church's name and address as well as the location, date and time of the game. You have just made my day, Manuela Santiago."

She replied, "I'm glad that I could be of assistance. Thomas Jefferson Robinson.

We said goodbye because she had to study for three exams that she had coming up next week.

I said, "Good luck on your exams." I quickly emailed Manuela all of the information concerning the fundraiser. The next morning I started making phone calls for additional donors and/or volunteers. There were several people that I called who stated that they wouldn't be able to attend but they would make donations. Thus far I had pledges of $120,000 from twenty people. I was blown away about having received that many pledges in such a short length of time. All I needed to do now was collect the funds.

I had my first day of training with Master Kim. Everything was grueling, as I had expected. We did a lot of stretching and ankle exercises in order to try and get more mobility back to my ankle. I was glad when 8 PM came. After practice he gave me some bandages, herbs and ointments. He said, "Jefferson, each night after you shower put the herbs and ointment on your ankle then wrap the ankle and leave on overnight. Do this every day, Jefferson. This will help take all of the soreness away, which will help your mobility."

I said, "Yes sir." I left and went home. When I arrived home I went in the kitchen and got a bottle of Ozarka water. While in the kitchen I saw a big plate of food that was left on the stove. There was a note which read, "I hope you enjoy your dinner, my handsome son. I'm glad to have you home. Love, Mom." I was glad she had left me food because I was starving. However, I went and took a shower first, then I got my foot massager out of the closet and filled it with water and turned it on and soaked my feet for about 20 minutes. Then I dried my foot and put the ointment and herbs that Master Kim had given me on my ankle and wrapped it tightly. The herbs and ointment were strong. I could feel it working right away.

I then went and grabbed my food and sat at the island and ate and watched TV. After dinner, I washed my plate and fork, then I tried calling Olivia; however, it went to her voicemail. I left a message to let her know that I was thinking about her and for her to call me when she had a chance. I was tired so I went to bed.

The next several days went back rather quickly. Master Kim was really working me hard each day. I felt the ointment and herbs working on my ankle as well. It wasn't as sore as it once was.

When I got home from practice that Friday I stopped by my parents' house prior to going home. Mom said, "Jefferson, I didn't take food by your house today because I figured you would be stopping by here. Your plate is in the kitchen on the stove, baby. You also have a lot of mail and a priority mail packet that was delivered today."

I said, "Thanks Mom." I gave her kiss and told her and Dad that I would see them tomorrow afternoon after practice.

When I got home I put the food and mail on the island then I went and took a shower. I then soaked my foot, put the herbs and ointment on my ankle and wrapped it for the night. I went and sat at the island in the kitchen and ate my food. I also slurped down two big glasses of Grandma's homemade lemonade that she had left in my refrigerator for me. I still hadn't spoken to Olivia; she hadn't returned any of my phone calls. I tried calling her again; however, it went to her voicemail. So I left her another message.

I must have opened about 20 letters from some of my friends and teammates. They had sent their donations. I couldn't believe it, but I had collected $150,000 from those envelopes. I was really pumped. Then the phone rang and it was Manuela.

She said, "Good evening, Jefferson, I have great news."

I replied, "I have great news as well."

She said, "My father and several of his friends have made a donation for your fundraiser. Are you sitting down?"

I said, "Yes."

She said, "I have checks in the amount of $250,000."

I was speechless. She asked, "Jefferson, are you still there?"

I said, "Yes. I'm here. That is truly unbelievable. Who said our God isn't mighty and powerful?"

She said, "My father gave $150,000 and I asked five of his other friends and they gave $20,000 each."

I said, "Thank you so much."

She said, "Don't worry, I didn't ask Mr. Medina, Escobar's father."

I said, "I would have taken his money as well. I collected $150,000."

She jokingly said, "Well, you did ok; it's a start."

I said, "Oh, you have jokes. How did you do on your exams?"

She responded, "I think I did well on each one of them. So how has your training been going?"

I said, "It has been hard but good. I'm very pleased with everything."

Manuela and I talked on the phone for two hours. I could have talked all night on the phone to her but I told her that I had to get up early for training the next day. We both said goodnight and hung up.

There was a knock at the door and I told them to come in. It was my brother Isiah. He said, "Little brother, I met with the Mickey Hammer the private investigator today, and it isn't good."

I asked, "What is it?"

He said, "Take a look at the photos and information for yourself. Olivia has been meeting this guy in Mobile every day since Monday. They would meet at the Holiday Inn in Mobile. They would go in the hotel for several hours then come out and go have dinner. It was as if she didn't have a care in the world." He said, "Mickey said he will stay on the case through Sunday and that if you wanted him to stay on after that just let him know."

I said, "No, you can tell him that after Sunday it will be ok; he can stop." I said, "Wow." I looked at the photos that Mickey had in the envelope. The guy in the photo was Jeremy Bosch. I was pissed.

I went over and got the priority mail package off the counter which was from the private investigator in New York. I opened the package and there was an envelope that was labeled photos; however, it also stated on the envelope to read the report first. I started reading the report and it stated that Olivia had been seeing Jake Goldstein. It showed photos of her wearing a wig and going to meet this Jake Goldstein at his apartment building, as well as him coming to our penthouse while I was at practice. I was floored but more importantly, I felt betrayed.

I wanted to go over to her parents' house that night and confront her; however, Isiah said, "Please Jefferson, calm down. You don't want to go over and see her while you're like this. Jefferson, you have to keep it professional."

I said, "Isiah, I have given all of myself to Olivia. She was the first and the only woman that I have ever been with. I have loved her since the moment that I first laid eyes on her." I couldn't help it; I started crying.

"Just let it out, little brother," said Isiah, "just let it out."

I just felt like hitting something. I was swinging at the air. Isiah said,

"Jefferson, you need to transfer all of your money out of those accounts as well as turn off all of those credit cards that are jointly held."

I said, "We only have the Platinum American Express and Visa jointly for credit cards. I can take her off those accounts right now. I will send an email to my broker and my Banking Manager at the bank to contact me as soon as possible." I logged into my American Express account and saw where she had been charging a lot of stuff. It looked as if a lot of the stuff that she was charging was stuff for the beauty salon and spa. There were over $145,000 worth of charges. I immediately contacted American Express and cancelled her card. I did the same thing with her Visa card.

I said, "There is about $250,000 in the Joint Checking account and another $350,000 in the Joint Savings account and another $750,000 in the Joint Investment Account. I will close all of those accounts with the exception of the savings account tomorrow." I said, "I'm going to transfer all of the funds out of the Savings Account except $10,000. I will leave that for her to live on. I will be contacting my attorney tomorrow to let him know to start the proceedings for a divorce. Isiah, I'm pissed. I want this divorce expedited." I hugged my brother. I said, "Thank you for being a great brother and friend. You helped to save my ass because this would have been much worse if I hadn't gotten the Prenuptial Agreement signed."

I said, "The most that I will be out of is a couple of hundred thousand dollars as opposed to several million dollars."

Isiah said, "It also helps that you have the photos and reports from two different private investigators in two different parts of the country," said Isiah. "Not to mention that you have one of her affairs all across all of the news outlets."

I said, "Thank you, brother. You can go home now. I'm about to get some rest."

Isiah asked, "Little brother, are you sure that you're going to be ok?"

I said, "Yes Isiah, I'm going to be just fine. Olivia has just awakened the sleeping giant."

The next morning I went to training with Master Kim. I trained very hard. After practice Tiger and I talked. I told him everything that had happened. He said, "Jefferson I told you that bitch was no good. I don't understand why she would marry you if she wasn't willing to make any kind of effort to make the marriage work."

I said, "Tiger, I gotta go home, shower and then go let Olivia know that I want a divorce."

Tiger said, "I'm coming with you. I'm going to go inside and shower and then I will meet you at your house." He said, "Whatever you do, Jefferson, don't leave or go there by yourself."

I said, "Don't worry, I will wait on you, Tiger."

I left and went home. When I had arrived home the usual suspects were there waiting on me: my parents grandparents, sister, and brothers. When I walked through the door Mom came up and gave me a hug. Then my grandmother gave me a kiss on the cheek.

She said, "Baby, do you need me to kick that heifer's ass?"

I said, "No Grandma, she isn't deserving of that kind of attention. I'm about to take a shower then go by Olivia's parents' house and tell her that I want a divorce."

"Well, we are going with you," said Mom.

I said, "I don't need all of y'all to go with me. Tiger is going to go with me."

Mom said, "Since you don't want us to go with you, at least take your brothers with you and Tiger.

I said, "Fine, they can go." I went and took a shower and got dressed. When I walked out the door Tiger had already arrived and was sitting in the kitchen with the rest of my family. I took several of the photos, one where she was kissing Jeremy and the other kissing Jake.

Prior to us walking out the door my phone rang. It was Olivia. I said, "Hello."

She said, "Hi, it's Olivia."

I said, "Wow, look who decides to call."

She said, "Jefferson, I tried using my American Express and Visa and neither one of them works."

I responded, "I know, because I cut them off. You had charged $145,000 on the American express and $35,000 on the Visa for what appears to be salon equipment, beauty supplies and massage equipment.

She replied, "You had no right to do that."

I replied, "I had every right to do just that. I'm the one who earned the money and I've have never spent that kind of money on either one of my credit cards, nor have I written any checks for that amount. I'm done talking over the phone. I will stop by your parents' house shortly, so that we can talk."

My family overheard the phone conversation. My grandma said, "That heifer has a lot of nerve to come off questioning you."

I replied, "I know, right?" I said to my brothers and Tiger, "Let's go."

Mom said, "Be careful and don't be alone with her."

I replied, "She isn't going to do anything, Mom."

Mom replied, "Be careful, son. When a person is desperate they will do anything."

My grandpa said, "Yes, the situation can turn hostile at any time."

I said, "Thanks for the advice" as we were walking out the door to leave. When we all got into Isiah's Chevy Tahoe Tiger said, "I will keep my phone recorder going at all times in my pocket."

Isiah replied, "I don't think that will be a bad idea."

Once we were almost to Olivia's parents' driveway we could see cars parked along both sides of the road. There were cars all both sides of their driveway as well. It appeared that they were having a party. Once Isiah parked the car Jackie said, "Ok guys, let's stay together and stay focused."

I said, "I will ask Olivia if I can speak to her and her parents in person, then that is when I will her know that I want a divorce. I will also explain why I want a divorce."

There were people standing on the porch as well as outside the house. Several people walked up to me and shook my hand and said, "I was just asking Olivia where you were, Jefferson."

I asked, "So what, y'all are having a party?"

He said, "Yeah, Olivia wanted to have a little gathering for everyone to stop by."

I said, "Oh, how nice."

When we walked into the house I saw Olivia and her parents sitting in the living room drinking beverages. When they saw me her father walked over and said that he wanted to talk to me. I said, "Sure Mr. Jacobs, but I would like to speak to you, your wife and Olivia as well."

He said fine so he called Olivia and his wife over and we all walked into his office across the hall for privacy. Tiger and my brothers were trying to walk in with me as well. I said, "I just need one of you to come in with me" so I selected Jackie to come into the office with me.

As soon as we walked into the room Olivia's father said, "I thought you were better than this, Jefferson."

I said, "What are you talking about?"

He said, "Removing Olivia from your credit card without telling her was downright awful. She was in the grocery line in Jackson with several thousand dollars of groceries for this party and neither one of her credit cards worked. Thank God her debit card did work."

I said, "Well, I did leave $10,000 in the account to ensure she had funds. First off, sir, if Olivia had answered my calls she would have known ahead of time that the credit cards didn't work, as well as why they wouldn't work. However, I haven't spoken to my wife in over a week. I had her credit cards turned off because she had charged $145,000 on the American Express card and $35,000 on the Visa card last week."

I went on to say, "Olivia wired $45,000 from our account to her friend Emily's account two weeks ago."

Olivia's mom said, "Well, Olivia and Emily had started a beauty salon and massage Parlor."

I responded, "I would have been ok if she had discussed that with me; after all, we are married and supposed to discuss major decisions like this with each other When I asked Olivia about the $45,000 wire she became irate and said, 'I don't have to discuss anything with you, Jefferson.' I said, 'We should have gotten a business plan and worked out the numbers of how much an investment like this really would cost.' However, she didn't want to hear what I had to say." I said, "After all, I did work for this money." I said, "The real reason that I'm here is so that you can hear it from me. I want a divorce."

Her father yelled, "You want a divorce? You just married my daughter and put her name across all of these news channels and newspapers like she is a bad person." He said, "You were the one who beat those guys up, not her."

I said, "Listen to what you're saying, sir. Your daughter cheated on me and I was still defending her honor from this creep who she cheated on me with. The guy was trying to grab her by her hair. I've said all that I have to say. This is the last conversation that I will have with you. Everything else will be coming from my attorney."

Olivia's mom said, "Jefferson, I think that it is time for you to leave."

I said, "No problem, Mrs. Jacobs. I'll leave. However you and your husband try to shield and protect Olivia from everything even when she is wrong, there is going to come a time when she is going to have to be held accountable for her actions, and that time has arrived."

Jackie and I then turned to walk toward the door when Olivia said, "I'm going to take you for everything that you got."

I stopped and turned around and said, "You've gotten all that you're going to get from me. Please be thankful that I left the $10,000 in your account, because you didn't deserve that much leniency." As I was walking out the door I placed the envelope with the photos on the table. I said, "You may want to take a look at these."

Jackie and I walked out the door. Isiah and Tiger asked if everything was ok. I said, "Yes, everything is great."

We were walking out the front door when Olivia came running up and threw a beer bottle. I was thankful that Jackie was there and told me to duck because that bottle would have hit me in the head. After throwing the bottle she said, "Fuck you, Jefferson."

I turned and said, "I do believe that is Jeremy and Jake's department."

My brothers, Tiger and I then got in the vehicle and left. Tiger said, "So aren't you glad that you didn't come over here by yourself?"

I replied, "I sure am, because it could have gotten out of hand real quick."

Jackie said, "Did you hear the tone in her parents' voice? They were blaming you for everything. They blamed you for having her name and face plastered over all the TV and sports channel, which was caused because of her cheating. They even blamed you for cancelling her credit cards after she ran up over $185,000 worth of charges. Hell, they even blamed you for Olivia not being able to charge several thousand dollars worth of groceries to the credit cards earlier today for their party."

Isiah responded, "You think that they could have at least said thank you, because after all, they still ended up charging the groceries to your debit card, Jefferson."

I responded, "I know, right? Isiah, could you schedule a meeting with Attorney McCorquodale for first thing Monday morning?"

Isiah responded, "Sure" as we arrived back at my parent's house. Isiah then said, "Jefferson, there is no need to meet at Attorney McCorquodale's office on Monday morning."

I asked, "Why is that?"

He said, "Because that is Attorney McCorquodale's truck parked in the yard. He is currently here."

I said, "That is even better."

When we walked in my parents' house, sure enough, Attorney McCorquodale was seated at the kitchen table with Dad and Grandpa finishing off a piece of my grandma's apple pie and drinking coffee.

Mom asked, "So how did everything go?"

I replied, "Everything was ok."

Jackie responded, "Let's just say I'm glad that we went over there with Jefferson because things were getting a little testy."

"What do you mean?" asked Dad.

"Well, Olivia's father made it seem as if it was Jefferson's fault that Olivia was all over the news for cheating as well as Jefferson cancelling Olivia's credit cards."

I responded, "I just want everything to be over. I want a divorce as soon as possible."

"Well, I have a copy of your prenuptial agreement, Jefferson," said Attorney McCorquodale, "however, please give me any other evidence you have as well as explain to me from the beginning everything that has transpired between you and Olivia."

I then explained everything as it related to Olivia, from the first time I met her all the way to the present time. After explaining everything to him, I then gave him a copy of the reports and photos from the private investigators in New York as well as in Alabama.

Attorney McCorquodale then said, "Based on all of this information, it should be an open–and–shut case. However, it isn't always as easy as it seems. First, I will put together the documents and have the divorce documents served to Olivia. Then I'm going to wait and see who her attorney is and their response." He said, " I will first make an offer to her attorney for a settlement based on the guidelines of the prenuptial agreement, which was a smart thing to put in place, by the way. Then we will go from there." Attorney McCorquodale went on to say, "I'm thinking that they will take the offer, especially based on all of the evidence of cheating against her." He said, "What really is going to bolster your case, Jefferson, is that her cheating allegations were blasted all over the news, as well as in newspapers. Her cheating is well documented."

I replied, "I'm ready to get everything done and over with, sir."

Attorney McCorquodale got up and said, "Jefferson, I will keep you posted." He then left.

"Son, you have made the correct choice to go down this road because it was only going to get worse with this girl," said Mom.

Tiger said, "Well, I have to go, Jefferson, but if you need me, call me."

I said, "Thanks Tiger, enjoy the rest of your day."

Then Dad, Grandpa and Jackie said, "Well, we have to go to Mobile but we would be back shortly."

Isiah said, "I have to go get ready for a date."

I responded, "I'm tired and I'm going home and take a nap." I asked, "Isiah, do you know of a company that could install security cameras?"

He replied, "No, I don't. However, you can stop by and ask the contractor who is building your house if he knows of someone while you're en route to your guest house."

Sure enough, when I was riding the golf cart past my main house I saw TMG Industrial's General Manager David Dubose. I stopped him. I said, "Good afternoon. First I would like to say that y'all have been doing a wonderful job."

David replied, "Thank you, sir. We have another two and one half, maybe three weeks, before your main house will be complete."

I said, "That is wonderful news." I asked, "Does your company install security cameras?"

He replied, "Yes, we have subcontractors that install security cameras."

I said, "I would like cameras around the main house as well as the guest house. Please provide me with a quote."

He replied, "Sure thing, Mr. Robinson. I will have you a quote by Monday afternoon."

I said, "Thanks." Then I walked to my guest house. I was exhausted.

I lay down on the sofa and took a nap. I didn't wake until 9 PM. I said to myself, "Man, that was a five-hour power nap." I felt really rested.

I then called Pedro. I said, "What's up, my friend?"

He said, "I'm currently at a dinner at Escobar's parent's house."

I asked, "Can you talk?"

He said, "Yes."

I said, "Well, I finally did it."

He asked, "So what did you do?"

I responded, "I told Olivia that I want a divorce."

He said, "That is awesome news, bro. That was long overdue."

I replied, "It sure was, especially after all that has transpired over the past several weeks with Olivia. My attorney is already drawing up the paperwork."

Pedro said, "Jefferson, that is the best thing that you could have ever done. Well, I gotta go, Jefferson. They are ringing the bell for some kind of announcement. I must go back inside the house."

I responded, "I'll talk to you later" and hung up the phone.

The next morning around 10 AM I got a phone call from Pedro. He said, "Hey, my friend."

I said, "What's up, Pedro?"

He said, "Well, I have some bad news."

I asked, "What is the bad news?"

He responded, "Escobar proposed to Manuela last night and she said yes."

I don't know why but it felt like a sword had stabbed me in the heart. I put on a strong face. I said, "I guess congratulations are in order for Manuela and Escobar. I'm happy for her."

Pedro responded, "I know my sister, and she doesn't love Escobar."

I replied, "Well, she did say yes."

Pedro replied, "Yeah, that was prior to her learning that you were getting a divorce. After she had gotten engaged I told her later that you stated that you were getting a divorce and her face dropped. She asked why I didn't tell her sooner. I told her that I had just found out about the divorce about five minutes prior to her getting engaged."

Pedro said, "Jefferson, this Escobar guy is no good. After he got engaged to Manuela he, some of his friends and his body guards went out to the club to party."

Pedro said, "Jefferson, I know that you care about my sister as well, so just tell her."

There was a knock at my door. I said, "Come in."

It was Tiger. I said, "What's up, Tiger? Pedro, I'll give you a call later. Tiger just stopped by."

Pedro replied, "Ok, tell Tiger I said what's up?"

Tiger asked, "So how are you doing, Jefferson?"

I said, "I'm doing ok. I was just on the phone with Pedro. Pedro told me that his sister Manuela got engaged to Escobar last night."

Tiger said, "Tell me that isn't true. Jefferson, you know that Manuela is in love with you, right? Take it from your boy, Manuela is the one for you. Therefore, Jefferson, you need to get off your pride and tell Manuela how you really feel, especially since you're finally divorcing Olivia."

I replied, "Listen to what you're saying, Tiger. She is currently engaged to Escobar."

Tiger replied, "But Manuela loves you, Jefferson."

I replied, "Now look at this; I'm getting relationship advice from the Asian Don Juan."

Tiger replied, "You have to admit that I have been correct about everything thus far. So how is your fundraiser coming along?"

I replied, "Well, I have currently raised $400,000 worth of donations for the church, which doesn't include any receipts from the auction or receipts for entrance into the gym."

He replied, "What an awesome job, Jefferson."

I asked, "So are you ready for the auction, Don Juan?"

Tiger replied, "So you are actually going to auction off us men as dates to the women who pay the highest bid."

I replied, "I sure am. It's not like you have to go on a date with them; it is only a lunch date. As it relates to the celebrity basketball game, Pedro has three players committed, I have seven, and my brother Jackie has several. The cost to attend the game is $15 for adults and $7.50 for kids. They will also get free autographed baseball cards and t-shirts. We will also be selling fried seafood plates."

Tiger said, "That sounds great. I'm about to head home. I will talk to you tomorrow."

I responded, "I'll talk to you tomorrow as well."

I then called Pedro back to see if everything was a go for the fundraiser. He said that it was. I told him thanks. I said, "I will talk to you later because I'm going to call your sister to congratulate her."

Pedro responded, "Jefferson, that would be great."

I then called Manuela. She said, "Hi Jefferson."

I responded, "I do believe congratulations are in order."

She replied, "Thank you." She then said, "I do believe that I can say the same for you. Jefferson, I'm glad that you are finally getting out of that terrible relationship."

I responded, "I do believe that you may be headed down the same path. I'm begging you, Manuela, if you don't love Escobar then don't walk down that aisle because it wouldn't be fair to him nor to you."

She replied, "Jefferson, I love you but your heart belongs to someone else someone who doesn't love you."

I replied, "I know, Manuela, and as sad as it sounds, I still love Olivia. I do care about you, however, I don't want to lie to you.

"Fair enough," said Manuela. "Well, I have collected some of the donation checks. I should have the remaining balance prior to me coming there for the fundraiser in a couple of weeks."

I said, "That sounds wonderful."

She said, "Thanks for the call, Jefferson, but I have to go study."

I responded, "Ok, talk to you later."

The next couple of weeks passed by rather quickly. My house was completed ahead of schedule. Today we were having fundraising activities at Leroy High School. Pedro and his friends had arrived at the school around noon. He and Manuela arrived around the same time. She and a couple of her friends had driven down from Tuscaloosa. I was surprised but Maria had flown down as well in order to be supportive of Pedro. It was brought to my attention that Pedro and Maria would be the coaches of my brother Jackie's team, which included several of Pedro's friends. Then I had nine of my friends show up, which included some of my college teammates, Ricky Williams and Butch Sullivan and Jamie Rollins, along with some professional players.

Our game started at 4 PM and the auction started at 7 PM. I asked Manuela if she would like to be my assistant coach. She said, "Sure, why not? I always like every opportunity that I can get to beat my brother." So I gave her an honorary Assistant Coach t-shirt to put on.

When the game started Pedro's team jumped out to a 10-point lead. My brother Jackie was pretty good in basketball, although he had retired from the NFL in football. Pedro had brought a couple of former professional basketball players as well. After halftime we were down by 12 points. Manuela came back after halftime dressed in a uniform. She said, "Jefferson, I want to play," however, Pedro was against her playing.

I said, "Wait a minute, can you play, Manuela?"

Manuela responded, "Well, I'm ok."

Pedro said, "No, she can't play, Jefferson."

I asked, "Why you don't want your sister to play, Pedro?"

I went to the scorer table and said, "Please add #40, Manuela Santiago, to the list." I said, "You're wearing my old basketball number as well as baseball #40."

She responded, "I know. Forty is my favorite number."

I have to admit she looked kind of sexy in her basketball uniform. We got the ball to start the second half. When Manuela got the ball she pulled up from the three-point line and sunk a deep three. Then we got a steal and passed to Manuela and she shot another three-pointer. We were only down six points now. When we had gotten the next rebound they gave it to Manuela and she shook a couple of guys and gave a behind-the-back pass to Ricky, cutting to the basket for two points. We were only down four points. It was give and go for the remaining of the game. We were down two points with eight seconds left. We had the ball so I called a timeout. I called play where we set a pick so that Manuela could take a three-point shot. I said, "Win or lose, the game is in your hands, Manuela." Then I said, "123" and we all said, "Roll Tide."

The fans were cheering loudly. We inbounded the ball and Butch set up an awesome pick, which freed Manuela and she knocked down a three-pointer with no time left on the clock. We all ran on the court cheering. I gave Manuela a big hug. I said, "You're too pretty to be a baller." Then the other team came over and congratulated us. I said,

"Pedro, why didn't you tell me that Manuela was an awesome player? Better yet, I'm shocked that you didn't recruit her for your team."

"Well," he responded, "Manuela was all-county, all-state, all-Florida and voted best Female Basketball Player in Florida. She had the opportunity to play basketball anywhere in the country on a basketball scholarship; however, one summer during her junior year in high school she was introduced to golf by Dad and she has been hooked every since."

I said, "I'm very happy that she came out of retirement today. Ok everyone, it is time for the final game of the night."

We had a total of nine people being auctioned off for a lunch date. Some of the participants in the auction were Isiah, Tiger, Tiger's brother Rabbit, Jamie Rollins, Butch Sullivan, Ricky Williams, and me. The first person to be auctioned off was Ricky Williams and the highest offer was $700. Then there was Isiah – the first offer was $500, then the next one was $750 by Sandra Wilson. Yes, that Sandra Wilson, my home decorator from New York. I had some questions for my brother. Next it was Tiger. He had several participants bidding on him. His price was driven up to $3,000, which was pledged by 78-year-old Ms. Johnson. Tiger was disappointed but he was a good sport and walked off the stage with Ms. Johnson. It was now my turn. I was the final participant. The first offer was $2,000. I looked u to see who had offered that amount and it was Olivia. I was shocked to see her here. Then Manuela said $2500. Then Olivia said $3200. Manuela was determined to not lose to Olivia, so she said $7,000. Olivia didn't respond. Olivia then put her head down and walked out of the building. The winner was Manuela.

It was time to total up the numbers. Our first amount was $12000, collected at the doors, $3500 collected from selling catfish plates; $13500 collected for the lunch auction and $150,000 raised by me, Jefferson Robinson, and the lead fundraising amount of $250,000 by Manuela Sanchez, for a grand total of $429,000, and I gave the checks collected by Manuela and myself to Pastor Johnson. She was extremely happy. I thanked everyone for coming and participating in our fundraising events.

I said, Manuela, "You and your girls, Pedro and Maria can stay at my guest house if you like. I will sleep on the sofa. My main house is complete but I haven't had an opportunity to decorate or furnish it at the present time.

They accepted the offer to stay at my guest house. Tiger came up and said, "Jefferson, I really did enjoy the fundraiser."

I said, jokingly, "Where are you and Ms. Johnson going?

He replied, "Oh, you have jokes, Jefferson."

My brother Jackie said, "Well little brother, my wife and I are going to call it a night and head home."

I said, "Ok."

My parents and grandparents walked up and said, "Y'all did a wonderful job." They gave Pedro and Manuela a hug.

Pedro introduced my family to his girlfriend Maria. Everyone was happy to meet her.

Grandma said, "That heifer Olivia had some nerve coming here trying to bid on Jefferson for the auction."

Grandpa said, "Yeah Jefferson, if it wasn't for your mom your grandma would have grabbed Olivia and beat the hell out of her."

I replied, laughing, "I'm glad that she didn't."

Then my brother Isiah and Sandra walked up. I said, "Sandra, I didn't know you were coming down."

She said, "Yes, Isiah told me that your house would be ready this week so I have been decorating and furnishing your house while you were out each day."

I said, "Really? You're amazing. I had noticed the outdoor furniture in the backyard but I didn't pay any attention to it. So where have you been staying these past few nights?"

She said, "I've been staying at the hotel in Jackson."

I responded, "Well, get your things because we are all staying in the main house tonight."

Isiah chimed in, "There is no need. I have all her things in the car because I figured you would say that, little brother."

I said, "Can you believe this guy?"

So we all left to go take a look at my new main house. Once we got to the house I waited until everyone had arrived before going in. Once everyone was there, I opened the door and walked in. Everyone's mouth dropped as they saw the inside.

"The house is masterfully done," said Mom. She said, "I love the entrance. When you walk in you see the grand stairway leading up stairs.

The dark color wood on the stairs is wonderful. I love the crown molding as well. Then you have off to the side your office with the built in dark mahogany shelves and large mahogany desk."

"So how many bedrooms do you have?" asked Dad.

I responded, "There are five bedrooms—master bedroom downstairs and four bedrooms upstairs—and seven bathrooms—2 1/2 bathrooms downstairs and 4 1/2 bathrooms upstairs. The total square footage is roughly 6,400 square feet. We increased it by 1000 square feet."

"Damn, it looks much bigger," said Grandpa.

My sister Eve said, "I love the bedroom, how the TV is built into the main wall at the foot of the bed with the dark wood entertainment center built into the wall, as well as how the sitting area is set up at the foot of the bed as well in front of the TV."

A large gas fireplace was built in at the bottom of entertainment center on the wall as well. The Master bedroom was also gorgeous.

"I bet you can fit 10 people in that shower," said Grandpa."

I responded, "At a minimum there will be one person but at a max two people."

We all walked into the kitchen, which was beautiful. The walls were white with a long counter with ceramic tile. The ceramic tile was grayish with black and the Viking stove was silver. The location which housed the refrigerator was white and looked like a wall. You couldn't tell by looking that it housed a big Sub Zero refrigerator.

The living room was gorgeous as well. The kitchen flowed into the living room, which was a large open space. It had a large TV with dark wood built in on top with a large fireplace on the bottom. Then if you looked to the left there was a large sliding door which covered the entire wall. When you slid the door back it brought the back patio into the home The door led to an outdoor eating area which had a long kitchen table and chairs. On the other side of the table was a built-in outdoor pit surrounded by four nice wooden chairs with lime green pillows.

The 15 feet in front of that was the outdoor pool. Then to the right of the pool was the outdoor cabana with a built-in outdoor kitchen, bar and fireplace. There was a flat screen TV that was built into the wall over the outdoor glass fireplace. There was also a flat screen TV on a swivel hanging from ceiling over the bar.

After seeing the outside we went upstairs to see the theater room. Prior to going into the theater room, directly outside the theater room and to the left was the game area, which had a nice regulation size pool table with mahogany wood and tan felt and a circular professional poker table which sits four and had all the cards and poker chips included. There was a half a bathroom to the left of the pool table. To the right of the pool table was a nice-size five-foot bar.

We then slid the sliding white wood doors back and walked into the theater room. The theater room had gorgeous white sectional sofas with tan and brown pillows to match the large built-ins on the wall that housed the large flat screen TV. The sofas sat on a large white rug with dark brown designs. There were hardwood floors throughout the house with the exception of the bathrooms, which had dark brown ceramic tile floors with ceramic grout.

There were four bedrooms upstairs. Each one of them had its own full bath. After we had looked at the bedrooms we all went down stairs to the kitchen. Everyone was talking about how beautiful the house was.

Grandpa said, "Yeah, it is also a big house. It is too big for a man to be staying here alone, if you know what I mean," as he looked over at Manuela.

I said, "Hey Grandpa, let me get out of the marriage that I'm in first."

He said, "I'm just saying, grandson."

Dad said, "On that note, we are going to let you young folks sit down and talk because it's past our bedtime."

Just before leaving Mom said, "Manuela, you had a great game today."

I said, "Yes, she did."

Dad then chimed in and said, "Jefferson's mom used to be a good basketball player as well." My

Mom looked at Dad and said, "Used to be?"

Dad said, "Well, I meant *is* a good player."

Mom said, "We better go before you put your foot in your mouth again. We will see you kids tomorrow."

My parents and grandparents then left and went home. I said, "I'm thirsty. I know I'm pushing it to ask if y'all went grocery shopping as well?"

Isiah responded, "Little brother, why don't you take a look in your refrigerator and let me know what you see."

I opened the refrigerator door and the refrigerator was freshly stocked with all of the foods that I eat. I looked in the pantry and both of them were stocked with food as well. I went and hugged Isiah and said, "I love you, man. I don't know what I would do without you."

A few tears came down both of our eyes. We then pushed away from each other and said jokingly, "Who sprinkled black pepper in the air? I got something in my eyes."

Then Pedro said, "There is something in your eyes" to the laughter of everybody.

"Jefferson, could you get our bags out of the car?" asked Manuela. "Because my girls and I need to take a shower."

I responded, "I sure can."

Pedro lifted his arms and said, "I believe everybody needs a shower."

So Pedro and I walked outside to get their bags out of the cars. I said, "I need to get something to wear from my guest house." Manuela said, "I'll walk with you over there as well because I haven't seen the inside of the guest house yet."

I opened the door to the guest house and walked in. "I love this place," said Manuela. "It is so warm and cozy." She asked, "So did Sandra decorate this place as well?"

I replied, "Yes."

She replied, "Sandra is very good at what she does."

I said, "Yeah, it appears that she and Isiah are getting cozy."

Manuela replied, "It sure does."

I said, "Let me grab an overnight bag to put some things in." I grabbed the bag with my things and stopped by the kitchen.

Manuela said, "I see that you have wine."

I said, "Well, it is just for show because I don't drink wine."

Manuela replied, "Well I do."

I said, "Take a bottle of your choice."

Manuela grabbed a bottle of Merlot wine to take with us to the main house.

We then left and went back to the main house. Once we were at the main house, everyone was sitting in the kitchen at the island. I said,

"Everyone, we should have enough bathrooms for those that are ready to take a shower."

"Thanks Jefferson," said Pedro, "but we were trying to figure out what we were going to have for dinner."

I responded, "Well, I have about 10 pounds of peeled shrimp and 10 pounds of catfish at the guest house that we can cook." Everyone said that sounded good. I said, "Plus I have a bowl of fresh banana pudding in the refrigerator and a pecan pie on the counter that my grandmother just baked today.

Pedro said, "My friend, you eat good while you're at home."

I replied, "Yeah, you can see why I work out and train so hard."

"So how is rehab coming along?" asked Sandra.

I replied, "Everything is coming along just fine. I will be furthering my training in Miami starting the first week of January."

"Well, that sounds good," said Sandra. She then said, "I'm going to go upstairs and take a shower."

Isiah said, "Me too."

I said, "Oh wait a minute, what is going on here?"

Isiah said, "Hey little brother, slow your roll."

I said, "You could have at least told me that you and Sandra have been communicating, that's all I'm saying."

Isiah responded, "I'm glad that you had Sandra come down to decorate your guest house."

I responded, "Well, I'm glad that I had her come down as well, especially seeing how happy you two are together."

Pedro said, "Maria and I are going to go upstairs and get ready as well."

Then Manuela's friends Melissa and Rosetta said that they were going to go upstairs and freshen up also." They asked, "So are you coming up, Manuela?"

Manuela replied, "No, not right now. I'm going to help Jefferson bring the food over so that we can feed y'all's hungry asses."

"Well ok, girl," said Melissa.

I asked, "Are you ready, Manuela?"

She replied, "Yes, I'm ready."

I said, "We can take the golf cart this time around since we have to bring some items back." We got on the golf cart and went to the guest house. Once we were at the guest house I went in the pantry and got several paper bags in order to carry the food back over. I opened the refrigerator and put the catfish and shrimp into the paper bags. I also got a 12-pack of Michelob Light out of the refrigerator and placed it in another bag. I went back to the pantry and got two boxes of the Zatarain's fish fry mix, a bottle of Tabasco sauce, a bottle of cocktail sauce, a bottle of Heinz Ketchup, a bottle of Miracle Whip Mayonnaise and a bottle of mustard. I said, "Would you please put these items in a paper bag, ma'am?"

Manuela said, "No problem, sir."

I then grabbed a loaf of wheat bread out of the bread box and a half gallon of Tanqueray Gin and a six pack of tonic water and a bottle of Crown Royal from the bar. I said, "Well, that should do."

"Is it ok to bring the 12-pack of Coronas out of your refrigerator as well as a couple of limes?" asked Manuela.

I responded, "Sure, you can bring them. My brother Jackie is the only person that drinks Coronas anyway; that is why I keep them in stock." I then got the Big Daddy Fry Machine from under the pantry, along with two bottles of Crisco oil, in order to fry the seafood. We then loaded everything on the golf cart and headed back to the main house.

"Why does it feel like we have been grocery shopping?" said Manuela.

I jokingly said, "I do believe we have been grocery shopping."

Everyone was still upstairs, so we brought everything in the kitchen and got set up. I said, "Manuela, you can go ahead and freshen up if you like. You can use my bedroom and shower if you like."

She responded, "It is ok. I can wait until we prepare the food first."

I said, "No problem. The seafood has already been cleaned and washed. We just need to season it. Manuela Santiago, this is how I normally cook seafood so pay attention and you may learn something." I said, "I season the seafood real well, then I take the Zatarain fish fry mix and place it in a one gallon Ziploc bag. Then I take a regular baking pan and pour the yellow mustard, either French's Yellow Mustard or Heinz Yellow Mustard, in the pan and season real well." I said, "while I'm doing this, can you pour the Crisco oil into the Big Daddy Fry Pan?

"I sure can, Chef," replied Manuela. She poured the oil into the Big Daddy Fry Pan, then I plugged the pan into the electrical outlet.

I said, "Once the temperature reaches 375 degrees the fryer is ready to start cooking. I normally cook the shrimp for three minutes and the fish for four or five minutes based on the thickness of fish."

I took the shrimp and placed it in the mustard mix and coated the shrimp really well. The red light on fryer meant that it was ready to go. Then I took the shrimp and placed into the Zatarain Fish and Shrimp mix and shook the Ziploc bag real well to ensure that the shrimp was coated. Then I placed the shrimp into the fryer and set the timer for three minutes. After three minutes I took the shrimp out and poured it into a large pan already layered with paper towels in order to catch the excess oil. I looked over and saw Manuela had already made a salad as well as toasted some French bread in case someone wanted to make sandwiches or shrimp po-boys.

Everyone started making their way down to the kitchen one by one. Pedro said, "I smell something good cooking."

Manuela and I had everything complete and it was now time to eat. I was starved. I told everyone that there were Michelob Light, Coronas, wine and other beverages if anyone wanted anything. Personally, I grabbed a Michelob Light, which went perfect with my seafood.

"Jefferson, you and my sister really did a great job preparing dinner," said Pedro.

I said, "Yeah, Manuela and I make a great team. She knows her way around the kitchen."

We ate dinner then laughed and joked around while sitting in the kitchen.

"Thomas, I'm getting ready to go take a shower," said Manuela.

I said, "Well, let me show you where everything is located." I grabbed her bag and took it into my bedroom. I told her that she could sleep in my room and I would either sleep on the sofa or upstairs in one of those rooms.

She replied, "Thomas, you can sleep in here with me if you like; after all, it is a king size bed. I promise that I won't bite."

I replied, "You may not bite; however, I can't say that I wouldn't bite.

You're so beautiful and I'm vulnerable right now. I'm in the process of going through a divorce and you've just gotten engaged."

She replied, "I care about Escobar but I love you, Thomas. I know Escobar isn't the right person for me; you are."

I said, "Manuela, I just don't want to complicate things right now. I want to finalize my divorce to Olivia prior to moving forward in another relationship because I want to have a clear conscience, knowing that I was faithful to her and gave everything I had while we were married. I also don't want Olivia nor her attorney to have any reason or proof saying that I wasn't faithful or committed to her." I asked, "Does that make sense?"

Manuela responded, "Yes, Thomas, that makes perfect sense." She said, "Well, if you will excuse me, I will take a shower."

I said, "No problem. I will go take a shower in the other bathroom downstairs."

Once I had showered I came back to the kitchen where everyone was still sitting, drinking and talking. Manuela was already there, standing near the island drinking a glass of Merlot.

"Oh, I almost forgot, little brother," said Isiah, "but the security company will be by tomorrow morning to install your surveillance system."

I said, "That is great news to hear. Sandra, I want to thank you once again for doing such a wonderful job with the furnishing and decorating of not only the houses here in Alabama but also the houses in Greenwich. Although I haven't seen the main house in Connecticut, I know that if it looks anywhere close to the guest house there or both houses here in 'Bama that it will be a masterpiece."

She replied, "Well, thank you Jefferson. I was told by the contractor as well as Jane that the house should be ready in a couple of weeks."

I said, "So they are finishing about three weeks ahead of schedule."

Sandra replied, "That is correct."

I said, "Everyone, I would like to extend an invitation for all of you to come to Greenwich for a housewarming gathering."

They all asked in unison, "So what date?"

I pulled out my phone and looked at the calendar and said, "How about New Year's Eve, Sunday December 31?"

I asked Sandra, "So do you think the house will be fully furnished and decorated by then?"

She replied, "Jefferson if the contractors are able to complete everything as scheduled the house will be ready."

I said, "Perfect, because I could stay in Greenwich for a week then fly to Miami to start work for Mr. Santiago. Well everyone, Greenwich it is for New Year's."

"Sounds great," said Pedro.

Maria looked at Pedro and said, "You see, sweetie, you have another reason to come back to Greenwich."

Pedro replied, "I already have every reason in the world to be there."

I said, "Aw, how sweet."

"So you're going to be working for Mr. Santiago?" asked Maria.

I replied, "Yes, I'm going to be in Miami training for two months so I decided to take Mr. Santiago up on his offer to work at his company."

She replied, "That is awesome."

I replied, "It sure is."

"Isiah and Jefferson, your dad and grandpa look so familiar," said Maria.

I said, "Well, they both retired from the government. Our grandfather retired about 10 years ago, after 45 years with the Department of Transportation. Our dad just retired after 35 years with the Department of Transportation."

She said, "Yes, that is where I know them from. I had seen a photo of a father and son team of high ranking administrators that worked for us."

"So exactly what do you do?" asked Isiah.

"Well I'm a financial analyst within the Department of Transportation," said Maria.

"Oh, how cool," said Isiah.

I said, "Our brother Jackie just received a job with the Department of Transportation as well."

"That is truly awesome," said Maria. She then changed the subject and said, "What a nice and sweet and not too dry bottle of Merlot."

I said, "I'm not a wine drinker and I can't take credit. All of the credit goes to Sandra."

Then Manuela and Maria said, "Thank you, Sandra."

We all drank and talked until about midnight, then everyone started saying that they were getting ready for bed.

I said, "Yeah, I need to go to bed because I have to train tomorrow."

"Don't forget that we have lunch tomorrow," said Manuela, "because I want my $7,000 worth."

I said, "Don't worry, I have Mom and Grandma preparing lunch for us. I'm going to take you horseback riding as well as on a picnic to one of my favorite spots. Therefore, you be ready when I get back home tomorrow afternoon."

"I would like to go horseback riding too, Pedro," said Maria.

I said, "We have enough horses for everyone to go riding if you like. Isiah can show you'll the horses tomorrow."

I then walked Manuela to my bedroom, gave her a kiss on her cheek and told her goodnight. I slept on the sofa in the living room.

I awakened the next morning to the smell of bacon. I looked in the kitchen and saw Mom, Grandma and Manuela in the kitchen cooking breakfast. It was around 6:15 AM. I got up and went and washed my face and brushed my teeth. Then I went in the kitchen and said, "What are y'all doing?"

My grandma said, "What does it look like we are doing? Cooking breakfast."

I said, "I know that, Grandma."

"Well Jefferson, Manuela had asked us yesterday what you normally like for breakfast," said Mom. "So we told her that we would come over and show her how to cook a country breakfast as well as cook breakfast for everybody."

A few moments later there was a knock at door and it was Grandpa, Dad, Jackie and his wife Suzette. They all walked in asking whether breakfast was ready or not.

Manuela said, "Yes, breakfast is ready."

Pretty soon everyone from upstairs came down for breakfast. They all were saying the smell of bacon and coffee woke them up. "There's nothing better in the morning as a wake-up call than the smell of bacon and coffee," I said. "We all owe it to Manuela for having this fine country breakfast prepared for us this morning. It was her idea to have the breakfast here this morning. I can think of no better way to christen the house than with family and friends sitting around the table eating a good breakfast."

I went over and gave Manuela a hug and kiss on the cheek and said, "Thank You." After I had finished my breakfast I went in the room and changed into my Gee (martial arts uniform) and grabbed my gym bag. I said, "Well y'all, I hate to leave good company but I have training to do."

Manuela walked over and said, "Don't be late for lunch."

I said, "I wouldn't miss it for the world." Then I left to go training. I had a great practice with Master Kim. I was getting mobility back in my ankle. The mobility and strength drills as well as the ointment treatments were working. Tiger and his brother Rabbit also trained with me today. After practice Tiger and I sat in the Dojo talking. I asked, "Tiger, so are you ready for your lunch date with Ms. Johnson?"

He said, "Yes, I sure am. I already have her some flowers and I'm taking her to Big Daddy's Grill for lunch."

I said, "Damn, I knew I was forgetting something. I'm going to have to go to Doshia's in Jackson and get some flowers for my lunch date with Manuela."

Rabbit came running in the Dojo and said, "Jefferson, you may want to come outside."

I asked, "Why?"

He responded, "Your wife is out front."

Sure enough, I walked out front and there was Olivia and her sister. She asked, "Jefferson, can we talk?"

I responded, "There is nothing to talk about. Anything that needs to be said can be discussed between our attorneys."

She said, "I got served with these divorce papers this morning and it finally hit me that this is real."

I responded, "You're damn right it is real. Olivia, it should have been real for you a long time ago. I was too damn good to you as well as too damn good for you. There are many women out there that would appreciate a warm, kind, loving, supportive and strong man like me; however, you didn't. So if you would excuse me, I have somewhere that I need to be."

I then jumped in my truck and left. My phone was ringing. It was

Tiger. "Yo Jefferson, you really told her ass. She left out here like a bat out of hell."

I said, "Well, she needs to realize that it is over between us."

Tiger said, "I think reality has set in, especially since she doesn't have your money to blow through anymore."

I said, "You damn, skippy. I will talk to you later, Tiger." I went to Jackson and picked out a dozen pink roses and went back home. I went to the guest house first and took a shower and put on my riding clothes, cowboy boots and cowboy hat. Today was a beautiful day for riding. I then went to my main house; however, no one was there. I then stopped by my parents' house and that is where I found Manuela, her girlfriends, Sandra, Suzette, Mom and Grandma.

I got out of the truck with the dozen roses as well as a card for Manuela. They were all sitting on the front porch. I handed Manuela the card and roses. She read the card and then jumped up and gave me a hug. She said, "Thomas, that was so sweet."

I said, "Where are Pedro and Isiah?"

Mom replied, "They went to pick up a few items for the grill a little later. Isiah wanted to cook out. Your dad, grandpa, Jackie and Maria are over at the office in the barn talking." She said, "Maria had told your dad and grandpa that they looked familiar. She stated that she had seen their photos at work."

Mom then went inside the house and came back with the picnic basket. She said, "I have y'all two homemade turkey and bacon sandwiches, two Dill Pickles, two twice-stuffed baked potatoes, salad and two slices of buttermilk pound cake and a canteen of Grandma's famous lemonade."

I said, "Mom, that sounds so good."

Grandma replied, "It not only sounds good but it tastes good also."

We then walked over to the barn. Dad, Grandpa, Maria and Jackie were in the office talking. I could see Dad showing everyone some paperwork. I yelled, "Hey what's going on in here?" as I walked through the office door." Dad started fumbling around trying to hide the papers. Everybody was looking suspicious. I jokingly said, "What, are y'all going over some black ops mission for the Department of Transportation?"

Grandpa said, "I got your damn black ops. You know to knock before you come into a room."

I said, "I'm sorry about that, Grandpa. I'm about to go saddle the horses, so Manuela and I can go for a ride."

Jackie said, "There is no need, little brother. The horses are already saddled. Storm and Star are saddled and ready right out back. They are currently grazing in the pasture by stalls."

I turned around to tell Manuela, "Let's go" but she was nowhere to be found. I called her name and she said, "I'm out back."

I walked out back and she had already mounted Storm. I said, "Hey, wait a minute, Manuela. Storm is my horse and she only allows a handful of people to ride her. You can ride Star." I was expecting Storm to start rearing up and causing problems but she didn't. She was very calm. I said, "It appears that she likes you. She normally never lets anyone ride her except me or my brothers." The next thing I knew, Manuela had taken off on Storm, headed down the pasture. I said, "I guess I will ride Star. Let's go, boy."

It was a beauty watching Manuela ride Storm. I had to catch myself because I believed that I was falling for her. Manuela was everything that I ever wanted in a woman. She slowed down so that I could catch up with her because Storm is such a powerful runner that it would have been hard for Star and me to keep up. I asked, "So where did you learn to ride horses like that?"

She replied, "In Venezuela we own this huge hacienda and every year during the summer months we would go there and stay for a month or so."

I said, "Well, it shows, because you are an awesome rider." I said, "Follow me" as we took a trail through the woods. We came upon this gorgeous pond that had a pier as well as a boat tied to the pier. We got off the horses and walked toward the picnic table underneath the tree.

"Thomas, aren't you going to tie the horses?" asked Manuela.

I replied, "No, they're not going to go anywhere."

Storm and Star walked over to the edge of the pond and started drinking water. I took all of the food out of the basket and sat on the table.

"Jefferson, this is really nice. Thanks for bringing me here," said

Manuela. She said, "I love the serenity of this place. It is so much better than being cooped up in some restaurant on a beautiful day like this."

I replied, "No, thank you for paying $7,000, which went for a great cause, to have lunch with me."

She replied, "Are you sure you're not just thankful that I saved you from Olivia?"

I replied, "I'm thankful for that as well."

She said, "Not only are the salad and sandwich good, but this buttermilk pound cake just melts in your mouth. I couldn't live here eating this cooking every day. I wouldn't be able to fit my clothes," said Manuela.

Laughing, I said, "well you see why I work out every day."

She replied, "Your grandma has to give me the recipe for this lemonade and your mom the recipe for the buttermilk pound cake."

I replied, "So not only do you cook but you bake also."

She replied, "Well, yeah."

I asked, "What is it that you don't do, Manuela Santiago?"

She thought about it for a moment and said, "I can't think of anything."

I asked, "So would you like to feed Storm?"

Manuela replied, "Sure."

I had two small Ziploc bags of carrots and another bag of sugar cubes. We then called the horses over to eat the carrots and sugar cubes. I told Storm if I had known that I wasn't going to be able to ride her I would have let her rider bring her treats.

Manuela said, "Don't worry, Storm" as she was rubbing her, "I will bring you carrots and sugar cubes the next time."

I looked at her and asked, "So are you coming back?"

She replied, "Sure, unless you don't want me to."

I said, "I would love to have you back here."

She asked, "Oh, is that a tree house?"

I replied, "It sure is. I will show it to you next time, but let's get back to see if Isiah has fired up the grill."

We got on the horses and made our way back to the open pasture. I knew Manuela was going to open up Storm so the only chance that

I had was to send Star in motion first. I said, "Let's go, Star. Come on, boy, let's go."

The next thing I knew Manuela and Storm came flying by me. I knew there was no catching Storm once she was in her stride. When I finally caught up Manuela had already walked Storm to her stall and was taking off her saddle. I rode up and said, "Let me do that for you."

She replied, "I can handle it. I've been taking saddles off horses since I was eight years old."

I replied, "Well, excuse me."

We both finished taking the saddles and bridles off both horses. Then we walked over to my parents house but no one was there. I said, "I bet I know where everyone is." So we jumped on the Rhino ATV and rode up the road to my house. Sure enough, that is where everyone was located, sitting underneath the cabana.

"So did y'all have a nice ride?" asked Mom.

Manuela said, "The ride was wonderful."

Mom said, "I see you were riding Storm. There are very few people other than Jefferson that she will let ride her."

I said, "Yeah, she really likes Manuela."

Manuela said, "If you'll will excuse me, I'm all sweaty and I'm going to go take a shower."

I replied, "I'm going to go do the same."

Manuela went into the main house in my bathroom to shower. I went to my guest house and showered. When I arrived back at the cabana Manuela, along with everyone else, was already eating.

I said, "The least y'all could have done was wait on me to eat; after all, you're at my house."

"Little brother, you were taking too long," said Jackie.

I said, "Well, thank you." I grabbed a plate and fixed me some food. I have to admit Isiah did an excellent job on the grill.

After eating we all sat around talking about everything from how nice the weather was to how fast this year has gone by. I asked, "So Dad what were y'all talking about in the office earlier?"

He replied, laughing, "Son, if I tell you I would have to kill you."

I replied, "I'm not ready to die yet so I don't want to know."

We all really enjoyed the rest of the day. I hated to see everyone leave the next day, especially Manuela. When I was cleaning up in my room she had left one of my t-shirts in the middle of the bed. I picked up the shirt and it smelled like her perfume. I looked down and there was a note. She said, "Thank you, Thomas, for such a wonderful weekend. Words can't express how much you mean to me. I'm going to take you up on what we discussed. I'm going to give my all to see if it works with Escobar as well as give you time to complete your divorce and to realize what you want. I'm praying that everything turns out in each of our favor. Forever Yours, Manuela. P.S. I slept in your t-shirt—just a little something to remember me by. I know I'm not playing fair."

I sent her a text because I knew she was driving. I said, "No, you're not playing fair but I'm glad that you did what you did."

The next month went by rather quickly. The training with Master Kim was great. The divorce paperwork was going along as planned. My attorney stated that everything should be finalized by April if there weren't any snags. I pretty much told him to do whatever he needed to in order to have it wrapped up prior to April. I told him that if we had to threaten to release all of the photos or text messages that Olivia had sent to other men, then please do it. But let her know that we were serious. I also added an additional $100,000 to the original prenuptial settlement amount, as well as I wouldn't sue to recoup any of the $245,000 that was taken from the joint account to use for the beauty salon and massage parlor in New York. My attorney replied, "Sure thing, Jefferson." I had a great Christmas spending time with my family. It was truly a magical time. I told them good bye as Isiah and I caught a JetBlue flight for New York.

CHAPTER SEVEN

Welcome To South Beach

James was at the airport waiting on Isiah and me when we touched down. He gave me a hug. "Nice to see you again, Mr. Jefferson."

I replied, "Nice to see you as well, James. You remember my brother Isiah."

"Yes sir. Hi Mr. Isiah."

James said, "Thanks, Mr. Jefferson, for the Christmas gift cards. My family really did enjoy them."

I replied, "No problem, James. I'm glad that y'all enjoyed them." I said, "James, when we get to Greenwich, could you stop by a grocery store as well as a liquor store? I need to do some grocery shopping."

When we arrived in Greenwich James took us by a grocery store which also had a liquor store next door. Isiah and I went inside to gather some items to last the weekend. When we came out James asked, "Did y'all leave any groceries for anybody else? It appears that y'all bought the entire store."

Isiah responded, "My brother has a tendency to go overboard."

While they were putting the groceries in the Suburban I went in the liquor store to get some alcohol. I got a case of Champagne, two half gallons of Tanqueray Gin, two half gallons of Crown Royal, four bottles of Merlot, four bottles of white wine, two cases of Michelob Light, two cases of Corona, four bottles of rum, four bottles of tequila, two gallons of Strawberry Daiquiri Mix, champagne glasses, plastic cups, one case of Canada Dry Tonic Water and six bags of ice. I then checked out and headed toward James and Isiah.

"Jefferson, do you think that you have enough alcohol?" asked Isiah.

I replied, "I don't want to run out of anything."

Isiah replied, "Well, little brother, you don't have that many people coming."

I said, "Sandra is coming, along with her parents, sister, brother and a couple of her girlfriends, then you have Pedro, Maria and her parents, Maria's two sisters, and her brother. Then there is Jane, my realtor, and her husband, as well as Jackie and Suzette. And don't forget Manuela and her friends from college, who are bringing their boyfriends. Oh yeah, Pedro invited a couple of his buddies as well. I'm also having food catered on Sunday afternoon as well." I said, "I'm excited about seeing the completed house."

Isiah replied, "Well, Sandra is going to meet us there."

I said, "She always meets us there."

Sure enough, when we pulled in front of my house there were Sandra and Jane both. I gave both of them a hug and then introduced Jane to my brother Isiah. She asked, "Where is your brother Jackie?"

I replied, "He and his wife fly in later this afternoon. He wasn't able to fly out with us."

She said, "I can't wait to see him. It has probably been over ten years since the last time that I saw him."

Sandra and Jane started helping us get the groceries and alcohol inside. It seemed like there was a never ending line of bags; however, Isiah finally came through the door and said, "This is the last bag." We all cheered. "However, we do have luggage."

We all laughed, then he and I went outside and helped James bring in the luggage. Isiah got Sandra's luggage out of her car.

James said, "Mr. Jefferson, I will see you later. I will be at the airport to pick up your brother Jackie and his wife, as well as Ms. Manuela, whose flight comes in 30 minutes later."

I said, "That sounds great, James." I walked James outside and gave him a $2500 check. I said, "This is for your airport runs today as well as your New Year's gift."

James said, "Thanks Mr. Jefferson." He then got in his car and left.

Isiah and Sandra had already started putting the groceries away. I said, "Thank y'all for putting the groceries away. I guess I can start stocking the bar with alcohol. I forgot to have a freezer installed in order to store the ice."

Sandra replied, "There is no need for ice" as she opened the garage door and pointed toward a commercial style ice maker in the corner.

I said, "Sandra, you have thought of everything. Well, I guess I will use the ice to place over the beer in the coolers."

Isiah said, "Little brother, it is a good thing that you brought these two coolers earlier at the store."

I replied, "It sure is."

Isiah said, "Jefferson, this is a beautiful house."

I replied, "Thanks Isiah. I was so busy bringing in groceries that I forgot to look at the furnishing and decorations that Sandra had done. Sandra, once again you have outdone yourself."

The kitchen was white with black marble countertops; the appliances were stainless steel. The cabinets were made of a dark wood finish which also hid the Sub Zero refrigerator. The microwave and dishwasher both were built into the side of the long island. The sink was in the middle of the island. Then there was a large bar in the kitchen next to living room. Everything was open and flowed very well. The design was on the same level as my main house in Alabama. However, this was an older home that had to be totally redesigned. I walked through the entire home and it was tastefully done. When I walked out from the kitchen onto the back deck I was totally floored by the pool with a small grotto, as well as the outdoor cabana with outdoor kitchen and gas fireplace with outdoor pit. Everything flowed so well. I loved it. When I made it back inside the house I had to give Sandra another hug. The doorbell rang and I yelled for them to come in; the door was open. It was Pedro and Maria, along with Maria's sisters and brother. They came into the kitchen and I gave them a hug. Maria introduced her siblings to Isiah and Sandra. Then I told them to make themselves at home.

"Jefferson, this is a beautiful home," said Maria.

I replied, "Thanks Maria."

Pedro was like, "Bro, this is an awesome place. It resembles your Alabama home, sort of."

I said, "Thanks, my friend."

They went outside to look at the patio, pool and cabana. They really did like everything. I said, "I don't know about y'all but I'm getting hungry. We have food in the refrigerator that needs to be cooked or we can send for takeout."

Isiah said, "Jackie just texted. He said that he, Suzette and Manuela are en route." He said, "James has already picked them up from the airport."

I replied, "Awesome. I guess we can wait a little longer until they arrive from the airport in order to eat." I said, "For tomorrow I'm catering food from Blackstone's Steakhouse. For Appetizers we are having Lobster Bisque, Sizzling Neuski Bacon, Maryland Crab Cakes, Lemon Peppered Shrimp and Smoked Salmon. For Entrees, Double Cut American Lamb Chops Blackstone's Chicken, Filet Mignon Crostini and Miniature Steak Quesadillas, Vegetables- Creamed Spinach, Sauteed Asparagus and Baked Potatoes, and House Salad. Oh, I forgot about the Dessert – Cheese Cake and Pecan Pie, and I have Ice Cream in the refrigerator."

"So do you think that you have enough food for tomorrow?" asked Sandra.

I replied, "I just want to make sure that we don't go hungry."

Maria said, "We will cook today."

I asked, "Who will be doing the cooking?"

She replied, "My sisters, me and Manuela."

I said, "Manuela isn't here yet."

She replied, "I just got off the phone with her and she is only a few minutes away."

Sure enough, a few moments later Manuela, my brother Jackie and Suzette came walking through the front door. I went and hugged my brother and Suzette and gave Manuela a hug and kiss on the cheek. Then James and Jackie came in the door with additional bags of groceries. I asked, "What, more groceries?"

Manuela replied, "Well, we need certain things in order prepare food for tonight."

I said, "Hey, my mouth is shut; do your thing."

James said, "If that is all I will see you on Tuesday morning, Mr. Jefferson."

I replied, "That will be all, James. Thanks for everything."

Everyone said, "Thanks James, and have a Happy New Year."

The girls said they were making Homemade Spaghetti, Lasagna, Garlic Bread, Italian Zucchini and for Appetizers stuffed mushrooms and Spicy Oil and Vinegar dip for the bread and a Caesar Salad.

I said, "Sounds good. We boys are going to get out of you girls' way." We went upstairs to the area outside of the theater room that had a pool table and a round poker table used for playing poker or cards. The tables also had a slot for poker chips.

Pedro said, "I'll be right back. My friends are about to pull in the driveway." When Pedro came back inside he introduced his friends to the girls downstairs. Then he came up and introduced his friend Jason Wheeler to everybody. Then I asked, "Pedro, I thought you had two friends coming over."

He said, "I do. Here he is, Ricky Williams."

I said, "Oh hell no." I went and hugged my boy Ricky Williams. He was a senior on the baseball team when I was a freshman at the University of Alabama. I said, "What's up, man?" We made so much noise the girls came running upstairs to see what was wrong. I said, "It's Ricky Williams from Coffeeville, Alabama." I asked, "Ricky, do you remember when I first came on the team you said, 'I'm glad to have someone else on the team from a small town with a crazy name besides me.'" I said, "Wow, this is an awesome surprise. I thought that you were playing for the Minnesota Twins?"

He replied, "I was until I got traded several days ago."

I replied, "Damn, I haven't watched the news lately so I wouldn't have known."

Ricky replied, "Well Jefferson, you were on the news a lot several months ago for kicking not one but four guys' asses."

I replied with a laugh, "I couldn't help it, Ricky, I couldn't help it. I tried to avoid the confrontation."

Ricky asked, "Jefferson do you remember when I stopped you from kicking Butch's ass at practice that day?"

I replied, "Yeah I remember. I'm glad you did stop me because Butch turned out to be a good guy."

Ricky said, "Butch is still playing for Minnesota but he wants out of there as well. He wants to come back south. He really wants to play for the Braves." Ricky said, "Jefferson, I'm glad to see that you're doing better."

I replied, "Ricky, I'm doing better physically, mentally, emotionally and spiritually." I said, "I'm just blessed to have a wonderful family and great friends beside me."

"Hey boys, the food is ready. Come and get it," yelled Maria.

The doorbell rang. I told everyone to go ahead and eat and I would get the door. Manuela said, "No, we will wait because we must say our prayers."

I replied, "Ok." When I opened the door it was Manuela's friends Melissa and Rosetta and Melissa's boyfriend as well as Sandra's friends Wilma and Jacqueline and Sandra's sister Amanda and brother Derek. I said, "Nice to meet y'all. Please come in." I came in the front and introduced them to everybody. I said, "Y'all have come just in time. You can wash up in either one of restrooms downstairs as well as upstairs."

Once they finished washing their hands they came back to the kitchen. I walked over to Manuela and gave her a hug for helping to prepare such a beautiful meal. Manuela said, "It is time to say our prayers so please grab your neighbor's hands." She led the prayer, which was beautiful. Then everyone got in line and went around the island loading food onto their plates.

They had prepared Lasagna, Spaghetti and Meatballs, Stuffed Mushrooms, Garlic Bread, Spicy Olive Oil and Vinegar Dip, Grilled Chicken Breasts and fried Pork Chops, House Salad and baked two Mrs.

Fields Apple Pies and a tray of Chocolate Chip cookies. Everything was great. I even went back for seconds.

After our meal we decided to play games. We played Taboo first, then we played Family Feud. We played games until two in the morning. Then Jerry and Ricky caught a ride back to their hotel by Sandra's friends. Everyone else went home. I told Jackie that he and Suzette, Pedro and Maria, Isiah and Sandra could sleep upstairs. Melissa and Davey and Rosetta could sleep in the guest house. I said, "Manuela you can sleep in my bedroom and I will sleep on the sofa." Everyone went upstairs and Manuela's friends went to the guest house, and I made sure that the house was secure. I turn around and Jackie was double-checking the doors and windows. I said, "I have everything under control, big brother." I then put the alarm on.

I went into my bedroom and got a pillow and blanket. Manuela said, "You know that you can sleep in the same bed with me, Thomas."

I said, "I'd rather not, at least not right now. Just leave me another t-shirt." We both laughed. I gave her a hug and kiss on the cheek and said goodnight.

I woke up the next morning to the smell of baking. I thought I was dreaming but I wasn't. I looked in the kitchen to see Manuela, Maria, Sandra and Suzette cooking up a storm.

I asked, "What is going on in here?"

They said, "What does it look like?"

I yelled upstairs for the guys to come eat breakfast. I then went into the bathroom to wash my face and brush my teeth. They had a spread cooked: turkey bacon, regular bacon, egg whites, regular eggs ham, omelettes, grits and homemade biscuits.

I said, "It looks good and smells good, but how does it taste?"

Manuela's friends rang the doorbell and about that time the boys were down from upstairs. We held hands and gave thanks to our Lord and Savior for the wonderful breakfast prepared before us. Then we ate breakfast. I said, "I have to admit, this is pretty good."

Manuela said, "I made the grits, turkey bacon and homemade biscuits.

I said, "You're giving my mom and grandma a run for their money on these biscuits."

Isiah said, "Don't be talking about my momma's biscuits." We all laughed.

After breakfast we sat around in our pajamas and talked until 2 PM. I said, "We better get up and get dressed. People will be coming over at 4 PM and they're delivering the food at six."

Manuela's friends went to the guest house to get ready. I then went into my bedroom in order to pick out some clothes to wear. I had picked out a nice navy blue suit with a cream dress shirt and black shoes and black belt Then I gathered my underwear, t-shirt and socks.

Manuela said, "Your outfit looks nice, Thomas."

I said, "Thanks." I went to the guest bathroom to shower. After showering, I went back to my bedroom and knocked on the door. Manuela asked, "Who is it?"

I said, "Jefferson."

She said, "Come in."

When I had gone in she said, "Just what I needed, an extra hand. Thomas, could you please zip me up?"

I said, "No problem. You look stunning."

She said, "Thanks." She was wearing this pink ribbed mini dress. I was floored by how beautiful she was. Her wavy hair came down to the middle of her back. She was about 5'9" inches tall but with her two-inch heels she was closer to 5'11" or 6' tall. I felt like grabbing her in my arms and kissing her. It had been a long time since I had been intimate. I could feel my testosterone in overdrive. She said, "Thomas, you look handsome in that suit. I love that color on you. It brings out the complexion in your skin."

I replied, "Stop, you're making me blush. I'm so embarrassed."

She said, "Stop silly, I'm paying you a compliment and you've got jokes."

I said, "I have to joke to keep my mind off how beautiful you are. I want to grab you in my arms so bad and passionately kiss you."

Manuela replied, "Thomas, why don't you? I want you to grab me in your arms so bad."

I replied, "Manuela, I know, but it just won't be right. I made vows to God, my Lord and Savior, and I won't break those vows. Even though Olivia committed adultery on me I can't go down that road. I have my attorney expediting things as much as possible in order to finalize this divorce. Manuela, these past occasions that we have shared together have shown me that you're the woman for me. However, I don't want to complicate things with you and Escobar. Like I said before, please put everything in it to see if that is what you really want because when I'm done with this divorce I want all of you: your mind, body, soul, spirit, and your love. If you can't give me everything, then I want nothing. Because I refuse to have to go through what I'm currently going through again. Manuela each moment that I'm in the same room with you, I find myself falling for you more and more."

She replied, "Thomas, can you at least hold me in your arms? Because I need a hug right now."

Before she could complete her sentence I had her in my arms. I said, "You feel so good, Manuela Santiago." There was a knock at the door. I asked, "Who is it?"

"It's Isiah, little brother."

I said, "Come in."

He said, "Hey, the food caterer is here. I'm not sure what all you ordered."

I said, "No problem, I'll be right there." Before leaving I grabbed Manuela by her right hand and kissed her hand.

She said, "I have to go straighten up my makeup."

I said, "I almost forgot; I came in here to put on deodorant and cologne. I don't want to be around everyone musky."

She replied, "Thomas, you are so crazy."

I went and put on deodorant and cologne. Then I went to the kitchen to meet the caterer. "Man, that's a lot of food."

"It sure is," said Sandra.

After the caterer had brought in all the food I checked the list to ensure that we had everything on the list. Everything was there. I asked, "So why did y'all come an hour early?"

The caterer replied, "We got a lot of orders at the last minute so we figured they would rather be early than late."

I said, "That makes sense." It was a $5,000 bill, plus I gave him a 15% gratuity. Hopefully that would help bring his New Year in with a bang.

It sure did put a smile on his face. He ran up and hugged me. He said, "Thank you very much, Mr. Robinson."

Manuela was walking out of the room around the time the caterer gave me a hug and thanked me. She asked, "What is it that makes people want to hug you so much, Thomas Jefferson Robinson?"

I replied, "It must be my smile." Then I did a quick smile for her.

She said, "You're so silly."

Everybody started whistling when she walked into the kitchen. Everyone said how much they loved the dress as well as her hair. She said, "Thanks."

The doorbell rang and it was Maria's parents, her brother, her sisters and one of her girlfriends. I escorted everyone into the kitchen. I said, "You clean up rather well, Mr. Sanchez."

He replied, "You clean up ok yourself, Jefferson."

There was a knock at the door and it was Melissa and her boyfriend, Rosetta and Jane and her husband. I said, "Jackie, someone is here to see you." When she saw Jackie she ran and gave him a hug.

"What has it been, 10 or 11 years since the last time that we saw each other?" asked Jackie.

Jane replied, "It has almost been 11 years." She told how they had met. She was a young realtor who sold Jackie his first home. "Well, actually she was a realtor in training," said Jackie. "She was working for this shady realtor who had tried to sell me a piece of property that had a lot of serious issues that hadn't been disclosed. I fell in love with the place and had called Jane to make the deal. When I met her at the house she said, 'Jackie, this isn't the right house for you. It has a lot of issues that the neither owner nor the realtor is disclosing. The homeowner is the realtor's brother-in-law.' She went on to say that this house had serious electrical and plumbing issues as well as foundation problems. She said, 'Now if you want to buy the house it won't be from me because I'm putting in my notice to resign today because I can't work in that kind of environment.' I said, 'Jane, thanks for being so honest. Once you get on your new job call me and I will make sure to buy my house from you, so now you have some leverage in your interview—that you have someone ready to spend a substantial amount on a home.'"

"Well, it worked," said Jane. "I landed a job in roughly a week and

Jackie as well as some of his teammates that he had referred to me purchased homes. The rest, as you say, is history. I became the top seller it the area, which allowed me to move back home six years ago and start my own company."

"That is a wonderful story," said Manuela. Manuela said, "You Robinson boys are something else."

A little later Ricky and Jason arrived, as well as a few other guests. I was glad to see that everyone was having a good time. However, I couldn't keep my eyes off Manuela. I watched her as she gracefully walked from the kitchen to the living room entertaining the guests.

There was food stretched out a country mile in the kitchen, from the island to the kitchen counter tops. There were individuals eating as the urge hit them. I had to check on the 16 bottles of champagne that I had chilling in the cooler next to the bar.

The time passed rather quickly; it was only 15 minutes now until New Year's Day. I told everyone to get ready. I had Isiah, Jackie and Pedro assist me in opening the champagne when there were only five minutes left. Manuela, Suzette, Sandra and Maria had already given everyone their champagne glass. The countdown was now on; everyone was counting down: "10, 9, 8, 7, 6, 5, 4, 3, 2 1...Happy New Year!"

Then we all put up our glasses for a toast and continued to hug each other and shake hands. When I got to Manuela, I gave her a hug but then she kissed me in the mouth. It was a long, passionate kiss.

"It's ok, you can come up for air now, little brother."

Afterwards, I said, "Wow."

Manuela said, "Happy New Year. This is for a wonderful year in 2007. It is so that you will know that I'm worth waiting for and that my love and heart belong to you and only you, Thomas."

I said, "Don't worry, Ms. Santiago, I'm definitely coming for you when everything is finalized. I just hope you will still be there."

"Don't worry, Thomas I will be waiting," said Manuela.

We all partied for the next several hours until three in the morning, then everyone went home. We had a brunch the next day, drinking mimosas along with our breakfast and leftovers from the night before.

Melissa and her boyfriend and Rosetta left directly after eating. They were driving over to Melissa's boyfriend's parents' house in Ohio. Sandra took Isiah, Jackie and Suzette to the airport to catch their flight later that afternoon. Pedro, Maria, Manuela and I hung out the rest of the day. Pedro and Maria went back to bed, while Manuela and I lay cuddling on the sofa watching "It's Wonderful Life", which I had on CD. "It's a Wonderful Life" is one of my favorite movies of all time. It pretty much sums up life in general, which is no one is a loser as long as they have family and friends that love them. It also lets you know that we all are special in some sort of way, that we all have a purpose in the world.

Pedro and Maria came down stairs around 6 PM that day. Manuela was in the kitchen warming up food. I asked, "What woke you love birds up?"

Maria replied, "The sweet aroma of food."

We all sat down at the island in the kitchen and ate. Pedro said, "I love it here in this area. It is so peaceful and quiet."

I said, "Greenwich is a beautiful place to live. It has really grown on me. You know Jane had stated the house next door is coming on the market soon." She said this old married couple lived there but the husband died last month and the kids brought their mother to live with them." She said that it will be available for showing within the next couple of weeks."

Pedro said, "That sounds great, Jefferson. Please text me Jane's number."

I said, "No problem, my friend. I just sent you the text."

Maria said, "Yes, that is a nice house; however, with a few updates it can become modern like yours, Jefferson." Maria said, "These past several days have been wonderful. I hope that everything works out for you and Manuela, Jefferson, because whether you know it or not you make a great team. You two have been wonderful hosts," said Maria.

Pedro chimed in, "If I may add, you two complement each other quite well."

I replied, "Thank you both for your gracious compliments. Everything that you have said I have already seen and said to myself a thousand times over the past several days." I said, "I have watched Manuela work the room, talk to and ask anyone if they needed anything. I have never had that in my previous relationship and I can't wait to have it with Manuela

Santiago." I added, "We both just have some loose ends to rectify because I'm looking forward to my future with Manuela."

"Thomas, thank you very much," said Manuela. She said, "It always helps when someone appreciates you and doesn't take you for granted. I'm looking forward to the day when I don't have to hide my true feelings from the world as well."

We stayed up until one in the morning watching movies and talking. The next morning James was there at 7 AM to pick Manuela and Pedro up to take to the airport. Their flight was leaving at 11 AM, headed to Miami. Maria said goodbye to Pedro then she left for work. I gave Pedro a hug. Then I gave Manuela a hug, then I kissed her and held her tight. I said, "Don't you forget that I'm worth waiting for, Ms. Santiago."

They then departed for the airport. I went back in the house and lay on the sofa. I felt lonely already. The doorbell rang. It was the cleaning company. I said, "Thank God, because there are a lot of things that need to be done."

Manuela and Maria had already taken all of the linen off the beds at guest house and main house and washed them. They had also re-made the beds. I went to the refrigerator and threw all the leftovers in the trash. I told Sarah, the head cleaning person, to clean everything else from the top to bottom. There were a total of five people on the crew. They did an excellent job in cleaning both houses. After they left I took a nap.

The next week went by rather quickly. James picked me up at 8 AM for my noon flight to Miami. During my flight I was just thinking about the next two months of my life. I was embarking on a job that could be a bridge to my post-baseball career—that was, if I decided to come back and play. Whatever the future held for me, I was going to be open and embrace it.

When my plane touched down I was shocked to see Pedro and Manuela there to pick me up. I asked, "What are y'all doing here?"

Manuela said, "I don't fly back to school until tomorrow afternoon, and Dad said that you're staying at the house."

I said, "I have reservations at the Marriott already."

Pedro said "Jefferson, you may want to cancel those reservations." Pedro helped me carry one of my bags. When we walked out the doors by baggage claim the driver helped load the bags into the back of the Suburban.

"How was your last week?" asked Pedro.

I replied, "Well I worked out and jogged about five miles with no pain. Well, actually I didn't jog the five miles all in one day. I jogged those miles over five days. It really felt good." I said, "I see that y'all are having great weather as usual in beautiful South Beach. I love coming here; it is so beautiful."

When we arrived on the sprawling 15-acre estate we stopped by the guest house and the driver dropped my bags off to my maid and butler for the guest house. Then we went to the main house to see Mr. Santiago, Mrs. Santiago and Manuela's sister Sophia. It was a large mansion, roughly 45,143 square feet, to be exact. It had 13 bedrooms and 17 bathrooms two gyms, spacious kitchen, gracious living room, 10-car garage, resort style pool, banquet size dining room, hair salon, billiards room, card room, theater room and cigar room. I could go on and on about all the amenities on this property. It was also a unique Intracoastal estate. His 75-foot yacht was parked at a private marina in his backyard. I was really impressed with this property.

When we walked through the door Manuela yelled, "We are here." She then took me to the kitchen where her mom and dad were sitting drinking tea. Mrs. Santiago rushed and hugged me and gave me a kiss on my cheek. Mr. Santiago shook my hand. "Hello Jefferson, how have you been?"

I said, "I have been getting better and better each day, sir."

He said, "Have a seat. Are you hungry?"

I replied, "No sir, not right now."

He said, "Well, you have your own maid and butler for your house. You can have your own cook if you like but I figured that you would be eating with us each night."

I said, "Yes sir, I would like very much to have dinner with you and your family each night. However, my training starts at 5:30 each evening and I should be done by 7:00 each night."

"We have dinner at 7:30 each night," said Mrs. Santiago. "Let me introduce you to our head staff: Elena is head housekeeper; she has been with us for the past 28 years. Then we have Felipe, head butler, who has been with us for 25 years. Rivera is our head chef. He is responsible for all meals at the property. You already know Carlos, the head of security."

"Yes, how are you doing, Mr. Carlos."

Carlos replied, "I'm doing fine, Senor Jefferson."

"Javier Garcia will be your personal driver as well as bodyguard while you are here. Your personal maid for your house is Anabella Padilla and your butler is Luis Marin."

I said, "Thank you sir." Carlos then dismissed all of the servants.

Mr. Santiago said, "So now Jefferson, let's talk numbers. How do you feel about $3,000 per week to start?"

I said, "Well Mr. Santiago, that is quite generous; however, I do not have any on the job training in Accounting. I was thinking that I would work for free these next couple of months until I understand everything that is expected of me."

"Jefferson, are you sure?" asked Mr. Santiago.

I replied, "Yes sir, I'm positive."

Mr. Santiago asked, "Don't you have expenses, mortgages to pay, Jefferson?"

I replied, "No sir, I don't. My home in Greenwich is paid for, as well as my new home in Alabama. I paid cash for both homes. My 2003 Chevy Tahoe is paid for as well. The only things that I currently pay are utilities, insurance, credit card fees, fitness/training fees and taxes. I used the monies from my endorsements to pay for my homes and the revenue from those endorsements currently covers my living expenses. I haven't touched my signing bonuses and salary from this year; all of those funds are currently in investments, CDs and stock. I also have two additional endorsement deals in the works for Green Star Ointment and Heal a Wrap, which has the potential to be quite lucrative. I'm currently waiting on call from my agent with an update."

"Well Jefferson, I'm glad to see that you handle your money quite well. But what about your pending divorce? How is that going to affect your financial stability?"

I replied, "Well sir, I have a prenuptial agreement in place stating that for each year that we are married she gets $100,000, plus for each child she gets $50,000. Plus I had a morality clause installed as well that stated if I committed adultery the previous numbers would double and she would receive $200,000 per year for five years after we divorced. However, if she committed adultery, she would leave the marriage with nothing and/or whatever she had brought to the marriage. Even though I have evidence that she committed adultery, I told my attorney that I would allow her to keep the $245,000 that she took from my account to start a beauty salon and massage spa with her friend in New York, as well as I would still give her the $100,000 even though we were not married for a year. I also told him that if she signs the divorce papers and everything is finalized prior to March 31 of this year I would increase the $100,000 to $200,000. So I'm currently waiting on updates."

"I very impressed, Jefferson, very impressed," said Mr. Santiago.

I replied, "Well sir, I have great teachers: my father, grandfather and brothers. I'm a good student. I listen."

"You're so mature to be so young," said Mrs. Santiago.

I said, "Thank you ma'am."

Mr. Santiago asked, "Carlos, what do you think about having Jefferson work under Eduardo in order to learn the system?"

Carlos replied, "Well Constantine, I don't think that would be a good idea. Because Eduardo is a jealous person and he will already feel threatened by having Jefferson around. I think that Jefferson would learn more and not only understand what Eduardo does but what the company does as a whole by working with Elizabeth."

Mr. Santiago replied, "That makes perfect sense. Carlos, I see why you have been my friend and closest confidant for so long. Jefferson, report to our office tomorrow morning and ask for Elizabeth. Carlos will give her a briefing so she will be expecting you."

I replied, "Sounds great, sir. I'm looking forward to working with your firm. I promise that I won't let you down."

Manuela asked, "Dad, are you done with your meeting?"

Mr. Santiago replied, "Yes, Manuela, I'm done."

Manuela said "Ok, come on Jefferson, I want to show you around the property."

Pedro walked with us to the foyer. He whispered "When y'all are done holding hands I would like to talk to you, Jefferson."

I said, "No problem, my friend."

Manuela then walked me upstairs to show me the different rooms.

She said, "You better behave yourself working with Elizabeth. Not only is Elizabeth smart, she is single and very gorgeous."

I replied, "Don't worry, I only have eyes for one woman and that's you."

I enjoyed our walk-through of the house. Then she took me down to the boat dock to give me a tour of her father's yacht. I said, "This is a beautiful boat. It is practically a house on water. This is my first time on a yacht."

Manuela replied, "When I come home for Spring Break I will have Captain Manuel take us out on the yacht for a cruise."

I asked, "Where is Captain Manuel presently?"

She replied, "He is currently on vacation in Venezuela.

As we were on the way back up to the top of the deck she pulled me into one of the state rooms and kissed me. She said, "I have missed you, Thomas Jefferson Robinson."

I replied, "Oh really? I have missed you as well." I kissed her back.

She said, "My father is having an engagement dinner for Escobar and me on March 18 while I'm home for Spring Break. Escobar's parents and my parents are inviting a lot of people to the event. Your family should be getting an invitation as well. I tried to tell my father prior to him planning the event but it was too late. My mother already knows that I love you. She doesn't like Escobar. My mother says that Escobar is a liar, womanizer and a bad person like his father Mr. Medina. However, my father and Mr. Medina have been friends since they were little kids. Mr. Medina once saved my father's life when they were young men.

"My father had just started Santiago Global Oil Company and several months later had a big oil strike. My father was made a multi-millionaire overnight. My father was really making a lot of money. My father then became the target for a lot of the drug dealers and Mafioso of the city. They wanted my father to pay them a percentage of his profits on a monthly basis; however, my father refused. My father then started receiving threats against not only him but against his family. He and my mom were married but we weren't born yet.

"He and my mom were living with his parents while the hacienda was being built. One night while my father was out of town masked men broke into my grandparents' home and held a gun to their heads. They ransacked the house and when my grandpa tried to stop them, they beat him severely. My father then hired armed men to protect him and the family. However, one night while he was working late armed men bombarded his office and beat him severely. They were about to sever his head until Pablo Medina and his bodyguards arrived and killed several of the armed men.

"Then for saving his life my father gave Pablo Medina 40% of his company Santiago Global Oil Company. Over the years my father started other companies that weren't affiliated with Santiago Global Oil which name later changed to Medina and Santiago Global Oil."

I replied, "The entire story sounds fishy to me. So what happened to your father's bodyguards that night?"

She replied, "Nobody knows. They were never seen again, nor were their bodies ever discovered." Manuela said, "Once Uncle Carlos finished his tour with the Army my father hired him to be the Head of Security as well as to put together a trustworthy and trained security team. Once Uncle Carlos had his team in place he fired the old security detail. Over the next several years it was becoming more and more dangerous in Venezuela. Mom was pregnant at the time with Pedro. Uncle Carlos didn't trust Mr. Medina. He told my father that he needed to relocate to the United States with his growing family. Once all the paperwork was in order, my father and Mom Uncle Carlos and his wife flew to Miami. We have been here very since. Pedro as well as Sophia and me were born here in Miami. We didn't start going back to Venezuela until I was eight years old."

"So that's why Escobar is so close to your family."

"Yes, Escobar currently runs 40% of Medina and Santiago Global Oil Company. My father purchased a high-rise building in downtown Miami several years ago and relocated all his businesses there with the exception of Medina and Santiago Global Oil Company. Medina and Santiago Global Oil Company is located in a five-story building in South Miami. Eduardo spends much of his time at that building working with Escobar."

I said, "Thank you for all the information. It is beginning to all make sense to me now."

We then walked up to the top deck, where we ran into Pedro. "Hey, I was looking for you two," said Pedro.

Manuela replied, "I was about to take Thomas to the guest house."

I can show him, Manuela, because Mom wants to see you," said Pedro.

Pedro and I hopped on the golf cart and rode to the guest house where I would be staying. "Wow." That is all I could say when I h walked through the door. It was a Mediterranean style one-story home. It had five bedrooms and seven baths. I said, "This is a wonderful home. So what did you want to talk about, Pedro?"

Pedro said, "I just wanted to get your thoughts about Maria."

I replied, "I think that Maria is a wonderful person. I think that she is perfect for you. It appears that she comes from a great family as well as; she has great genes. My advice is to always look at the mother first, prior to getting serious with the daughter. If the mother ages terrible or is ugly, please run; don't pass go."

"Well, I don't have to worry about that," said Pedro, "because she has a beautiful mother."

I asked, "Why are you asking all of these questions, my friend?"

Pedro replied, "I sort of kind of purchased this." He pulled out this huge two-carat engagement ring. It was gorgeous. I gave him a hug. I said, "Congratulations, that is a nice ring."

He said, "Thanks, I paid a little over $100,000 for the ring."

I asked, "So when do you plan on proposing to her?"

Pedro replied, "I plan on proposing to her in March during Manuela's engagement party."

I said, "That would make sense. You will already have a lot of family and friends present."

Pedro said, "Manuela doesn't know about this yet. Nobody does but you, Jefferson."

I said, "Don't worry, your secret is safe with me, my friend."

Pedro said, "I start Spring Training next month so that will help the time pass a lot quicker."

I replied, "Spring Training always makes time pass a lot quicker."

It was almost 7:30 PM. We then went back to the main house and washed up for dinner. After dinner that night I said goodnight to everyone and went back to the guest house to go to sleep.

The next morning I was all excited. I was up bright and early. I brushed my teeth then jumped in the shower. After showering I picked out a gray suit with a white shirt and a black tie with a hint of gray stripes, a black belt and black shoes. I then walked into the kitchen, where I had smelled bacon cooking. However, to my surprise there stood Manuela making grits, bacon and egg whites with two slices of toast.

I said, "You didn't have to do this."

She said, "But I wanted to. I wanted to be the first person to ever prepare breakfast for you as you start your first day of work in a private business setting."

I said, "Thank you, Ms. Santiago. I'm so glad that you prepared me breakfast, because you know that your breakfast is right up there with my mom and grandma's breakfast."

Manuela gave me a hug and said, "I'm so grateful that you are here working at my father's business. I plan on joining my father's company after my graduation next May."

I said, "I'm quite sure that your father will be ecstatic when that day arrives."

Manuela replied, "I'm currently taking a course overload for this semester, the summer and the fall as well."

I said, "That is wonderful." Then I said, "I don't want to be late for my first day of work so I must be going."

Manuela gave me a hug and kiss on my cheek. My driver Javier was waiting outside the house for me. "Good Morning, Mr. Jefferson," said Javier.

I said, "Good morning," as Javier was opening the door to the Chevy Suburban. During the drive, I asked Javier if he was originally from Miami.

"No sir, I'm originally from Venezuela. Senor Carlos and I served in the Army together."

I said, "That is awesome. I like Senor Carlos."

Javier said, "Yes, he is a great man." Javier dropped me off in the front of the building. I went inside and caught the elevator to the 30th floor and asked for Elizabeth.

Elizabeth came out and said "Hi, my name is Elizabeth Alvarado."

I said, "Jefferson Robinson, nice to meet you."

She replied, "No, your name is Thomas Jefferson Robinson, #40 with the New York Yankees."

I asked, "Oh, you watch baseball?"

She replied, "Yes, I'm a big Yankees fan. You had a hell of year until your injury."

I said, "Thank you, but I'll be back."

She replied, "Welcome aboard." I went to her office and she closed the door. She said, "I was told to teach you everything about our businesses and what it is that we do. I saw your transcript that you were a good student. You graduated Cum Laude from the University of Alabama." Then she said, "Roll Tide."

I said, "Thank you."

I asked, "So Elizabeth, where did you attend school?"

She replied, "I graduated from Miami University." Then her door flew open and it was Escobar and Eduardo. Elizabeth said, "I would appreciate it if you knock prior to entering my office."

Eduardo said, "Hi Jefferson, I heard that you would be coming aboard for the next couple of months." He shook my hand.

I reached out to shake Escobar's hand but he didn't shake my hand. I said, "Ok."

Escobar said, "So you couldn't make it in the Big Leagues, so now you beg Constantine for a job to work at his company. We don't need losers on board our team."

I asked, "From what college did you graduate, Escobar?"

He replied, "I didn't need to graduate from college; I have hands on experience."

I said, "I know it was hard work having your father give you the position that you currently have. I would love to continue this conversation; however, Elizabeth and I were in the middle of a meeting and unless you have business to discuss concerning Medina and Santiago Global Oil, then we need to get back to that meeting." I then held the door open as they left. As they were on their way out I said, "It was nice seeing you again, Eduardo"

"I'll be stopping by to check on our investment over the next several weeks."

After they were gone Elizabeth said, "Jefferson, you handled that very well. I like you already."

I said, "Elizabeth, I want to learn everything that I can about what you do and what everyone else does, especially Eduardo and Escobar. I don't mind having homework. I don't currently have any on the job experience but I'm a quick learner."

She said, "For starters, we have several companies here at this location. They all fall under Santiago Global Holdings. The companies are: Santiago Iron Company, $260 million in revenue; Santiago Gold Company, $200 million in revenue; Santiago Minerals Company, $800 million in revenue; Santiago Global Chemicals, $180 million in revenue; Santiago Transportation & Tanker Company, $120 million in revenue; and Medina & Santiago Global Oil Company, $400 million in revenue, for a combined revenue of $1.96 billion.

I replied, "Mr. Santiago has built some strong and viable companies. Of all the companies, which company is least profitable and/or concerns you most? Wait, before you say anything let me write the company that I think you may say on a sheet of paper. So I ask again, what company is it?"

She replied, "Medina and Santiago Global Oil."

I flipped over the name that I had written down and it was the same name. She said, "You're not only smart in the books but you have common sense."

I said, "Thank you."

She said, "Mr. Santiago wants desperately to find a buyer for his 60% of Medina and Santiago Global Oil because he wants to sever his ties with Pablo Medina."

I replied, "I can contact several investment bankers that I know as well as I have several friends who fathers are big time oil men in Texas. I will check with them and let you know."

Elizabeth said, "That sounds great; keep me posted."

It was now 5 PM. I was like, where has the day gone? I told Elizabeth that I had to go to training at 5:30 PM. She said, "No problem. I will see you tomorrow morning."

When I arrived downstairs Javier was there waiting on me. He then took me to meet Presario for my first day of training. When we were pulling into the parking lot I saw Escobar talking to some guy. I could see the guy give Escobar a manila folder and Escobar got in his car and left. I waited until Escobar had left the parking lot prior to going into what appeared to be a storefront that sold vitamins and supplements.

I walked into the store and asked for Presario. The young lady asked, "May I ask your name?"

I replied, "Tell him Jefferson Robinson is here to meet him."

She replied, "Wait right here while I go get him." The guy who came out and said that his name was Presario was the same guy that Escobar had met earlier. Presario asked me to come into his office. Prior to sitting down I asked, "Could I use your restroom?"

He replied, "Sure, the restroom is around the corner to your right."

I said, "thanks."

While in the restroom I decided to turn on the recorder on my cell phone just as a precaution. I then flushed the toilet as if I was using it, then I washed my hands and went to meet Presario. He said, "You were referred by Dr. Dawson."

I replied, "Yes, that is correct."

He replied, "Dr. Dawson refers a lot of his patients to me."

I replied, "Dr. Dawson stated that you were an excellent trainer and could get me back to where I needed to be."

Presario said, "Yes, there won't be a problem getting you back to where you were and beyond."

I asked, "So when do we get started training?"

Presario responded, "I'm going to give you some ointment to place over the area of your injury as well as some supplements to take. Now you take these for two weeks and once they're gone, come back and I will give you another two weeks' supply."

I said, "But what about the training?"

He replied, "Jefferson, you will have to train on your own time; however, if you place the ointment on your injury twice daily as well as take the supplements, you will be in great shape within the next 60 days. Trust me, Jefferson, I have never let Dr. Dawson down yet."

I asked, "So what is in this ointment and supplements."

He responded, "All I can say is that they are all natural herbs."

I asked, "What is the cost for the ointment and supplements?"

He replied, "The cost is $10,000 for a 30-day supply. For a 60 day supply I will give you a deal of $ 17,000."

I replied, "That is a lot of money for supplements."

He replied, "It isn't a lot if you want to get back on the playing field. You can pay the girl at the register and I will see you in two weeks."

I said, "Thanks." I shook his hand and went to the register to pay for supplements. I gave the girl my Platinum American Express card in order to pay for the supplements. Once I got my supplements I got in the car with Javier and left. I had a very bad feeling about these supplements.

During my drive home I called Mr. Carlos and told him that I would like to meet with him. He said, "Sure Jefferson, what time would you like to meet?"

I said, "I should be by the Santiagos compound in about 15 minutes. We can meet at the guest house."

He said, "Fine, I will see you there."

When I arrived at the guest house Carlos was out front waiting on me. He shook my hand and said, "Buenos noches." Carlos went and hugged my driver Javier. Carlos and I then walked inside the house and went and sat at the kitchen table.

He asked, "So what is it you want to talk to me about, Jefferson?"

I replied, "I was referred by my surgeon to a trainer here in Miami who is known for getting athletes back to their peak performance after severe injuries. Therefore, the trainer and I were scheduled to meet this evening at 5:30 to start my training. However, when Javier and I pulled into his parking lot I saw Escobar talking to a man who gave him a manila envelope prior to Escobar getting in his car and leaving. I waited until Escobar had gone before getting out of the vehicle and going into the storefront. The man I was there to meet was Presario Gonzales, which turns out to be the same man that had given the manila envelope to Escobar earlier. During my meeting with Presario he sold me a 30-day supply of ointment and supplements for $10,000. When I asked Presario about my training he stated that he doesn't train; he just provides ointment and supplements." I said, "Mr. Carlos, this whole deal stinks. I called you because I wanted to see if you can use your resources and have the supplements as well as the ointment tested."

Carlos replied, "Sure, I can have someone take a look at these items and I will get back with you in a couple of days, Jefferson."

I replied, "Sounds great, sir, thank you."

After my meeting with Mr. Carlos I went and washed up for dinner. Prior to dinner I called Manuela. I said, "Hi, did you arrive back in Tuscaloosa ok?"

She replied, "Yes, I've just arrived back at my dorm. How did your first day at work go?"

I replied, "Everything was great with the exception of Eduardo and Escobar barging in on a meeting between Elizabeth and me."

She replied, "I'm quite sure that was interesting, nonetheless."

I replied, "Yes, it was, but I was able to handle the situation."

She asked, "So how did your training go today?"

I responded, "Well, it was quite interesting to say the least." I explained to her what happened.

She said, "That sounds strange. I wonder what Escobar was doing there."

I said, "I'm not sure but I had Mr. Carlos take the supplements and ointment and have tests run on them. I'm not going to use either the supplements or the ointment, nor am I going to go back to see that guy, Presario. I will continue to train on my own." I said, "Well, you have a good evening young lady. It is close to 7:30 pm and I don't want to be late for dinner."

"Yeah," she replied, "my mom doesn't like when you're late for dinner."

When I arrived at the main house for dinner Mr. and Mrs. Santiago were just being seated. Mr. Carlos and Sophia came in shortly after I did. During dinner Mr. Santiago asked, "Jefferson, how did you like your first day at the company?"

I replied, "I enjoyed my first day, sir. I was very intrigued by all of your companies." I said, "I told Elizabeth that I want to learn everything. Elizabeth is very knowledgeable."

He replied, "Yes, Elizabeth is the glue that helps hold everything together."

Mrs. Santiago inquired about my first day of training. I said, "Mrs.

Santiago, let's just say that this person isn't a trainer and I won't be going back to see him. I will work out and train myself."

After dinner, I told them goodnight and that I was going to head back to the guest house because I had a lot of reading to do. When I arrived back at the guest house I went and sat at the kitchen table and pulled the reports out of my brief case in order to go over them. Prior to reading the documents I decided to call my brother Jackie since he played professional football to see if he had heard about this guy Presario Gonzales. "Hey little brother," said Jackie, "how are you doing?"

I replied, "I'm doing fine." I explained to him everything about Presario Gonzales as well as Escobar.

Jackie replied, "Jefferson, you did the right thing by not taking those supplements or using that ointment because my gut is telling me that those items are some form of steroids."

I said, "If those are steroids then Dr. Dawson is in on the deal as well."

Jackie replied, "Please let me know the moment that Carlos gets the test results back."

I said, "As soon I hear something I'll give you a call."

Jackie said, "Sounds great, little brother. I'll talk to you soon."

After I got off the phone with Jackie I put in a call to several investment bankers as well as a couple of friends to see if anyone had interests in acquiring ownership in a Venezuelan oil company. My friend William (Billy) Lewis said that he would talk to his father and get back with me over the next couple of days. His father was no other than multi-billionaire Rory Lewis, a big time oil man in Texas. After speaking to Billy I started poring over the different reports about Mr. Sanchez's companies.

The next morning I was up at six and I went to one of the gyms on the property and worked out and rode the treadmill. After working out I went and showered and got dressed and went to work. I told Javier prior to him dropping me off at work that I would probably be working until 6:30 tonight.

"No problem, Mr. Jefferson, I'll be here by 6:30 PM to pick you up."

When I arrived at the office I stopped by Elizabeth's office to give her back the reports. I said, "Good morning, Elizabeth, how are you?"

She replied, "I'm fine, Jefferson, how about you?"

I replied, "I'm doing great. I just wanted to give you these reports back."

She asked, "So did you have a chance to go over the reports?"

I replied, "I sure did. I was up until two in the morning looking over all the reports. I wanted to talk to you about something."

She said, "Jefferson, can it wait until after our staffing meeting this morning?"

I said, "Sure."

She said, "We have a meeting at 9 AM in the conference room. I want you to meet the rest of our Accounting and Finance Group, as well as some of our Department Heads."

I said, "Sounds great."

She said, "Just a heads–up, Mr. Santiago will be in attendance as well." She said, "Your email address is already set up so when you turn on your desktop just go to Microsoft office and pull it up from there. I will be sending you an email shortly of who all will be in attendance, as well as their job titles."

I said, "Thanks" and then I went to my office. When I got to the office and turned on my computer, sure enough, the email was there with a list of department heads and personnel who were going to be in attendance. I printed a copy of that list so that I could study it prior to the meeting.

When the clock struck 8:50 AM, I made my way to the 31st floor to attend the Board meeting. When I arrived almost everyone was there, seated at the conference table. I said, "Good morning" and with my notebook and pen available took a seat at the table. When Mr. Santiago walked in the room everybody quickly stood up and said, "Good morning sir."

He replied, "Good morning" and asked if everyone was present.

Elizabeth responded, "Yes sir, everyone is present."

He then started the meeting off, "I'm not sure if you know it or not but we have a new person on our team."

Then Bryan Rivers, the Chief Operations Officer, said, "Yes sir, we have Jefferson Robinson, Right Fielder with the New York Yankees, who finished the season with a .375 batting average."

"Well thank you, Bryan, I wasn't aware that you were a big baseball fan," said Mr. Santiago. "Jefferson is going to be with us over the next several months as he fully recovers from an ankle injury that he suffered during the playoffs. Everyone make sure you treat Jefferson good because I'm hoping to have him aboard permanently." He finished by saying, "I know that Jefferson is going to bring the same fire, tenacity, devotion and attention to detail as he brings on the baseball diamond. I'm confident of that and I want y'all to make him feel at home."

I replied, "Thank you, Mr. Santiago, for giving me the opportunity to be a part of your great organization. I promise you as well as the rest of this team each day I'm going to bring my best. Therefore, please don't get upset if I ask you a lot of questions; it is just that I want to learn as much as possible."

The meeting went great. After the meeting I went to my office. A few moments later Elizabeth stopped by my office to see what I had wanted to discuss earlier. I replied, "I wanted to tell you about what happened when I went to meet the guy that I was supposed to train with yesterday."

She said, "So what happened?"

I explained to her everything that transpired. She said, "That sounds shady. Presario Gonzales, who owns the vitamin shop as well as several strip clubs, is one of our team member's boyfriend."

I asked, "Who might that team member be?"

Elizabeth responded, "Mia Acosta, one of our Senior Accountants."

I said, "Something is going on here; however, I just can't put my finger on it yet."

When I arrived home that evening Mr. Carlos stopped by the guest house. He said, "Good evening, Jefferson, how are you?"

I replied, "I'm doing fine, Mr. Carlos."

He said, "Well, your suspicions were correct as it relates to the supplements and ointments from Presario. They both are forms of steroids as well as illegal and probably shipped here from another country." He asked, "Have you contacted this Presario guy since you purchased these items?"

I replied, "Yes, I told him that I decided to work out on my own but thanks for his assistance. Mr. Carlos, I have a feeling that he and Escobar are doing more than just distributing steroids. Elizabeth told me that

Presario also owns several strip clubs as well as he is the boyfriend of Mia Acosta, a Senior Accountant at Santiago Holdings."

Carlos responded, "That isn't good."

I said, "I think we need to see if she is taking information from the office and/or giving Escobar information about the other companies."

He stated, "I will talk to Constantine tonight and I'm sure that he won't mind if we monitor Mia's desktop as well as put her under surveillance."

I said, "There is something else kind of strange that I have noticed; however, I need to gather additional evidence before I come to you and Mr. Santiago."

Carlos said, "Jefferson, that is good enough. I'm on my way to talk to Constantine right now."

I then called my brother Jackie. I told him everything that Mr. Carlos had told me. He said, "I'm glad that you didn't take any of that stuff, little brother. What is the name of the place Presario owns?"

I said, "It is called Just In Time Supplements and Herbs."

He asked, "Where are the steroids now?"

I said, "Mr. Carlos' friend is currently holding on to the steroids. I even have the recording on my phone of my initial meeting with Presario."

He asked, "Do you really?" I said, "Yep, I sure do."

He replied, "Make sure you don't delete it; you may need it for evidence."

I said, "I won't. Jackie, I have another call coming in. I will talk to you later."

On the other line was my friend Billy. He said, "Hey Jefferson, my father would like more information about the Venezuelan Oil company."

I said, "That is great. I will get with the Vice President of Finance and put together a portfolio as well as the financials and have it overnighted to you tomorrow."

Billy replied, "Jefferson, that sounds great. Once we go over the information I'll give you a call back."

I said, "Thanks Billy."

The next morning when I arrived at the office I went straight to Elizabeth's office. I said, "I have great news."

She said, "What might that be, Jefferson?"

I said, "We may have a potential buyer for the oil division."

She said, "Who might that be?"

I said, "Rory Lewis, the owner of Lewis Oil out of Dallas, Texas. He is a multi-billionaire."

She asked, "So how do you know him?"

I replied, "His son Billy and I graduated college together. They would like to see a portfolio of the company as well as the financials."

"Well Jefferson," said Elizabeth, "let me get with our legal counsel and draw up a Non-Disclosure Agreement and have it sent to them to sign prior to us sending over any documents."

She had the Non-Disclosure Agreement (NDA) drawn up and I emailed it over to Billy. They had the Non-Disclosure Agreement signed and sent back over right away. Elizabeth then began the process of having all the information gathered to be sent out via Express later today.

A little later that afternoon as I was stopping by Elizabeth's office I had seen Mia exiting her office. I asked, "So what did Mia want?"

Elizabeth replied, "Mia was inquiring about all the information being gathered about Medina and Santiago Oil."

I asked, "So what did you tell her?"

Elizabeth said, "I told her that we were putting on a presentation for some potential partners."

It was a grueling day; however, we were able to have the documents requested by Billy sent overnight to him. Elizabeth said, "Jefferson, once we get a response from Mr. Lewis we will then inform Mr. Santiago about the possible deal."

I replied, "Sounds good."

Over the next couple of weeks Elizabeth, Billy and I went back and forth discussing the potential deal. I buried myself, learning as much as I could about Mr. Lewis' company as well as learning about my work at Santiago Holdings. I was going over all the reports as well as financials. I was really learning a lot about the company. I became more fascinated with the work that I was performing as each day went by.

Manuela and I would speak over the phone daily and she would say how much she missed me. I was still in negotiations with Olivia as it related to my divorce. My attorney said the final sticking point was that

Olivia wanted a new car in order to finalize the divorce. However, she didn't want a regular car; she wanted a brand new $90,000 Range Rover Sport, fully loaded. I told my attorney, "No way."

He said, "Jefferson, if you want to get rid of this no-good excuse for a wife, then I suggest that you agree to purchasing the vehicle and we will have everything settled within the next couple of weeks."

I told him that I would send a $90,000 cashier's check over the next day. The next day I went to the bank and got the cashier's check, then I sent it via overnight to my attorney. Who would have thought that I would be where I was currently right now, about to get a divorce, not playing baseball and working in Miami for a multi-billion dollar corporation.

For the past couple of weeks I would go down to the port several times each week to check the reports on the tankers. I noticed that on all the shipments coming back from Venezuela the actual weight log showed more than the tanker would normally weigh coming from somewhere else with supposedly the same amount of fuel. Something just wasn't adding up. I decided to just go down to the port and stake out the area on the days that the shipment would come in from Venezuela. Everything looked normal to the naked eye; however, I was curious why there were a lot of large boxes being unloaded from the tankers even though we were transporting oil, not cargo. The oil had already been transported to the fuel trucks; however, there were 18-wheelers being loaded with boxes as well. It was now 7:00 at night and I saw Eduardo walk out of the office on the docks and walk out to meet Escobar as he arrived at the docks in his car. The two of them stood outside and talked prior to going into the office. I didn't go any further.

I immediately left the area without being seen and made my way back to the main street to catch a cab back to the guest house. The next day Elizabeth, Yadiel Figueroa, the Chief Legal Counsel, and I had a conference call with Billy, their legal counsel and the Vice President of the Lewis firm. The Vice President for Lewis Oil (James Stephens) stated that they were willing to give Santiago Holdings $240 million dollars in cash plus 80,000 acres of land which currently had active oil and natural gas wells in exchange for Santiago holdings' 60% stake in Medina and Santiago Global Oil.

Elizabeth stated for them to make their offer official and get it back to us in writing within the next 48 hours.

Billy stated that they currently had everything all drawn up and would have it to us prior to close of business today, as well as originals sent overnight to us. We said great and hung up the phone. After we got off the phone Elizabeth asked Yadiel whether or not he thought that what they were offering was a great deal. His response was it all depended on the value of those 80,000 acres and the current revenue being generated from the property.

Elizabeth stated that now it was time to contact Mr. Santiago. She gave him a call and explained everything as it related to the deal. Mr. Santiago stated that once we had the offer and had the opportunity to look over the offer, we could then meet. The offer came over from Billy as planned later that afternoon. Elizabeth, Yadiel, I and a host of other personnel from legal looked over the document. Elizabeth scheduled a meeting for 9:00 the next morning in order to meet with Mr. Santiago. I looked over the offer for the next couple of hours.

Billy called me around 5:30 p.m. I was still at the office. He asked, "So what do you think, Jefferson?"

I replied, "Everything looks good; however, I need more information on these natural gas wells."

Billy replied, "Check your email. I just sent you over information about those wells as well as the property." He went on to say that his father was very fond of me and he hated to see me suffer such a gruesome injury. He also said that those 80,000 acres were prime real estate and that if we sold the land itself it would generate revenue alone close to the amount that we were selling our interest in Medina and Global Oil for. Billy said, "Jefferson, my father wants to break into the oil industry in Venezuela."

I responded, "Perfect, I think the natural gas industry is really going to take off based on my readings and research."

Billy replied, "Jefferson, as soon as you hear something, please give me a call."

I replied, "Sure thing," then we hung up. I went over the information that Billy had sent over. It was quite informative. I looked at the clock; it was after 7 PM. I quickly hurried downstairs to meet Javier and head home for dinner. I just barely had enough time to wash my hands and meet everyone in the dining room for dinner.

I said, "Good evening" as I sat down to dinner.

Mrs. Santiago said, "We have missed you the past couple of dinners, Jefferson."

I replied, "I apologize, ma'am. I have been quite busy."

Mr. Santiago said, "Jefferson, Elizabeth sent me a copy of the offer from Lewis Oil earlier today. It looks like a great opportunity, so what are your thoughts?"

I replied, "I think that it serves a major purpose for several reasons, the first being that you are definitely not going to lose any money. Because after doing my due diligence I was told that the 80,000 acres is prime real estate. My friend Billy told me that himself earlier this evening over the phone. However, prior to him telling me I had already researched the matter.

"Reason #2, you will be adding a new revenue stream. Before you had only oil but now you have natural gas as well. The third reason is that modern shale gas drilling has experienced two distinct stages of growth, the first being in the 1980s and scaling up during the second stage currently. Based on research and current predictions Santiago Holdings should more than triple their investment from the Natural Gas Division alone. Then the fourth and final reason is that you will be free of the Pablo Medina Partnership." I concluded, "Mr. Santiago, based on research and facts, sir, this is a great deal on paper; however, it is a better deal off paper. My gut feeling is telling me that it is time to rid yourself of your business relationship with the Medinas."

"Jefferson, you are wise beyond your years," said Mr. Santiago. "I knew there is a reason why I like you. Well, enough about business. Let's eat; we will discuss business tomorrow," said Mr. Santiago.

Immediately after dinner Mr. Carlos walked with me outside as I was getting ready to go to the guest house. He said, "They have found evidence that both Mia and her assistant have been downloading company information to removable disks on numerous occasions." He also stated that they were going to make some changes after our meeting tomorrow morning.

I also told him about what I had discovered from paperwork from the tanker business as well as cargo being removed from the tankers each time the tankers return from Venezuela. I said, "I think that they are moving drugs."

He said, "I think we should inform Constantine."

I said, "I don't think that would be a good idea right now, because if we let him know what is going on and something comes out in the news prior to him signing the deal it will appear as if he was in on it as well." I said, "No, my thinking is that once he sells his percentage of the business he can then decide whether or not to continue to allow them to use his tankers. We can also confront Eduardo and Escobar at that time."

Carlos said, "Jefferson, it sounds like a strategic move. We will wait before we tell Constantine."

Once I had arrived back at the guest house I looked over the offer once more to ensure that I didn't miss anything. My phone rang and it was Manuela. I said, "Hi gorgeous."

She asked, "How was your day?"

I told her about how we had gotten an offer from a company to buy her father's percentage of his oil company.

She said, "That is great news, Thomas. My semester is busy since I'm taking the maximum credit hours allowed. I have barely spoken to Escobar." She said that each time she talked to him he stated that he was too busy to talk. The brief moment that she was able to speak to him she told him that they needed to talk; however, his response was that they could talk at their engagement party.

"Well, I guess you both will have the opportunity to talk at his party." I didn't tell her about the activities that had been going on at the port. However, after I had told her about the vehicle that Olivia wanted in order to finalize the divorce, she totally flipped. She said, "Jefferson, please tell me what the hell you saw in this girl?"

I responded, "Well, she and I dated for so long that I didn't care or I didn't notice all of her flaws."

I had a call coming in from Pedro. I said, "Manuela, I have a call coming in from your brother so I'll call you back tomorrow."

She said, "Ok, goodbye."

"Hey Pedro, what is happening, my friend?"

He said, "I hear you have been busy."

I said, "Yes, I have been enjoying everything. I love working at your father's company."

He said, "Well, he loves having you there." Pedro said, "I will be home tomorrow."

I replied, "I thought that you wouldn't be back until the engagement party."

He said, "I wasn't planning to be; however, Maria called and stated that she will be there in Miami for business for a couple of days so I decided to take some time off from training and come hang out for a couple of days." Pedro asked, "How has your training been going?"

I responded, "I have been utilizing a hitting coach for the past week. I feel great behind the bat."

Pedro said, "You have a very full plate, my friend."

I replied, "You just don't know how full my plate really is. I'll see you tomorrow. I'm fixing to get ready for bed."

The next morning I awakened around 5 AM and went and worked out. I was feeling excited about today. I really wanted to close this deal as soon as possible.

When I arrived at work that morning Elizabeth had everything in place for our 9AM meeting. While we were in sitting in the conference room waiting on Mr. Santiago's arrival she stated that instead of transferring Mia and her assistant, she would probably lay them off with a nice severance package. However, she wanted to finalize this deal prior to finalizing the decision.

When Mr. Santiago arrived he got right down to business. He stated that there were a few concerns regarding this deal; however, those concerns were addressed over dinner last night. He asked if anyone else found anything they felt might impede this contract. Everyone said everything looked good. He said, "The next order of business is to contact Pablo and let him know my intentions as it relates to selling the business."

He picked up the phone and dialed Pablo's number. He had the call on speaker. "Hello Pablo," said Mr. Santiago.

"Hi Constantine," said Pablo.

He said, "I have you on speaker and I'm calling to let you know my intentions as it relates to Medina and Santiago Global Oil."

"What's going on, Constantine?" asked Pablo.

"Well, I have a buyer for my 60% of the business."

"What are you talking about, Constantine? You can't sell your half of the business," said Pablo.

Mr. Santiago responded that he started the business and if he wanted to sell half of his business he could. Pablo stated that if Mr. Santiago sold his percentage of this business then he would do the same. Mr. Santiago said, "That is up to you if you want to sell your percentage of the business."

"So how much are you getting?" Pablo asked.

Mr. Santiago said that he was getting $160 million. I was wondering why Mr. Santiago would say that we were getting $160 million when it was really $240 million.

Pablo then said, "Well, I want $180 million.

Mr. Santiago responded, "How do you expect to get more than I'm getting when you own 20% less of the company?"

Pablo responded "Because I'm Pablo Medina."

Mr. Santiago responded that he would make the call and let him know something shortly, then he hung up the phone.

Elizabeth asked, "So Mr. Santiago, how did you know that he would want more money?"

He responded, "Because Pablo is a very, very jealous and greedy man. I knew that he would want to make more money than me. Ok Jefferson, let's call Lewis Oil and see if we can close this deal."

I said, "Yes sir." I called Billy to see if he was at his office yet. He said that he was. I asked him if he and his father and their legal counsel could be available for a conference call in five minutes. He said sure. When I called him back in five minutes he had everyone present. I then introduced the Lewis Team to our team. I told him that everything was ok with the offer and that we would be ready to meet and sign the deal to make everything valid. Then I said however, we ran into one issue: the 40% partner of the company wanted to be bought out for $180 million. Mr. Lewis quickly responded that he didn't want to buy the junior partner out of the company because he wanted to keep Venezuelan ownership in order to keep local ownership and presence. Mr. Lewis said, "Furthermore, if there isn't a minority partner from Venezuela then the deal is void."

Mr. Santiago then told me to put Mr. Lewis on hold. I told everyone to hold on for a moment. Mr. Santiago then stated that he would buy out Mr. Medina's share for $180 million in order to salvage the deal; however, Mr. Lewis would have to pay Pablo Medina the $180 million in order to close the deal. Then the Lewis company would own Pablo Medina's 40% share of the company then wire Santiago Holdings $60 million dollars for an additional 20% ownership, which would give Lewis Oil 60% ownership and leave Santiago Holdings with 40% ownership. Everyone was shocked as well as excited about this opportunity. I then took them off hold and explained to Lewis Oil what Mr. Santiago had said. Mr. Lewis and his team were onboard. Everyone was excited.

Mr. Lewis and Mr. Santiago each stated that they were looking forward to the partnership. Elizabeth then stated that we would have the contract drawn up on our end per our arrangement and the Lewis Company needed to draw the contract up between them and the Medina Company for Pablo Medina. We set a closing date for the following Thursday. Mr. Santiago then called Mr. Pablo back and informed him of the great news. Mr. Pablo was excited. Mr. Santiago said, "This is a great day" after he had gotten off the phone with Pablo Medina. Mr. Santiago said, "Let's get the contracts drawn up so that we can get this thing finalized. We have a wonderful opportunity in front of us. Not only do we get to keep our oil interest in Venezuela but now we can expand those interests into prime areas in the United States as well as expand our interests in the natural gas arena." Mr. Santiago said, "Let's keep the portion about Santiago Holdings becoming the minority owner to the Lewis Company private." He stated that as far as everyone else was concerned we were selling our Medina and Santiago Oil Company to Lewis Oil.

After the meeting Elizabeth gave me a high-five. She said, "We make a great business team."

I said, "We sure do. We just have to close the deal."

She agreed as she went to ensure that the additions were made to the contract. That evening when I arrived at the Santiagos' for dinner, not only were Pedro and Maria there but to my surprise, Dad and my brother Jackie were there also.

I said, "What are y'all doing here?"

Dad asked, "So you aren't you happy to see your old man?"

I said, "Sure I am" as I hugged him and my brother. I also hugged Maria and Pedro.

Dad said, "Well, I came down with Jackie for several meetings. It just so happened Maria was at one of those meetings as well, and she invited us to come to dinner tonight."

I said, "You could have at least let me know that you were coming."

He replied, "It was last minute for me. I only came to formally introduce Jackie to an old buddy of mine."

I jokingly asked, "So are you sure that y'all don't work for the FBI or CIA or somebody instead of the Department of Transportation?"

Jackie responded, "I wish that we did because I'm tired of looking at plans about new highways and over-paths and turnpikes, etc."

Everyone started laughing. Mr. Santiago said, "You should be proud of your son because not only is he a hell of ballplayer but he is damn good businessman." He said, "He learns quickly."

Dad responded, "Yes, he is a quick learner."

Mrs. Santiago then asked, "Mr. Robinson, did you and your family get our invitations for Manuela's engagement party in almost three weeks?"

Dad responded, "Yes, we sure did and we will definitely be there."

Mr. Santiago said, "Thomas, you and Jackie will be our guests. Either you can stay here at the main house or at the guest house with Jefferson."

My father said, "Constantine, thanks for the offer; however, we already have our hotel rooms."

Mr. Santiago said, "Good enough. Well, at least be our guests for the engagement party."

Dad responded, "Fair enough, we will be your guests for the party."

After dinner we said good night to the Santiagos then Dad, Jackie and I walked back over to the guest house. While we were sitting at the kitchen table I told them about the strange activities that had transpired at the port concerning our tankers. I said, "I'm willing to bet money that Escobar and his father were shipping drugs."

Dad asked, "Well, did you contact the authorities?"

I replied, "No sir, I didn't want to get Mr. Santiago in trouble."

Jackie asked, "So how do you know that he isn't involved?"

I said, "Well, I'm confident that he isn't involved." I said, "After next week we won't have to worry about dealing with Pablo Medina or his son anymore."

Jackie replied, "Isn't Manuela going to marry his son?"

I said, "Let's just say I don't think that is going to happen either."

After an hour Jackie and Dad stated that they had to leave because they had an early meeting tomorrow prior to them flying back to Alabama. I gave them a hug and had Javier drop them back off at their hotel. The next week went by rather quickly. It was finally contract signing day. We had our legal counsel present as well as Pablo Medina's legal counsel along with Escobar Medina, who had Power of Attorney to legally sign the contract, although as a precaution we had a neutral party in Venezuela witness Pablo Medina sign and notarize the contract then scan and email the document to us. Then we had Escobar sign and execute underneath his name as well as have the document notarized again. Then the $180 million was wired to Pablo Medina's designated bank account.

Once Pablo Medina had sold his interest in the oil company Escobar quickly left the building to go celebrate because his father was wiring $50 million to his account. Mr. Santiago signed the contract selling his 20% of Median and Santiago Global Oil to The Lewis Company. He then also signed showing that he and Mr. Lewis were now the owners of the newly-formed Lewis PMS Global Oil Company. However, there was one hiccup that we had hit. In Venezuelan bylaws it stated that the local company or Resident Company had to be owned 51% by a native of Venezuela in order to count as a Venezuelan company Therefore, Mr. Santiago had to pay an additional $32 million in order to purchase the 11% from The Lewis Company. So now Sanchez Holdings owned 51% of Lewis PMS Global Oil and The Lewis Company owned 49%. Mr. Santiago and Mr. Lewis signed the new contract then they shook hands to seal the deal.

Then everyone screamed and clapped. Mr. Santiago then said, "I would personally like to thank Elizabeth and Jefferson for all of their hard work in order to make this deal happen. I would like say to Jefferson that you are a natural at business and I hope that you would stay aboard." He said, "I would like to say to The Lewis Company that we are pleased to be in partnership with your company. I know that based on your experience in the industry we can go to new heights."

It was now time for Mr. Lewis to speak. Mr. Lewis said, "I would like to thank Jefferson also for showing the same mental toughness and tenacity that he shows on the baseball diamond inside the boardroom as well. It is his friendship with my son Billy that allowed this deal to happen. I would like to say to Mr. Santiago and the rest of the Santiago Holdings team that I look forward to a long and prosperous relationship with your firm. Once again, thank you."

We sat around drinking champagne and beer and eating catered food. It was a great day. I was truly blessed to be part of such a great organization. Just as I was about to call Manuela to tell her the good news she called and said, "Congratulations."

I said, "Thank you, ma'am. The deal has now been completed."

She said, "I hate to see Dad sell his business."

I started laughing. She asked, "What is so funny?"

I said, "I forgot, you don't know, do you?" I then explained to her what had transpired and that her Dad was still the majority owner of the company, just with a different name.

She responded, "That is totally awesome."

I said, "So in actuality he just added two more revenue streams to Santiago Holdings with the creation of Santiago Natural Gas, which owns 80,000 acres in Texas and Oklahoma, which also includes oil wells. So now he has oil in the states as well."

Later that evening after we had eaten dinner, Mr. Santiago, Mr. Carlos, Pedro and I had gone into Mr. Santiago's study. He broke out the Cuban and Venezuelan cigars as we sat around and drank cocktails and smoked cigars. Mr. Carlos then said, "Constantine, there is something that Jefferson and I must tell you." Then Mr. Carlos told him about the loading and unloading of cargo from the tankers as well as the weight differential of the tankers on days when they came back from Venezuela. I also showed him the footage taken of the activities at the port.

Mr. Santiago asked, "So why are you all just now saying something about this?"

I replied, "Mr. Carlos wanted to tell you right away; however, I wanted to wait until this deal was done prior to letting you know. Just in case they were raided or caught prior to the deal closing, I didn't want you to be a culprit because of your prior knowledge."

"Well thank you for waiting," said Mr. Santiago.

Pedro said, "I can't believe that they are transporting drugs using your tankers, Father. Then to top it off Eduardo is involved in this conspiracy as well."

Mr. Santiago said, "I'm going to wait until Pablo is in town for the engagement party before confronting him. In the meantime we will let Eduardo continue to work there until we finish all of Medina and Santiago Global Oil business. Once we have severed all ties with Medina and Santiago Oil and everything is transferred, I want to have that office closed down and all new business take place at our building. I want us to take the 27th floor, which is vacant, and convert it into The Lewis PMS Global Oil Company."

Pedro asked, "What is the meaning of the initials PMS?"

Mr. Santiago replied, "It stands for Pedro, Manuela & Sophia.

The next day Elizabeth and I began the process of separating all the business transactions for Medina and Santiago Global Oil and converting everything into Lewis PMS Global Oil. We were letting all of our clients know about the name change and the merger of the majority partner with the Lewis Company. We let them know that Mr. Santiago was still the majority owner and that they would continue to receive the same great service. We also let Bryan Rivers, the Chief Operations Officer know to get started on the buildout of the office space on the 27th floor.

After work, I had Javier take me to a variety of stores to do some shopping as well as get a special gift for Manuela. I asked myself, "What can I get her that will make her remember me and that day for the rest of our lives?" I needed to search no further. I knew just the gift.

CHAPTER EIGHT

The Art Of Betrayal

It was now the day before Manuela's engagement party. She was flying in this afternoon from college for spring break. She had taken her last final exam at 10 AM. I told Javier to pick my parents, grandparents, Jackie and Suzette, and my sister up from the airport at 1:30 PM and take them to the guest house. My brother Isiah and Sandra weren't arriving until 5 PM. They were flying in from New York. Isiah had taken vacation and flown to New York to spend time with Sandra. I told him that he could pick them up and take them to the guest house and that I wouldn't be ready until 6:30 PM. I was doing a final walk-through of the renovated 27th floor when Elizabeth had stopped by to tell me that she was about to leave.

"They have done a wonderful job on this floor," she said.

I replied, "They sure have." I hadn't noticed but it was almost 6:30 p.m. I said, "I didn't realize the time. I need to leave as well."

Elizabeth asked, "So are you seeing anyone, Jefferson?"

I replied, "Technically, no I'm not, because I was waiting for my divorce to be final. I didn't want to have anything on my conscience. However, my divorce was just finalized yesterday. My attorney emailed me a copy of the divorce earlier today. Therefore, I'm getting ready to go give a big kiss to this wonderful woman I have fallen in love with over these past several months. She flies into town today."

Elizabeth replied, "Whoever she is, she is a very lucky woman. So will I see you at Manuela's Engagement party tomorrow?" she asked.

I replied, "I wouldn't miss it for the world."

Elizabeth gave me a kiss on the cheek and a long embrace. She said, "We not only make a great business team but I'm confident that we would have made a great team in every other way." She said, "If your relationship doesn't work out you know where to find me." We then said goodbye.

Javier was waiting on me when I walked out the front door of the building. When I got in the car I said, "You have had a very busy day today, huh Javier?"

He replied, "Yes sir, Senor Jefferson, a very busy day."

He said, "You have a very beautiful family."

I said, "Thank you. They didn't give you too much trouble, did they?"

He replied, "No senor, they didn't give me any problems."

When I arrived at the guest house I told Javier that he could have the rest of the evening off. I was expecting to see my family when I walked through the door of the guest house; however, no one was there. It was about 7:05 PM so I took a quick shower and changed into some linen pants, a brown long-sleeve shirt and brown loafers. I then walked into the main house and everyone was standing around in the kitchen.

Mr. Santiago said, "My boy Jefferson" as he walked up and shook my hand and gave me a hug. Then I hugged my grandpa and grandma.

Then I gave my sister Eve and my mom big hugs. Then I hugged Sandra, my brothers, Uncle Abraham and Dad. I looked around; however, I didn't see Manuela. Then I felt some warm hands over my eyes. I already knew who they belonged to. I then turned around and gave her a big hug and a kiss on the cheek. I asked, "Where are Pedro and Maria?"

Mrs. Santiago said, "They should be here at any moment from the airport." She then said, "I feel left out. What, I don't get my normal kiss, Jefferson?"

I replied, "Oh, I'm sorry Mrs. Santiago: as I gave her a hug and kiss on the cheek. Then I gave Sophia a hug as well.

A few moments later Pedro and Maria walked through the door. Pedro yelled, "So was everybody waiting on us before eating?"

We all said, "Yes, we were." We were all starved. He and Maria hugged everybody. Then we sat down to eat dinner.

I said, "I would like to tell everyone that it is official."

"What is official?" asked Eve.

I said, "I'm officially divorced. I received an electronic copy of the divorce earlier today via email."

My grandma had to get up out of her seat and come give me a hug and kiss. She said, "Thank you, Jesus!"

Mom looked at me and said, "God is good."

I replied, "He is good all the time."

Everyone else said, "Congratulations."

I said, "I also would like to say something else." I stood up. I said, "You know, in life bad things happen but at the time you don't realize that it was actually a good thing. Because that is what happened with my previous relationship, my previous marriage. If you all recall the last time that we all had dinner together, I was about to go propose. However, prior to me going to propose this other young woman had told me that she loved me and that she had loved me for a long time. I was taken aback because I didn't see it coming. However, it didn't stop me from proposing to the woman that I married. Fast forward to my wedding day: I saw this person with another man and I was jealous. I had this little voice inside telling me that I was marrying the wrong woman. This little voice then turned into a yell: *Don't marry this woman.* However, I didn't listen. Instead, I made one of the biggest mistakes of my life. However, like I said before, things happen for a reason, right? Over the course of the next seven months this person helped raise money for a fundraiser, helped me fry seafood and prepare a meal for friends; she even helped me clean the house. She did something else very special; she woke up early one morning and gathered Suzette, Maria and Sandra and prepared on old fashioned country breakfast. The breakfast was great, by the way. I know Mom and Grandma were proud of her; after all, they were the ones who gave her the pointers on how to prepare the meal. Let me tell you that after she had prepared that big breakfast, the deal was done. However, there was more. During the New Year's Eve party she was not only beautiful in the pink dress that she wore but she was the perfect hostess. It was at that moment, as I looked across the room and watched her talk and laugh, that I realized that I had found my true love." I said, "Mr. and Mrs. Santiago, I not only love you both and love this family, but I love your youngest daughter Manuela Juliana Santiago. Mr. Santiago, with your blessing I would love to ask your daughter Manuela Juliana Santiago to marry me."

Mr. Santiago replied, "Jefferson, I didn't see this coming but you definitely have my blessing, son."

Then I turned to Manuela and got on one knee. I said, "Manuela Juliana Santiago, I'm sorry for taking so long to realize that the love I wanted and the woman that I wanted was right under my nose all the time. These past months have been the best months of my life. It feels so good loving somebody when somebody loves you back." (Then my uncle said in a low voice to Dad, "That damn boy is quoting Teddy Pendergrass.") I said, "Will you marry me?"

She replied, "Oh yes, Thomas Jefferson Robinson," as she kissed me passionately. I then put a two-carat pink diamond on her finger.

The next thing I knew Pedro stood up. He said, "There is something that I would like to say." He said, "I have always wanted a brother and even though my parents weren't able to give me one, I'm grateful that God brought me you, Jefferson." Pedro came over and gave me a hug. He said, "Welcome to the family, my brother." Pedro then said, "I have something else to say. I was going to say this tomorrow; however, I said, what the hell—why not tonight."

Mr. Santiago said jokingly, "Is it another wedding proposal?"

Pedro then got on one knee He said, "Maria Sanchez, this past year with you has been truly wonderful. I used to have eyes for multiple women; however, I now only have eyes for you. When I'm with you I hate leaving you. I can't breathe without you; you complete me." (My Uncle Abraham whispered to Dad again, "Now this damn boy is quoting Toni Braxton.") Then he and Dad started laughing.

Pedro said, "Maria Sanchez, will you marry me?"

She replied, "Yes Pedro, I will marry you. This is such a special day. I wish that my parents were here."

"We are here sweetheart," said her father from the back of the room as he and Mrs. Sanchez and her sisters and brother walked into the room.

The butler brought additional place settings. We all then ate dinner. While we were finishing our dessert Mr. Santiago said, "I would like to say something and no, I'm not about to propose." We all laughed. He said, "I would like to say that this is one of the proudest moments in my life. I could not be prouder of the man and woman that my daughter and son have chosen to marry. Jefferson and Maria, you both were heaven sent. You know, I had been preparing a speech to say tomorrow night as it relates to the previous man that I thought that Manuela was going to marry. However, the words that I wanted to put on paper I couldn't say to the audience because everyone would have thought that I was crazy. However, now my job has been made a million times easier because of the man that I know Jefferson to be." He said, "The times that I have met Maria the woman I have known her to be, so with that let's raise our glasses—salud."

Maria asked, "Pedro, did you have this planned, flying my family in town?

He replied, "Well yes, I did. I was going to propose tomorrow night but when Jefferson surprised me and said that he was going to propose tonight, I said why not tonight? It all worked out because your family were able to catch an earlier flight."

Maria then kissed Pedro and said, "Thanks for making me so happy."

After dinner we sat in the living room and talked till the early morning hours. The next morning Mr. Santiago called me and Pedro to his study. He said, "Well men, we have a dilemma here. I have called for Pablo and Escobar Medina to come to the house at 1PM today. I wanted to talk to them first as opposed to having them come to the restaurant tonight; that way they will have time to stop their friends from coming to the restaurant." He said, "However, the backup plan is for their guests, the ones that show up, have them attend dinner at Sonny's at no cost. Sonny's is directly across the street from Wyntria's, where we are having the dinner party." He said, "I currently have the name cards and invitations and all of the programs being rushed to show an engagement dinner for Pedro Felix Santiago and Maria Alexandra Sanchez and Thomas Jefferson Robinson III and Manuela Juliana Santiago."

I responded, "Thank you sir."

He said, "I also called y'all here today in order to let you know that this could get ugly. Pablo is a proud man and may think that this is a sign of disrespect." Mr. Santiago said, "I also called Eduardo here today because I want to settle all family business. Y'all can leave but be back here in my study by 12:30 PM."

Pedro and I then went back to hang out with Maria and Manuela. Mr. Santiago told Carlos to increase the security for the dinner tonight as well as increase security at the compound. Pedro and I went to his father's study at 12:30 PM. When we got there Mr. Santiago and Carlos were already there talking.

Mr. Santiago said, "I want you both to only speak when spoken to when they get here."

Pedro and I said, "Yes sir."

He said, "Any little thing can send Pablo over the edge."

Sure enough, Carlos's assistant escorted Pablo, Escobar and Pablo's bodyguards into the room at 12:55 PM. Mr. Pablo Medina walked in and kissed Mr. Santiago on both sides of his cheeks. He then shook Carlos's hand. Then he walked around and gave Pedro a hug. "What is this, Little Pedro is now this big time Americano Baseball Player." Pablo said, "And this must be Negro Jefferson Robinson that I have heard so much about." He shook my hand and said, "You don't look so tough."

"So why do you have all of these security guards in our meeting?" asked Mr. Santiago. Mr. Pablo Medina had four security guards in the room with us and two outside the door as well as four security guards sitting in one car and two sitting in his vehicle.

Pablo responded, "These four guys go wherever I go. So what is it that is so important that have you bring me over here to meet as opposed to discussing later tonight at the dinner tonight? Is it that you feel bad about double-crossing me about the oil company deal?"

"What do you mean, I double-crossed you?" asked Mr. Santiago.

Pablo responded, "I know that you're still the majority owner after you had stated that you were selling your interest in the business."

Mr. Santiago replied, "Pablo, you had every opportunity to keep your interest in the business. After you wanted to sell your share of the business as well, Pablo, I had to purchase your share in order to salvage the deal. Because the buyer would only do the deal if there remained a local content owner. I was only able to increase ownership from 40% to 51% because government regulations said that we had to do it that way in order to operate."

Pablo said, "You cheated me on the amount that you paid me also."

Mr. Santiago replied, "Pablo, you and I both know that you weren't cheated. Pablo, you have done quite well over the past 20 years in the amount of money you have received from the business. Therefore, I don't see how you can sit here and say that you were cheated when you received $180 million from a company that you have never stepped one foot into. I put my money blood, sweat and equity in Global Oil."

Pablo responded, "I guess you have forgotten that I once saved your life."

"No, I haven't forgotten. How could I?" said Constantine. "You remind me every chance you get." Then there was a knock at the door. It was Eduardo. "You're late," said Constantine.

"I'm sorry," said Eduardo.

Pablo said, "Well, to make it up to me I would like to use your cargo ships and tankers to transport cargo from Venezuela to here."

Mr. Santiago responded, "I've been told that you have already been using my ships and tankers. My answer to you is no on using my ships and tankers. You will not use my ships to transport your drugs."

"I told you, Father, Eduardo's loyalty is with them," said Escobar.

"Yes, you did, son," said Pablo.

Eduardo jumped up all scared and ran to Pablo and said, "I didn't say anything, sir. I swear I didn't."

Mr. Santiago replied, "Eduardo didn't inform me of anything

although he should have because he is my nephew and I have taken care of him his entire life. However, I'm glad to know that he is a part of this conspiracy. Therefore, Eduardo, enclosed in the envelope is a check for $2 million. Please consider it a severance package. I would hope that you don't go spend it all on strippers. I took you into my home and raised you as if you were my son, and this is how you repay me. This is the worst betrayal of them all; you're my sister's child. Eduardo, please leave my study and leave my presence because you're dead to me."

Javier escorted Eduardo off the property. Mr. Santiago said, "Pablo, to answer your question it wasn't Eduardo who told me about your activities. It was your carelessness with documenting the weight of the ships as well as coming down to the port to load boxes that weren't even on our load documents."

Pablo said, "So this is how you treat me. We are almost family. Our kids are about to be married."

Mr. Santiago said, "Well, that is what I wanted to talk to you about as well, Pablo. Manuela has called off the engagement to Escobar. She no longer wants to marry him." said Mr. Santiago.

"This is blasphemy,' said Pablo. "How dare you wait till the day of the engagement party to make this announcement."

Mr. Santiago replied, "Pablo, Manuela has been trying to tell Escobar over the past several weeks but he never wants to talk to her. However, I didn't find out until last night that her heart belongs somewhere else and it's not with Escobar."

"You piece of shit," said Escobar as he looked over at me.

Mr. Santiago responded, "No, you are the piece of shit. I know that you have been messing around with countless women, screwing strippers and doing drugs. Therefore, Escobar, don't blame anyone but yourself."

Escobar started cursing. He said, "Fuck this family. Fuck Manuela and fuck you" as he tried to hit me. I quickly caught his hand and took him to the floor and punched him in the face. Pablo's guards went for their guns; however, they were far too slow because Carlos and Mr. Santiago had already had their 9 millimeters drawn and pointed at the guards.

Pablo said, "Constantine, calm down."

Mr. Santiago replied, "I'm very calm. I just get pissed when I have a snotty nose punk curse my daughter and curse me in my own house. I can't believe that I almost allowed your disrespectful thug son to be a part of my family. Pablo, it is time for you, Escobar and your personnel to leave my property. Please contact all of your guests and let them know that there won't be an engagement dinner tonight as it relates to Escobar and my daughter. I will have his and Eduardo's office furniture, computers and all of their personal items delivered to wherever you want them sent. However, they are not to come to the property or they will be escorted off the premises. I believe that concludes all of our business together, both professionally and personally."

Pablo replied, "Constantine, you think that you are so smart. However, it is over when I say it's over. You wait until the day of the engagement dinner to cancel the entire engagement. I have a problem with that. You cheat me out of my portion of your business. I have a problem with that. I no longer have resources to transport my cargo to the United States. I have a problem with that. How does that make me look? I have very important people that I have made promises to in order to have that cargo delivered to the U.S. These are the kind of people that you don't break a promise to," said Pablo.

Mr. Santiago replied, "I have no control over who my daughter chooses to fall in love with or marry. However, I'm glad that she had a change of heart as it relates to your sorry-ass son. As it relates to the buyout of your portion of the business, you had every opportunity to keep your ownership but you were the one who suggested selling your interest in the business because of your greed. Everything was done legally and fairly. I'm thankful that my staff noticed the inconsistencies of the weight of our tankers, which threw up red flags.

"Pablo, when is making millions and millions of dollars not enough? I will tell you when it isn't enough; it is when greed comes into play. Pablo, your greed has you in this situation with whomever you made promises to have cargo delivered to, which isn't my concern."

Mr. Santiago said, "Carlos, please have security escort these individuals off my property."

"Constantine, you haven't heard the last from me," said Pablo. "I promise you."

Mr. Santiago said, "Pablo, I have made you a very, very wealthy man. I'm sorry that you feel that way."

Escobar walked out cursing. "Fuck the Santiagos. I will make every last one of you pay, especially that little bitch Manuela and her negro boyfriend."

Carlos ensured that they had left the property. Then he came back into the study. "Constantine, they have gone," said Carlos.

"So have all of our devices been planted?" asked Mr. Santiago.

"Yes sir, our inside guy has planted the listening devices in all the vehicles including Pablo's."

Jamie then brought the device into the study and attached it to the speaker phone. We could then hear Escobar and Pablo talking about what they were going to do. They stated that they were going to fire bomb the restaurant tonight once they knew that everyone was in the restaurant. They talked about making the entire family and me pay dearly.

"Carlos, contact your resource down at Miami Dade and let them know to have some undercover cops camped out near the restaurant tonight," said Mr. Santiago. "Please give them the description of the vehicles as well as license plate numbers; also give them information on Escobar's goons as well. We will need to beef up the security here at the compound as well as at the restaurant tonight. We also need to be wary of everything coming to and from the restaurant as well."

"No problem, Constantine," said Carlos. "Jamie, make sure that we have our best guy listening to their conversation at all times."

"Pedro and Jefferson, y'all be careful also," said Mr. Santiago.

"We will leave here at 5:30 PM in order to get to the restaurant a little early," said Carlos.

When Pedro and I walked out of the study Maria and Manuela were sitting out in the foyer waiting on us. They ran up and hugged us. Manuela asked, 'Is everything ok, Jefferson? I saw Escobar leaving the study and they were very upset. Escobar was cursing while walking out and when he saw me, he called me a bitch."

I said, "Don't worry, sweetheart. I will never let anything happen to you."

The four of us started walking to the guest house. I looked out at the yacht sitting in the back of the estate. I said, "Wait here, I need to ask Carlos something."

I ran back inside the house and knocked on the study door. Mr. Santiago said, "Come in."

I went in and said I just had a quick question. "Do we have any boats or security that guard the entrance to the waterway that leads into the back of the property?"

Carlos said, "No, we don't. We just have men protect the back perimeter."

I said, "Ok. How about personnel on the yacht that guards the entrance?"

Carlos said no. I said, "Just a suggestion—if we can plant maybe four guards on the yacht with night vision goggles just in case."

"No problem said," Mr. Santiago. "Carlos do we have enough personnel to make this happen?"

"Yes," said Carlos.

"Thank you, sir." I then turned around and walked back outside. I thought that Manuela would have walked to the guest house already but she was there waiting for me. I said, "Thanks for waiting," then I gave her a big kiss. I said, "You taste so good."

Manuela replied, "You haven't tasted me yet."

I said, "I sure haven't, but I'm planning on changing all of that later." We then held hands and walked into the guest house. Everyone was in the kitchen standing around the long island and sitting around the island and sitting at the kitchen table talking. My grandma and Mom were talking about how much they love South Beach and that they could get used to living in Miami.

I said, "Yes, Miami is a beautiful place. I smell something good."

Mom and Grandma had made fried chicken, potato salad, fried green tomatoes and two big pans of homemade buttermilk biscuits. I said, "You all know that we are going to a dinner later."

Mom said. "Everybody knows that once you eat that diet food, you're hungry 10 minutes later."

Grandma said, "I don't see anybody else complaining except you, Jefferson."

I looked around and said, "You're correct, Grandma."

Manuela was the first one in line, grabbing a piece of fried chicken, potato salad and fried green tomatoes. Manuela said, "I have never had fried green tomatoes." While I was fixing my plate Mr. and Mrs. Santiago and Sofia walked into the kitchen. Uncle Abraham said jokingly, "I'm glad that y'all could make it to the little house."

Mr. Santiago said, "Looks like we are just in time." Mrs. Santiago then went and hugged Mom and Grandma. Then Mr. and Mrs. Santiago got a plate as well. We all sat down around the island and the kitchen table and ate. Maria's father said, "This is some good down home cooking."

My grandma brought out two pitchers of her famous lemonade. Mr. Santiago said, "This is some of the best fried chicken that I ever had, and these fried green tomatoes really complement everything."

Manuela said, "I agree, Father, these fried green tomatoes are so good."

Mrs. Santiago asked who made the potato salad and lemonade. Grandma said that she had made the lemonade and that my sister Eve made the potato salad. She replied, "Everything is so good."

I said, "You haven't had the dessert yet. You have Mom's famous buttermilk pound cake and Grandma's pecan pie." Grandma also put on a big pot of coffee. Mr. Santiago said, I think I'll try a slice of pound cake and a cup of coffee.

Everyone was saying how good the dessert was. Mr. Santiago said, "I don't think that we have to go to dinner later. What do y'all think?"

Dad said, "It is time to take a nap."

Manuela said, "Oh, we are having dinner later so y'all better save room."

I said, "Don't worry, sweetheart, I will have room for dinner."

She said, "Thank you, sweetie" as she gave me a kiss.

I said, "I was hoping that you were going to give me you last piece of pecan pie."

She said, "I love you Thomas, but this pie is so-so-so good."

After we had finished our dessert Mr. Santiago said, "I would like speak to everyone for a moment. As you know Manuela was engaged to Escobar Medina, whose father is Pablo Medina, who is a notorious gangsta and my former business partner from Venezuela." Then he explained how he met Pablo and how Pablo became his business partner.

"Well Pedro, Jefferson, Eduardo, Carlos and I met with Escobar and Pablo earlier today. Needless to say, it didn't go well. Escobar and Pablo blamed everyone except themselves. Carlos has beefed up the security here on the compound as well as at the restaurant tonight. Pablo was told to contact all of their guests and tell them that the dinner was cancelled. However, just in case that he doesn't our security team will be checking the guest lists and the guests who aren't on our lists will be directed to a restaurant across the street for them to enjoy a free meal and drinks."

Then I got a call from Elizabeth, who said to turn on the TV, that the Feds had just arrested Presario Gonzales. She said they raided his vitamin shop as well his strip clubs. She said, "It appears that he was a big time drug dealer as well."

I said, "Thanks Elizabeth." I quickly turned on the TV.

Manuela said, "What's wrong, Jefferson?"

I said, "That was Elizabeth and she said that Presario Gonzales was just arrested. She said, that his vitamin shop was raided, as well as his strip clubs. When I turned on the TV the reporter stated that he was selling steroids to high school, college and professional athletes. The reporter also stated that he was a drug dealer selling cocaine and heroin at his strip clubs here in Miami. I was so thankful that I didn't take the ointment or the supplements that this guy sold me. My sister Eve asked, "So aren't you afraid that your name may come up since you did purchase ointment and vitamins from this guy?"

I said, "You are correct because I paid with a credit card. However, I have nothing to hide. They need to get my surgeon, because he is the one who referred me to Presario. I think it is only a matter of time before they get Escobar because he is in bed with this guy. I know he is."

"Well, it is getting close to time for to leave," said Mr. Santiago. "We are going to go get ready."

Manuela gave me a kiss and said that she would see me shortly. I then went to my room and showered and got dressed. I was wearing a white linen suit with a nice short-sleeve black linen shirt, black belt and black loafers. Once I was dressed I went to the living room. Dad and Jackie were already in the living room talking. Dad said, "So what else happened today during your meeting, Jefferson? I know Constantine didn't tell us everything today."

I then explained to Dad and Jackie what had taken place. Dad said, "Well, I'm willing to bet that they have a warehouse somewhere storing all the cocaine, especially if you said that they had just gotten a shipment in on Wednesday. Escobar is probably nervous right now since Presario was arrested earlier today. That is why we have to be very aware tonight, because when a dog is wounded that is when he is more dangerous."

"I agree," said Jackie.

Javier then came in and said that the vehicles were ready. My parents, grandparents, Uncle Abraham and sister Eve were in one Suburban. Isiah, Sandra, Jackie and Suzette were in another vehicle. Maria's family was in a vehicle that directly followed Isiah's vehicle. Mr. and Mrs. Santiago, Sophia, Carlos and the driver were in another vehicle. Maria, Pedro, Manuela, Javier, a bodyguard and I were in the last vehicle, followed by a Suburban with four security personnel. There was also a lead vehicle that had four security personnel that led the caravan of cars. Carlos also had four motorcycles with security personnel riding on them as well within the caravan.

Everything went as planned as we were en route downtown to the restaurant. When we arrived at the restaurant there were additional personnel there as well. Carlos also had undercover personnel at the nearby coffee shop and hotel as well as the restaurant directly across from where we were having the dinner. Mr. Santiago was expecting 100 guests, all of which were present. Everyone was seated at different tables; however, there was one large table in the front of those tables, which is where Manuela's family, Maria's family and my family were seated. Manuela and I sat next to each other and Pedro and Manuela sat next to each other.

Mr. Santiago stood up and said, "I would like to thank everyone for coming out tonight. I would just like to say that I'm a very proud father. These past two days have been some of the best days of my life. It feels good to see your children grow up and chase their dreams, fall in love and be happy. I know some of you are a little confused, especially after seeing a change as it relates who Manuela is engaged to, as well as instead of one engagement there are two. Well, if you are surprised imagine how I felt when I found out about it last night. It seems like everybody knew that there was a change in the air except me." Everyone started laughing.

"However, I'm so thankful for the change. Because my daughter Manuela deserves to have someone that cares about her, someone that is respectful to her, but most importantly someone that loves her. I'm positive that she has that someone in Jefferson. The same is true for my oldest child, my son Pedro. I must admit I thought that I had another 10 to 15 years before he gave up his playboy ways. I'm grateful for Maria. So with that being said I'm going to turn it over to the future brides and grooms."

"Thank you, Dad," said Pedro. "I would like to thank everyone for coming out this evening in order to share the engagement of Maria and me as well as my beautiful sister Manuela and my best friend Jefferson. This is a special evening and I want to say thank you."

Manuela then stood up and said, "Good evening everyone. I guess you were expecting to see another groom sitting here but sorry, that's not happening. I would like to say that I have loved Jefferson since the first time that we met. However, he was clueless. He was in love with someone else he gave his all to; however, that person didn't appreciate him. I almost made the same mistake of marrying someone that didn't appreciate or love me the way I'm supposed to be loved. I had asked God to give me a sign that I was making the right choice marrying Escobar. Then the next time I spoke to Jefferson he stated that he was getting a divorce. He then told me about on his wedding day how he had this little voice telling him that his bride wasn't the right person for him; however, he ignored that little voice and his wedding turned out to be a disaster. He told me not to make the same mistake. It didn't take much because Escobar wasn't worthy to be my husband. I know deep down that Jefferson is my soul mate and I want to spend the rest of my life with him and oh yeah, have a lot of babies. So with that being said, let's eat drink, dance and have a great time."

The waiters and waitresses started serving food to the guests. I could hear my Uncle Abraham say, "This is some damn good bird food." Everybody started laughing.

"Wyntria's is one of my favorite restaurants," said Manuela.

I said, "Yes, the food is good." I saw Carlos come whisper in Mr. Santiago's ear. Then I saw them go to the back.

"Constantine, my resources at the Miami Dade just told me that they intercepted some of Pablo's men down the street with pipe bombs and assault weapons," said Carlos. "They also told me that they have a warrant out for Escobar's arrest because Presario is singing like a canary. He is telling everything."

"Excellent work, Carlos. Because of your due diligence, we have stopped a massacre tonight."

Elizabeth came up to me and said, "Congratulations, Jefferson. You and Manuela make a wonderful couple."

I said, "Thank you, Elizabeth."

The engagement dinner was wonderful. We had a great time. Prior to us leaving, Mr. Santiago called me and Pedro into the back room and gave us an update on everything. I said, "Thank God for Carlos." After we met with Mr. Santiago everyone loaded up into the vehicles and went back to the compound. We arrived back at the compound around 11:30 PM.

We all went to the main house for drinks. Dad then stood up and said, "I would like to make a toast to the couples tonight. I would like to wish you much love and success. May you always trust and love each other. Then for the boys, don't forget to take the garbage out." Everyone laughed. "I also would like to thank Constantine and Alejandra for being such wonderful hosts. We have truly enjoyed our stay here these past couple of days. I also would like to extend an invitation to you all to come to Alabama for our annual Mother's Day Cookout which will be held on Saturday, May 13. We normally have a lot of family and friends in town for this event."

"Well Thomas, please count on us being there said," Mr. Santiago.

"That is great news," said Dad. He then said, "I believe that I had a few too many drinks so my wife and I are getting ready to head to the guest house and go to bed."

Prior to Dad leaving Carlos called Mr. Santiago into the hall to inform him of the latest with Pablo and Eduardo. Mr. Santiago then came back in and said, "Everyone, I was just informed by Carlos that Law Enforcement and Drug Enforcement Agents have raided several warehouses near the port and found cocaine and employees belonging to Pablo and Eduardo. Based on that information and the testimony of Presario, Eduardo has moved up the most wanted list. Therefore, we are going to be on heightened alert; however, there is no reason for panic, for you'll just go to the guest house and get some rest."

Uncle Abraham said, "That left over fried chicken is calling my name." So he left with my parents, grandparents and sister and went back to the guest house. Manuela, Pedro, Maria, Isiah, Sandra, Jackie, Suzette and I all decided to go hang out at the yacht. First we had Elena make us some sandwiches from the kitchen, then we walked over to the yacht. They had security personnel stationed there as well. We went to the main deck and prepared some glasses of alcohol, played music on the iPod and then begin to eat our sandwiches.

The song "Let's Get It On" by Marvin Gaye came on and I grabbed Manuela by the hand and we stood up and started dancing. She said, "I love you, Thomas Robinson."

I said, "I truly love you, Manuela Santiago."

Manuela said, "Let's take a walk down below to one of the rooms."

I said, "You don't have to tell me twice."

We told everyone that we would be back soon. They all started laughing and making cackling sounds. No sooner had we walked in the room and closed the door than we were all over each other. I picked her up against the wall as I took her shirt off. We were like wild animals. We made love it seemed like forever. After we were done Manuela lay on my chest as we lay in the bed. She said, "That was everything that I thought it would be and more."

I said, "I don't smoke but I need a cigarette; that's just how good it was." We started laughing. We then went for round two. Afterwards we hurried up and got dressed and went back up to the main deck. Everyone started clapping. We stayed there talking until three in the morning, then I kissed Manuela and I went back to the guest house with my brothers and their mates as Pedro, Maria and Manuela went to the main house. The next morning Mom and Grandma were up bright and early and cooked a huge Alabama breakfast, with homemade buttermilk biscuits, grits, eggs, bacon, ham, and toast. They also had help from Manuela, Maria, Sandra, and Suzette. We also had fresh fruit, strawberries, grapes, and cantaloupe.

As always, the smell of the good bacon woke me from my deep sleep. I slept on the sofa because I gave my room to Uncle Abraham. I then went to the restroom, brushed my teeth and took a quick shower. When I walked into the kitchen everyone was already in there eating. There were Mr. and Mrs. Santiago, Maria's family, Pedro and Maria, Manuela, Sophia, Sandra and my family. I said, "Thanks everyone for waiting on me."

Manuela said, "I haven't started eating yet. I was waiting on you."

I said, "Thank you, sweetheart" as I walked over to give her a kiss. Even Carlos and Javier were in there eating. I said, "Even you, Mr. Carlos?"

He responded, "Well, I had to grab a quick bite so that I can get back to work." Everybody started laughing.

Grandma said, "Even the girls were in here helping cook this breakfast."

I said, "That is great." My phone rang and it was my agent Jerry. I said, "Hey, what's up, Jerry?"

He said, "I will be emailing the contract for the ankle wrap endorsement over to you and Isiah a little later today. However, I was checking to see if you are going to try to attend Spring Training camp in Tampa."

I said, "I know that training camp already started; however, I was going to at least attempt to attend in a couple of weeks."

"Jefferson, based on your injury," said Jerry, "if you didn't want to play anymore that would be ok. We have a large insurance policy as well as because you were injured in a game the majority of your remaining contract is guaranteed."

I said, "That sounds great. I have some good news; my divorce was final last week."

"Oh, that is good news," said Jerry.

I said, "I also have even better news. I got engaged to Pedro's sister Manuela on Friday."

"Well congratulations, Jefferson. She seemed to be a wonderful young lady," said Jerry.

I said, "I will keep you posted, Jerry; my breakfast is getting cold."

Dad asked, "So you are going to attend spring training."

I said, "I'm going to give it a shot. But my heart isn't in it anymore. I love what I'm currently doing; however, I owe it to myself as well as the

Yankees to give it a shot. Well, I have some good news. I have another endorsement. This one is for ankle wraps. Isiah, you should be receiving an email with the contract and all of the details. It is a three-year, $1.5 million deal." I went and kissed Manuela and said, "Thank you for helping prepare this awesome breakfast." Everyone laughed and talked and then my family and Maria's family got ready to go to the airport. All of their flights were flying out in the afternoon. Everybody said goodbye as they left for the airport. We really had a great weekend.

CHAPTER NINE

I Bet You Never Thought

During dinner at the main house that night it was only Manuela's parents, Sophia, Mr. Carlos, Pedro, Maria, Manuela and me. Manuela was in town for another week prior to her going to college and Maria and Pedro were flying out the next afternoon.

"So have y'all decided when you would like to get married?" asked Mrs. Santiago.

Maria said, "We were discussing November 18th of this year, the week before Thanksgiving."

Manuela said, "We were thinking about December 16th of this year, the week prior to Christmas."

"That would be wonderful," said Mrs. Santiago. "That doesn't give us much time. We need to starting planning."

"I agree, Mom," said Manuela."

We would like to have our wedding in Miami. Preferably this time in a church," said Jefferson.

Maria said, "We would like to get married in Connecticut in a Catholic church since we are both Catholic."

Mrs. Santiago said, "Just let me know if you need anything, Maria. I mean anything."

After dinner the men went to Mr. Santiago's study and the women went to the kitchen. "Jefferson, so what are your plans next month once you attend spring training in Tampa Bay?"

"Well sir, my heart isn't in playing baseball anymore. However, I must attend Spring Training to ensure that is the case. I owe it not only to myself but my team as well."

"Jefferson, don't rush. Take your time," said Mr. Santiago. "Jefferson, it is because of you that Santiago Holdings is free and clear of any dealings with Pablo and Escobar Medina as well as we have a new company here in the states. It is because of you that my daughter didn't make the major mistake of marrying Escobar. I t is because of you that my company isn't blasted on the news as it relates to drug charges. You have done so much not only for my businesses but for my family," said Mr. Santiago. "I know that it has been a crazy ride these past couple of months but it is because of you that this entire conspiracy is unraveling," said Mr. Santiago. "**I bet you never thought** that you would experience such a crazy past several months, huh Jefferson?"

"Well, no Mr. Santiago, I didn't; however, I would do it over and over again for this family, the people that I love."

"Well, you take as much time as you need; your position will be waiting on you once you come back."

The next day Manuela and I rode with Javier as we took Pedro and Maria to the airport. We also had four security personnel riding behind us in a Suburban. After dropping them off at the airport Manuela and I went to go grab lunch at Capital Grill. While having lunch I told her that I would fly out with her on Saturday when she went back to Tuscaloosa. She said, "That is nice of you."

I said, "I want to ensure that you make it back safely as well as we can have a couple days of time alone."

She responded, "I would like that very much." Manuela went to work at the office with me over the next several days. Her office was right next to mine. I enjoyed working with her. She was a natural working in the office; everyone was drawn to her. Not only was she beautiful but smart as well.

On Friday morning, her last day there, her father called us into his office. He said, "Manuela, you and Jefferson work well together."

She said, "Yes Father, I enjoy working with him. We make a great team."

I looked at her and said, "Yes we do, sir."

"I can't wait until the day that I have you both aboard full time. I want you to be careful, sweetheart, when you get back to school. Be mindful of your surroundings," said Mr. Santiago.

"I will, Father," said Manuela.

"Jefferson, the same goes for you. I know that you report to Spring Training on Monday so you be careful as well."

"If it is ok with you, sir, I asked Elizabeth to send me reports and things that I can address out of the office on a daily basis. She currently has a secure laptop for me to utilize. "Yes, that is fine, Jefferson."

The next day we said goodbye to Manuela's family as Javier took us to the airport. We had a good flight to Tuscaloosa, then we caught a cab to the Marriott Hotel. We both were tired when we checked in so we took a nap. When Manuela woke up she saw me staring at her. She said, "What is wrong?"

"I was just thinking how I'm the luckiest man in the world." I said, "I love you, Manuela Santiago." We ordered room service and then watched movies the rest of the evening.

On Monday, after I ensured that she was safely back on campus, I caught a cab to the airport to catch my flight. I arrived in Tampa Bay, Florida that afternoon and reported to Spring Training the next day. All of the guys came up and congratulated me when I walked in the club house. The skipper came over and said, "Welcome back." The practice went well. I hit the ball great; however, it was kind of difficult running the bases.

After practice the Skipper called me into his office He said, have a seat Jefferson you looked pretty good today. He said, "Jefferson, **I bet you never thought** that you would experience such a gruesome injury, especially so early in your career. However, you have handled it like a veteran. You have worked hard and gave it your all. It isn't easy to make it to the Big Leagues but you have never taken your ability to play this game nor playing the game for granted. Whatever you decide to do in life, I know that you are going to be successful doing it. Therefore, give it your all while you here and let the chips fall where they may."

I said, "Thank you sir" as I left his office. I went and showered. Several of the guys had asked if I wanted to go out for some drinks I said, "No thanks. Maybe some other time." I then caught a cab back to my hotel.

The next several weeks of spring training went great. I played well in the games. During our game against the Minnesota Twins I hit a line drive to the short stop . I was racing to beat the throw and stepped on the bag wrong and tweaked my ankle. I was able to get up and walk off on my own, even though I was limping.

It was at that moment, as I was sitting on the table in the locker room as the doctor was looking at my ankle, that I knew that I didn't love playing baseball anymore. If you knew me, you would know that baseball has always been my first true love. However, I knew now that I didn't want to spend the next 10 to 15 years being away from Manuela 90 to 100 days per year. I wanted to be able to come to her beautiful, smiling face each night when I left work. After I had taken my shower I stopped by the skipper's office and told him that I wanted to retire. He didn't try to talk me out of it; he understood.

The team scheduled a conference for me to announce my retirement a couple of days later. To my surprise my family, Manuela and Manuela's family were present for my announcement. I was surprised that I wasn't sad about leaving the game that I love.

Pedro called me on my cell to congratulate me and apologize that he wasn't able to be there for my retirement because he had a game. He did say that he had just purchased the house next door to my house in

Greenwich, Connecticut. I said, "Not to worry because Sandra is going to take good care of you."

He said, "Yes, Sandra said the renovations should be done by July."

I said, "That is awesome. We are going to be neighbors. I have a reason to keep the house now."

He said, "Yeah Jefferson, **I bet you never thought** that we would soon be brothers-in-law as well as neighbors."

I said, "I know, Pedro."

After the news conference my family and Manuela's family went out to dinner at Bern's Steak House for our final night in Tampa Bay. Mr. Santiago said, "I would like to propose a toast to Jefferson. I would like to say congratulations on your retirement but most importantly welcome to the family and welcome aboard."

I said, "Thank you, sir."

My sister Eve asked, "So do you have any regrets about walking away from your first love, the game of baseball?"

I said, "No, I don't, little sis. I'm at peace with my decision to walk away from the game. Everything just felt right about me leaving. I'm looking forward to the next chapter of my life with Manuela and working at Sanchez Holdings. Plus I still have my endorsements."

"Yeah, it was great seeing Jerry again today," said Dad.

I said, "Well, he says that I should have a lot more endorsement opportunities coming across his desk. We will use the money from endorsements to pay for our new home."

Mr. Santiago said, "You will do no such thing. After the amount of money that you have saved as well as brought to the company, the least that we can do is buy you and Manuela the home of your choice."

I said, "That is nice of you, sir. Speaking of houses, Pedro just informed me that he just closed on a house in Greenwich right next to mine."

Manuela said, "I'm glad that he purchased that house. It had a lot of charm."

I said, "Yeah, wait until Sandra finishes putting her touch on it. Well sweetheart, at least we can keep the house now since we are neighbors to your brother and future sister-in- law."

"Sounds wonderful to me," said Manuela. "Well family, I forgot to tell everyone that our wedding date is December 16th of this year."

"That is awesome," said Eve.

My Uncle Abraham said, "I believe that you're going to be ok this time around, nephew."

I said, "I guess that I can take that as a compliment, Uncle Abraham."

Mom said, "We only have a couple of weeks until the cookout. I just want ensure that everyone will be there."

I said, "Don't worry, Mom, we will be there."

The next day I flew back to Tuscaloosa with Manuela to ensure that she arrived safely back on campus. I stayed the night at the Marriott and flew back out the next day to Miami. Javier picked me up from the airport. "Buenos noches, Senor Jefferson. Welcome back."

I said, "Thank you, Javier."

When I walked into the guest house Anabella came running and gave me a hug. "Welcome back, Senor Jefferson."

I said, "Thank you, Anabella. I will only be here a couple of weeks and then we will be headed back to my parents' house for our Annual Mother's Day Cookout on May 13."

"That is wonderful, Senor Jefferson."

The next couple of weeks in Miami went by rather quickly. I flew on the private plane with Mr. and Mrs. Santiago, Sophia, Carlos and six security personnel, along with the two pilots, I asked Mr. Santiago if he had heard anything about the whereabouts of Escobar. Carlos said his resources were saying that Pablo was back in Venezuela; however, Escobar was still here in the Florida area. He said, "I told everyone to not let their guard down."

We arrived in Mobile around 1 PM and there were three Suburbans waiting to take us to Leroy. We arrived at my parents' house around 2:30 PM. I told Carlos that he and several of his team members could sleep in the guest house as well as we had several rooms in the new barn. Mr. and Mrs. Santiago were my parents' guests; they would be staying at their house. When we got there Sandra, Maria, Pedro and Manuela had already arrived. They were at my main house. We stopped at my parents' house first, where my parents and grandparents were sitting on the porch drinking lemonade. When we arrived they got up and hugged Mr. and Mrs. Santiago, Sophia and Carlos first.

I said, "What's up? I can't get any love."

Mom told Mrs. Santiago, "Come on girl, let me show you to your room. I'm sorry that it's not the Taj Mahal."

Mrs. Santiago said, "What are you talking about, Anna Mae? Constantine and I weren't born with silver spoons in our mouths. When we got married my family was too poor for us to stay there so he and I stayed with his parents. There were 14 of us in a three-bedroom house with one bathroom inside and an outhouse out back. Some nights we had to warm our bath water. So I'm able to adapt to any situation," she said jokingly.

Mom said, "Alejandra, you are my kind of girl."

Mrs. Santiago then said, "You have a lovely home."

Mom also showed Carlos his room across the hall from Mr. and Mrs. Santiago. He was never too far from Mr. Santiago's side. I then took Carlos and showed him the property. He wanted to set up perimeters before nightfall as well as for the cookout tomorrow. After showing him the perimeters I showed him the barn where we had three bedrooms, as well as my guest house, where there were two bedrooms and a sofa. Carlos went back to my parents' house. I went to my main house.

When I walked through the door the guys were around the bar and the girls were in the kitchen. When I walked in I said, "It is nice to see that everyone has made themselves at home." My beautiful fiancé came, in jumped in my arms and gave me a kiss. I said, "Hi beautiful."

Isiah, Jackie, and Pedro were sitting around the bar drinking. I gave everyone a hug. Then the doorbell rang. I said, "Come in." It was no other than my man Tiger. He came running in and gave me a hug. I said, "What's up, Tiger?"

He said, "Congratulations to you and Manuela."

I said, "Thank you. You already know everybody with the exception of Manuela's friend from college, Rosetta. Rosetta, please meet Tiger. So what are you drinking?"

"I would like a Crown on the rocks." I made him a Crown on the rocks then I made me a Tanqueray and Tonic. I said, "What's going on here in the kitchen?"

The girls said, "We are going to be cooking dinner tonight."

I said, "So what is on the menu?"

Manuela said, "We are having a seafood dinner tonight. We have Lobster, Fried Shrimp, Fried Catfish, Baked Catfish Shrimp Scampi and Grandpa Robinson is cooking the Shrimp Boil (which includes Shrimp, Corn on the Cob and Potatoes)."

I said, "I can't wait." Grandpa was out back at my cabana preparing the seafood boil.

"My parents, your parents and grandparents will be coming here for dinner tonight as well. Suzette made a big pot of rice for the Shrimp Scampi. I see you are using my technique to prepare the fish and shrimp, sweetheart," I told Manuela. The food was finally ready by 6 PM.

Manuela said, "Since it is so gorgeous outside we are going to eat out by the cabana and on the patio."

"That sounds great to me."

We all then went outside where Dad and Grandpa were doing the Shrimp Boil. They also had Mr. Santiago helping them. Mom, Grandma and Mrs. Santiago were sitting by the pool drinking Sangria. They were laughing and having a great time. When we brought the food outside everybody got their plate and sat at the patio tables as well as the table under the cabana.

I said, "Please wait prior to eating. Manuela would like to bless the food."

After blessing the food Uncle Abraham said, "This my favorite niece right here. There is no way in hell that white girl would have done that."

Isiah said, "Uncle Abraham."

Manuela and Maria also saw to it that the security was well fed. I looked over and saw Rosetta and Tiger becoming real friendly. Everyone was having a wonderful time.

Carlos came to Mr. Santiago around 9 PM and said that he had some bad news. He stated that Eduardo had caught Anabella out shopping and beat her up pretty badly. She took a severe beating before telling him where we were. "Constantine, I don't want to scare everyone; however, we need to be prepared when they get here."

Mr. Constantine then called Dad, Grandpa, Jackie, Isiah and me out by the cabana. He explained to us what had happened. I was pissed. Dad said, "We don't want to interrupt the girls having a good time tonight because I doubt if they are able to make their way here tonight, therefore, why don't y'all walk over to my house."

Mom asked where we were going. Dad said that he needed to show us men something. Then Dad called Maria to come bring something back from the main house. When we went into Dad's house he took us all downstairs into the basement. He then removed a little ornament on the wall that had numbers for a code. He then pressed a code and the wall opened into a stairway. We went down the stairs into this hidden room that had cameras which showed the entire property and stretched out to the highway. Anyone sitting in this room could see anyone prior to them getting on our property from any direction.

My grandpa then opened this gun case and brought out additional weapons. There were assault weapons, 9 millimeters, night goggles, and walkie talkies. He then said, "If you take this door here it leads to the barn. This door here leads to Grandpa's house. Once you get to the barn there is another door that leads to Jefferson's house and another door that leads out near the tree house."

I said, "What is it that you and Grandpa really do, Dad?"

He said, "Your Grandpa and I both retired from the Central Intelligence Agency (CIA)."

"Hell, you mean the CIA," I replied. I said, "If you and Grandpa retired from the CIA then that means Jackie and Maria are CIA as well."

"That is correct," said Jackie.

Maria then said, "I wanted to tell you, Pedro; however, I had to wait until after this mission was over."

Grandpa then said, "Several years prior to me retiring I had been on the heels of Pablo Medina, who is a notorious, ruthless criminal in Venezuela. I had been tracking him for his arms dealing, not his drug dealing. However, the trail went cold after he became a business owner with Santiago Global Oil. He continued dealing drugs; however, he went dark as it relates to arms dealing. My boss then pulled us off his case. I wanted this bastard because he was responsible for several of my friends being killed on a mission in Venezuela. He was directly responsible. After I retired, Thomas's missions were mostly dealing with Panama and Afghanistan. However, when Jefferson started telling us about this

Presario character as well as when he mentioned Escobar and Pablo Medina's names, I knew that it had to be the same Pablo Medina. We were in Miami to meet with my old contact from the Drug Enforcement Agent. We brought Maria down to meet with them as well."

"So that was you as it relates to the raid of Presario's supplement store and strip clubs?" I asked.

"That is correct," said Dad. "The same goes with the raid of Escobar's warehouses. We may might not be able to get him for the arms dealing; however we can sure get him for the drugs."

"It was the best thing you ever could have done," said Constantine. "I'm glad to be rid of Pablo from my business as well. It is my hope to be rid of him for good because I don't want to have to keep looking over my shoulders."

Dad then said, "Carlos, you can have a couple of your men come down here to monitor the property while the other men get some rest, because we will need them fresh tomorrow."

"That sounds good said," Carlos. "In the meantime, we can go out and enjoy the rest of our night."

Grandpa said, "I don't think they will try anything as long as we have all of these people here tomorrow. We can shut everything down earlier than usual tomorrow. We can have all the women come down here where they will be safe."

Constantine said, "Well you don't know my wife. She can handle a gun better than the average man."

I replied, "So can Mom and Grandma. We can have them come here for safety as well as give them weapons."

Then we left out of the secret space and walked back into the basement. Dad opened the refrigerator door and got two cold bottles of Sangria out and gave them to Maria. He said, "We had to have a reason for bringing you over."

Carlos took two of his men to my parents' house to the secret room in order to monitor the property. When we got back Manuela said, "We were about to send a search party out for y'all." She then asked if everything was ok.

I said, "Everything is fine." I was shocked my parents, grandparents and Mr. and Mrs. Santiago were still going strong at midnight. Everyone was having a great time enjoying each other. However, I couldn't help but think about what was going to happen tomorrow not if, but when Escobar and his goons arrived. As I looked at my father and grandfather I thought about what they had to go through over the years while fighting to keep our country safe. They risked their lives each time they left this small town of Leroy; however, we never noticed anything out of the ordinary. They were always there for birthdays, holidays, baseball games and Tae Kwon Do Tournaments. Then there was my brother Jackie who graduated in finance from the University of Alabama, retired from playing football in the National Football League and is now doing the same job as my father and grandfather. It made me proud to be a member of this family.

My grandparents were now up dancing to Johnny Taylor's "Disco Lady." Our family loves old school, music especially the blues. The next thing you know my parents and then Manuela's parents were out there dancing also. We all stood on the sidelines cheering them on. I was sitting in a lounge chair when Manuela came and sat in my lap. She said, "Thank you, Jefferson."

I said, "Thank me for what?"

She said, "For just being you. Thank you for all that you have done for my father's business, for my family, but most importantly, thank you for loving me. I have never seen my parents this happy and having so much fun. This is one of the happiest days of my life. I love you, Thomas Jefferson."

I said, "Thomas Jefferson Robinson," laughing.

She then gave me a kiss. Pedro and Maria came and sat next to Manuela and me. Pedro said, "Mom and Dad are having a wonderful time."

I said, "Yeah, Jimmy Smits and Wanda De Jesus are having a ball."

Manuela hit me on the arm. I said, "It is true. That is who they look like."

I hadn't even noticed Rabbit, Tiger's brother, was here also. He was sitting talking to Sophia and Eve. He must have come while we were at my parents' house. Uncle Abraham was over by my parents' house next to the grill. He was roasting a pig and he had a goat wrapped in foil sitting on top of coal roasting underground. Manuela wanted to walk over to see the pig. Marie and Pedro walked over with us as well. When we walked over to Uncle Abraham he said, "Yeah nephew, you might learn something watching your uncle."

It was past one in the morning. I said, "I'm watching, Unc." A few moments later I saw my grandparents, parents and Manuela's parents walk over to where we were. Mrs. Santiago said, "Look Constantine, they're roasting a pig. Do you remember how we use to roast pigs like that in Venezuela?"

"Yes dear, I sure do."

Uncle Abraham said, "I bet you they won't taste as good as mine."

Mrs. Santiago said, "Well, time will tell, Abraham. I will let you know tomorrow."

My grandparents said, "We are turning in for tonight. We will see y'all bright and early tomorrow."

Uncle Abraham said, "Goodnight, Pop."

Then my parents and Manuela's parents said goodnight as well as they went inside the house. My Uncle Abraham and his girlfriend Sylvia and his other two friends Jimmy and Robert and their girlfriends would probably be there all night cooking and drinking. They would probably take turns sleeping in the little house next to my parents' house., The little house had a bathroom with shower a bunk bed and a sofa bed along with stove and refrigerator. We told Uncle Abraham goodnight and that we would see them tomorrow morning. When we arrived back at my house they were still going strong in my backyard.

"Sweetie, I'm ready to go to bed," said Manuela.

I said, "Ok, we can go in a little bit."

She then repeated herself. "Sweetie, I'm ready to go to bed right now."

I said, "Oh well, let's tell everybody goodnight." We then got up from the chair holding hands and told everybody that we would see them tomorrow. We then went in the house. I said, "Let me get a bottle of Ozarka water."

She said, "Well, I will be in the bedroom."

I grabbed a bottle of water out of the refrigerator and went to the bedroom. When I walked through the door she was lying on the bed completely naked. I went to the bathroom and got the massage oil, then I came back in the bedroom and turned off the lights. I then got undressed and got on my knees beside her and put massage oil over her back as she was lying on her stomach and gave her a full body massage for 30 minutes. I caressed every part of her body. She said, "Mr. Robinson, you're doing a marvelous job."

I said, "Well, it is my neighborhood."

We then made love for the next few hours and fell asleep in each other's arms. I was up bright and early the next morning. I washed my face and brushed my teeth and put on a pair jeans, cowboy boots and work shirt. I gave Manuela a kiss; she asked where I was going.

I said I was going outside to see if my uncle needed any help. I went out and Uncle Abraham was still going strong. I said, "You still at it, Unc?"

He said, "Well, I slept for about four hours, nephew, but I'm ready now."

I then went inside to see Dad, Mom and Grandma had just finished cooking breakfast. Manuela's parents were already downstairs sitting at the kitchen table talking. They asked where Manuela was.

I said, "She is still sleeping. I'm just in time for breakfast." I quickly washed my hands and fixed my plate after everyone else had fixed their food. Then I fixed my plate and sat down to the table to eat. While we were eating Mom asked Dad whether or not there was any movement concerning Escobar coming here today. I said, "Mom, how do you know about that?"

She replied, "Mamma knows everything."

"So you and Grandma have known about your husbands' real occupations all of these years?"

"Yes, that is correct, son. If you truly love someone, there is no such thing as secrets. You tell the truth regardless of how bad it may hurt."

"Amen to that, sister," said Mrs. Santiago.

Mom said, "We will get through today as we have gotten through every other obstacle."

Grandma said, "There are some strong men at this table; however, there are some strong women sitting at this table also. Some of us gave birth to some of the men sitting at this table. And you know what? We know how to shoot too."

Then Grandma, Mom and Mrs. Santiago gave each other a high-five.

"Dad and Grandpa, is there anything that you'll need me to do?"

"Well, the Barbecue Master, Isiah, will be on the grill. Your Uncle Abraham has the Goat and Roasted Pig ready. We have all of the sides available: potato salad, Baked Beans, Corn on the Cob, Boiled Seafood, Boiled Crawfish, Watermelon. We also have the desserts as well. Well I'm going to go see if my sleeping beauty is awake yet."

When I walked back outside Isiah was already on the grill cooking. Jackie was assisting him. I said, "Hey brothers I'm glad to see y'all are up."

Isiah responded, "Well, some people have work to do."

Jackie said, "I know you are nervous about Escobar, little brother; however, everything is going to work itself out. Dad and I contacted some of our friends with the Drug Enforcement Agency (DEA) to let them know that we were expecting company later today. They currently have all the small airports under surveillance in Mobile, Mississippi, Chatom and Jackson. They want to nail this Escobar creep as bad as Grandpa wanted to nail Pablo. They currently have several teams that should be arriving shortly." Sure enough, three SUVs pulled up in front of my parents' house. There were two guys who got out of the vehicle and went inside the house.

Isiah said, "I will stay and man the grill."

Jackie and I went in the house after the agents. Shortly afterward Maria walked into the house as well. One of the men was Jim Dean; he was a Caucasian male, medium build, in his mid-60s. He came inside and hugged Grandpa and Dad and also Mom. He then introduced the man with him, who was Billy Reed. Dad told him he could talk in front of everybody.

He said, "Some of our sources in Florida have told us that two private planes carrying roughly 12 men each had departed from outside Miami with coordinates headed to Mobile Alabama. We aren't sure who is on the plan; however, they were confident that it could be Escobar. If that is Escobar it will put them getting here around 6 PM or maybe a little before today. Therefore, we need to have this place clear of all civilians prior to that time."

Dad introduced them to Mr. Santiago and Carlos then showed them to the private room downstairs. I followed them to the room as well. Mr. Jim said, "This is perfect, Thomas. My men can take over here; you can have your men go get some rest. They will need it for later. Dad told Carlos that his guys could go grab some food and rest and meet back here in the room by 4 PM. Dad told Carlos and Jim that their men could get anywhere on the property from this room without being seen.

Jim said, "That is perfect." He would have the men get all of the gear out of the vehicles and bring it down to the room. He would then have them go park the vehicles in the barn. Then Dad, Carlos and Jim went in another room to strategize and put a plan in place.

Mr. Santiago said, "Jefferson, I think we need to go back upstairs and let the professionals get to work."

I said, "I do believe that you are correct, sir."

It was now 11 AM and there were a lot of people showing up. Isiah had the majority of the meat prepared on the grill. So I went to check on Manuela. She and the other girls were in the kitchen sitting around the island drinking coffee. I said, "Good morning ladies" as I walked in the kitchen and kissed Manuela. "I'm glad to see that you sleeping beauties are awake." I told the girls that there was a possibility that Escobar and his crew are on their way to our location. I explained that the DEA would know exactly when they touch down in Alabama as well as when they will depart from the airport. Everyone was getting nervous.

I said, "We have a plan and will be shutting the cookout down a lot early tonight as opposed to years past where we go into the wee hours of the morning."

Pedro then walked downstairs. "Where is Maria?" asked Pedro.

I said, "She is next door by my parents' house; she should be here shortly."

"What is the status of everything, Jefferson?"

I then updated him on the status of everything. I told everyone that we were in good hands, so let's go out there and enjoy ourselves. I asked Manuela if she wanted to go down to the barn so that I could let Storm and the rest of horses out to go out into the pasture. She said, "Sure sweetheart, let's go."

When we had walked out I said, "We have a nice crowd of people out there."

When we walked to the barn Storm ran up to the fence for Manuela to pet her. I said, "Manuela, she likes you."

She replied, "I like her too."

I said, "Wait here while I go to the barn and grab some carrot sticks out of the refrigerator for Storm."

When I got back to the fence I gave the carrots to Manuela to feed to Storm. I grabbed Manuela and pulled her close to me. I said, "I already knew you were the one for me. However, when I saw Storm react to you the way she did that just helped to solidify things. I love you, Manuela. I know that you are nervous about what may or may not take place today but I just want you to know that I will never let anything happen to you. I'm hoping that we can get some closure today as it relates to Escobar. You and your family deserve closure. I just found out last night that my father and grandfather retired from the Central Intelligence Agency (CIA)."

"Are you serious?" asked Manuela.

I said, "Yes, I'm serious. My brother Jackie just recently joined the CIA as well."

She said, "Get out of here."

I said, "This next one is going to really blow you away. Maria is CIA as well."

"Thomas, close the front door," said Manuela. "I can't believe it."

I said, "Well, believe it."

"Thomas, this is so crazy."

"When I was by my parents' earlier today I asked my Mom if she knew. She said of course she knew. My grandmother said she knew as well about my grandpa."

"Thomas has Maria told Pedro?"

"No, she hasn't told him as of yet. However, all of that is going to change today." I said, "Let's walk back over and enjoy the cookout."

The cookout was great. Everyone was having a great time. Dad stood up around 2 PM and said that we would be wrapping up the cookout around 5 PM today because of unforeseen circumstances. Everyone jokingly started booing. He said, "However, once today is over I promise that we will do it again the Saturday before Father's Day this year. So what do y'all think about that?" They started cheering. "Although we are shutting down earlier than normal today I want everybody to take to-go plates with you."

When 5 o'clock came we still had about 20 people other than my family, Manuela's family, Sandra, Security and the DEA that were content with staying. Jim Dean came out and told Dad that Escobar and his men had just touched down in Mobile. He stated that his resources said that besides the 24 people that they had flown in from Miami with him that they had recruited a dozen more guys from their Mobile contacts. He stated that they had a caravan of about seven SUVs headed North on I-65.

The remaining guests finally left around 5:30 PM. Dad told everyone to come inside. Once inside he explained to us everything that was going happening. He stated that there was a hidden space downstairs that had pathways to either to the barn, the tree house, my grandparents' house or my house. He went on to say, "These are dangerous individuals that are coming to our house; however, it is our goal to take them down without any casualties." He said that Jim Dean and his team were in the house as well as placed at the barn and throughout the property. He also stated that local authorities were already strategically placed once this individuals turn down our road and come to our house. He said, "At no time will any of you be in any danger. Once the bullets start flying, because they will, we have bullet proof plates that will protect the windows and the outer cover of the home. He said, "You're in good hands. My father and I both retired from the Central Intelligence Agency and Jackie and Maria are CIA as well. Mr. Jim Dean, who is a good friend of mine, is leading the DEA in this effort. Therefore, if you're hungry or thirsty get food and beverages and go downstairs to the private room."

I could see Pedro and Maria talking in the kitchen She said, "I was going to tell you, Pedro. However, I was hoping to have this Escobar thing behind us first."

Pedro said, "It doesn't matter what line of work you're in. I just want you to come back to me."

"I promise I'll always come home to you, my love."

Jim said, "I think it would be wise if we had some of the men and Agent Sanchez at least be outside when they come toward the house so nothing will look out of place. Pedro, Isiah, Jackie, Grandpa, Dad, and I volunteered to go outside. He also had several of Carlos's security personnel out walking around guarding the house as well. One of Jim's agents came and told Jim something. Jim came and yelled to us, "Game time; they are five minutes away."

Dad, Jackie, Grandpa and Maria checked their weapons. Dad said, "As soon as you see those vehicles come in sight I want you and Pedro to get your asses inside, Jefferson."

I said, "Ok Dad." Moments later we saw a caravan of vehicles careening down the road headed toward my parents' house. Pedro and I started walking hastily toward the house. We had just entered the house when we heard gunfire erupt. I looked around and saw Dad and Grandpa running up the steps shooting. Jackie and Maria were right behind them. There were a lot of bullets flying. They quickly hit the switch that lowered bulletproof plates around the windows which had openings to fire their weapons through.

Dad told us to get our asses downstairs. Carlos' personnel took cover behind their vehicles and started shooting as well. I also heard a helicopter flying overhead. When we arrived downstairs Pedro's mom and father hugged him. My mom and grandma hugged me as well. Then I hugged Manuela's neck. The gunfire went on for about 15 minutes. Then, just as quickly it started, it stopped. Then 10 minutes later Jackie and Maria walked into the room. They said, "It is over."

He said, "Grandpa was shot in the arm; however, he appears to be ok."

The agents wouldn't allow us to go upstairs until everything was secure. Finally, after we waited about 45 minutes, Jim Dean came down and said that the area was secure. We all went upstairs. Grandpa was sitting in the doorway of the ambulance. Grandma and Mom went running to him. Grandma said, "Are you ok, Thomas?"

He said, "Yes baby, I'm ok. I was just nicked by a bullet. They are going to take me to the hospital just as a precautionary measure."

Dad then walked over from talking to the local authorities. Mom ran and hugged him. My sister Eve, Jackie and I hugged him as well. I felt like a kid again. Everything felt so surreal. I was so thankful that he, Grandpa, Jackie and Maria were ok.

He then walked over to where Manuela, her parents, Pedro and Maria were standing. He said, "You don't have to worry about Escobar anymore; he was killed during the shootout. He was given the opportunity to surrender but he chose not to. There is a young man that was shot who said that he was your nephew. His name is Eduardo. He is currently being loaded into the ambulance if you would like to see him."

"I don't want to see him," said Mr. Santiago.

Pedro said, "I would like to see him." So my father took Pedro over to see Eduardo. "Eduardo, all I want to know is why?" asked Pedro. "My father gave you everything. We grew up like brothers. You're family."

"I wanted more said," Eduardo. "Escobar and his father made me feel important. They told me I could have made millions of dollars."

"Eduardo, you could have made millions with Dad. He had you listed in the paperwork as having ownership in Sanchez Holdings. However, after you betrayed him he removed your name from the documents. You betrayed us, Eduardo. You're not only dead to my father but you're dead to our family. I hope you rot in jail."

Pedro then went back by his family. My grandma went to the hospital with Grandpa. There were a lot of personnel walking around with DEA on their jackets, local authorities and some CIA agents mixed in as well. I overheard Jim telling Dad that they had nine law enforcement personnel injured. Two of Carlos' personnel were injured and there were eight fatalities for Escobar's men (including Escobar Medina) and seven injured for Escobar's men as well. There was a lot of yellow tape scattered throughout the property.

We decided to go over to my house in order to relax. We all went to my house with the exception of Mom and Dad. They went to the hospital to be with Grandpa and Grandma. We went into the kitchen and sat down. Mr. Santiago said, "I need a drink." Everybody said they needed a drink. So I opened a bottle of Sangria and Merlot for the women. I made Mr. Santiago a scotch on the rocks and a Tanqueray and tonic for me. I tried to give Jackie a Corona. He said, "No little brother, I need something stronger." I made him a Crown Royal on the rocks. He was trembling as he took a sip.

I said, "How was your first time in action?"

He said, "You can practice for it; however, it moves so fast when it is live. Dad and Grandpa were so calm as they were shouting out orders as well as shooting at the bad guys."

Manuela came and placed her head on my shoulder. I kissed her on the top of her head and said, "I love you."

We just sat around in disbelief and talked over the next hour. Dad and Mom walked through the door, followed by Grandpa and Grandma. Everyone started clapping when they saw Dad and Grandpa and went and gave them a hug.

Mr. Santiago's phone rang; when he answered it was Pablo Medina on the other end of the phone. He said, "Constantine, I want you to know that you and your family are dead. I want you to experience the same pain that I'm feeling right now."

Dad asked, "Who was that?"

He said, "Pablo." Mr. Santiago didn't have to say anything else because everyone already knew what was said during the conversation. Mr. Santiago then stood up and said, "I would like to thank you and your father Thomas for helping to keep my family safe. I have worked my entire life to do things the right way and to keep my family from experiencing the kind of violence that my wife and I experienced growing up in Venezuela. Then to have this happen here in the United States and involve my family and friends…it makes me angry. I mean really angry. Pablo has made millions and millions of dollars from my blood, sweat and tears over the past 20 years and for him to do this to my family and friends is unbelievable."

Dad then said, "Greed makes people do crazy and unbelievable things. I want you to always remember that we will always have your back, Constantine."

I said, "Dad, you and Grandpa have experienced so much over the years working in the CIA; however, **I bet you never thought** in your wildest dreams that you would experience a day like today. I just want you to know that I'm proud of you and Grandpa and that I love you, I love this family and I love everyone in this room."

Printed in the United States
By Bookmasters